AF406348

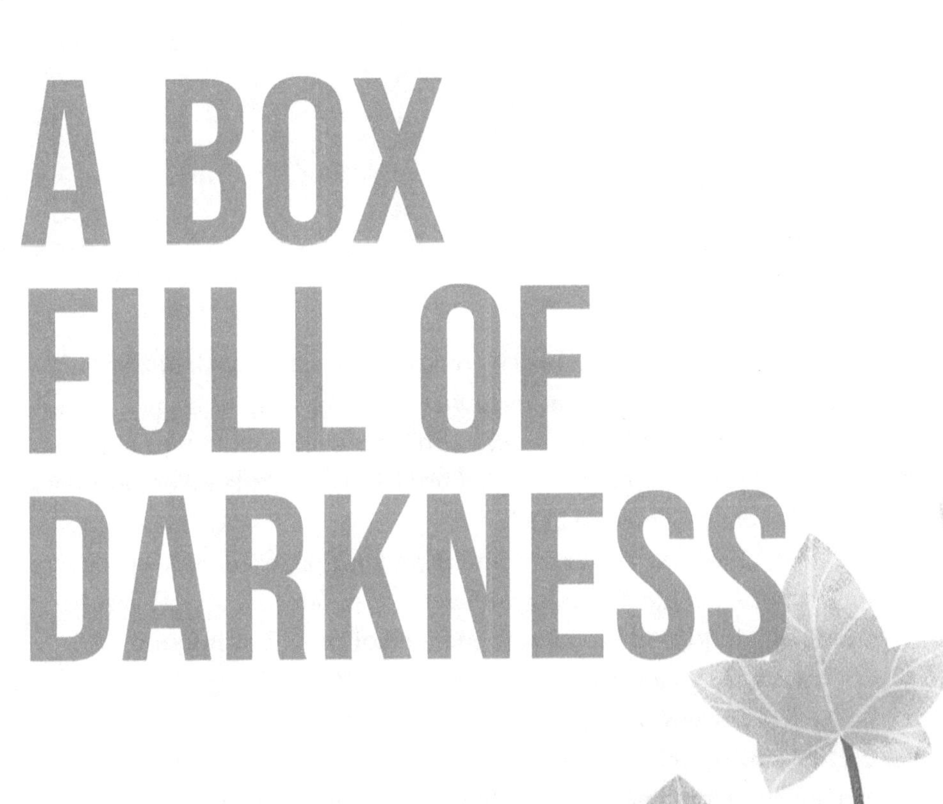

A BOX
FULL OF
DARKNESS

To David

*Someone I loved once gave me
a box full of darkness.
It took me years to understand
that this, too, was a gift.*

—Mary Oliver

Chapter One
October 2025

Tessa Halifax wakes draped over the sofa's armrest, her cheek pressed against the pebbled gray leather upholstery. She pushes herself upright, gasping for each ragged breath. It takes her a moment to place her surroundings, even though she spends most of her waking hours here. Her fingers dig into her own knees, underneath the hem of her black skirt. Her gaze jumps around the room, seeking a focus object. It lands on Leo, sitting at her feet, looking up at her with his intelligent brown eyes. He must have been the one to wake her, as he always does. Tessa reaches down to stroke her service dog's head, and he nuzzles against her palm.

She remembers the grounding technique she learned with Taliyah. Five things she can see. Four things she can feel. Three things she can hear. Two things she can smell. One thing she can taste.

She can see Leo. She can see the enormous dark wood bookcase, and the latest report on clean energy sitting on one of the shelves. The Vice President must have picked it up for her after she so carelessly fell asleep while reviewing it. Tessa can see the photo resting on one of the other shelves, of Ryan and Matt standing at the peak of Mount Elbert in Colorado. They are both heavily bundled up, with broad smiles on their faces. She can see Ryan's desk, and the chandelier sparkling above her, and the black marble fireplace in the corner of the room.

Four things she can feel. Frightened, lonely, regretful, and sad. So deeply, desperately sad.

That's not what she's supposed to be thinking about. Tessa reaches down and feels the soft fur on Leo's head. That's one thing, at least. She skips to three things she can hear. Leo's breathing. The ticking of the grand-father clock in the corner of the room. It's just past nine-thirty at night.

(She can hear Owen's voice, in snatches of memory. He promises to love and cherish her from this day forward, always, always. She can hear him saying goodbye to her before he departed on that final trip for work.)

This isn't what she was supposed to hear. Tessa almost places her hands on her ears, as if blocking out the sound could be so easy. Two things she can smell. The roses and lilies from the flower arrangement on the coffee table. One thing she can taste. Tessa stands up, narrowly avoid-ing stumbling on Leo, and heads for the carafe of lemon-infused ice water resting on a table on the far side of the room. She pours herself a glass of water, her hands shaking, and gulps down a mouthful.

The door opens. The Vice President steps inside, holding one large to-go paper mug of tea. He makes the effort to nudge the door shut quietly, which is unlike him. Ryan turns, and the frown that has been etched on his brow all day deepens as soon as he sees her. "What's wrong?"

"N-Nothing." Tessa leans against the table to steady herself. Leo followed her here from the sofa. He stands close by her legs, as if trying to keep her upright. "I'm sorry f-for falling asleep like that."

Her speech gives her away. She didn't stutter after working for twen-ty-four hours straight during election season. She didn't stutter under high stress in combat, or in the meeting rooms of the Capitol and the West Wing.

The Vice President strides over to her. He presses the tea into her hand and places one hand on her back, leading her to the sofa. Tessa lets Ryan guide her, with Leo walking on her other side. She sits, and Ryan sits close beside her on the sofa. Their bodies angle toward one another, knees almost touching. Leo settles at her feet.

She is cold, despite the blazer she wears over her silk blouse. She might benefit from the tea, but Tessa leans over and sets it on the coffee table. Her hands are still shaking.

"Was it the hospital?"

She nods, unwilling to elaborate further. Even after almost a year of therapy, she still isn't entirely comfortable discussing her feelings aloud. Ryan sighs. "I'm sorry. I should have asked someone else to come with me instead. I just — I knew it would be a hard day, and I thought it would help to have you there."

"I'm glad I could be there for you." Tessa rubs the space above her heart. It does nothing to alleviate the vice-like tightness that grips her chest.

"I'm sorry." Ryan's complexion is ashen.

"Don't apologize. It's not your job to mind my feelings." Leo sits upright, pressing against her legs, trying to comfort her. "It just–" She can't speak. Seeing the soldiers in rehab, and the soldiers lying there in their hospital beds, reminded her of the last time she set foot in a hospital like that.

The tears that she has tried to hold back since waking from her nightmare spill out. Tessa presses her hands over her mouth, trying to hold back her sobs, and turns away. Ryan wraps his arms around her, drawing her into his chest, holding her close. The tenderness of the touch only makes Tessa weep harder. She bows her head, ashamed of the display of emotion. All she can feel is pain and near-crippling shame at this breakdown. It has been a full year. She should be past this.

"I'm so sorry, Tess." Ryan rubs her back. His embrace is grounding, tight and firm without being stifling or forceful, holding her together. She turns her face against the solid warmth of his shoulder, and she cries until her eyes and head throb.

Ryan holds her until her tears subside. At least this fit of crying, as intense as it was, burns itself out quickly. Tessa withdraws, self-consciously wiping at her nose and face with her sleeve.

Ryan stands up so abruptly that Leo startles. He strides off and returns with a box of tissues clutched in both hands. "Here."

"Thank you." Tessa takes a couple, wiping at her face. The sensitive skin underneath her eyes is swollen to the touch, and her face is hot. Ryan sits by her side again, placing a hand on her back. She balls up the soft, damp tissues in her hands, squeezing them hard. "I wish I could — I wish all of those memories were just *gone*."

She almost recoils from her own bold words. Would she erase the joy of all those years with Owen, just to spare her from the pain of the end? Tessa shakes her head, trying to clear it. "I'm sorry about all this. Let's call it a night. I'll be fine by Monday."

Ryan rises, holding his hand out to her. It's still strange to see his hand without the silver ring on it. Tessa automatically places her hand in his and lets him help her to her feet. "If you apologize to me again, I'll fire you."

Ryan has employed this threat at least once a month for all the years that she has worked for him. She forces a wan smile. "All right."

Ryan retrieves his black wool overcoat from the coat rack and shrugs it on. He removes her camel-colored wool coat from the rack, and Tessa allows him to help her into it. She goes to the coffee table to fetch her still-hot peppermint tea, and fastens Leo's service dog harness, patting the top of his head. "Ready to go home for the night?"

Ryan watches them. "Do you want to stay over at the residence?"

Tessa stops in the middle of a sip of her tea. "What?"

"I'm not sure if you should be alone."

Tessa's face flames with heat again. "With all due respect, I'm fine." This is almost as bad as the weeks and months immediately after last October. Her friends and colleagues all loved her as a sister. They threw her birthday parties every year. They spent weekends and evenings together, even when they weren't working. They attended her wedding, as she did theirs. They all looked at her differently afterwards, their expressions laden with compassion and pity.

"You don't sound fine." Tessa can hear the edge to Ryan's voice. It makes her pulse quicken, before she realizes that it isn't a hard, angry edge. It isn't something to be afraid of. He's just worried about her.

"I can't stay the night with you." That came out wrong, and Tessa rubs her temples. "I can't spend the night at the residence."

Ryan checks his watch. "It's past ten, and it's Friday night. It's been a quiet couple of days."

It has been a quiet couple of days, which means that there won't be reporters lurking near the residence. Ryan's security detail is trustworthy. And she doesn't want to go home alone, to her one-bedroom Capitol Hill apartment.

It won't be like it was last year. She has recovered a little bit, at least. She has Leo now, and he helps to keep her grounded. Barring a few occasions — Valentine's Day, Owen's birthday, and their anniversary — what would have been their anniversary — she hasn't had a truly bad night since Leo came into her life.

"I'll be alright." Ryan doesn't appear convinced, until she elaborates. "I'm seeing Rosalie for dinner tomorrow."

That mollifies him. "Fine. Come on, I'll walk you to your car."

They discuss the Summit of the Americas next month as they walk, two Secret Service agents following Ryan at a discreet distance. Tessa grimaces as they step outside of the Eisenhower Executive Office Building. The skies, heavily overcast during her and Ryan's visit to Walter Reed earlier in the evening, have burst open since they returned. The wind buffets the umbrella that Ryan opens and holds over their heads, threatening to turn it inside out. How had she missed hearing the rain earlier? She should have put Leo's raincoat on.

At this hour, her car is one of the couple left in the parking area. "Text me when you get home," Ryan tells her, as Tessa fishes her car keys out from her bag.

The headlights of her car flash as she unlocks the door. She opens the back door first, letting Leo jump in and get away from the rain. "I will. Good night."

"Night."

It is a short drive from the EEOB to her apartment building. Leo rises from his well-mannered seated position in the backseat as soon as she parks. She pulls out Leo's bright yellow raincoat from her satchel and shakes it out. "What do you think? Do you want to brave the weather?"

A crack of thunder sounds overhead. Leo is too obedient to balk, even though Tessa knows the dog isn't a great fan of his raincoat. She puts it on him, pops open her own umbrella, and takes him for a short walk before they enter the building.

Her apartment is on the top floor, the fourth. Tessa does not dwell on coming home to a dark, empty apartment. She removes Leo's leash and service dog vest, hanging them up beside her own coat. "Stay." If not commanded otherwise, Leo's instinct is to follow her around the apartment.

She grabs a towel from the linen closet, and uses her hair dryer to blast it with hot air until it is pleasantly warm to the touch. Tessa finds her dog where she left him, standing in the middle of the living room. His black-and-tan fur is sodden from the rain, giving him an unusually disheveled appearance. Tessa smiles at his patience as she wraps him in the warm towel. "Let's get you dried off."

She towels Leo down, rubbing vigorously at his wet fur. He wriggles, tail wagging, tongue lolling out the side of his mouth, clearly enjoying the sensation of the warm towel. He shakes himself again, and Tessa runs a hand over his flank. He's dry enough that she will spare him the ordeal of the blow dryer.

She retrieves her phone from her coat pocket and taps out a text. *Home.* Her phone buzzes a second later, indicating that Ryan "loved" her message.

Tessa stands near the table, oddly adrift. She doesn't know what to do with herself. On a normal night, she might be able to get away with watching an episode of something on Netflix. The evening at Walter Reed ensured that this hasn't been a normal night. Her fingers itch with the temptation to pull out her laptop and get back to work. She manages to hold herself back. Her homework for this week with Taliyah was to refrain from working at home. *You already work unusually long hours,* Taliyah said. *I know that work has been an escape for you, but I think it would be helpful for you to find other ways to self-soothe.*

They came up with a list of ideas. Watching shows, listening to podcasts, reading books, texting friends, exercising. Every one of those has proved effective over the last week, but none of those days took a toll on her like today.

Someone nudges her leg, and Leo looks up at her. She attempts a smile, sinking down and petting him. "I'm fine."

She doesn't bother standing up again. Phone in hand, Tessa flicks over to her podcast app, finds the newest episode of Freakonomics, and presses play. She listens to the entire episode while sitting on the wooden floor, Leo curled up at her side. The episode ends, and she pulls herself to her feet. Exhaustion sinks in, making her eyelids heavy, slowing her thoughts. She should sleep. The memory of her earlier nightmare still makes her shrink from the idea.

But maybe it is out of her system now. Maybe the nightmare was her way of processing what she saw in the hospital, and the feelings the visit brought up.

Tessa holds onto that hope like a talisman. She sheds her work clothes in favor of black leggings and a faded old Barnard t-shirt. She gets ready for bed, letting her hair down from the claw clip holding it in its updo, putting it into a simple ponytail. Leo is stretched out at the foot of the bed. The dog's eyes are open, and he remains alert until Tessa slides under the covers. "Good night, Leo. Thank you for being with me today."

She says this every night, and she means it. She will never forget those two months before she got Leo, just before the end of last year. She stumbled through those eight weeks like a walking corpse.

Tessa reaches to turn out the bedside lamp. She hesitates, struck by a premonition of what will happen. She will plunge the room into darkness. She will lie down, curling into herself, pulling the covers over her. She will try to think about work, but she will think about the hospital instead. She will remember.

She hasn't done this in a little while. It feels like a step backward. Tessa gets her phone from her bedside table and reopens her podcast app. She presses play, and clings to every word, focusing on the topic at hand — *Nuclear Power Isn't Perfect. Is It Good Enough?* — until she finally drifts off to sleep.

Chapter Two

January 2006

"I-I'm sorry I missed class yesterday."

"That's all right." Ms. Hunt looks up from her lesson plan for the day. Around them, the classroom rustles with activity as Tessa's classmates pull books from their backpacks and flip to the pages they marked. "Are you feeling better?"

Tessa ducks her head, blushing. "I-I'm fine now."

"You still sound congested." Her English teacher opens the glass jar on her desk and offers her a plastic-wrapped lemon-shaped candy. "Here. These help."

Tessa takes the lemon candy and stammers her thanks. Her dad hadn't even commented on her cold. She slips it into the pocket of her hoodie, and keeps her palm curled around it. Ms. Hunt explains the assignment and sends her off to the library, hall pass in hand. Tessa stops in the bathroom to blow her nose. She can't breathe any better than she did yesterday, but she didn't want to stay home again.

The librarian looks up from her computer when Tessa enters the library. "Hi there, Tessa. We missed you yesterday."

"H-Hi, Mrs. Taras."

"Oh, hon, you don't sound so good."

"I-I didn't want to miss my classes today." Tessa self-consciously raises her wrist, covered by her too-long sleeve, to her nose. At least it's not running again.

"Now that's a solid work ethic."

Tessa turns, startled. There's a soldier in her high school's library, looking completely out of place in his heavy camouflage top and matching pants. He stands beside an exhibit table draped with a black US Army tablecloth.

"Rowan University?" the soldier asks. "My cousin went there back in '99. Are you headed down that way in fall?"

Tessa glances down at her worn gray hoodie. "No. It was a g-gift." It was marked down to two dollars at the local Goodwill. She grabbed it right off the rack, thrilled by her luck.

"Nice gift. It's a good school. Are you a senior?"

She doesn't really want to get drawn into a conversation. It would be rude to ignore his question, though, so Tessa nods. "I-I am."

She takes a small step back toward the shelves. The soldier's cheery demeanor doesn't change. "That's an exciting time. Have you been thinking about college or any other career paths?"

It's all she's been thinking about for the past six months. "Yes, I'd like to go to college, b-but–" Tessa clamps her mouth shut, too embarrassed to finish the sentence.

The soldier's expression softens into one of understanding. "I get it. It's expensive. I wouldn't have been able to go if I hadn't enlisted. That's why I'm here today. I'm hoping to share my story with seniors and let them know what a great option the Army is for them. Enlistees can get their college tuition paid. You'll also get a stipend for housing and another one for your textbooks."

Tessa takes one step toward the table. After writing several essays, she has scraped together about fifteen-hundred dollars in scholarships. That's not quite enough to cover a single semester's tuition at Atlantic Cape Community College in Hamilton. She'll also have to pay for textbooks, apartment rent, and groceries. "That s-sounds good."

"It really is. It's a life-changing opportunity." The army recruiter takes a business card off the table and hands it to her. "I know a lot of young people your age are tempted to go the student loan route, but let me tell you, you don't want to get tangled up with those. The interest rates will really get you. I have friends from high school who did that, and they're still trying to get rid of that debt a decade plus after graduating college."

"And it's complicated." Mrs. Markham, the guidance counselor, gave her a few printouts on student loans. Tessa read them several times, puzzled over them, and still hadn't been able to figure it out.

"You've got that right. Whether you go for one of the federal loans, or if you go through a bank or another private lender, they all come with their own kind of headaches. The Army's process isn't like that. It's real straightforward. You're eligible for all those education benefits I mentioned once you've served for three years. All you have to do to start using your benefits is fill out a quick application."

Tessa looks down at the business card. "W-what would I do in the Army until then?" All she knows about the military is what she has seen on TV these last few years. Brief video clips of grim-faced, uniformed soldiers clutching long machine guns, standing clustered together in the deserts of Iraq and Afghanistan.

"I'm glad you asked. We can train a high school grad like you in over a hundred and fifty different jobs. We have something to suit everyone."

Tessa flips the card over, studying the phone number and address there. *US Army Recruiting Station, Elizabeth, NJ. 299 N. Broad Street.*

"That's the nearest recruiting station. Feel free to give us a call anytime. We would love to sit down and talk with you and share some more details about what we do."

After saying goodbye, Tessa heads back over to the stacks. The librarian stops her as she passes the front desk, beckoning her to come closer. "If you go in and talk to them, make sure that they mention a signing bonus," she whispers. "My nephew enlisted last year, and his enlistment bonus was twenty thousand!"

That's enough for her to pay rent on her own apartment for *years.* "T-thanks."

∞∞∞∞∞

It is a thirty-five minute walk home. She stops at the Save-A-Lot on the way, notes what's on sale, and grabs those things, along with her usual cheap staples. The rest of her walk is slower, as she's weighed down by her backpack and the bags of groceries. It isn't her typical reaction to coming home, but Tessa is relieved when she finally arrives at 45 Hawthorne Court.

She gropes with her key in the lock in the dark. Tessa pushes the front door open and flicks the entryway light on. She is greeted by silence. She hadn't noticed this yesterday, when she'd had the time to do something about it, but the living room needs to be vacuumed. The surface of the coffee table is dusty too. Shame makes Tessa's shoulders hunch up towards her ears. Mom always kept the house looking good, even when she was sick. She should do better.

Tessa turns on the small radio sitting on the kitchen counter and turns the dial to the local news station, just so she can have some voices in the house. In the past, she used the TV for this kind of white noise, but she sold that on Craigslist more than a year ago.

She puts the groceries away and cooks dinner. She fixes her dad's plate first, and stops in the hallway, at the door to his office. A light is on inside, which is a good sign. Sometimes he just sits there in the dark, the only light coming from his desktop computer. Both her hands are full, so she can't knock. "Dad?" Tessa carefully modulates her voice. Her father doesn't like to be startled. "I have dinner for you."

Several seconds pass without a response. Maybe he has his headphones plugged in. The aroma of the quesadillas makes her mouth water.

"Leave it."

Sometimes he lets her come in and give him his dinner. Sometimes he opens the door and takes it from her himself. This must be a bad day. She sets the plate and the glass down in front of the door and retreats to the kitchen.

Tessa shovels down her hot quesadillas while reading her book for English. She reluctantly puts *Parable of the Sower* down at a little past eight, pushing her empty plate away. She has to do dishes and clean up the kitchen before she gets started on calculus homework.

She buries her head in her hands and groans softly, before giving herself a hug. This relentless monotony has been her life for the past five years. School, cleaning, cooking, grocery shopping, and work on the weekends. This is what her life is going to be like once she graduates too. Except instead of getting to leave the house every day to go to school, she will just leave to work at her job. Even once she gets more hours after graduating, saving up for college will take a while. Completing the nursing program will be a total of $22,000, and doing radiology tech will be even more — $32,000.

The librarian's words come back to her, unbidden. *My nephew enlisted last year, and his enlistment bonus was twenty thousand.*

Tessa rifles through her notebooks and textbooks until she finds the US Army brochure the recruiter gave her. She should really get started on her calculus homework. She sits back down at the table and opens the brochure instead.

∞∞∞∞

Tessa wakes up at five in the morning on Saturday, bundles up in her coat and scarf, and walks twenty minutes to get to her job. There's no one out in the neighborhood this early on a Saturday morning. There are only a few cars on the road, their headlights slicing through the predawn darkness.

Jesy is leaning against the front desk, texting on her shiny pink Razr phone, when Tessa walks in. "How are you?" she asks, putting her phone down. "Is school going okay?"

"I-it's fine. I have a presentation in S-Spanish class on Thursday that I'm worried about."

"It won't get busy in here for another couple of hours. Turn one of the TVs to Telemundo and put subtitles on. Or watch some videos on their website. You have to do, like, total immersion to get good at Spanish."

Jesy went to Elizabeth High too, though she graduated two years ago. She knows just how unhelpful their Spanish textbooks are. "I'll try anything at this point."

Jesy gets her purse out from the shelf underneath the front desk. "I wish I could hang out for a while, but I have to head out and get some rest before Liza's baby shower."

"Bye, Jesy."

Jesy grins at her. "*Adios,* Tessa. ¡Qué tenga un buen día!"

Tessa cringes, and Jesy giggles all the way out the front door. Once she's gone, Tessa approaches the desktop computer. She should go to the Telemundo website, but she navigates to another one instead.

The golden banner at the top of the page is the first thing that catches her attention. *Get up to $15,000 in enlistment bonuses. New 4-year enlistment options.* Tessa scrolls down on the page, her heartbeat quickening.

22

Discover the career for you and opportunities you never knew existed. Benefits for now. Security for your future. Her gaze jumps over each of the subheadings. *Education. Money and pay. Skills and training. Health care.* Finally, at the bottom of the page, *how to join. Contact a recruiter. Call 1-888-550-ARMY.*

Tessa catches herself picking at the skin around her cuticles, a nervous habit. She shouldn't call from home. Her dad will get mad at her for tying up the phone line. She doesn't want him picking up the phone on the other line and overhearing her conversation either.

Why? Would he be mad? Why would he even care if she joins the Army? *Of course he'll care,* Tessa thinks bitterly, uncharitably, before she can stop herself. *If you move out and join the Army, who's going to take care of him?*

Before she can lose her nerve, she grabs the phone and dials the number.

ooooo

Sunday, Monday, and Tuesday crawl by with agonizing slowness. Tessa frets about her appointment at the Army recruitment center on Wednesday. What if the Army doesn't think she has what it takes to join them? What if they think the way she talks is a red flag for weakness, for timidity? (Would they be wrong?)

She has trawled every inch of the Army website by now. The website goes into depth about how members of the Army protect the nation and its people. About how Army soldiers have strength of body and character. There are so many references to toughness, to fortitude, to *strength.* Not just being *strong,* but *Army strong.* The men and women photographed on the website personify steely toughness and determination. They stand with their backs straight. Resolve shines from their eyes, in the set of their jaws, in how high and proud they carry their heads.

Tessa looks at herself in the mirror, at her limp blonde ponytail, the ever-present dark circles underneath her brown eyes, and the few stubborn acne scars on her jawline that won't go away. She tries to stand up straighter and push her shoulders back. She tries to think of strength and resilience. She still sees no resemblance to the women on the Army website.

Tessa stops by the locker room to change after school. She still makes it to the recruiting station in twenty minutes, even though she is walking in the slightly too small leather loafers she got from Goodwill. She stops at the side of the building, and pulls her sleeve up to check her battered watch. She's early.

A memory of her mom returns, unbidden. *You can do it, Tessie. You're my brave girl.* Tessa squeezes her eyes shut. Tears prick at the insides of her eyelids.

The center is busier than she expected it would be. Four young men sit in chairs pressed against the wall, filling out paperwork. Three of them have backpacks resting at their feet. She checks in with the uniformed woman sitting at the front desk and takes a seat, looking around while she waits. The walls are painted a dull shade of green, and a few large framed posters of soldiers in a desert landscape hang on the wall.

Another soldier emerges from the back of the recruitment center. "Tessa Halifax?"

Tessa stands immediately. "P-present." She remembers Mr. Gabriel's advice during junior year career fair. *A strong handshake exhibits confidence in your abilities.*

The recruiter holds her hand out. "Staff Sergeant Andrea Drake. Thank you for coming in today."

Tessa makes every effort to give Drake a handshake that projects strength and confidence. "Thank you f-for taking the time to meet with me." *Stop stuttering,* she chides herself.

Staff Sergeant Drake leads her back to a small conference room, and she indicates one of the chairs around the round table. Drake sits across from her, setting a notebook and a shiny black folder emblazoned with the now-familiar US Army logo in front of her. "It's nice to meet you, Tessa. That's a lovely outfit, by the way. It's always nice to see a young woman who knows how to present herself professionally."

Tessa blushes at the praise. She changed into her career fair clothes after school, all of which she snagged from the thrift store last summer. Her clothes were so much more plain than the other girls in her class, with their impeccable skirt suit sets, and silk blouses, slacks, and high heels. It's a relief that the recruiter doesn't think she looks shabby. "Thank you."

Drake opens up her notebook, consulting a page of neat notes. "I see here that you're a senior. That's an exciting time, with lots of decisions to make about the future."

Exciting isn't the word Tessa would use to describe her senior year, with all the stress about scholarships and money, and the increasingly unbearable prospect of continuing to live with her dad after graduation. On top of it all, there's the jealousy of hearing about her classmates, who are heading to Rowan University and to Rutgers, to Seton Hall and Montclair and the Stevens Institute of Technology. "It is exciting," Tessa says meekly, anyway.

Drake goes over some basics with her, like what basic training entails, and the length of a commitment to the Army. There are four year, six-year, and eight-year commitments. There are enlistment bonuses, and quick-ship bonuses. "Those are for people who can commit to going to basic training right away, within thirty days of enlistment. You don't enlist until you go through MEPS — that's a visit to our Military Enlistment Processing Station. If you decide you want to enlist, you can do that right after your graduation. Does that make sense?"

"Yes." Tessa looks down at the questions that she wrote in her notebook. One thing stands out as a priority. "D-do all Army soldiers have to go to Iraq or Afghanistan?"

Drake hesitates. "No, not all. It depends on your MOS — that stands for military occupational specialty. But as you know, we are at war. We can't guarantee that enlistees will or won't go to a war zone. I get that going to war can be an intimidating thing to consider, but the training that the Army provides ensures that our soldiers have the skills to succeed in their missions while deployed."

Tessa bites the inside of her cheek. That wasn't the answer she was hoping for.

Drake seems to pick up on her mixed feelings. "Again, it depends on your MOS. There are some occupational specialties that have a higher chance of seeing combat than others."

"T-that MOS is decided by how I do on the ASVAB entrance test?"

"It is. What are your thoughts so far? There's no pressure to make a decision right now, or even to know exactly where you stand. I just want to know what's on your mind."

The truth is that it isn't as ideal as it sounded from her conversation with the recruiter at her high school, or from her exploration of the Army website. What are her other options, though? Take out a college loan that will take forever to pay back? Or live with her dad for an extra year or two, pick up more shifts at work, and save up for Atlantic Cape?

It's just another year or two, and she's put up with five already. It shouldn't be so bad. It should be bearable. But–

She has to get out. The prospect of living at home with her dad for another year or two — god, the basic training that the recruiter described sounds better than that. She can learn those skills, at least. Being at home with her dad just makes her feel hopeless and stuck and stunted, the same struggling thirteen-year-old and fourteen-year-old and fifteen-year-old she was back then. Worse, it makes her feel *helpless*. Unable to change anything. Unable to bring her mom back, or snap her dad out of it and make him love her. Unable to even make the house feel like home again, no matter how much she tries to keep it clean.

"I'm interested i-in taking the ASVAB after graduation. What can I do to study for it?"

Drake gives her a warm smile. "I'm glad to hear that. There are study guides and practice tests available…"

∞∞∞∞

Tessa carves out an hour every night for sitting with the ASVAB prep books that she checked out from the library. In March, her recruiter schedules her for a visit to the Military Entrance Processing Station in June, just after her graduation. "This is where you'll take your ASVAB test. You'll choose your MOS and get sworn in at this point. After that, you'll ship out to basic training."

Jesy is the only person Tessa tells about her plan to enlist, save for the librarian who helped her find the ASVAB test prep books. There's only one more person she has to notify. She has a check-in with her recruiter at the beginning of the next month, and Drake gets right to the point after they exchange greetings and settle down in her office. "Have you spoken with your dad yet?"

Tessa fidgets. "N-no, I haven't."

"Graduation isn't that far away, and things will move fast after that. Do you want me to come by and speak with him? I can certainly do that. I've done it a few times before."

Her dad loses his temper with coworkers and students, people outside the house, people besides her, all the time — but he couldn't do that with a soldier, right? *He flipped out on a bunch of different bosses,* Tessa reminds herself. "I-I don't know how he would take that. I-I should do it by myself. I'll do it soon, I promise."

Drake gives her a long look. "All right. Please let me know how it goes. If the conversation doesn't go well, remember that you can call or text my cell anytime."

"Thanks." Tessa stares at the conference table. Her recruiter, like Jesy, probably now thinks that her dad is crazy and terrible. She doesn't know how that makes her feel. She doesn't love him, not like she loved her mom. She can say to herself, in the privacy of her own mind, that her dad is terrible. She still doesn't like the idea of *other* people thinking that. Of other people knowing that about her.

"Do you have any questions for me? Anything about the ASVAB, or basic training?"

"You mentioned last time that I could go to the same b-basic training location where you went, because that's where they train men and women together. W-were there many other women there with you?"

"There were two other women in my platoon. We had thirty-five total, for context."

She and the two other women must have been completely outnumbered. Not for the first time, Tessa's recruiter seems to read her mind. "I have to admit that was definitely a change, after coming out of high school. It was…" Something unreadable, a departure from the staff sergeant's usual pleasant professionalism, flits across her face. "There was a short adjustment period. I did form a close bond with the other two women in my platoon. They're my best friends to this day. Women in the Army are cut from a different cloth. We look out for one another. I'm sure you'll have the same experience with the other young women in your platoon."

Tessa broods about that conversation late that night, as she tries to fall asleep. Boys haven't been her only bullies over the years, but they have been the worst. Colton and Brady mocked her stutter throughout seventh and eighth grade. *W-w-what is wrong with her? Jesus Christ. She c-c-can't even talk.* That only served to make Tessa clam up more, leaving her terrified to answer questions in class or participate in group discussions. In ninth grade, Cory Alberts asked her to the Winter Formal as a joke. Even now, Tessa can't think about that — about the delighted acceptance she stammered out, and then how Cory had burst out laughing, and how Colton and Brady laughed with him — without her throat seizing up.

She spent the rest of her time in high school avoiding boys like the plague. The thought of being surrounded by them at basic training makes her curl up on her side in bed, pulling the covers around her, as if that will be enough to shelter her.

∞∞∞∞

Tessa spends the next week agonizing over how to talk to her dad. Her recruiter gave her a pamphlet on how to tell parents about an impending enlistment. The advice boils down to *having a reasonable discussion* and *sharing as much information as you can.*

Tessa imagines how that would go. *I chose this because I need to get away from this house and because I hate living with you. You barely make any money, because you can't work anywhere for more than a couple of years, because people can't stand you. So you can't pay for me to go to college like so many other kids' parents can. I chose this because I don't want to take out loans and spend the decade after I graduate trying to pay off that debt.*

She's overthinking this. He won't even care. He doesn't see her and he doesn't talk to her, so it won't make a difference to him if she's here or at Atlantic Cape in Mays Landing, or if she's at an Army base in Germany or Japan.

Tessa spends her Saturday shift at the gym on edge, and Jesy tries to cheer her up by buying her a meatball sub from the deli for lunch. She drives her home too, even though Tessa says that she can walk to clear her head and mentally prepare for the conversation.

She fixes her dad's dinner, and makes herself walk down the hallway toward his study. *I can call Jesy if I need to,* Tessa reminds herself. She's not as alone as she was in the past, in the years before she met Jesy.

Tessa cradles the bowl in the crook of her arm and knocks on the door. "Dad? I have dinner f-for you."

Silence. The computer chair creaks on the other side of the door. "Come in."

Tessa tentatively steps inside. It's dark, the blinds closed even though it's still light outside, the spring days growing longer. The only light comes from the dim yellow desk lamp and the glow of her dad's computer screen. He sits at his desk, a Word document in front of him — probably a student's paper. He doesn't turn to face her.

Tessa places his food on his desk, careful not to disrupt the stacks of scientific journals, other papers, and books scattered around the desk. Habit and instinct tells her to turn around and flee, but she remains still.

The only personal memento on her dad's desk is a framed photo of her mom standing in front of the *Just Sold* sign on their house's front lawn. Mom looks so stylish in her short-sleeved yellow printed dress, cradling a bouquet of red roses and beaming at the camera, radiant with joy. Tessa's arms ache with how much she wants to hug her mom again.

Her dad finally tears his gaze away from his computer, frowning at her. His expression is always severe, his mouth twisted into a hard line. That particular frown makes her feel about an inch tall, like a little kid again. He isn't used to her sticking around for so long. She normally drops off his food and leaves without another word.

Tessa used to try more. For her mom's sake, and for her own. She would ask him how his day was, and if things were going okay with his classes. She would try talking to him about school. Maybe she should have kept trying for longer. But she tried, and he didn't. That made her sad and hurt, and then it made her angry and hurt, and then she stopped trying entirely.

"What is it?"

He sounds a little irritable, a little impatient. Not a good sign. She has to get this over with as quickly as possible. "I'm m-moving out after graduation next month. I-I'm enlisting in the Army."

Her dad physically recoils from her, as if she has spat into his food. "The Army? That's what you want to do with yourself?"

His tone is even more scathing than it was when Tessa made the mistake of asking him for help with her algebra homework in ninth grade. It takes all of her strength to keep herself from flinching. *Don't stutter,* she orders herself. "Yes."

Her dad isn't impressed by her resolve. His expression darkens. "You know who joins the Army? People who are too stupid or weak to think for themselves. People who need someone to tell them what to do, because they don't have what it takes to make their own way for themselves. People who are okay with being used as mindless cannon fodder."

He stabs a finger at her to make that last point, standing up from his chair, towering over her. Tessa reflexively takes one step backward. "This isn't how I raised you."

If she were braver, she would yell that he hasn't raised her at all. Tessa takes a shaky breath, willing herself not to cry. "I-I-I just wanted to let you know." She stutters over every word.

That only makes her dad angrier. He steps away from her, gesturing his frustration. "You think you can make it on the front lines? You can barely string a sentence together. You won't last a week in the Army. Just listen to me."

It isn't the first time he has commented on her stutter. The words still hit her like a slap. "Y-yes," Tessa manages to say, with all the dignity she can muster. "I can make it. I will."

She turns on her heel and strides out of her dad's office, slamming the door behind her, ignoring how he yells out after her. But he doesn't follow her as she runs down the hallway and into the backyard. Tessa sinks down onto the overgrown grass that she hasn't had the time or energy to mow, bracing her elbows on her knees and burying her face in her hands. Her dad's face twisted with fury. *People who are too stupid and weak — mindless cannon fodder — you can barely string a sentence together — you won't last a week-*

Tessa starts to cry, rocking back and forth in the grass. She wants her mom. Mom was never, ever mean to her. She never said anything unkind, to Tessa or anyone else.

Today reopened the cracks inside, and she can't stop crying. She stays out until twilight fades into true darkness, wiping at her nose and her eyes with the sleeves of her t-shirt. She can't breathe through her nose, and her eyes are swollen, and her head hurts, and she's exhausted to the bone. She hadn't even bothered eating dinner. And she has to be up at five for work tomorrow.

Tessa pulls herself up to her feet. She looks at the house, with the kitchen light shining through the window, and every fiber of her rebels against the thought of going back inside. If she could walk to the Army recruiting station and find her recruiter and beg her to let her leave for military processing tonight, she would.

One month. Just one month until she can leave here and never come back. Tessa bows her head, wipes her face again, and heads inside.

Chapter Three

June 2006

Tessa's dad doesn't attend her graduation. She hadn't expected him to. She sits in her plastic chair on the football field in her cap and gown, surrounded by her classmates, half-listening to the valedictorian and the principal speak. She tries not to react after the ceremony finally comes to an end, and parents and siblings flood onto the field to find and embrace their graduates. Moms hug and kiss their graduates, and dads clap them on the shoulders. So many of the other girls get bouquets from their families. Tessa's chest hurts. She makes her way through the crush of people, her diploma in hand, looking to leave the field as fast as she can. She just needed this to take to the Military Entrance and Processing Station office on Monday.

To her surprise, she is waylaid by a few teachers on her way out. Mrs. Taras, the librarian, and Mrs. Hunt from English, and Mr. Gabriel from US Government, all of whom wrote letters of recommendation for her, back when she had been applying for scholarships. Tessa finally leaves the football field feeling a little dazed, like she is sleepwalking. She has had fleeting encounters with this sense of warmth before. When she got a perfect grade on an essay, and her teachers wrote *Amazing job!* at the top of her paper. When she and Jesy hung out together.

The parking lot of Elizabeth High is overflowing. Tessa catches sight of a familiar, beat-up silver Honda CRV, duct tape holding the tail light together. Jesy leans against the car door, texting.

"Jesy?" Tessa's voice cracks with incredulity. "I-I thought you were scheduled to work tonight."

Jesy hugs her, and Tessa gets a noseful of Bath and Body Works Japanese Cherry Blossom perfume. "I switched shifts. We're going out."

The Olive Garden in town is packed with graduates and their families, so the food comes slowly, but Jesy and Tessa enjoy lingering over their shared appetizer of spinach-artichoke dip and breadsticks. They gossip about what's going on with Britney Spears and their other favorite and least favorite celebrities, and complain about what a letdown the new Twilight book was. It's late by the time they finish their dinner and dessert, and Jesy refuses to let Tessa pay her half of the check. "Nope. You can get me Dunkin this weekend if you want, but I got this."

Tessa has gone to bed over the last several nights in an anxious tangle of nerves. Tonight is different. She curls up in bed, holding her old stuffed dog close. She doesn't go through an excruciating mental replay of the last fight she had with her dad. She isn't haunted by the memory of her mom's final year. Of how thin she got, and how she struggled to grip her favorite cherry Chapstick to put it on her lips, and how Tessa would apply it for her.

(She still thinks of her mom. She imagines her mom sitting at the table with her and Jesy at Olive Garden.)

ooooo

Tessa spends her Saturday after work packing. She doesn't intend to come back home again.

She folds her things into the TSA-approved carry-on gym bag that she found at the thrift store. The packing list that Staff Sergeant Drake printed out for her is sparse. She packs up the things that she wants to hold onto, using empty cleaning supply boxes she took home from work. The only things she'll keep are her old stuffed dog Leo, her mom's photo albums, and the few pieces of her mom's clothing she squirreled away before her dad went on his alcohol-fueled cleaning out of her closet. She takes a cab to Safeguard Self Storage and walks back, her stuff secured in a 25 square foot unit that will cost 55 dollars a month.

A knot forms in Tessa's stomach halfway through her last shift at Fundamental Fitness the following day. She should be excited to be leaving this behind. She is still hit by waves of melancholy throughout her shift. Fundamental Fitness has been an escape for her. A safe place. The gym is as familiar to her as her own home, and a thousand times more comfortable. She'll miss coming here.

Jesy insists on driving her home. They stop at McDonalds for ice cream on the way, and they eat Oreo McFlurries in Jesy's car, parked in the lot.

"Enjoy it while you can." Jesy speaks around a mouthful of ice cream. "I heard the food's kind of shit at basic training."

"I don't care. It's going to be ten weeks where I don't have to cook or do dishes or grocery shop. I can just show up in the cafeteria and *get* f-food."

"Well, when you put it like that…" Jesy muses. "Hey, they're paying you for being there, right? We should go see Beyonce in concert when you get some time off."

They discuss that all the way to Tessa's house, and they fall silent when Jesy pulls up at the curb. Tessa has been dreading this all day. But it's not goodbye forever. They were just talking about when they can see each other again.

"It's not really goodbye," Jesy says, reading Tessa's mind.

"I-it's not." Tessa takes a deep breath, trying to keep herself from crying. "Thank you for everything, Jesy."

Jesy twists to face her, holding her arms out. Tessa hugs her tightly, trying to put everything she couldn't say into that hug.

For once, there isn't much for her to do when she gets home. Tessa goes to sit in the backyard. She mowed the lawn in the front and back yard one last time on Friday. The fresh-cut grass prickles against her bare feet and her legs, underneath the hem of her gym shorts. She has no idea when it'll get mowed again.

Tessa sits there for a long time, in the shade of the hazel alder tree. A gentle breeze stirs the branches, pushing the fluffy clouds along the blue sky. She saw so many other girls crying after graduation, and on their last day of school, as they wrote in each other's yearbooks. The melancholy has come for her too, now, just a few days late. The realization that she is on the final page of this chapter in her life. She's on the cusp of something new.

She will leave Elizabeth tomorrow. She'll enlist in the Army and forge a new life for herself. She will never live with her dad again. Whatever struggles and challenges the future has for her, it won't be the same as this.

And she can bear it. Whatever it is, she can bear it.

ooooo

Tessa keeps an eye on the clock as she finishes her breakfast the next morning. Her ride should be here any minute now.

She still hasn't made a decision.

She should say goodbye. She could call it through the door, just casually, the way she used to tell her dad she was going to school. But she and her dad haven't spoken a word since their fight last month. She hasn't even been into his office to hand him his food. Tessa just sets the plate on the floor in front of his room, knocks twice, and then leaves. She has never gone this long without seeing him, and it makes her feel a little bad.

She could at least write him a note and slip it under his door, the way she used to when she was going to spend the night at Jesy's house. *At a sleepover with my friend, I'll be back tomorrow.* What would this note say? *At Army basic training, I'll be back never? Thanks for nothing for all these years!*

Her mom taught her that if she couldn't say anything nice, to not say anything at all. She has nothing kind or constructive to say to her dad.

(Guilt nags at her. Her mom wouldn't want her to leave things like this. Even years before she got sick, she knew that Tessa and her dad weren't close. She tried and tried to get them to connect with one another, but it never went anywhere.)

A yellow cab with the Elizabeth Taxi logo stenciled on the side pulls up to the curb. Tessa abandons that train of thought. She's spent enough time over the last five years ruminating about her dad, trying to understand why he is the way he is, and trying — and ultimately failing — to be compassionate of the fact he clearly has something wrong with him. Her dad and this failed relationship aren't her priority anymore.

She gathers her things and locks the front door behind her. She doesn't anticipate needing her house key again. Habit compels her to slip it into her bag, just in case.

The cab driver pulls away from the curb after confirming her destination, and Tessa can't help herself. She turns and takes one last look at the house. Suddenly, she remembers the photo on her dad's desk, of her mom standing beside that *Just Sold* sign, beaming and holding her flowers. She must have had such high hopes for that house, and for her family, and for the life that all of them would live there. There's a wrenching, tearing feeling inside her gut, and Tessa faces forward again. The driver turns the radio on to the local news. Tessa tries to listen, but she keeps thinking of that picture of her mom in the front yard of the house.

She had been so desperate to get out, to get away from her dad. That was still the house where Mom lived. It still had the kitchen where they would cook and bake together, and the yard where they would sit together and talk, and the sofa where they would hang out to read or watch TV. All the joy and warmth fled from the house after Mom died, but still. She's going to a place that has no touch of her mom left in it at all. (Nowhere she ever goes after this will have any touch of her mom left in it at all.)

Don't think of it like that, Tessa chastises herself. She still has her mom's clothes and albums, safe in the storage unit in town. She'll pay to have them shipped to her once she knows what base she will end up stationed in. And she still has *herself.* She remembers what her mom taught her and gave her. Memories of watching 60 Minutes every Sunday evening, and going for evening walks around the neighborhood when the sun set. Browsing at Borders bookstores together on rainy days, and going to the Elmora Farmers Market to buy tomatoes in summer, and watching ducks swim across the pond at the park. She'll remember her mom every time she does those things, no matter where she is.

They left early enough from Elizabeth that they don't run into much traffic on the drive to Bordentown. Tessa double-checks that she has all her things as soon as she exits the taxi. Her heart flutters with nerves. She's never been in a hotel before.

Her jaw drops when she walks through the glass double doors. It's the fanciest place she's ever been in. The floors are gray wood, polished to a high shine, and draped with a long rug the color of a coffee with extra milk. Even the overhead lighting is stylish, with light emanating from interlocking circles. When she checks into her room, she finds that amazing too. It has a big flatscreen TV, and the bathroom is sparkling clean, the way she never could quite get it at home. The bed is large, and so plush that she sinks down a few inches when she sits.

The dining room, downstairs lounge, and lobby have filled up by the time she returns downstairs. Tessa gets a small table near the floor-to-ceiling window and discreetly studies the other hotel guests while she eats. It's easy to guess who is here for military processing and who may not be. There are a lot of young men her age, or maybe a few years older. She would bet that they're military applicants too.

She's one of the first to arrive at the briefing, and the room fills up quickly. It's a lengthy recap of everything that her recruiter already told her about what to expect tomorrow. When the briefing finally wraps up, Tessa heads straight for her room for a change of clothes, and then to the gym.

She isn't the only one who had the same idea. She makes a beeline for the one open treadmill and focuses on the wall-mounted TV as she runs, reading the captions on CNN as they flicker by. Christiane Amanpour addresses invisible viewers from the CNN newsdesk.

"We have more details on the killing of Abu Musab al-Zarqawi, the most wanted insurgent in Iraq, last week. Acting on a maze of intelligence and tips, the military targeted a safe house north of Baquba, in which the leader of al Qaeda in Iraq was staying. A Jordanian-born Sunni militant with a $25 million U.S. bounty on his head, al-Zarqawi was believed to have the blood of thousands on his hands as leader of the group behind numerous beheadings, assassinations and bombings…"

Each sentence is punctuated by video clips of the US troops surrounding al-Zarqawi's compound, interspersed with photos of the F-16 warplanes used for the attack and photographs of the now-dead terrorist. Tessa presses the speed button on the treadmill twice, increasing her pace. Could she be ordered to help with a mission like that?

The 5K clears her mind. Tessa showers, has a quick dinner, and gets ready for bed. It's weird, going to sleep somewhere that isn't her own room or Jesy's bedroom. She snuggles into the soft bed, trying to get comfortable, and hugs her spare pillow in lieu of holding her stuffed dog.

ooooo

The following day at the military entrance and processing station drags on. She goes through intake, taking the career aptitude test, the medical examination, and balance, hearing, coordination, and vision tests. After lunch, all the potential recruits are herded to a large waiting room to discuss the results of their tests. Career counselors call them back one by one. Tessa crosses and uncrosses her legs, and folds her hands in her lap. Her earlier confidence about her career aptitude test performance leaks away the longer she waits.

A soldier strides through the doorway. "Halifax?" he calls.

Tessa springs up so fast that she nearly trips on her own feet. "I-I'm here." She sounds breathless, even though she's just been sitting around for the past hour and a half.

The soldier introduces himself as Sergeant Briscoe. He leads her to a tiny cubicle, with most of the available space taken up by large filing cabinets. Tall but neat stacks of paperwork almost completely cover his desk. "Congratulations, Ms. Halifax." He gestures for her to take a seat. "You scored a 93, meaning that you're qualified for most jobs the Army has to offer."

The hours spent studying and dozens of practice tests had been worth it. Tessa clasps her hands together in her lap to keep from trembling with excitement. "T-thank you."

Tessa leaves the cubicle an hour later, clutching a folder with her brand-new contract in hand. None of this feels real. There hadn't been any openings for her first choice of job, as a civil affairs specialist working to help Iraqi civilians amidst all the upheaval. She got her second choice — military working dog handler. The sergeant emphasized that it didn't come with an additional job signing bonus, and he seemed like he was kind of nudging her toward one of the areas that did. Infantry, engineer corps, field artillery, or air and missile defense. She turned him down. She likes her choice way better. She'll get to work with dogs.

After months of waiting to graduate, all of this is happening so fast. She will head to Fort Leonard Wood for basic training in three days' time. The Army is even paying for her plane ticket out to Missouri. *Missouri.* Tessa knows next to nothing about Missouri. She's never left Jersey, save for the occasional trip to New York City.

It's another hour of waiting around before she and a batch of forty other new recruits are led to the ceremony room. They stand shoulder-to-shoulder in the small space, facing a podium emblazoned with the Department of Defense insignia at the front of the room. The wall behind the podium is lined with flags. It's all a little intimidating, leaving

Tessa feeling out of place, out of her depth. She's the only girl in the room.

There's a glass partition to their left, separating their room from an observation area filled with family and friends of new recruits. There are a lot of parents holding cameras. Tessa redirects her gaze to the front of the room, to the officer who is walking out to stand at the podium. She swallows the bitter taste in her mouth.

You know who joins the Army? People who are too stupid or weak to think for themselves. People who need someone to tell them what to do, because they don't have what it takes to make their own way for themselves. People who are okay with being used for mindless cannon fodder.

Her dad was wrong. She's going to help people. She's going to help keep people safe.

The officer asks them to raise their right hands. He leads them through the oath. They repeat after him. Tessa tries her hardest, and she does not stutter.

"I, Teresa Halifax, do solemnly swear that I will support and defend the Constitution of the United States against all enemies, foreign and domestic; that I will bear true faith and allegiance to the same; and that I will obey the orders of the President of the United States and the orders of the officers appointed over me, according to regulations and the Uniform Code of Military Justice. So help me God."

Her voice blends right in with the others in the room, all of them speaking as one. It gives her chills.

Chapter Four

June 2006

Tessa's ticket scores her a window seat on her flight to basic training. She comes just short of pressing her nose to the window with fascination as the plane begins taxiing down the runway, and she has to bite back a gasp when the plane finally takes off. It's incredible, how fast the trees and the buildings, the cars and the highways, go from large in scale to as miniature as the toys she played with as a little kid.

The flight goes by fast. The travel instructions printout in her MEPS* folder directs her to go to the USO* lounge at the airport to await the basic training bus. The lounge is filled with about thirty other recruits. None of the other recruits appear much older than her, and almost all of them look over when she steps in. Upon seeing that she isn't anyone important, they turn their attention back to the TV, or the USO magazines or newspapers they were perusing.

(Almost all of them. Several of their gazes linger on her, in her jeans and her button-down plaid top, which is uncomfortable.)

There is only one person whose stare doesn't bother Tessa at all. She returns it, relief flooding through her. She isn't the only girl here. The other girl looks around Tessa's age, but she's gorgeous — slender and fine-boned, with brown skin and curly black hair twisted into a bun. She's the kind of girl that Tessa would normally observe from afar and be intimidated by. Then again, she had felt the same way about Jesy when they started working together.

Military Entrance and Processing Station
United Service Organizations

Tessa can hear her best friend's voice in her ear, urging her on. *Don't be so scared all the time. Most people are nice.*

Tessa summons all of her courage. She sinks down in the armchair across from the other girl, setting her duffel bag down at her feet. "H-hi. I'm Tessa."

That was dumb. Why should the girl care what her name is? Should she have asked the girl's name first?

The girl smiles, leaning in toward Tessa. "Hi. I'm so glad that I'm not the only girl here," she says, in an undertone. She definitely has a New York accent. "These guys looked at me like I was in the wrong place when I came in."

"I-I can imagine."

The girl sticks her hand out. "I'm Rosalie Soto. Where are you from?"

They learn that they're sort of neighbors. Rosalie is from the Bronx, where Tessa and Jesy used to hang out with Jesy's cousins. "I miss it already," Rosalie says mournfully. "I went looking around here for food after my flight landed and I couldn't find any real bagels." She jerks a thumb in the direction of the snack and coffee bar behind them. "They actually have a good Reuben though, if you want to grab one before we go. My uncle warned me about the food in basic."

"That's a good idea. I'll be right back." There's no line, and Tessa returns to her spot, unwrapping her sandwich. The first bite is heaven.

Rosalie catches the look of bliss on her face. "Right? It tastes like home."

"It doesn't even need salt and vinegar chips in."

"Salt and vinegar, huh? I always do jalapeno chips."

Something Rosalie mentioned earlier draws her attention, and Tessa lowers her sandwich. "Your uncle went to basic training?"

"Yeah, back in the 80s, forever ago. My cousin too, in 2000. Both of them say it probably hasn't changed much since they went."

"It's so nice that you know people who went through it. I've just been trying to find out everything I can about it online."

"You're the first in your family?"

Tessa suppresses a wince at the memory of her dad's reaction to her news. "Y-yeah."

"What made you want to enlist?"

She's glad Rosalie asked. She wanted to ask her the same thing, but she wasn't sure if that was considered too personal of a question to ask someone you just met. "The education benefits for college."

Rosalie nods. "That's why my uncle and cousin enlisted. It worked out. They got to go to officer training school and everything."

Tessa listens, impressed. The salary that she's going to get as a Private Second Class, after completing basic training, is kind of low. Twenty thousand a year, though everyone emphasized that she would get paid more with every year she stayed in the Army. They also said that officers got paid more, if she was interested in attending officer training school after getting a degree. "Are you going to do that too?"

"Maybe. They said I should, but I don't love the idea of college. It could just be the degrees my uncle and cousin got, though. They're both in finance. It's super boring."

Tessa balls up the paper her sandwich was wrapped in and tosses it into the nearby can. "What MOS are you doing?"

"74D. Defense against chemical, nuclear, biological, and radiological weapons, and WMDs. There's a lot of demand for that right now."

Tessa shivers at the mention of nuclear weapons. They watched the horrifying video footage of the Hiroshima bomb in her history class. It took her hours to fall asleep that night. She tossed and turned in bed, unable to shake the mental image of that mushroom cloud billowing into the sky. "I-it's scary, but you'll help keep people safe." It makes sense to her, too. Rosalie lived in New York City. The terror of 9/11 hit close to home for her.

"I hope I can. What about you?"

"31K. Military working dog handler."

"Oh, with the bomb sniffing dogs! I've seen them on the subway and Port Authority."

"Yeah. I've always liked dogs," Tessa explains, a little self-consciously. Her rationale is maybe a little childish, but it's the truth. "I like the idea of working with one as a partner. My recruiter said it's amazing what they can be trained to do — that they can do things people can't."

Rosalie gives Tessa a small smile. "It sounds like both of us could end up protecting New York."

It does seem likely that she and Rosalie could be deployed to bases at home, rather than in the Middle East. "Maybe." Impulsively, Tessa adds, "I-I'm glad we met today."

She immediately regrets speaking up. She doesn't want to be weird. Rosalie is already nodding her agreement, though. "My family told me that the most important thing I could do early on was find a friend and stick to her."

Tessa thinks back to Staff Sergeant Drake's words, months ago. *Women in the Army are cut from a different cloth, and we look out for one another.* "My recruiter said the same thing."

When the basic training bus finally arrives, Tessa and Rosalie sit together. They talk through most of the two-hour drive, keeping their voices down. Tessa learns that Rosalie is the youngest of three siblings. Her brothers and her parents work in the trades. They share the same taste in books, and they have enjoyed several of the same hangout spots in the city. They both like to cook and work out. Rosalie ran the United Airlines Half Marathon last month, which Tessa thinks is incredibly impressive. "I-I've never run more than a 10k."

"That's long enough. I won't do a half again. The training was too much." Rosalie gives Tessa's shoulders a speculative look. "Do you lift? I've been trying to get into it all year."

They fall into a nervous silence when they arrive at the Fort Leonard Wood visitor gate, clutching the straps of their duffel bags. Dozens of recruits are lined up in front of each bus here, a uniformed soldier at the head of each line, gesticulating and shouting orders.

Tessa and Rosalie stick close together as they line up. They spend the remainder of the day getting their personnel records processed, enduring more medical tests and exams, and attending various orientations. The drudgery goes on for three and a half days in total. There is a physical fitness test, yet more orientations, uniform issue and fitting, and immunizations. They set up financial matters, receive ID cards, and undergo security interviews. The days pass with waiting in shuffling, slow-moving lines, and signing endless pieces of documentation. Tedium doesn't begin to describe it.

"I'm looking forward to starting basic training for real," Tessa tells Rosalie over dinner on their third day.

Rosalie shakes her head grimly and saws off a chunk of her meatloaf. "You're going to regret that."

ooooo

Tessa does, a mere two hours into their first day after beginning basic training. She and Rosalie end up in the same platoon, which is their only stroke of luck. Drill and ceremony training starts at once, as their drill sergeant lines them up on the field and teaches them the ten stationary drill commands. After a few hours, their platoon finally gets the hang of it. Tessa makes the mistake of thinking they will be allowed to take a break, or perhaps eat lunch.

Instead, the drill sergeant instructs them on the correct procedures for responding to the other orders he barks out. "Mark time! Half step, march! Column right, march! To the rear, march! Change step, march!"

There are so many different commands that it makes Tessa's head spin. She doesn't know what she's doing anymore. Neither does anyone else. Any semblance of competence they demonstrated during stationary drill falls apart. The consequence for setting one foot out of place or letting posture slip is steep. "Get it together!" Drill Sergeant Davis yells. He makes them all drop to the ground and do push ups until they're on the brink of collapse. Then he orders them to repeat the march. This goes on for hours, in the sweltering, humid heat of the Missouri summer. Tessa and Rosalie exchange looks of helpless misery.

"Eyes forward, recruits!" Drill Sergeant Davis stabs a finger at both of them. "You think this is your social hour?"

Tessa is so flustered at being chastised that she screws up her mark time. The guy to the left of her shoots her a contemptuous look as they all drop to the grass for more pushups. "Jesus Christ."

The drill sergeant storms over, looming above him. "What was that, recruit?"

"N-nothing, sir!" For once, she isn't the one stammering. Tessa still wilts, her arms trembling as she does yet another push-up.

Tempers flare once after that, too. One of the guys in their platoon, Perez, accidentally turns left instead of right, ruining their march. Nichols shoves him in the back, sending him stumbling into Tessa. "Are you stupid, man?"

Drill Sergeant Davis moves rapidly, lunging into Nichols' face, coming just short of grabbing him by the collar. Nichols almost trips over his own feet in his haste to stumble back. The rest of them quickly put space between themselves and the drill sergeant. "Do not *ever* put your hands on one of your fellow soldiers like that ever again!" he roars, and Tessa thinks that even her dad would have found him frightening. "Do you hear me, recruit?"

Nichols almost sobs out his, "Sir, yes, sir."

Drill Sergeant Davis finally pronounces them all pathetic, and regards the platoon with disgust. They are herded inside for a hurried fifteen-minute lunch and yet more briefings on the Army core values. Loyalty, duty, respect, selfless service, honor, integrity, and courage. The platoon returns to the field for more hours of practice before dinner. It goes marginally better this time.

Dinner is rushed. "I keep thinking that I could be at home right now." Rosalie takes a forkful of her limp boiled carrots. "Sitting on the roof with a cold drink, tanning and reading."

"I don't feel that way." As much as today has sucked, Tessa would still take this over what she was used to at home. At least she's not lonely here. "But I'm so tired. My brain is fried."

Their day still isn't over. After dinner, Drill Sergeant Davis gathers their platoon into a briefing room. He launches into a lecture about the importance of teamwork, complete with historical examples of Army operations where good teamwork made or broke the mission. He paces back and forth in front of them as he speaks, his hands balled into fists at his side. "The stakes in the situations you will be in cannot be higher. The stakes are the success of the mission, and there is nothing more critical than the mission. In many cases, trusting your team and squad cohesion are matters of life and death. When you are out there in the field, you need to look out for your squad and protect your squad like they are your own family, like they are your own brothers and sisters."

Drill Sergeant Davis pauses to let that sink in. Tessa tries to wrap her mind around that. Her own experience of devotion to family has been limited.

"That attitude does not kick in overnight, or on your flight to the Middle East. It is a state of mind that I will instill in you here, and you will never forget it. I do not want to see any childish squabbling and petty in-fighting again. I won't tolerate that shit. This is a diverse group here.

You need to act right with one another and treat each other with respect. Do you hear me?"

"Sir, yes, sir," they chorus.

"Good. You're dismissed for mail call. You two recruits, hang back."

Tessa and Rosalie exchange quick, unhappy looks. They remain seated, and Drill Sergeant Davis waits until the last of their fellow platoon members has left the briefing room. He folds his arms over his chest. "There are some special considerations for you two recruits. I'm sure you've felt this already. The stereotypes, or the judgment or awkwardness from being the only females in the room."

"Y-yes, sir," Tessa murmurs. Rosalie echoes her. She would normally deny that, just because it seems like the polite thing to do, but she feels like Drill Sergeant Davis might get at least a little bit of what they're going through. He is Black, and he's probably dealt with stereotypes and judgment and awkwardness from being the only Black person in a room.

"It's not the same, but I kind of get it," he says briskly. "I'll tell you what my drill sergeant told me when I was a new recruit. Whatever the emotions coming from other soldiers, the one answer is to work hard. Work twice, thrice, as hard as the others. Never let them hear you complaining, and never make excuses. Push yourself as hard as you possibly can — to your limits, and beyond. Your work ethic will speak for itself. Your skills will speak for themselves. You work hard, and you make it so that no one can argue with or doubt your competence as a soldier. You do this, and you will force them to respect you."

He speaks with such conviction, such fervor. Tessa finds herself nodding along with Rosalie. "Yes, sir."

"I've trained dozens of female recruits over the years, and they've all been successful. No washouts." Drill Sergeant Davis points between them. "You two are going to be battle buddies. You'll do everything together, and I mean everything. You're not going anywhere alone. You're going to be responsible for each other's safety and well-being. Get it?"

His lips press into a hard line, and Rosalie's brows draw together. "Yes, sir." Tessa's words come out more like a question.

"Look, I am going to be real with you. You two need to be careful. Act right."

Tessa's shoulders stiffen.

"Trust your unit in the field," Drill Sergeant Davis continues. "I wasn't joking around earlier when I said that trust and unit cohesion are life or death in the field. But keep your guard up otherwise, on base, in the barracks. Make friends with the guys, sure. That's important, to get them to see you as a person. Talk to them, have conversations with them — but don't do anything that they could perceive as being flirtatious. Shut it down if *they* try to get flirtatious or sexual, too, so they don't get the wrong idea and try to follow that wrong idea to any conclusions. Don't party with the soldiers in the barracks or put yourself in any questionable situations. You don't want to get mixed up with any of that and put yourself at risk of date rape."

Her mind is blank. Rosalie's mouth is hanging open.

Drill Sergeant Davis huffs a small, humorless laugh. "The things your recruiter won't tell you, am I right?"

Tessa still can't speak.

"Do you understand me, recruits?"

"Y-yes, s-sir," Tessa stammers. Rosalie's reply is so quiet that Tessa can barely hear it.

A flicker of sympathy crosses the drill sergeant's face. "It's a tough lesson, sure. But it's better you both learn it here and now from me, rather than learning it the hard way from experience. Don't forget this. Watch out for yourselves and each other. Now, you have personal time until lights out at twenty-one hundred hours. You're dismissed."

Tessa and Rosalie trudge back to the women's barracks. Tessa rubs at her chest. It hurts. The thought of facing the rest of the platoon after that sends her reeling. Drill Sergeant Davis practically told them to think of the other guys as potential rapists. How could he ask them to think of the members of the platoon as brothers on the field, and then tell them to keep their guard up around them? To be friendly, but not too friendly? The cognitive dissonance is immense.

Rosalie's jaw is tight, her face flushed. She is four inches shorter than Tessa, but fury fuels her stride. Tessa has to quicken her pace to keep up. "That was fucked up."

"D-did your uncle and cousin ever warn you about…"

"No. Maybe — kind of? But not so bluntly, you know? They told me to find a friend and stick to her, and be careful, and not let anyone give me any shit. That was it. But this must be a real problem if he warned us like that."

"I-it's okay." Tessa speaks with a resolve that surprises her. "We'll listen to him. We'll watch each other's backs. Safety in numbers."

"Yeah, but what about when we're not here anymore? We're not going into the same MOS. We won't be doing advanced individual training together either."

Tessa doesn't want to think about that. That's intimidating enough, without thinking too far into what Drill Sergeant Davis told them about not letting their guard down on base. (Weren't they supposed to be safe on base?) "L-let's just get through these ten weeks first."

Chapter Five

June – December 2006

First call is at four-thirty every morning. By five-hundred hours, Tessa and Rosalie are in the company yard with the rest of the platoon, running and doing calisthenics while Drill Sergeant Davis yells at them to work harder; run faster.

Tessa makes his advice her mantra. She repeats it to herself as her shoulders, arms, and core burn from doing pushups. She repeats it as she does pullups, her arms trembling. *The one answer is to work hard. Work twice, thrice, as hard as the others. Push yourself as hard as you possibly can — to your limits, and beyond.*

Every day, Tessa coaches Rosalie through pushups, planks, and burpees. "Five more. You can do it. Keep your elbows in. Keep your core tight, hips low."

"I'm gonna die," Rosalie gasps, during the pushup phase of her thirtieth burpee.

"N-never let them hear you complaining." Tessa finishes her fortieth burpee, wiping the sweat from her forehead. "Make it look effortless."

"I'm gonna…throw up in your shoes…"

They acquit themselves well in their hand-to-hand combat training. Rosalie has to coach Tessa through Victory Tower, an exercise where they navigate through obstacles at extreme heights. They rappel down 50-foot walls, and cross rope ladders and bridges swaying forty feet in the air. "You got this, Tess!" Rosalie encourages, resting a comforting hand on Tessa's shoulder. Tessa breathes through the sick, swooping feeling in her stomach as she inches along the rope bridge.

They get classroom instruction on first aid training, map reading, and land navigation. They get exposed to a tear gas chamber. They are introduced to their standard-issue weapon, the M16A2 assault rifle, and they both pass their weapons proficiency tests. Neither of them are at the top of their platoon in weapons proficiency, but that's fine. They're not like the other guys, with their dreams of being Army Rangers or snipers. Rosalie is going to be working in chemical weapons defense, and Tessa is going to be working with her dog as a partner. Neither of them should need to draw their weapons unless there's an emergency and they are under attack.

They head straight into field training exercises focusing on simulated combat scenarios, including nighttime combat operations and military operations in urban territory. The atmosphere of relief in the platoon when Drill Sergeant Davis announces that they have all successfully completed basic training is palpable. All Tessa can think about is her dad telling her she wouldn't last a week in the Army. He was so wrong about her.

"Your recovery week starts now," Drill Sergeant Davis says. "Graduation is next Saturday at nine-hundred hours. You'll spend the rest of this week repairing anything that you're not taking with you to your advanced individual training, and practicing for the graduation ceremony."

He dismisses them, and Tessa and Rosalie head back to the barracks. She never thought she would miss that spare, grim space, shared with four other female recruits from other basic training platoons. After two nights of camping during the field exercise, even the lumpy bunk bed is going to feel like the height of luxury.

"My parents are going to want to come to graduation, but it's still summer, so flight tickets are going to be expensive," Rosalie frets. "How long do you think it'll take to drive?"

"Maybe sixteen hours. Would your brothers come with your parents? They could help with the driving too."

"I don't know. It depends on if they can afford to take the time off work. They'd want to, though. Are you going to invite your dad?"

Tessa shrugs, keeping her gaze straight ahead. "No. He wouldn't come even if I did." She is going to be the only person in her platoon without family attending her graduation. Everyone has mentioned their families in passing over the last several weeks. She doesn't know the whole story about anyone's life, just the fragments they share, but from those fragments, everyone else's lives sound so *normal*. Even amidst all the imperfections in their families, all of them are loved. All of them are valuable parts of their families. She would bet that all of them have been missed, over these last nine weeks.

There is no awkwardness in admitting this to Rosalie. There is none of the self-consciousness she would have felt ten weeks ago. They have gotten close, after spending ten weeks by each other's side, day and night, providing encouragement, support, and companionship whenever needed.

Rosalie makes the small huffing sound she always makes when she's mad. "Well, my parents will show up for you too, then. They'll be so happy to meet you in person."

The thought of anyone being happy to meet her is a foreign one. Tessa's skepticism must show on her face, because Rosalie nudges her in the ribs. "Don't be like that."

"Ouch! I'm looking forward to meeting them too."

"The girl who did the impossible and helped me get these muscles." Rosalie rolls her right sleeve up, flexing her bicep, and Tessa laughs.

"Hey! Don't laugh at me! Just because you're still more ripped than I am, you think you're the boss?"

The other girls aren't back in their barracks yet. Tessa grabs the broom from the closet and begins to sweep, while Rosalie goes to fill up the mop bucket with water. "The others never pull their weight around here. When was the last time you saw them cleaning?"

They work in silence for a little while. She should be happy today. She should feel nothing but happiness and pride and accomplishment. The melancholy that settled over her earlier when she thought about graduation and her dad still lingers. This time, it is harder to speak up about it. Tessa tries, anyway. "H-have you been feeling like you're saying goodbye a lot lately?"

"No." Rosalie sloshes the mop in the bucket and flops it onto the ground halfheartedly. "What do you mean?"

"T-to your parents and your brothers, when you left for basic training, and your friends. And now we're getting ready to do it again."

"It didn't bother me, because I knew I'd see them again soon-ish." Rosalie studies her, and Tessa busies herself by intensifying her sweeping.

Horrifyingly, her throat begins to tighten, just like it did when she said goodbye to Jesy.

"Hey. Are you okay?"

"I-I'm just–" Tessa sweeps faster still. She didn't cry after hundreds of frustrations and missed shots on the weapons range. She didn't cry during the simulated combat exercises, even though she was so overwhelmed that her hands shook. She won't cry now. "I guess I'm nervous about going to AIT."

Without Rosalie. She leaves that unspoken. "Me too." Rosalie crosses over to Tessa, plopping down on the nearest bunk bed. "It's going to feel wrong to not have you around."

At least she isn't the only one who feels that way. "Y-yeah. Same here." She isn't going to see Rosalie again soon-ish. She doesn't know when she's going to see Jesy again, either. She doesn't have a family like everyone else does. She just has her friends, and they're not going to be anywhere near her for a long time.

"You know what, though? Drill Sergeant Davis said that we do get some cell phone use in AIT. You have my number, and you've been getting paychecks. Go get a phone as soon as you're out of here and we can stay in touch."

Tessa sniffles. "I will. I-I need to text my friend Jesy too and see how she's doing."

"Yeah! And who knows, we might end up stationed at Fort Hamilton in the city." Rosalie springs to her feet. She bridges the distance between them, hugging Tessa tight. "It's going to be okay. I promise."

ooooo

Rosalie's parents and brothers show up for graduation. They bring a bouquet of flowers for Rosalie, and one for Tessa too, even though they don't know her. Mr. and Mrs. Soto hug her and give her their warm congratulations, and Mrs. Soto pats Tessa's upper arm. "So strong," she marvels. Raul and Ramon thank her for "keeping an eye on this brat," before dodging away from the punches Rosalie aims at them.

It is so hard to say goodbye. "Be careful," Tessa tells Rosalie, echoing the advice their drill sergeant gave both of them yesterday.

"I will." Rosalie hugs her. "You too. And hey. This isn't goodbye."

The barracks are depressingly empty after Rosalie leaves, and Tessa is glad to catch her own flight to San Antonio the following day. She is equipped with a brand new cell phone bought from the Post Exchange — a pink Razr, just like Rosalie and Jesy's. Her only two text threads are with them.

Reporting to AIT at Lackland Air Force Base would have been terrifying just ten weeks ago, but the brusque TSA agents at the airport don't make her cower. Nine weeks of basic training stripped away almost all of her dozens of old fears. It is strange how the training changed her.

She doesn't quite recognize herself anymore, without the fear and self-consciousness that have been her constant companions for as long as she can remember. Early on in basic training, Drill Sergeant Davis told them this would happen — that the training would change them. She hadn't fully believed it at the time.

ooooo

Advanced Individual Training is even more rigorous than basic training, without any of the respite that came with having Rosalie around. Platoon Sergeant Rawlen is no less demanding than Drill Sergeant Davis. The other members of Tessa's AIT platoon are all men. Some of them act like she doesn't exist. Some treat her as an afterthought, like a kid tagging along behind them, even though she just completed the same basic training that they did, and she is as much of a soldier as they are.

A few members of her platoon are friendly and normal. They talk to her the way they do everyone else. They ask her where she's from, where she went to basic training, and most importantly, if there are any sports teams she follows.

A couple of her classmates are friendly in a way that leaves Tessa unsettled. They smile at her too widely, in a way that doesn't reach their eyes. They don't keep their gazes on her face. They are always too quick to make room for her to stand or sit beside them. They keep inviting her to parties at the barracks, or to come over to watch a movie.

Tessa keeps her distance from them. She declines every invitation to socialize. She can never forget Drill Sergeant Davis's warning, especially because she doesn't have Rosalie here to look out for her. She and Rosalie check in with each other over text every evening as soon as they're back in the barracks, to make sure that they're both safe.

Tessa spends the first part of her training learning textbook techniques for dog handling, canine first aid, and understanding canine behavior. It's all interesting enough, but she counts down the days until the second phase of her training begins. "Y'all are meeting your dogs at the start of next week," Sergeant Rawlen announces. Tessa spends the weekend in a state of nervous excitement.

She meets her dog at six-hundred hours on Monday morning. He is the largest dog she has ever seen in real life, squarely built and strong, with long golden-brown and black fur, and big, pointy ears. He is an imposing figure. Tessa takes a moment to resolve her nervousness before extending a fist for him to approach and sniff. Dogs can sense when humans are anxious, and that can put them on edge as well.

The dog pads forward, sniffing her hand. All around her, fifteen other Belgian Malinois echo the gesture with her classmates. Her platoon sergeant and a few other, seasoned, military working dog handlers observe them.

The dog looks up at her. Tessa is struck by the cleverness in his expression. Somehow, this dog appears smarter, kinder, and more trustworthy, than half the people she has encountered thus far in the Army. This is a dog she could walk into an unsecured building with. This is a dog she could walk with on base after dark, and feel safe.

"Hi there, big guy," she greets, a little awestruck.

The dog presses his cold nose against her hand in response, allowing Tessa to pat his head. One of the older dog handlers comes to join them. "This is Spencer. He's a year old now, and he aced his basic training. The rest is up to you here. If you both get certified at the end of your training, you could head to the same duty station together, domestic or overseas. There's a high need for new MWDs in Iraq and Afghanistan right now."

There is one obvious reason why the military installations in Iraq and Afghanistan would need new military working dogs. They're huge countries, with hundreds of US military installations on their soil. Tessa's mind immediately jumps to the other reason. It leaves her just as uneasy as she was when she began learning about canine first aid. About how to field-treat a bullet wound on a dog.

She rests a protective hand on Spencer's head. "I won't let anything happen to you," she says quietly, as soon as Sergeant Travis has moved over to check on Richards and his dog. "You're safe with me."

ooooo

Tessa spends twelve hours a day with Spencer, teaching him and learning alongside him. They master patrol work first, and searching and scouting, before moving on to bomb detection. They are tested on their bomb detection capabilities and how well they can handle conditions under gunfire as a team.

"How's it going with Spencey?" Rosalie asks her, when they talk over the weekend.

"Don't call him Spencey. It's not dignified." Tessa leans against the washing machine, listening to it hum. "I-I don't know, maybe it sounds stupid. But he inspires me to be better and stronger, so I can be worthy of working with him."

"It doesn't sound stupid at all. Everyone has someone to motivate them."

Tessa embraces the fact that her biggest source of daily inspiration is a dog. Spencer is so tough, so brave and resilient. Nothing fazes him. He is always alert, eyes and ears flickering toward every sound with alacrity. When he's focused, he zones in on a target with frightening intensity. He walks with confident ease, never balking at her commands. He always keeps his head held high. Her dog is a good soldier. She needs to be on his level for them to get certified together.

Her dog is a good soldier, but he is also a good dog. Having a military working dog is not at all the same as having a pet, as Sergeant Rawlen emphasized during their first day of advanced individual training. It is easy to form a bond, nevertheless. Tessa plays with Spencer between each of their training sessions. She brushes him, and takes him for walks and runs on base, after their official work day is over. She talks to him, because she loves how he listens and seems to understand her.

Tessa learns when the look in Spencer's eyes and the set of his ears means he is unimpressed. He hates taking baths, and he never looks as unenthused about her as when she is wielding a hose to rinse mud off his fur. She learns the wagging of the tail that reveals enthusiasm, and the slight lowering of the head that betrays exhaustion.

Tessa is fairly confident in saying she made zero impression on Sergeant Rawlen during the first part of the platoon's training. Now that they have their dogs alongside them, Rawlen finally takes notice of her. "Your communication is great with the dog, Halifax." He has the entire platoon observe how Tessa and Spencer communicate during a person-borne improvised explosive device exercise. "See how she's balancing her verbal and nonverbal commands, choosing which to use in which situation, and how she's making sure the dog has her attention before she delivers any command."

All her friends, both in and out of the platoon, tell her that she and Spencer are going to ace the certification test at the conclusion of advanced individual training. Tessa still spends night and day worrying about the test. "Why are you like this?" Jesy asks her on the phone, affection and exasperation mingling in her voice.

"If I don't get certified, Spencer will go to someone who does. I can't imagine us splitting up, after all the time I've spent with him." The mere thought of Spencer walking at the side of a faceless uniformed soldier makes Tessa's eyes sting.

"You're going to get certified. You've been training so hard, I bet you could pass that exam in your sleep."

Sleep is a hard commodity to come by on the night before her and Spencer's certification exam. Tessa tosses and turns in her lumpy bed in the barracks, hoping that Spencer is sleeping better in his kennel. She is exhausted and sick with nerves the following morning, unable to even eat breakfast. Her spirits still lift when she greets Spencer at the kennel. He is bright-eyed, tail wagging, and he presses his cold nose into her palm. "You're right." Tessa strokes his furry head. "We're going to do this."

The certification test takes hours. She and Spencer conduct practice searches of a variety of areas — individual vehicles and vehicle convoys, barracks, luggage, warehouses, and various open areas. A panel of examiners watches them like hawks the entire time. Spencer identifies every single one of the fake explosives in just under two minutes, just like he did during their training. He signals the presence of several explosives from as far as fifty feet away. "Good boy," Tessa whispers, petting him between each exercise. Spencer leans against her legs, basking in the praise.

The other components of the test go just as well. The simulated firefight is the most harrowing, but Spencer handles it like a champ. The sound of the gunfire is rattling enough that it makes Tessa want to cry out, but Spencer's focus remains unbroken. He isn't shaken.

They don't get their results immediately after the test. The panel of examiners confer, while Tessa and Spencer sit beside one another in the grass, breathing hard, leaning against one another. "Y-you did great." Tessa pats Spencer on the back. She hasn't stuttered in weeks, but she's jittery with adrenaline. The adrenaline and exertion made her flush with heat in her heavy battle uniform. The sweat has cooled on her body, leaving her with an unpleasant chill, longing for a shower.

Spencer turns to the side, and Tessa instinctively follows his gaze. She springs to her feet, almost stumbling in her weariness, and salutes.

"At ease."

Tessa tries to relax at Sergeant Rawlen's command. His expression is as inscrutable as always. Objectively, she knows she and Spencer did well. Her heart still races, still convinced he will tell her she failed and has to start over with another dog.

"Congratulations, Halifax. And congratulations to you too." Rawlen holds a fist out for Spencer to sniff. "There's an official announcement that'll be coming soon, but you two made it through."

All the breath leaves Tessa's body in a gasp. Yellow spots creep into her vision, which hasn't happened since the most physically demanding days of basic training. She's literally lightheaded with relief. Spencer stands and presses against her legs, keeping her upright. "T-thank you, sir."

Sergeant Rawlen regards her with faint alarm. "Hey now, don't pass out or anything."

"O-of course not, sir. Thank you for letting us know ahead of time."

"Yeah. Hopefully y'all have a lengthy career ahead of you."

Tessa clears her parched throat. She and Spencer are badly in need of some water and lunch, now that they've caught their breath. "On my first day with Spencer, Sergeant Travis said that we could be deployed together if we passed our certification."

"That's right."

She shouldn't ask, but this has gnawed at her for the past several weeks. Tessa shifts from foot to foot. Spencer looks up at her, picking up on her unease. "May I ask, sir — I know that you may not have an answer for me — but may I ask if you know anything about whether I'll be directed to a duty station or deployed?"

Rosalie just learned that her duty station will be at the Aberdeen Proving Ground in Maryland, with the 20th CBRNE* Command. "Not home, but close enough." she relayed over the phone. "Thank God. I'm really hoping you end up close by."

Sergeant Rawlen looks at her out of the corner of his eye. She really shouldn't have asked. It's the question on everyone's mind, but no one gets an answer until the higher-ups deem it time for them to know where they'll spend the next three years of their lives. "You'll go where you're needed."

Tessa hangs her head, her face burning. "Yes, sir. Of course."

She is just about to apologize when Rawlen sighs. "The details are still being worked out. You'll go where you're needed most. But if I were you, I'd start getting my mind around a deployment to the Middle East."

He heads back to rejoin the panel of examiners. Tessa stares after him. The instinctive protest that swelled inside her withers and dies on the vine. There is absolutely no saying *no* in the Army. Insubordination is not an option. She will go where she is needed most, to serve the mission.

It isn't as though this is coming out of left field. *There's a high need for new MWDs in Iraq and Afghanistan right now,* Sergeant Travis said, on her very first day with Spencer.

She should spend today dizzy with happiness over her and Spencer's win. Tessa rewards him with a nice long play session with all of his favorite toys (the red ball, the large crocodile chew toy, the stick-bordering-on-branch he loves to fetch and drag back to her). She goes out to dinner with her friends in the platoon to celebrate. They all recount their triumphs with their dogs during the certification exams. Each of them brags about their dogs, asserting that their dog is the best dog. Tessa tries to take as much joy from it as she can, even though part of her is screaming on the inside.

*Chemical, Biological, Radiological, Nuclear, Explosives

She finds texts from Rosalie and Jesy on her phone as soon as she gets back to her room in the women's barracks. Jesy's text asks if she's free for a call tomorrow, and Rosalie asks if she's home. *Yes,* Tessa texts back.

Rosalie calls before Tessa has even finished changing into her pajamas. "Congratulations! I knew you guys could do it! Give Spencer a hug for me too!"

Tessa can't help but grin as she flops down on her bunk. "Thanks. I will."

"You sound tired." The hundreds of miles of distance between them do nothing to blunt Rosalie's perceptiveness, but it goes both ways. About thirty seconds into their phone call last night, Tessa accurately guessed that Rosalie had a stomach ache.

"I am." Tessa picks at the skin around her cuticles "I-I heard something from Rawlen today. I asked him if he had any idea about where my duty station would be, or if I would get deployed overseas."

Tessa catches Rosalie's shocked intake of breath. "That was bold. What did he say?"

"He didn't give me any details." A lump forms in Tessa's throat. "But he told me to start getting my mind around the idea of a deployment to the Middle East."

Silence falls on the other side of the line. "Oh," Rosalie says faintly.

Maybe it was naive of them, but for their ten weeks of basic training, and for the past eleven weeks here — they have just talked about getting stationed on some base in the United States. About using their newfound skills to protect innocent civilians in their own country.

Both of them enlisted, dreaming about the education benefits, the career benefits, the enlistment bonuses. At some point, somewhere along the line, that Army messaging sunk its teeth into them. They still dreamed about the education benefits and that fifteen-thousand dollar enlistment bonus, collecting interest in their savings accounts. But they dreamed about protecting the homeland too. Protecting American people from biological warfare, or domestic terrorists planting homemade pressure cooker bombs in large crowds. Neither of them wanted deployment to Iraq or Afghanistan. They both thought that they could, and would, make a difference here at home.

Tessa covers her mouth and nose with her arm, trying not to make a sound as she cries. She doesn't want to worry Rosalie.

"You're going to be okay," Rosalie promises. "You're going to be fine, Tess. I know we all know about the bad stories, but there are thousands of soldiers coming back from their deployments there. There were thousands that came back from Desert Storm, too. My uncle came back from that. He got home okay. You will too."

That assurance cuts through some of the terror. Tessa wipes her face on the sleeves of her t-shirt. "I-I'm so scared. Everyone says that our training prepares us, and I guess it does, but — I still don't feel ready."

She isn't ready to face live gunfire. Live grenades and improvised explosive devices. If she failed in her exercises in basic training or advanced individual training, the worst that could happen was failure and humiliation. If she fails in Iraq or Afghanistan, the worst that could happen is that she could *literally fucking die.*

"I know." Rosalie's voice breaks. "I wouldn't feel ready either. But I have to believe that you're going to get through it."

"I-I just wish I could take Spencer and run away somewhere." She and Rosalie had been forced to listen to a hundred reminders of the penalties for desertion during basic training. Reduction to the lowest enlisted grade, forfeiture of all pay and allowances, dishonorable discharge, confinement for five years.

"No, don't. They would find you. You could never get a passport or apply for any job where you need a background check. You'd have to like — flee to Mexico or something."

Tessa hacks out a dry, humorless laugh. "You've heard my Spanish. I couldn't get by in Mexico."

"Oh, God. I can't even imagine." Rosalie sounds like she's laughing through her tears too. "We'll just pray that you get through this deployment, just like we prayed for my uncle. My parents always say that brought him back home safe."

Tessa's chest aches. She prayed when her mom was sick, and those prayers hadn't been answered. She prayed that her mom wouldn't die, but her mom died anyway. When it was clear that she would die, Tessa prayed that it would be peaceful, at least, like falling asleep, but it wasn't. Her mom, who never did anything to hurt anyone, ever, suffered, the entire time. That was the last time she prayed. Why would these prayers be any different? But she supposes it's the sentiment that counts. "Thank you."

After their talk, Tessa huddles under the covers. The worst case scenario for being deployed to a war zone is that she dies. But if she dies, she'll be with her mom again. After all this training as a soldier, she knows that bullets and bombs and IEDs kill a lot faster than cancer does. At least it will be quick, and then it will be over, and she'll be with her mom. She exhales, slow and shaky. It's perverse, but it is comforting.

Her fingers tighten around her blanket as a thought occurs to her. She won't go to Iraq or Afghanistan alone. Spencer will be with her. He'll look out for her, and she'll look out for him. She made a promise to protect him, on the day they first met. He must be asleep in his kennel right now, with his chew toy beside him.

Tessa relaxes fractionally at the thought, before lapsing into a fractured, uneasy sleep.

Chapter Six

December 2006 – December 2007

Two weeks pass between Tessa and Spencer's graduation from Advanced Individual Training and the beginning of the next part of their journey. They are attached to the 94th Engineer Detachment, 5th Engineer Battalion, the only combat engineer unit with mine detection and specialized search dogs.

Those two weeks have a surreal quality to them. There are endless pre-deployment training sessions and briefings. There is the rush to get her and Spencer's equipment and weapons in order. Tessa double- and triple-checks the fit on Spencer's tactical vests, harnesses, goggles, boots, and his impact protection vests.

She and the rest of the 5th Engineer Battalion soldiers who are deploying out are dispatched into one of the basic training classrooms. They sit packed in close quarters, as several soldiers from Legal Assistance assist them in writing out their wills. Tessa stares at the document, pen in hand, mind blank. The only things she has that she really values are Spencer, and her keepsakes from her mom, back in the storage unit in Elizabeth.

Tessa makes Jesy and Rosalie the beneficiaries for the contents of her checking and savings accounts. The keepsakes from her mom, her mom's clothing and photo albums… She can't even think about what to do with those if she dies. Tessa wipes her damp palms on her uniform pants. *Brian Halifax,* she scribbles. She adds her old home phone number on the line beside it.

There's a line asking for her next of kin. The guy sitting next to her raises his hand. "What does next of kin mean?"

"Your closest living blood relative, including spouses and adopted family members," the lady from Legal Assistance explains.

She has renounced her dad, in all but name. She didn't even say goodbye to him when she left home. She hasn't called him once to check on him in the six months she's been gone. She hasn't asked Jesy about him, if she's seen him around Elizabeth, at the grocery store, or whatever. She hasn't looked up his name on the Internet to see if he's still an adjunct at Felician College. He could be dead, for all she knows. She should leave that next of kin line blank. Her dad isn't her family. But that wasn't the question, was it? He is her closest living blood relative.

Brian Halifax, Tessa writes, again.

Would he care if she died? Would he spiral into sanity-shattering grief, the way he did for her mom? Surely not. Surely he would just think about her with contempt, and think, *I knew you wouldn't last a week on the front lines. I told you so.*

ooooo

It is a fourteen-hour flight from Fort Leonard Wood to Baghdad. Tessa exercises Spencer until he's ready to drop, in preparation for the flight. The C-17 carries 102 troops, counting her and Spencer. Tessa tries to sleep, like the soldiers on either side of her, but she jolts awake every time the plane hits a patch of turbulence. She strokes Spencer's head periodically, marveling at the dog's composure. He betrays no discomfort at the hum and roar of the plane engines, or the fact that he hasn't been able to use the bathroom in ages.

They finally touch down at Camp Victory in Baghdad. This city has occupied her nightmares since the day she learned of this deployment. The landscape of her nightmares was barren, buildings reduced to rubble, cities almost entirely leveled by bombs, smoke spiraling toward the sky. The images were torn right out of the evening news that she has seen since 2003, and from video clips taken during combat in the Anbar campaign, the First and Second Battles of Fallujah, the Battle of Najaf, and several more.

She should be apprehensive, but she's just eager to get out of this plane. For Spencer's sake, more than her own. Her dog is as well-behaved as always, but the eagerness is evident in the way he wags his tail, shifting from paw to paw.

Tessa disembarks with her fellow soldiers. It is such a relief to be back on solid ground that she almost doesn't even care where that solid ground is. There is a chill in the air, but it's fresh air, after more than a dozen hours of breathing the recycled oxygen in the plane. Tessa gulps down a big breath. The scent of diesel, dust, and burning trash fills her lungs, and she dissolves into a coughing fit. Not so fresh after all.

Several uniformed soldiers are there to greet them. There are long tables set up a distance away, piled with paperwork. Tessa hangs back from the main body of troops, leading Spencer a short distance away. "You can go," she tells him softly. "You're a good dog for waiting so long."

They rejoin the crowd, though they linger near the back. Tessa's limbs and back are stiff from the long flight, and her eyes throb. If past experiences arriving at basic training and Advanced Individual Training are any indicator of the future, she has painstaking hours of in-processing, shuffling incremental steps ahead in slow-moving lines, ahead of her.

"Private Halifax?"

Tessa turns sharply. Spencer turns with her, moving in perfect synchrony. A young man stands a short distance away. There are Sergeant's stripes on his uniform jacket, and *Chao* is embroidered onto his coat. It is early in the night, but his weariness is written in the pronounced dark circles underneath his eyes and the set of his shoulders.

"Yes, Sergeant?" Her instinct is to think that he's going to rebuke her for leaving the other soldiers to let Spencer go to the bathroom.

Sergeant Chao holds two bottles of water, and he extends them to her. "Welcome to my fire team."

She certainly hadn't expected her fire team's sergeant to greet her upon arrival. Tessa stares, taken aback, and takes the bottles. She hadn't realized how parched she was. "Thank you." She sets her pack down and pulls Spencer's collapsible bowl from one of the side pockets. She fills his bowl with one of the bottles of water first, and he dives right in. Tessa takes a long draft of her own. It's perfectly cold and crisp, and she sighs with relief. "Thanks," she repeats. "That was perfect."

The soldiers she is with begin to fall into lines in front of each long table. Tessa joins the back of one of the lines, Spencer and the Sergeant accompanying her. Sergeant Chao gives her a small smile. It doesn't reach his eyes — but not in the creepy way that some guys have, where they smile with their mouth, but their eyes are cold or flat. The Sergeant's eyes are sad. "I remember when I got off that plane for the first time. Fourteen hours of flight time behind me and two hours of processing time ahead. I thought I would have killed for a bottle of water."

Tessa catches his choice of words. *For the first time.* This isn't the Sergeant's first deployment. Chao looks down at Spencer, who is regarding the Sergeant curiously. This time, his smile is genuine. It makes the corners of his eyes crinkle up. "This must be Spencer."

"How did you–" Tessa catches herself. The staff sergeant who commands their squad must have briefed Chao on her and Spencer's arrival. Each staff sergeant commands a squad of nine to ten soldiers. Sergeants, in turn, command small teams of four. "Yes. Spencer, you can say hello to the Sergeant."

Spencer sniffs the Sergeant intently, and his tail starts to wag. Chao remains still. "That's a stamp of approval, I hope. And you can call me Ryan. Our team keeps it pretty informal."

The line shuffles forward. "I'm Tessa. It's nice to meet you."

"Same. It's such a relief to have you both here. I've been begging Staff Sergeant Huber for a military working dog and handler since I got promoted. They can do things that we just can't, with finding those deep-buried IEDs and landmines. The squads that have them take fewer casualties than the ones who don't."

Ryan's desire for a military working dog on the squad and fire team makes sense. Combat engineers are often given the role of route clearance. It's critically important, given how common landmines and IEDs are on this battlefront.

"Huber's promised them before, but every single time a pair shows up, they end up attached to another squad." A note of frustration creeps into Ryan's voice, and he sticks his hands into his pockets. His mouth turns down at the corners. "We heard about you two weeks ago. Until this morning, I've reported to work every day expecting Huber to tell me that you've been reassigned."

It's a baffling feeling, to have her and Spencer's presence be so keenly anticipated. Barring her mom, and Jesy and Rosalie, no one has ever really wanted her around. "We're fresh out of AIT." Maybe it would be wise of her to remind the Sergeant of that, so that he can temper his expectations for them. She wants to help Ryan and her new team. The burden of expectation and responsibility weighs heavy on her shoulders regardless. She doesn't want to let anybody down.

"Yeah. We heard that you both graduated top of your class."

Ryan outranks her — he is *four* ranks ahead of her — but there is actually respect in the way he regards her. There was a time she would have brushed off a comment like that, but Tessa remembers Drill Sergeant Davis's advice to her and Rosalie, back in basic training. *The Army is full of people who will want to take your accomplishments away from you, because of who you are. Don't take your accomplishments away from yourself.*

So Tessa just nods in acknowledgement. "It sounds like you've been here for a while." Ryan isn't old, but there's something about his demeanor that strikes her as — seasoned? Weathered? It's very different from the guys in her platoon at basic training and AIT.

"I'm three months into my second deployment here. I spent eleven months here, from March of '03 to February of '04."

Tessa places the dates in her mental timeline of the war. March of 2003. Ryan must have been involved in the initial invasion of Iraq. The invasion lasted just over one blood-soaked month, with twenty-six days of major combat operations culminating in the six-day long Battle of Baghdad. They studied that in basic training. The guys in her platoon hadn't been able to stop yapping about how "cool" it was.

Tessa watched the same video footage they did. She saw the air strikes blowing apart buildings, and the surface-to-air missile launches sending planes careening out of the sky, and the M1 Abrams tanks rolling through the streets of Baghdad. It didn't look *cool* to her. It didn't look real. It looked like chaos. It looked terrifying. Ryan had been in the middle of it.

She doesn't ask any further questions. She knows how easily certain memories can get triggered, and the devastating effects they have when they do.

Ryan clears his throat, and rakes his fingers through his inky dark hair hard enough that it must make his nails scrape against his scalp. He's distracting himself. (Tessa recognizes that because she does the same thing, when she's trying to give her cuticles a break from picking at them.)

His hair is a good deal longer than the male soldiers in front of her in line, and it's smooth and shiny and nicer than hers.

"Anyway," he says, clearly forcing a change in subject. "We have you and Spencer for the next eleven months. You'll be a valuable part of our team. I'll introduce you to the rest of the guys later tonight, if it's not too late by the time you get done with all this."

He waves an impatient hand at the long line ahead of them. Ryan keeps her company in line, chatting with her about her flight, and Fort Leonard Wood, and her experience in AIT with Spencer, until she is finally done with her intake. Tessa wouldn't normally be up for conversation after such a tiring day, but Ryan is easy to talk to.

"They'll have an orientation tour for new arrivals starting soon." Ryan indicates the clumps of soldiers that stand about, rubbing at their eyes, or munching on granola bars fished out from their packs. "You can join one of them, or I can show you around."

Tessa hesitates. Drill Sergeant Davis's advice to her and Rosalie is never far from her mind. *Keep your guard up on base and in the barracks. Don't do anything the male soldiers could perceive as being flirtatious. Don't put yourself in any questionable situations.* Even with her male friends in AIT, who she genuinely liked, she was never alone with any one of them.

However, both her drill sergeants also taught her to trust their instincts. There is nothing about Sergeant Ryan Chao that gets her guard up. He talked to her like a person the entire time. He hadn't found a way to subtly or unsubtly ask if she had a boyfriend. He hadn't checked her out.

She won't be alone with Ryan, anyway. Spencer will be with her. "I'll go with you."

Ryan begins their tour of the sprawling Camp Victory complex, pointing out landmarks as they pass. They stop at the women's barracks, and he waits outside for Tessa to drop off her heavy pack in her room and freshen up.

Ryan shows her the gym, the medical facilities, the kennels and vet center, and the armory, keeping up a running commentary as he does. Camp Victory houses thousands of troops. Somehow, Ryan appears to either know or know *about* most people who work in the various sectors of the base. His knowledge extends from the lowest-ranking non-commissioned officers to the higher-ranking officers.

Tessa is treated to a summary of which armory staff to go to for weapons needs and which to avoid. She also receives a rundown of which of the medical staff have been helpful to Ryan and the soldiers on his squad. "Dr. Agarwal is a genius. She saved my friend's leg during my first deployment here. Dr. Medina is great too, *and* she's kind and humble. Not like Dr. Barr — he's talented, sure, but he acts like he's Jesus, walking on water every day." Ryan rolls his eyes. "Stay away from Hendrix and Powell. I wouldn't trust them to bandage a paper cut. I don't know much about the vets or vet techs here. I can ask around for you, though. I'm sure you want your guy to be seen by the best."

Tessa then receives a detailed analysis of Staff Sergeant Huber's personality and character. Huber is higher up than both of them on the chain of command, and the things that Ryan says about him are downright insubordinate.

"I have no idea how Huber got promoted to his current rank." Ryan kicks a pebble on their walking path, making it skitter ahead several steps. "Actually, I can guess. He's a doormat whose main priority is kissing ass so he can try to get ahead, and that makes the higher-ups like him. He's good for pushing paper, but he's…" He doesn't even make an attempt to conceal his disgusted grimace. "He's weak. He can't or won't look out for his soldiers in any way that matters."

His bitterness is evident. He has been burned by Huber before, even if he hasn't shared the details yet. Ryan's features settle into something tired and sad when he's not actively talking. Tessa wonders if he's aware of that, because he seems to try to talk a lot. Unlike the vast majority of people who talk a lot, Ryan isn't annoying, stupid, or boring. He answers every one of her questions immediately, and he never makes her feel like anything she asks is stupid.

Ryan takes her to the dining hall, and shows her where she can get the best food. Tessa falls upon her burger, fries, and salad without self-consciousness. The first time one of the guys commented on her eating in basic training, Tessa stared down at her empty plate wordlessly, while Rosalie asked him if he was some kind of moron. By the end of basic training, when Nichols asked her if she was trying to out-eat a sumo wrestler, Tessa told him to fuck off.

Ryan sits across from her and does not comment on what or how she eats, which earns him yet another point. He props his elbows on the table as he takes a bite of his giant peanut butter cookie. He reconsiders, breaks off half, and sets it onto her napkin. "These are the best they have. You'll probably be tempted by the chocolate chip at some point, but they always let you down."

Tessa smiles, taking another forkful of her salad. "Thanks. You can have some of my fries if you want."

"Nah, cookies and fries don't go together. I feel like I've been talking this entire time. Sorry. Tell me about you."

Her mouth is full. Tessa gestures apologetically, and Ryan sighs. "I should have asked you to talk while we were walking, and saved the monologue for now instead."

"It's fine. And you weren't monologuing. You answered my questions."

Ryan looks unconvinced. "You look super young. Did you enlist right out of high school?"

Not just young, but *super* young. Maybe Ryan's observation skills aren't as sharp as she thought. There is no way that she looks *super* young. "Yeah. I graduated in June."

"I did the same thing." Ryan sets his cookie down, as if he's lost his appetite midway. "9/11 happened in my first semester of senior year. I dropped my college plans the next week, and enlisted right after graduation."

Tessa does some quick math. He's Class of 2002, four years older than her at twenty-two. He is also folding and unfolding the corner of his napkin, staring down at it, his brow furrowed in a frown. He catches himself and looks back at her, making an effort to smooth his expression. "Let me guess — you're from North Jersey?"

"Yep. New York City?" The accent gave him away at once, just like it had with Rosalie.

"Queens," Ryan replies proudly, breaking into a smile. Unlike his other smiles, this one isn't fleeting. "Have you ever been?"

"No. I've only been to Manhattan, the Bronx, and Brooklyn with my friends."

"You've missed out."

Tessa is distracted from her reply. The dining facilities have been relatively empty at this hour, with dozens of long tables left empty. Now there's someone approaching their table. He has dark hair like Ryan, and he wears rectangular glasses with thin silver frames. He smiles, and raises a hand in greeting as if he knows her.

He must have mistaken her for someone else. Tessa gives him a small wave nevertheless. Ryan twists around to see who has caught her attention, and then he slumps forward onto the table in mock disappointment. "Oh, it's just you."

"Please ignore him, if you haven't started to already." The soldier settles beside Ryan, extending a hand to Tessa. He has a Corporal's insignia on his uniform coat, and *Han* is stitched onto the breast pocket of his jacket. He looks no older than Ryan, but he has a silver wedding ring on his left hand. "I'm Matt. Ryan probably told you all about me and the guys already."

"I'm Tessa. And um–" She should have asked about her new teammates. She thought about that earlier, while she was in line for processing. She had gotten so wrapped up in listening to Ryan she forgot to ask.

Matt catches the nervous glance Tessa throws at Ryan, and he shakes his head in disapproval. "Man, you've been gone for hours. How do you not even mention us?"

Ryan balls up his napkin and tosses it at Matt. "Because I was so ashamed."

The easy way they interact with one another leaves Tessa with a sharp pang of longing for Jesy and Rosalie. "He'll start bullying you too, soon enough." Matt throws the napkin back at Ryan. "Make it clear that you won't stand for it."

"Spencer won't let me give Tessa any attitude."

"Who?"

Tessa takes a drink of water to conceal her amusement. "Look under the table."

Matt does, and then he yelps and nearly falls off his seat. Tessa and Ryan both dissolve into laughter. "Holy shit, that is a huge dog!"

Ryan rolls his eyes. "You've seen military dogs before."

"Uh, yeah, but not at close range. Not just sitting there, looking right at me, two inches from my leg." Matt shivers. "I didn't expect him to be chilling here."

"Don't worry." Tessa reaches down to pet Spencer. "He's very nice." He's so calm, in fact, that it has always unnerved her to have to work on controlled aggression with him. The ability to relentlessly pursue and subdue an enemy combatant is a non-negotiable skill for any military working dog. She doesn't recognize Spencer when he is like that. At one word from her, though, the switch flips, the aggression turns off, and he is her measured, reliable dog again.

"And we heard he's very good at his job." Matt inclines his head toward her. "Just like his handler. You guys are going to be a game-changer for us."

"What can Spencer and I expect tomorrow, and moving forward? What kind of work will we do?" She knows the answer in theory, but nothing beats hearing from soldiers who work directly in the field.

"There are a few things we do here." Ryan counts them off on his fingers. "We fill the gaps on understaffed EOD teams. That's–"

"Explosive Ordnance Disposal," Tessa finishes.

"Right. We also support infantry missions by aiding mobility of troops. We'll make a bridge, for example, or clear terrain with explosives. We'll impede the mobility of soldiers on the other side as well. We also work with mine-detecting equipment while the infantry directly engages enemy combatants. I hoped…" There's no hiding the irritation in Ryan's tone. "When I got back, I hoped that by now, our priorities would have shifted to helping rebuild infrastructure. Schools, hospitals, that sort of thing. God knows the whole province needs it. But we're doing the same old shit we were in 2003."

Matt immediately looks around, checking whether any other soldiers are in earshot. "Chill," he murmurs. "Come on, man. Not in the dining hall."

The rebuke has a very *we've been over this* tone. Ryan subsides, with only an ill-tempered shrug. "It's tough out there. But we look out for each other. I'm not going to tell you not to worry. I know that's impossible, especially before your first time in the field. But Matt and I have your back. Curtis's a good guy too. He'll look out for you."

The fear that gripped her when she first learned about her deployment, the fear that wrapped itself around her every night since, comes creeping in again. She isn't ready to leave the sanctuary of the base, this tiny slice of safety amidst a war front. The fear seals her throat shut and makes her palms grow damp. Tessa forces the same resolve she did during basic training, where she first learned how to be brave. "Thanks. Spencer and I are here for you guys too."

ooooo

Before her first mission, Tessa revisits the lessons she taught herself in basic training. She locks away every part of herself that is vulnerable to being seized with fear. She inhales and exhales slowly, focusing on the Army ideals of courage, determination, and strength. There is no place for anything else. All that she allows to remain on her mind, in her heart, is the skills she needs to be a soldier. To be a military working dog handler, top of her class. Spencer's partner.

She pets him, and presses her forehead to his own. "We've got this," Tessa whispers. He doesn't need convincing. She does.

ooooo

Her first field operation entails two days spent on the border between Baghdad and the troubled Al-Anbar province. Her platoon sergeants swore that their field training exercises would mimic the front lines, perfectly preparing their soldiers to carry out their missions overseas.

It only takes a couple of hours to realize how wrong they were. No field training exercise did justice to this experience. It takes every bit of Tessa's resolve to keep her shit together amidst the sound of the distant explosions and gunfire, the heavy machinery, the shouting. She grips her weapon too tight, white-knuckled with terror, because every explosive device that Spencer detects is real. Every IED is capable of blowing Ryan, Matt, or Curtis to bits while they scramble to disarm them. She fights hard against the mental fatigue that comes with being on top of her game, constantly vigilant at all times.

She needs to be capable. She needs to follow Ryan's orders, and to lead and guide Spencer to protect and defend them all. So she does.

ooooo

Camp Victory hasn't even been her home for a week. Tessa is still so grateful to see it approach in the distance that tears well up in her eyes. Their team will get one day off at most, and then they'll head out and put themselves through this again. She can't think about that now. At least they got home.

They return to their base and turn in their vehicle. "Get some rest." Ryan rubs his eyes. The constant exposure to dust and smoke has left all of their eyes reddened and teary since they set out. Thankfully Spencer has his goggles for eye protection, and he doesn't balk at wearing them for extended periods of time. "We're heading toward Camp Justice tomorrow morning, to provide extra security."

That's less time off than she expected. Tessa's disappointment is reflected in Matt and Curtis's expressions. "I tried to get us shifted to duty later this week." Ryan stares straight ahead as they trudge away from the motor pool. "Huber didn't want to hear it."

"Don't beat yourself up. You tried."

Matt nods in agreement with Curtis, but Ryan's jaw just tightens. "Trying doesn't do shit."

Tessa surprises herself by speaking up. "It does. Some people wouldn't even try."

Ryan doesn't seem convinced, but he doesn't argue either. He knows he's outnumbered. It's strange. He led them well out there, and he praised all of their work on the drive back to Camp Victory. He still seems so angry, as if this mission was a failure rather than a success.

Matt heads off to the Morale and Wellness Center, intent on sending an email to his wife Grace. He was restless last night, saying that he normally emailed her every day, and he hated missing a day when he was off base.

Curtis accompanies him. "I'll come with you. I've got to let my moms know I made it back okay."

Tessa has emails to send too, but she hangs back with Ryan. She has something to ask first. "Did Spencer and I do okay out there?"

She hasn't been able to shake the concern that she didn't do enough. That she could have done better. Maybe Ryan just didn't point that out during the post-op briefing because he didn't want to call her out in front of Matt and Curtis. For all that he talks shit about a lot of other people, Tessa has noticed that he's kind to the people on his team. He didn't roast Matt for being anxious about missing an email to Grace. He didn't say, *it's just one night, man. Ease up.* Instead, he said, "You can email her tomorrow and tell her that you defused two bombs for us." When Curtis said that he hated sleeping out in the field, Ryan didn't tell him to suck it up and stop complaining. He said, "It's not like it was before," and gestured to Spencer. "No one's going to get the jump on us now."

Ryan glances at her as if surprised by the question. "You guys did great."

Tessa's shoulders sag with relief. "Good. I'm glad."

"Now it's time for you to turn it off."

Tessa blinks, startled by the non sequitur. "What?"

"What did you do to turn it off, back in basic training and AIT?" Ryan asks patiently. "The girl I talked to a couple nights ago wasn't the same as the one I've seen for the past two days."

It makes sense. Ryan hadn't been the same off base as he was when they first met. Compared with the talkative, irreverent guy she had met, Ryan on the field was focused, professional, adult.

"I talk to my friends. Or I play with Spencer, or I brush him. That lets him know he's off duty too." Playtime and cuddles turns Spencer from a military working dog to simply a dog, happy and relaxed. Tessa loves seeing him like that.

"Play with your dog, then. Moving forward, you'll want to switch off and get back to yourself as soon as you're able. Otherwise it's just…" Ryan trails off. "It takes a toll, being on like that."

Ryan, Matt, and Curtis have referenced past missions that took them off base for weeks straight. She can't imagine sustaining her mental fortitude, her vigilance, her suppression of her normal emotions and personality, for that long.

ooooo

Every time she leaves Camp Victory, she switches from being herself, to being a soldier — a perfectly trained, perfectly efficient part of a larger machine. That shift was easy to make in training. She and her teammates were never in real danger there. It isn't so easy here. Sometimes Tessa the person, subject to human frailty, comes creeping in when she is least wanted. Tessa staggers away from her team, collapses to her hands and knees, and throws up in an alley after witnessing the aftermath of a suicide car bomb explosion outside a university in Baghdad.

Ryan briefed them on the drive over, saying it was a mass casualty incident. She braced herself when she heard that. She still hadn't been ready for the wailing and the screams that cut through the acrid smoke, the anguish and the desperation on the civilians' faces. The smears of blood on the streets. The body parts scattered on the road.

Ryan follows her into the alley and helps her to her feet. Tessa's face burns just as much as her throat, and she's hot with shame. "I'm sorry."

"Don't apologize." Ryan releases her, rummages in his pocket, and pulls out one of the hard candies he gives to Iraqi children their team run into on their missions. "Here. It'll settle your stomach."

Tessa's hand shakes as she takes the candy. "If a dog had been there– A dog and handler should have been patrolling there." If a military working dog had been there, he would have found the bomb before it went off.

Ryan notices her hands shaking. He gives her hands a reassuring squeeze, trying to steady her.

"We should provide more security in the city." Tessa's lips are cold. Her entire body is cold, despite her heavy uniform. They should help keep civilians safe. So far, everything her team has done has been to support their fellow troops in their engagements against Iraqi combatants. The civilians are far more vulnerable. They don't have the defensive or offensive resources that they have. They're just regular people trying to live their lives.

"Yeah," Ryan murmurs. "We should."

ooooo

Car bombs tear through the market in central Baghdad again just a week later, killing eighty-eight and wounding almost two hundred more.

ooooo

Her first firefight comes and goes, subsiding just as soon as it erupted. Tessa can't stop shaking afterward. Curtis and Matt pat her on the shoulder. "It's going to be okay," they say. "It'll pass."

Ryan comes to sit beside her, where she huddles against the ruins of a concrete wall. Spencer sits on her other side. "Breathe in for a count of five. Then breathe out for the same count." He makes her do that ten times, until she stops shaking. When Tessa apologizes, hating herself for her weakness, he waves it off. "You have nothing to be sorry for."

⚬⚬⚬⚬⚬

The weeks crawl on, one mission after another, as they attempt to wrest control of Baghdad back from Iraqi insurgents. The soldier in Tessa refuses to recede, even when she's off duty. Someone slams their dinner tray down on a table in the dining facilities, and she startles violently, the way she does when she hears gunfire in the streets of the city.

She lies awake at night, unable to stop envisioning the next firefight or attack their team will face. She imagines Ryan or Matt or Curtis fumbling during bomb disposal, and the explosive tearing them limb from limb. She watches Spencer trot or run, terrified that he's going to miss his footing and sprain or break a leg.

Even Spencer shares some of her struggles. He becomes just as quick to startle as she is. It takes him longer to relax, to transition from military working dog mode into "regular" dog mode, when she brushes him and plays with him in their short breaks between missions. When he is allowed to be a regular dog, just Spencer, he hovers near her, unwilling to take his eyes off her. He seeks her out for comfort more than he ever did before. It breaks Tessa's heart to know that he is becoming just as fearful as she is.

Sometimes she is so afraid of everything happening off base that she forgets Drill Sergeant Davis's warning about being careful on base. Then she looks over her shoulder, looking twice at every man that passes who isn't Ryan, Matt, or Curtis.

She wants to ask her team if this is normal. She was an anxious person before enlisting, but not like this. Her anxieties were routine. She was afraid people would be mean to her or make fun of her or think she was stupid. She doesn't fear mundane things like that now. She's terrified of catastrophe — accidents, ambush, maiming, death. And catastrophe lurks around every corner.

Tessa doesn't ask her team if it is normal. Drill Sergeant Davis told her and Rosalie they could expect stereotyping because they are women, and she doesn't want her team to think she's crazy. She and Spencer have done well for them. They respect her. She doesn't want to throw that away by making them think she's crazy or unreliable. Tessa doesn't say anything to Rosalie and Jesy in her emails, either. She doesn't want to make them worry. *I'm hanging in there,* she writes, every time they ask about how she's doing.

Tessa doesn't ask her team if what she is feeling is normal. She thinks they cotton on anyway. "Sleep okay?" she asks Curtis in the morning, and he shrugs.

"Not really," he admits. "Bad dreams."

That makes her feel less alone. "Me too."

Matt comes to find her every time there's a basketball game on at the Morale and Wellness Center. "Hey, Tessa, your team's playing," he says, every time any East Coast team plays.

"They're not interchangeable," Tessa protests. Ryan and Curtis join them to watch games, even though Ryan jokes that he has trauma surrounding basketball from high school gym class.

Ryan asks her to come to the gym with him every day that they're on base. "I need a spotter. Curtis wants to run, and Matt would rather read than lift." Tessa suspects the real reason is that he remembers the comment she made about Fundamental Fitness one day over dinner, while the team had been chatting about their jobs before enlisting. *That place was my sanctuary,* she said.

So Tessa spots him on his lifts. Ryan does the same for her. The gym is just as much of an escape now as it was in high school. There is no room for terror in her mind, or the dread of what the next day holds, when she is trying to bench-press one hundred and twenty pounds.

Tessa tries to hold onto what she can, to keep herself from getting lost in this world of sustained fear and tension. She holds onto the time she spends with her team, training and playing with Spencer, racing beside Curtis on the treadmill, lifting with Ryan, watching sports with Matt. They keep her sane, the four of them. They are the only silver lining, the only comfort, to living in this hell on earth. At the same time, that only serves to make her more anxious. The thought of anything happening to any of them is unbearable.

She holds onto her regular emails with Rosalie and Jesy. To her memories of her mom. Tessa holds onto all of that with both hands, digging her fingers in. She tries to think of that before she goes to bed every night, and not what she sees every time she steps into the city of Baghdad. The bloody aftermath of truck bombs and car bombs and suicide bombs. The dead civilians. The broken, lifeless soldiers.

ooooo

Tessa limps through the first five months of her deployment. "You're eligible for leave next month. Fifteen days," Ryan tells her, as they plod back from the gym after a workout. Spencer flanks her, as always. Not all of the working dog handlers keep their dogs with them on base all the time. They have the option of boarding them at the kennels. She doesn't want to be away from Spencer, and vice versa.

She could go back to the States. To safety, and sanity, and Jesy and Rosalie. She could hug them and be hugged in return. She could be half a world away from this unceasing stream of violence and death.

"I'm not going to take it."

"What? Why? You should."

"You skipped yours." And Ryan has family — his aunt, who sends care packages monthly. He has a home to go back to.

"That's different. I wasn't going to leave you all. I have responsibilities to this team."

Tessa raises an eyebrow, curling Spencer's leash around her hand. "And I don't?" If something happened to her team, or to Spencer, in her absence… Her knees almost give out at the thought.

"Another dog handler could step in to guide Spencer on our missions," Ryan says, after a pause.

The thought of someone else working with Spencer stings. "Well, another Sergeant could have stepped in to lead our team while you were gone," Tessa retorts.

Ryan scoffs. "Yeah, no."

"Exactly. I'm not going anywhere."

It comes up over dinner one night. "Your leave must be coming up," Curtis says. He has just returned from his own visit back to his family in South Carolina. The dark circles under his eyes subsided a bit while he was gone.

Tessa takes a bite of her sandwich. "I'm skipping it."

"You too?" Matt sighs, and then looks at Ryan. "See, you set a bad example for her. There's something seriously wrong with both of you."

"Oh, so being committed to keep your dumb ass alive is seriously wrong now?" Ryan grouses. He gives Tessa a *back-me-up* look, and she just shrugs.

Chapter Seven

June – December 2007

Operation Phantom Thunder launches on the sixteenth of June, with major offensive operations against al-Qaeda and other extremist terrorists operating throughout Iraq. Their operations off base become even longer and more grueling. There are close calls. Not with bomb detection, but in explosive firefights.

It's a miracle every time the five of them return to base intact. There are new lines around Ryan's eyes, and his orders change. He never has them spread out now, even if that is the best tactical approach. One of them always has to cover another. The responsibility of being their Sergeant, their leader and protector, has never sat easy on him. It takes even more of a toll now. Even when they are off duty, he talks and laughs less.

"Are you okay?" Ryan asks them every time they return to base, even when his voice is rough and scratchy with exhaustion after hours in the field, and shouting orders. "Do you need to talk about anything?"

The question is always sincere, never rote. Tessa only ever shakes her head mutely. Ryan has his own burdens to bear. She doesn't want to add to them. What would she say to him? That she misses the person she was, who had no firsthand experience of urban warfare? Who never saw a dead body in real life, let alone a thousand of them, mangled by explosives and gunfire? That she regrets coming here? That she never wants to return? That there's no way in hell she could ever bring herself to come back if or when she has a second deployment here? Ryan, Matt, and Curtis are all on their second deployment. How the hell did they make themselves get on that plane, the second time around? She can't do it. She won't, and damn the consequences.

There is someone waiting for their team upon their return to the base today. Private Yoder is on Fire Team B, the other fire team on Staff Sergeant Huber's squad. "What's up?" There is weariness in Ryan's tone. Their past several times returning to base have been marked by receiving another order to go out, sometimes with as little as five hours between operations.

"The Staff Sergeant wants to see you." Yoder nods toward Tessa.

Her ears are still ringing from gunfire, even though she had her ear protection in. It takes a few moments for Yoder's words to register. "Me?" The Staff Sergeant hasn't spoken to her more than a couple times over the past six months. Just words of quick thanks, in passing, for her and Spencer's work on their fire team.

"Yes. He says it's urgent. Please come with me."

Ryan, Matt, and Curtis exchange glances, just as taken aback as she is. There is no reason Huber should ever want or need to speak with her urgently.

"I'll come too," Ryan says, at once.

Tessa follows Yoder to the Staff Sergeant's office, flanked by Spencer and Ryan on either side of her. Huber can't be unhappy with her and Spencer's performance. They have maintained a hundred percent IED detection rate on all of their operations since they arrived in Iraq.

Her stomach plummets. What if Huber is reassigning her to a different fire team? Beside her, Ryan's hands are balled into fists at his sides. The same thought must have crossed his mind. He will fight to keep her, but rank is everything. If Huber has decided to make a change, none of them will have any recourse.

Tessa's steps are leaden as she trudges into Huber's office. Huber looks up from his paperwork. Not for the first time, she wonders if Ryan's repeated excoriations of the man have influenced her too much. Instead of standing tall, shoulders back, chin up, the typical soldiers' posture, Huber's shoulders are perpetually slumped, his head deferentially ducked, as though he is trying to make himself appear smaller than he is.

"Private Halifax." Huber's eyes flicker over Spencer and Ryan. His lips flatten into a thin line, making him look even grimmer than he did a moment previously. "And Sergeant Chao. Have a seat."

Tessa lowers herself into the chair across from Huber's desk, doing her best to mask her trepidation. Ryan is coiled and tense next to her. Huber straightens the stack of paperwork in front of him, and he doesn't meet her gaze.

"There's no easy way to say this." He clears his throat. "Private, I received word this morning that your father has passed away. My condolences for your loss."

The words hang between them. Huber still grips his fax, and Ryan takes a quick, shocked intake of breath. This makes no sense. "What?" Tessa asks stupidly. Her mind spins, counting up the months. It has been a year since she left home to enlist. Cancer stole her mom with terrifying speed, but she was still sick for more than a year. "But — but he wasn't sick."

She stammers on every single word. She hasn't stuttered in so long. Heat rises in her chest, in her face. This can't be happening. Was he sick? Was he sick like her mom, and she didn't even realize? Did she leave him while he was sick with cancer, to die alone?

"Tessa," Ryan says quietly.

There is such pity on Huber's face. "No, Private. It was a car accident. I understand that he was driving at night, in conditions with poor visibility."

Not cancer. She has seen video footage and pictures from fatal car wrecks before, in the newspaper, on the local news. Cars twisted and crumpled like soda cans, glass shattered in windshields and windows. At least it was quick. Hopefully it was so quick that there was no pain, or fright.

A moan still tears itself from her throat. Tessa presses her hand over her mouth, quelling the urge to vomit. Her stomach cramps and heaves. Why the hell was he driving? He never drove. The car was a beat-up piece of shit that barely ran, and he hadn't paid the insurance on it in years.

The question answers itself. Her dad never drove, because she was the one who got their groceries. He must have started going out after she left. Her tears overflow, and Spencer stands up, pressing himself close to her legs. She blindly reaches for his head. Ryan's hand is on her shoulder. "Tessa," he says, low and urgent.

"I'm very sorry for your loss, Private. I can process the paperwork for your compassionate leave today. You can fly back home tomorrow to be with your family."

"N-no." Tessa wipes at her face. "I-I don't have any more family. It was just him."

"Yes, but still–"

"I-I don't want to go back to the States and be alone." Tessa forces herself to take a slow, deliberate inhale. She can't break down here, in front of him. She wouldn't be alone if she went back. She could stay with Jesy in Elizabeth. But she can't go back to Elizabeth. She can't confront this. If she hadn't left Elizabeth, her dad would be alive.

She hadn't even said goodbye. She could have called him after basic training, when she bought her phone, to at least try to make things right between them. She hadn't. She threw her dad out of her life like trash, she moved on with her life and left him behind, and then he just *died.* "I would rather stay here. I can focus on the mission, and on helping my teammates."

"Well…" The Staff Sergeant shifts uneasily in his office chair. "All right. Come find me anytime if you change your mind. Sergeant, if you have any concerns about Private Halifax's well-being or capability to carry out the mission, bring that to me."

"Right," Ryan says tersely, and then remembers himself. "Yes, Staff Sergeant Huber. Will do."

They leave Huber's office, Spencer's paws tap-tapping on the floor. Ryan says her name. Tessa can't respond. She doesn't know where to go. She moves automatically, mechanically, and finds her way to the dining facilities. They are empty at this hour, in the lull between lunch and the dinner rush. She sits at the table where their team always sits. She pets Spencer, trying to focus on the sensation of his fur against her palms.

"Stay here," Ryan tells her.

As if she's going to run away somewhere. Tessa can't imagine moving again for a long time. She barely has the strength to remain upright.

Ryan returns with a bottle of water clutched in one hand, and a cookie on a plate in the other. He sets both in front of her, and sits across from her. "I'm here. If you want to talk. It's okay if you don't."

The beads of moisture condense on the bottle of water. There is so much in her mind, her thoughts tangled in chaos. *It's my fault.* Tessa doesn't say it, because Ryan would try to dissuade her from it, the same way any of her friends would. *It's not your fault,* Jesy would argue. Rosalie would throw her hands up. *You couldn't stay there and take care of him forever. What about living your own life?*

"At least…" Tessa manages not to stutter. "They're together now."

"Yeah?" Ryan asks carefully.

Their team has talked about their families before. Curtis's moms, his sisters, his huge extended family. Matt's parents. Ryan's aunt. Tessa listened to every conversation and never volunteered any information, save for the fact that her mom was a Knicks fan too. Ryan, Matt, and Curtis are sensitive enough that they must have noticed the past tense. They never pressed with further questions.

"My dad n-never really wanted to be alive, after my mom died. And… and now my mom isn't alone, either." Her dad was difficult and strange, in Tessa's eyes, but her mom had loved him so much. And he loved her. The only times he ever seemed like a real, normal person, with normal emotions, like tenderness and care, was when he was with her, when he was taking care of her.

"That's a comforting way to look at it." Ryan tries to smile, but it's small and sad. "Did I ever tell you why I lived with my aunt?"

"No." Tessa takes a small bite of her cookie. The sweetness is sharp and shocking on her tongue, a distraction from the remote numbness that has settled over her.

"Both my parents died when I was a kid. Car accident. I… remember being really bitter about it, really angry about it, because it felt easier than being sad." Ryan throws air-quotes around *easier.* "I hated that I lost both of them. Not *just* one, but both, in one sick accident like that. I was so damn angry at them for making that trip together and leaving me at my aunt's place. One of them should have stayed back with me, right? I was just five. Maybe too young for an overnight without my parents."

She has never met another person her age who has lost a parent. Let alone two. Everyone at school, everyone she knew at basic training, *everyone,* still had both their parents. It is alienating to be a young person who has lost a parent, when most people have their parents until well into their own adulthood. Most people have kids before their parents die.

Ryan grimaces, running his fingers through his hair, making it stand on end. "I know how hard this is. I'm here if you want to talk, all right?"

"All right." It comes out as a whisper. Tessa breaks a chunk off her cookie and offers it to him.

∞∞∞

That night, there aren't only the memories of what happened in the city today, running on a loop in her mind. There isn't only the fear of what tomorrow holds. There is her dad in the old car, his fingers gripping the wheel tight. *Poor visibility.* Rain, slick on the roads. That busy intersection near the grocery store. The glare of headlights coming in through the passenger-side window as someone runs the light while her dad makes the left turn.

Tessa knows how bodies can break under trauma, now. Not the trauma of cancer and illness, but the trauma of blunt force impact and major lacerations. She can imagine her dad limp, motionless, slumped, behind the wheel. Thinner than he was when she left him. His hair lanker, his face paler.

She presses her fist to her mouth and curls up in a ball. When she trusts herself to speak, she whispers Spencer's name. He hops up into the narrow bed with her, and stretches out beside her, letting her put both arms around him and press her face into his back.

∞∞∞

She throws herself into her work with the team to distract herself. Being Tessa the soldier has its own terrors, and it brings her face-to-face with horrors every day. The mass shootings, the bombings, the airstrikes. But it spares her from thinking about her dad, and her own failures as a daughter.

Both her parents might be gone now, but she doesn't feel alone. Spencer, Ryan, Matt, Curtis, Jesy and Rosalie, are her family. Any day she can keep them safe makes her life worthwhile.

∞∞∞

They are returning from a standard operation in the field. Spencer's body language changes as soon as they turn the corner, and Tessa's heart beats faster. "Where is it?" Beside her, Curtis tenses. "We have a problem up ahead," he calls to Ryan and Matt. Ryan is behind the wheel, Matt at shotgun.

Tessa follows Spencer's gaze. Her heart sinks. Two cars, both parked ahead of them on the street. Their vehicle is out of the blast zone, for now. "We can't go forward. Those cars aren't safe."

Two armored trucks come skidding through the turn and onto the street behind them, blocking their point of exit. All their eyes lock onto the trucks in the rearview mirror. Matt whirls around, his lips forming a curse. Ryan's knuckles are white on the steering wheel. "Don't panic," he orders. "We've got this."

Tessa has known fear intimately during her time in Iraq, but never like this.

∞∞∞

It unfolds in a nightmarish blur. They are outnumbered two to one in the firefight. Tessa prays that these trucks aren't loaded with explosives too, that nobody shoots Spencer, that they will all make it through this and back to base. It doesn't look likely. They're outnumbered two to one.

She doesn't order Spencer to fight. He can run with explosive speed and land a crippling bite to an insurgent's leg or arm, making them drop their weapons. But they have friends who could land a shot on him, and she learned what AK-47 bullets can do to a dog. Maybe it's selfish and unprofessional of her, maybe it's not being a good soldier, but she can't bear to see her dog get shot today.

"They have the numbers," Ryan grits out. "We have the skill. Don't lose your nerve. We're all going back home tonight."

They are outnumbered two to one. She shouldn't believe him. She does anyway.

Tessa takes cover behind the vehicle and keeps her hands steady on her gun. Distantly, she remembers how she struggled with pop-up and moving targets, once. Distantly, she remembers how she once believed she wouldn't have to shoot her rifle often, because she was a dog handler. Even now, she has time to berate herself. *Stupid,* she thinks. *Stupid.* She drops one insurgent with a shot directly to the head, and then another.

One of them throws a grenade at their vehicle, at where they're taking cover.

Ryan explodes forward, ready to throw himself on it. The scream tears itself from her throat, the fear even more acute than it was when the ambush began. "No!"

Matt and Curtis grab Ryan, fingers fumbling in the back of his armor, dragging him back. The explosion rocks her entire world, sending Tessa crashing to her knees. The vehicle is still standing somehow, engulfed in flames.

The radio is in there, clipped to the dashboard. If they're stuck out here without a radio, they're screwed. Tessa lunges forward, deaf to the gunfire, to the shouting. Fire obscures the vehicle door, but she doesn't hesitate. She ignores the blinding agony in her hands as she wrests the door open, groping around the interior until her ruined hands close on the radio. She yanks it free of the dashboard.

The exchange of gunfire hasn't stopped. The chaos is worse now, with the fire and the plumes of smoke billowing outward, darkening the street, scorching her lungs. Even if the four of them die, maybe Spencer can get away. She turns to him, gesturing toward one of the abandoned buildings lining the side of the road. "Go! Take cover, Spencer!"

Shots fire on her side of the street. It sounds like Ryan, Matt, and Curtis are still standing. Before Tessa can say a word, before she can grip her gun again, Spencer tears off into the smoke. Toward the insurgents.

ooooo

She can't say how long it lasts. Eventually, the gunfire from the other side of the street peters out. Tessa turns the radio over to Matt, and he radios over to Camp Victory. "We need a medic team out here as fast as possible. We have one soldier down with a gunshot wound and one with a severe burn injury. Here's our coordinates."

Curtis is on the ground, his pants leg dark with blood, breathing hard. Ryan applies pressure to the wound. "Hang in there. Hang in there. We're going to get you home."

She staggers over to join them. Even in his state, Curtis's jaw goes slack with shock when he catches sight of her. Ryan twists around, not releasing Curtis. "Tessa, your hands–"

Their first aid kit is burning up in the vehicle. Tessa grits her teeth to keep from blacking out, fumbles at one of her pockets, and pulls out a roll of bandages. She clumsily lobs it at Ryan. She would help, but…

Dread blankets her. Ice runs through her veins. She doesn't want to do this. She wants to lie down in the street and cry, or die.

She makes it to the other side of the street. She finds eight insurgents, dead and dying.

She finds Spencer.

∞∞∞∞∞

There was a time when Tessa might have cared about being perceived as hysterical, or crazy. That is the last thing on her mind now. Curtis is the one who has been shot, but she's the one who needs the sedative from the medic team, after the medics wrap Spencer in a white sheet and carry him into the back of the transport.

The rest of the night is a haze. Ryan and Matt refuse to leave her and Curtis's side as their wounds are evaluated; as Curtis is whisked off into surgery and Dr. Medina assesses Tessa's burns. The flames ate at her hands through her gloves. The doctor's voice drifts to her as if from a great distance away. *Third degree burns. Infection is a major concern. Stabilize for now. Medevac to Landstuhl. You'll need specialized treatment on a burn ward and rehab.*

"I'm going to go pack your stuff up for you," Matt says gently. "Is that okay, Tessa?"

Tessa nods.

Ryan stays with her as Dr. Medina places an IV drip for fluids, and cleans and debrides her hands. When she weeps, he dabs at her face with soft tissue, his own face twisted with agony. "She's hurting. Can you give her anything for the pain, Doc?"

Tessa can't tell him that she isn't crying because of her hands.

Ryan stays with her after her hands are bandaged, as she drifts in and out of sedation-and-shock-induced fog. "Spencer," she manages to whisper. She hasn't said anything since the transport. Her voice is raw from screaming and weeping. "His body."

She can't say anything more. Ryan calls one of the nurse aides and asks him to please get in touch with the veterinary department. One of the vet techs that Tessa recognizes from Spencer's check-ups comes to visit shortly afterward. Sarah tells her that there is a cemetery at Fort Lewis in Washington for military working dogs. That Spencer will be buried with full military honors. She thanks Tessa for Spencer's service, and she says Spencer was a brave soldier, a brave dog. She hugs Tessa around the shoulders when she cries.

ooooo

Curtis makes it out of surgery okay. He is still asleep when one of the nurses tells Tessa that the daily Medevac flight is preparing for departure, and she will be on it. "What about Curtis?" Ryan looks anxiously between her and Curtis. He hasn't gotten a moment's sleep through the night. "I was hoping they could go together. I don't want her to be alone."

"He probably needs another day or two to stabilize here," the nurse replies. "Transport staff will be here to assist you in a few minutes, Private Halifax. I'll give you some time to say your goodbyes."

Matt hangs her duffel on her shoulder very carefully. "I have all of your stuff packed in there. I emailed Jesy and Rosalie too, to let them know." He hugs her and kisses the top of her head, like a brother would do for a little sister. *Be safe,* she wants to say, but she can't. Who will protect Matt and Ryan from IEDs now that she and Spencer can't? Who will help Matt get home safe to Grace?

"Heal up, Tessa. Take care, all right?" Matt's voice breaks. He leaves to go sit with Curtis, waiting for him to wake up.

Ryan's eyes shine with unshed tears. He moves like he would take her hands, but he remembers the bandages. He places his hands on her shoulders, making her look at him. "Tessa," he says. "I saw what Spencer did."

Tessa had, too. Spencer tore into one insurgent's thigh, opening his femoral vein. He crushed another's leg with the force of his bite. He ripped another's throat out. Her dog, who loved nothing more than playing with his red ball and his stuffed crocodile toy, died while ripping a man's throat out.

"We wouldn't have made it out without him. We were outnumbered.

He evened the odds. He gave us the chance we needed. We owe our lives to him. We'll remember that. All of us, always." Ryan wraps his arms around her. His tears drip down into her hair. "Be safe, okay?"

"You and Matt too." Her voice is hoarse, barely audible.

The transport staff arrives to take her away. Tessa loses her family, again.

Chapter Eight

December 2007 – January 2008

The two weeks that follow are the same as the two weeks after her mom died. Tessa barely registers anything around her. The change in environment, from Camp Victory to the burn ward at Landstuhl Regional Medical Center in Germany. The skin grafting. The reconstructive surgeries. The rehabilitation. The assessments by the nurses and doctors and therapists.

The only things that reach her are the nightmares and the flashbacks, and the empty space by her side that makes her want to scream. Tessa cries for Spencer, and for everything that happened in Iraq. She cries at night, and every morning after she wakes up.

Jesy and Rosalie call, and Tessa crumbles when she hears their voices. They cry on the phone with her, sharing her grief, letting her know that she isn't alone. She would do anything to hear from Ryan and Matt, to know that they're okay, but she can't get in touch with them. Her hands are too messed up to email. To do much of anything, really. Feeding herself, getting dressed, even brushing her teeth and using the bathroom and showering, is agonizing. Once, she would have thought of her brave Spencer for inspiration to push past the pain. She can't bear to do that now.

She asks about Curtis, but the nurses tell her that their colleagues on the trauma ward haven't seen him. He may have been sent directly to Walter Reed National Medical Center in Maryland instead.

A psychiatrist comes to talk to her. She diagnoses Tessa with post-traumatic stress disorder and puts her on an antidepressant. She recommends Seroquel, an antipsychotic, for PTSD as well, but the term *antipsychotic* makes Tessa nervous and she refuses it. She has just returned to her room after a challenging rehab session when a knock sounds on her door. She turns, glancing toward the doorway. "Come in."

A woman in uniform enters, introducing herself as Sergeant Marta Diaz, with the Medical Evaluation Board. Tessa doesn't get why she's here. Maybe she would have gotten it a few weeks ago. A few months ago. Her mind's edge has been blunted by fear and pain; by pain meds and the new antidepressant. "Yes?" she asks cautiously.

"First of all, I want to recognize you for your service overseas. Your fire team's Sergeant and the squad's Staff Sergeant have both given you and your partner the highest commendations for your work during your deployment. They credit you and your partner for saving lives with your IED detection skills." Diaz's expression softens. "I'm very sorry for your loss, Private."

Tessa's eyes fill with tears, but she tries to maintain her composure. It's bad enough that she has cried in front of all of her doctors, her psychiatrists, and her physical and occupational therapists. "T-thank you."

"I wanted to talk to you about what's next. Obviously your focus should be on making a full recovery from your injuries."

Tessa glances down at her hands. "I'm working on it."

The rest of Diaz's statement sinks in, and fear comes with it. Are they going to send her back to Iraq? Will they assign her to another military working dog? She can't work with another dog, not after she let Spencer down so badly. She can't look at a dog who isn't Spencer.

"We care deeply about our soldiers." For the first time, Tessa notices that Sergeant Diaz is carrying a black folder. "Especially soldiers like you, who have given so much in the line of duty. The Medical Evaluation Board has reviewed your case. Based on your physical condition and recent psychiatric diagnosis, they believe that a medical discharge is in your best interest."

Tessa blinks. "W-what?" She hadn't wanted to return to Iraq, but a medical discharge? What does that even mean?

"Don't worry. This would be a medical discharge under honorable conditions. You'll be a combat veteran, so you're entitled to all VA benefits, including retirement, education, home loan, and insurance benefits."

Her mind is working so infuriatingly slowly, as it has since that day in

Iraq, the day she lost Spencer. It sticks on *education*. Education benefits. The reason she enlisted in the first place. She'd been so desperate for free college, for that stipend for housing and textbooks. She'd been so fucking stupid. "I can still get the GI Bill?"

"Yes, you can." Diaz hesitates. "Don't worry, Private. This isn't the end of the world for you. We'll see about getting some help for you to sign the necessary paperwork."

Tessa watches her depart. Her hand aches. Not from the burns, but from the impossible impulse to pet Spencer.

There was a time when nothing would have made her more excited than the prospect of going to college for free. She won't be restricted to an affordable community college program. She could even go to Rutgers if she wanted. Now it is impossible for her to sum up any enthusiasm for the idea. She can't imagine sitting in a crowded lecture hall, reading a textbook. Not after the things she has seen, and the things she has done.

(She wanted to be a nurse, once, like the nurses who helped her mom when she was sick. She doesn't want to see blood, or a dying or dead body again, ever.)

But she can't *not* go to college. What will she do with herself otherwise? All of this, the whole ordeal in Iraq, everything she has been through so far, was with that in mind. She can't squander that opportunity.

Tessa checks the clock, does a slow mental calculation of the time difference between Germany and the East Coast in the US, and reaches for the phone. She has to talk to Jesy and Rosalie.

ooooo

The wound dressings come off her hands the next day. The skin on both hands is mottled, uneven, warped. Frankly, it's disgusting. It would have reduced her to tears once, when she was in high school. Back when she used to fret over the acne on her jaw and the dark circles underneath her eyes. Now, Tessa can't bring herself to care. She just wants to brush her hair, and get dressed, and use her hands, without pain. Her physical and occupational therapy isn't progressing as fast as she would like.

She stands by the window, taking in the view as the sun sinks beneath the horizon. It is December, and the sun sets early now. On this day last year, she and Spencer had been preparing for their deployment to Iraq. The last year has aged her a decade. Her sweet Spencer will never get the chance to be an old dog, enjoying a peaceful retirement.

There is a knock on the door. Tessa turns, expecting to see a nurse. Her mouth falls open.

"Surprise," Ryan says. There is a stiffness to his posture, something wrong about the set of his right shoulder. He looks even more haggard than she remembers, but he holds a bunch of sunflowers in one hand, and he's smiling.

Tessa collides with the foot of her hospital bed in her haste to make it to him. Ryan moves to meet her, hugging her with his left arm. "Hey, Tess."

Relief washes over her, robbing her of the ability to think, to speak. All she can do is cling to him. Tessa finally lets go, stepping back. "W-what are you doing here? How are you here?"

Ryan hands her the flowers, and gestures toward his right shoulder. "I broke this and my collarbone in the field last week. Fallout from an explosion."

An IED. Her worst nightmare for both of them, made reality. Tessa reaches for his arm. "Is Matt okay?" Matt can't be alone in Iraq, the only one of the four of them still there.

"He's fine," Ryan hastens to assure her. "He's okay. He got free of the blast. And it's the end of his deployment. I convinced Medina to let me stay on base after my surgery until I knew he was on the flight back home. He flew back yesterday, so I got on the plane this morning."

"Okay. Good. Have you heard from Curtis? He's not here."

"He's doing inpatient rehab at Walter Reed. He's worried because he's been emailing you and hasn't heard back, but I told him that you probably haven't been able to check, with your hand injuries."

"Yeah." The tension begins to seep from her, leaving her weary to the bone. Tessa slumps against the wall. Ryan got caught in an explosion, Curtis got shot, she has third-degree burns to both hands, and Spencer paid the ultimate price.

"This was my second team," Ryan says quietly. "The first one I was leading. I lost friends the first time around, too. I saw friends medevaced out. I hoped that this time, it would be better. I hoped that I could keep you all safe."

His voice breaks on the last word. Tessa leads him to the chair, and they sit across from one another. "It's not your fault."

She fell to the depths of sorrow over Spencer. Along the way, she found anger. At herself, for not protecting him. At the bastard who shot him. At the system. Fool that she was, she consented to enlisting. She knew the risks. The risk that she would be killed, the risk that she would become a killer. She consented, out of greed, and her own naivete. Spencer was just a dog. He hadn't made a decision.

She never found anger at Ryan. Ryan never did anything but care about all of them.

Ryan props his elbows on his knees and puts his face in his hands. When he finally looks up at her again, his face is a mask of anguish. "I don't think it's ever going to get better. This war is never going to fucking end. It's been going on for years now."

She has had time to read the newspapers and watch the evening news over these last weeks. She has seen the other soldiers in the rehabilitation gym, almost all of whom have worse injuries than her, with missing limbs or severe brain injuries. "There's no end in sight."

Ryan clenches a hand into a fist, and then grimaces at the pain that must go shooting up his arm. "I've been reading too."

Tessa regards him cautiously. "What have you been reading?" Ryan, alone among the four of them, is addicted to the news. He has been, ever since she met him. *He wasn't like this in high school,* Matt muttered to her once.

While Tessa, Matt, and Curtis emailed their friends and family back home, Ryan trawled the depths of the New York Times, the Wall Street Journal, the BBC, and the Associated Press websites. Every time he sat down to watch TV with them, he had a newspaper in hand, or a copy of Time magazine. Every time he and Tessa went to the gym at Camp Victory, Ryan glanced up at the TV screens, his attention flickering between the screens airing CNN and Fox News. Sometimes fascination played on his face. Sometimes he looked away in what appeared to be outright disgust.

"All kinds of things." The legs of Ryan's chair squeak as he moves it closer to her. "You know about Pat Tillman, right?"

"I know he died in Afghanistan." She remembers seeing him play for the Cardinals, and she remembers when he enlisted.

"Did you know it was friendly fire? Did you know that before he died, Tillman called the invasion and occupation of Iraq illegal? He was shot three times, at close range, in the head. The higher-ups burned his stuff too. His uniform. His journals."

Ryan talks fast, his voice rising. There is so much to digest, and she can't take things in as fast as she used to. Now that he mentions it, Tessa does recall some news stories back in 2004 — her sophomore year of high school — about Pat Tillman's death being due to friendly fire. A tragic accident. Tessa's mind sticks on one thing. "Why did he call the invasion of Iraq illegal?"

The rest of it dawns on her. She and her fellow soldiers learned about the dangers of friendly fire. Friendly fire and being shot three times at close range in the head don't go together.

Ryan drums his fingers on the armrest of the chair. "There are a lot of reasons. The big thing is that the invasion violated the UN Charter and international law."

He must pick up on the blank look on her face, because he adds something. "You know how part of the reason why we invaded was because Saddam supposedly had weapons of mass destruction?"

That, Tessa remembers. She nods.

"Yeah, well, it's been almost five years, and no significant WMDs have been found in Iraq since the invasion."

That tugs at a fragment of memory from last summer, just before Tessa reported for basic training. The only reason she remembers it is because of how scary she found that headline. "Wasn't there a report saying that they found hundreds of chemical weapons?"

"I remember that." Ryan talks still faster, as if he can't get the words out quick enough. Like they've been pent up in him ever since they last saw one another. "But did you know the Department of Defense itself said those weapons weren't even usable? The DoD *itself* said that these weren't the weapons that America and the rest of the world believed that Iraq had. Those weren't the WMDs that this country went to war for."

Her body reacts to the implications before her mind catches up. Tessa's eyes fill with tears. "W-what are you saying?"

She doesn't need to ask. All of that human suffering — for nothing?

Ryan doesn't answer directly. He stands and walks to the window, his footfalls plodding, even more slow and weary than they were in Iraq. "Human rights organizations are coming out with more stats every year. They're saying thousands of Iraqi civilians have died because of this war we started."

The bombing outside of the university in Baghdad, the car bombs that hit the markets, the chlorine bombs, the suicide bombs. It's increasingly difficult for Tessa to catch her breath. How does Ryan manage, thinking about this all the time? It's no wonder that it all weighed even heavier on him than it did on the rest of them. She thought it was just the responsibility, the fact he was their Sergeant. She was wrong. It was the weight of this knowledge.

"What…" Tessa has to search out her train of thought. *Why are you telling me this?* The answer is self-evident. She was a part of it. She shouldn't get to be spared the ugly truth.

Ryan returns from the window and sits at the foot of her bed. "None of it should have happened. People who should have known better got us into this." He pounds his fist against the bed. Tessa startles, and he gives her an apologetic look. "Sorry."

"It's fine." She draws her knees up to her chest. Restless energy brims from Ryan now, a sharp contrast to his weariness earlier. Tessa casts back to her memories of her high school American Government class, when Mr. Gabriel asked them to research issues and write a letter on a topic of their choice to local elected officials. "What do you want to do about it? Should we write to the House representatives who voted for the war? Or write to some representatives to ask them to vote for ending the war?"

"Letters aren't going to do shit. There are a lot of anti-war activists who have been organizing, and they've been in the news. But they're getting nowhere. They have no real political power. They have no real lobbying power and no influence on Capitol Hill."

Tessa frowns at him. "Then what are you going to do?"

She has seen genuine smiles from Ryan a hundred times before. This small smile is not one of them. It's cold, and that is not something that she has ever associated with Ryan. "The answer isn't activism. It isn't demonstrations and peaceful protests and grassroots movements." Disdain colors his voice. "They did that during Vietnam, after Vietnam, and we still got into Afghanistan and Iraq. The answer is getting our hands on real political power, and stopping this. Or preventing this from happening again."

She had been fascinated and moved by learning about the anti-war activism in Vietnam, and struck by the courage of the protestors. Tessa opens her mouth to defend them. Instead, it's her turn to scoff — disbelievingly, not dismissively, like Ryan had. "What are you going to do? Run for Congress?"

"Yeah, I think I will."

Tessa gapes at him. "Are you crazy?"

"Matt said the same thing. Look." He stands up, pacing in front of her bed. "What's that quote? Be the change you wish to see in the world? I'm going to do that."

"You can't just..." Tessa thinks back to her Government class again. *Representatives must be 25 years old and must have been U.S. citizens for at least seven years.* Ryan's not twenty-five yet, but he will be, in two years.

"I can. I'm not an idiot. I know it's harder for people who don't already have a lot of money, power, and influence, but it's not impossible." He sits down on her bed again. "I've been thinking about this for a while, and I have a plan. I need to get at least an undergrad degree first. I'm thinking about international relations, but I'm not sure yet. My four-year enlistment is up now, so I'll be able to use my education benefits."

It's astounding. She spent her time in Iraq trying to get from one day to another while keeping a tenuous hold on her sanity. Meanwhile, Ryan had been plotting out his future. "It sounds like you have it all figured out." Tessa has to fight to keep the bitterness from her reply. Ryan has a plan to be the change he hopes to see in the world. Meanwhile, she doesn't even know what her next week looks like.

"I'm working on it." Ryan looks at her intently. "I figure they're hitting you with a medical discharge, like they are with Curtis. What are your plans?"

Tessa shrugs one shoulder, lifting her hands off her lap. "I need to get these to the point where I can type and hold a pencil. I've been thinking about college, but that's as far as I've gotten." Jesy and Rosalie have both been so enthusiastic about giving her ideas for potential majors. Psychology, public health, criminal justice, journalism, women's studies, animal sciences, history, social work... All of them have sounded interesting enough, but none of them have really clicked.

"I know this is going to sound insane. But you should do this with me."

She can't hold back a small, humorless laugh. "You want me to get into Congress?" Imagining herself in Congress, as competent and influential as Nancy Pelosi or Hillary Clinton, is such an outlandish mental image.

"Yeah, I do. You and I can start a coalition of anti-war Representatives. Or, if you don't want to go that path, you could help me do it. Matt said I can't do this alone, and he's right. I'll need support. People who believe in the cause. You and Matt and Curtis — you guys were right there with me. You know how important this is. I have a couple of friends back home in the city who will definitely be on board with this."

It takes several moments for her to process it. To Tessa's surprise, the tiniest flicker of enthusiasm stirs within her. American Government had been her favorite subject in school. She loved it. Majoring in political science, being an aide to a member of the House… She would have loved that idea during her senior year of high school. Besides, this will give her a purpose to work toward. That's more than she has right now.

"Okay," Tessa says. "I'm in."

ooooo

Ryan visits every evening after they are both finished with their respective rehabilitation sessions. They talk and eat dinner together. Tessa isn't even self-conscious of how clumsy she still is with her utensils, because it's just Ryan. They commiserate about their rehabilitation, and vent about the side effects of the antidepressants they have both been prescribed for their PTSD. "I'm getting these headaches." Ryan massages his temples, scowling. "And I feel agitated…even more agitated than usual, I mean. I can't hit the gym like I want to, either."

Tessa feels a pang of sympathy. She can't lift weights with her hands being as messed up as they are, but at least she can run on the treadmill, and use a stationary bike. "That sucks."

"How's the Zoloft going for you?"

"I don't feel like it's really helping." Tessa awkwardly grips her fork to take a bite of her carrots. "It's keeping me up at night." She misses Spencer all day, and even more acutely at night. "And it's giving me a… brain fog, sort of. I either need to get used to it or stop taking it before I start school."

College is another big topic of discussion. They go to the patient lounge, which has a few computers, and do Web searches on colleges. Tessa keeps gravitating to the Rutgers website, gazing at their political science page.

"I'm thinking of applying to Columbia," Ryan remarks offhandedly, one evening after dinner, while they sit in the computer lab.

Tessa turns to stare at him. "Isn't that an Ivy League?"

"I did pretty well in high school." Ryan uses the scrolling wheel on his mouse to scroll up and down aimlessly. She knows that he's just doing it because he likes the soft *click-click-click* it makes. "I went to Brooklyn Tech. My physics teacher kept telling me that I could get a physics, engineering, or chem scholarship at NYU if I wanted — but I had other ideas."

Tessa murmurs something vague in acknowledgement. It's jarring to think of Ryan as a scientist, like her father had been. Ryan is so expressive, so passionate, so caring, so good with people. Not at all like her dad.

"I have to believe that not going that path happened for a reason. Anyway." Ryan turns away from his computer, giving her his full attention. "You can do better than Rutgers. It's not even in the top twenty of poli-sci programs."

"I didn't know that I should aim that high."

"Don't sell yourself short. Your SAT scores were high, your GPA was high, *and* you're a veteran now. You could get into Columbia. That's ranked number eight for poli-sci, by the way." Ryan rolls his computer chair over to her. "You should check out their website."

"Are they paying you or something?" Tessa grouses, but she doesn't roll her chair away.

Ryan reaches for her keyboard and types in the Columbia website for her. "Matt's leaning toward Columbia over NYU as well. Poli-sci major, like you. You guys can take classes together."

ooooo

They get through their weeks of rehabilitation, and make plenty of long-distance calls back home. Ryan calls his aunt and his friends, and Tessa calls Jesy and Rosalie.

It is unsettling to realize that she doesn't have a home anymore. The house in Elizabeth stopped being a home when her mom died, and Tessa figures it has returned to the bank, anyway. Fort Leonard Wood was home, and then Lackland Air Force Base was home. Camp Victory was home, if only because Spencer, Ryan, Matt, and Curtis were there. Now she has no base where she will report to duty, and no dog at her side. She might make Columbia University her home one day, but that won't be until the fall semester. She is adrift from now until September.

"Oh, my God," Jesy says, when Tessa confesses this on the phone. "Don't say that. I'm moving in with Alyssa at the end of this month. I'll check with her first, but I don't think it'll be a problem to have you move in too."

Tessa drops the soft ball she was squeezing for her physical therapy exercises. The two of them used to hang out with Alyssa, Jesy's cousin, when they headed over to New York City. "Seriously?"

"Uh, yeah. I'm not about to let my girl be homeless."

It seems paradoxical, considering she's on an antidepressant, but these days, Tessa is even quicker to tears than she ever has been before. "Thank you."

ooooo

She and Ryan are both discharged from inpatient rehab in Landstuhl during the same week. Tessa leaves with instructions to continue her physical therapy exercises for both hands, a referral to outpatient occupational therapy at the VA Health System back in the States, and six months of refills for her antidepressants. The doctor and the psychiatrist both said they were willing to prescribe her anti-anxiety meds, an antipsychotic, and sleeping pills too, but Rosalie told her a horror story about her uncle's experience with sleeping pills and antipsychotics after Desert Storm. That scared Tessa enough that she declined all other drugs.

She and Ryan talk about college applications on the flight. Despite her attempts to distract herself, the pain in Tessa's chest gets worse with every hour that passes. "What's wrong?" Ryan asks, dropping his train of thought about college application essays.

"I just–" Tessa rubs at her collarbone, trying in vain to alleviate the tightness in her chest. "I was just thinking about how Spencer sat with me, the last time I made this flight. He was — he was so good on the flight. I remember being so impressed with him. But I was always impressed with him."

Her eyes sting with tears, and Ryan places a comforting hand on her back. "Spencer was great."

Tessa nods, trying her best to regain her composure.

"Hey." A small smile touches Ryan's lips. "Do you remember that time you and the guys made him steal my boot?"

Tessa laughs through her tears, wiping at her cheeks. "Yeah, I do. You called him — what did you call him? A ridiculous, insubordinate beast?"

"You got so mad at me that you threatened to kick my ass." Ryan grins. "I think that was my first time seeing that feisty side of you."

"The first of many."

At least, amidst all the horror and pain that unfolded, and all the horror and pain of how it ended, at least she has this. The memories of the softness amidst it all. Tossing the red ball for Spencer, cuddling with him at night, playing with him when they were off duty. Spencer was taken from her much too soon, but at least nobody can take those memories from her.

ooooo

She is so nervous about returning to the States that she almost throws up during the landing. She is a different person than she was when she left here in December of '06. The things she has seen since, the things she has done– She has changed. From what she has seen in the news and online, life here hasn't.

Even being in the airport doesn't feel right. JFK International is so crowded, so packed with people. All Tessa can think of is the possibility of a suicide bomb going off. There are so many people with so many bags, and they could be carrying God knows what in those bags. A small, rational voice tells her that these people all got through airport security, but still. She needs to get herself and Ryan out of here.

Tessa strides so quickly through the airport that Ryan has to jog to keep up, even though he is taller than her. Even though she ignored his protest and picked up his duffel bag along with hers, so that the strain of carrying it wouldn't weigh on his mending collarbone. She eschews the slow-moving escalator and rushes down the stairs separating the arrivals area from baggage claim, and she stops dead.

Jesy and Rosalie stand near the elevator. Rosalie holds a bouquet of flowers. Jesy sees Tessa first and tugs on Rosalie's arm, her face lighting up with excitement and relief. They rush over and hug her so tightly that she staggers back, colliding with Ryan.

"You're home, thank God," Rosalie sniffles.

Tessa catches the scent of Jesy's Japanese Cherry Blossom Bath and Body Works perfume, as she holds her tight. "Welcome home, Tess."

Chapter Nine

January – October 2008

Adjusting to being back in the States is just as much of a struggle as adjusting to being out of the military, and not having a job anymore. She doesn't have a purpose. She doesn't have a mission.

Tessa allows herself a single weekend to recover from jetlag and get settled into her and Jesy's new apartment with Alyssa. On Monday morning, she heads right over to the corner bodega she spotted on her first night back, the one with the handwritten *Help Wanted* sign taped to the window. She asks for an interview.

Tessa's shifts at the bodega are long. Customers stare at her disfigured hands when she rings their items up. "Do you want something different?" Jesy asks. "They're hiring admin staff at the office, and you could totally do that."

Tessa declines every offer. The bodega is fine. It is a relatively safe space to rest while she licks her wounds.

There is no truly safe space. Every car that drives past makes her remember car bombs. Routine construction noises are terrifying. Her gaze jumps from person to person to person as she navigates the streets of the city. She has to keep an eye out for potentially dangerous people or suspicious objects. Her teammates' life and her life could depend on that. She is a world away from Baghdad now, but Tessa constantly forgets that she isn't in a war zone anymore.

Adrenaline floods her system every time she catches sight of a car parked up ahead on the street. Or worse, when she has to walk on the sidewalk beside a parked car. She crosses the street to avoid parked cars whenever she can. Tessa instinctively looks down to her side for Spencer, searching for his reaction; for him to let her know if she's safe or not.

She has heard and read that other combat veterans have the sensation of phantom limbs. She misses Spencer like she would miss an arm or a leg. Spencer let her know if she was safe. Spencer kept her safe, right until the end. This once-beloved city, and her entire world, feels infinitely more dangerous and frightening without her partner and protector.

Once, in happier times, she loved how New York City was full of dogs. She would mentally count the dogs she and Jesy saw while walking in Brooklyn. Tessa hates that now. There is no reason that seeing someone's poodle or chihuahua or Shiba Inu should remind her of Spencer. Her dog, in appearance and skills, bore no resemblance to these safe, coddled city dogs. But it does. Every dog she sees reminds her that these dogs are living safe, coddled lives, and her dog lived and died in a war zone.

Sometimes she passes newsstands or TV screens blaring headline news about the war in Iraq or Afghanistan. Tessa flinches away like she's warding off a blow.

There is no truly safe space, even in the tiny little apartment that she, Jesy, and Alyssa are turning into a home. Even there, a neighbor slams a door and Tessa perceives it as a gunshot. Even there, she is cooking dinner with Jesy, or showering, or brushing her teeth, or watching Breaking Bad with Jesy and Alyssa, and a flashback seizes her by the shoulders and shakes her until her teeth rattle in her skull.

It is exhausting and discouraging and demoralizing. She doesn't want to live like this. Afraid, wracked by grief, in pain. She doesn't have her Army service weapons anymore, but she could still find a way to end it. Hundreds of New Yorkers do every year, even if they don't have firearms. She could be with her mom again, and with Spencer.

It's such a tempting prospect. It comforts Tessa as she lies in bed, awake between nightmares.

There are roadblocks, though. Insurmountable barriers. Cooking dinner together and watching shows, working out, and running errands with Jesy and Alyssa. Regular phone calls with Rosalie and regular texts from Ryan, Matt, and Curtis. Ryan is living with his aunt again and working at the LGBT burlesque club she owns. Matt is working at his parents' convenience store, and Curtis is applying for internships.

Tessa weighs her options. She won't put Jesy and Alyssa through the trauma of finding her body. The logical answer is to disappear and then kill herself, but she can't bring herself to do that to her friends. She has no choice but to survive.

ooooo

It is President's Day, a federal holiday, and a long weekend. This doesn't apply to Tessa anymore — the military observes all federal holidays, but the bodega observes none. But it does mean that it's a long weekend for Rosalie, and she takes the short flight from Baltimore to New York City to see her family and Tessa. Rosalie's Friday is full with family commitments, and Tessa works a double shift at the bodega to accommodate having Saturday off. She, Jesy, and Rosalie go thrifting, and then to the orchid show at the botanical gardens. It is opening weekend at the orchid show, and it is crowded enough that Tessa has to fight off a panic attack in the bathroom. Thankfully, they leave unscathed.

"Are you sure you can't come tonight?" Tessa asks Jesy that evening, back at their apartment, while Jesy rifles through her closet.

"I'd rather be at your fancy Manhattan burlesque club party than at this thing." Jesy rolls her eyes. "I *hate* fundraising nights."

Rosalie pulls out her phone. She and Jesy both have iPhones now, but Tessa has no interest in giving up her pink Razr yet. It was her lifeline during her short time in the military, and she has a sentimental attachment to it. "I'll text you the address so you can come by if your thing wraps up early."

They help Jesy pick out a wig and an outfit for the fundraising night, and see her off before heading to the subway. "So, Ryan and Matt will be there," Rosalie says. "I feel like I know them already, from hearing you talk about them for so long."

"You met them at the airport too. Just for a second."

"Right, right. That Ryan's kind of cute, isn't he?"

Rosalie gives her a meaningful look, which Tessa ignores. Both Jesy and Rosalie have asked her a half dozen times each if there's "anything going on there." *I have known you for years,* Jesy pointed out several months ago, *and I've never heard you mention a guy once. Not ever! But now it's Ryan this, Ryan that…*

"Grace will be there — that's Matt's wife. Ryan's other friends are coming too, Booker and Javier. He's known both of them since high school."

"Have you met them?"

"No, but he's told me both of their life stories, so I kind of feel like I know them already. I think you'll like them. They sound cool."

It is well after dark by the time they arrive in Manhattan. Tessa has never been to the Maple Rose before. Her pace slows enough as they approach that Rosalie hangs back, looking at her inquisitively. "What's up?"

"I'm a little, um." Tessa's face flames, even in the frigid February air. "Nervous. I've never been to a place like this before."

"Me neither." Rosalie bites her lip. "I did a Google search because I wasn't sure what burlesque even is. It sounds classy, though. Like, they said it was provocative *and* comedic, not super sexual stuff like a strip club."

Tessa exhales hard, stuffing her gloved hands in her pockets. "All right. Let's do this."

"Besides," Rosalie goads, "Ryan's going to be there, so it'll be fine, right?"

"I will take you back to Victory Tower and push you off it," Tessa threatens, and Rosalie laughs.

Tessa's lips part in surprise as they walk into Maple Rose. The interior is deceptively large, and the club is crowded, considering that it is early in the night by New York City standards. It's like stepping into a time capsule. The warmth is a welcome relief from the biting cold outside, and the lighting is just as warm — low and rich golden-amber. The decor is unlike anything she has ever seen. An enormous chandelier glitters above them. The long bar glimmers with gold and black marble, and hundreds of glass bottles of liquor line the shelves behind the bar. The booths and the barstools alike are upholstered in velvet. The curtains on the stage are drawn, and a jazz quartet plays there. The centerpieces on the tables boast vividly colored flamingo feathers and peacock feathers.

"Whoa," Rosalie breathes. "This place is insane."

Ryan's head pops up over the top of one of the booths. He beams and gestures enthusiastically, and Tessa and Rosalie weave through the crowd to join them. Their party of five is already squished into the booth, and Tessa hesitates. "Should we bring over a couple of stools from the bar?"

"No, there's room." Grace waves them in, and nudges Matt. "Scooch over."

Tessa and Rosalie squeeze in, and Tessa ends up next to Ryan. Instead of sitting next to Tessa, Rosalie subtly maneuvers to sit beside one of Ryan's friends instead. This is either Booker or Javier, and he is incredibly broad-shouldered, with brown skin and thick dark hair. Tessa raises an eyebrow at Rosalie, and Rosalie kicks her under the table.

Ryan and Matt both start speaking at the same time, trying to introduce Tessa and Rosalie. Ryan swats Matt on the shoulder and attempts to problem-solve by talking louder than his friend. "Booker, Javier, Grace, here are Tessa and Rosalie. Tessa and Rosalie, here are Booker, Javier, and Grace."

All three of Ryan and Matt's friends have genuine, ready smiles, kind eyes, and warm handshakes. That is where their resemblance ends. Grace is petite, with wavy dark brown hair cut in a stylish bob, and a cochlear implant tucked behind her right ear. Booker's sharp haircut and sweater-and-blazer combo look like they've been torn out of the pages of a high fashion magazine. Javier towers over all of them, even sitting. He's dressed casually, in a flannel shirt.

They fall into conversation. The easy way that Booker, Javier, Matt, Ryan, and Grace finish each other's sentences, even seeming to share their trains of thought, reveals how long they have all known one another. They still take care not to make Rosalie and Tessa feel like outsiders, which Tessa appreciates. None of them stare at her hands.

"So, are you guys in college?" Rosalie asks, taking a sip of her Coke.

"We all graduated last summer." Javier gestures to Booker and Grace. "I got a business degree to help my parents run their store. Booker did communications, and Grace did sociology."

"Matt and I are way behind."

Tessa picks up on the self-conscious edge to Ryan's joke. "Me too."

"Not like this. You're still way younger than us. We'll be the oldest freshmen on campus."

"Don't worry, bro. We'll tutor you guys." Booker turns to Tessa. "I heard you were thinking about Barnard?"

"Yeah," Tessa replies, surprised. Ryan must have mentioned it to him. After a couple years of exposure to an almost all-male environment in the Army, she found the idea of an all-women's college intriguing.

"I know a few people who went to Barnard, and they all loved it," Booker says encouragingly. "The academic experience and the whole culture of the college."

"Oh, good. That's a relief. Do you know the Barnard alums from work?"

"Yeah, I do."

"Also, Booker knows everybody," Grace adds.

"*Everybody*," Javier emphasizes.

"Booker has contacts in all five boroughs," Matt says, very seriously. "Even Staten Island. Booker has contacts in all fifty states, and Washington DC. Rumor has it that he even has contacts abroad."

Booker rolls his eyes. "It's called being social."

"I'm plenty social," Ryan complains. "I still don't have the kind of network you do."

They linger over the several rounds of drinks and appetizers that Ryan buys for their table, insisting that everything is on the house. The jazz quartet makes way for a burlesque show as the night goes on. They stay where they are, talking and eating cheese fries, instead of making their way closer to the stage. Their opulent surroundings seem completely routine to Ryan and his friends. To them, the Maple Rose is just as routine as the McDonalds where she used to hang out with Jesy. They've been coming here to hang out with Ryan since their freshman year of high school, after all.

It is close to midnight when Grace looks at her phone and blanches. "I have to be up at seven for volunteering tomorrow. I should be asleep right now."

"And I'm opening the store tomorrow." Javier hangs his head.

Their little party disperses, but not before making plans to meet up again in a couple of weeks. "You should join us anytime you're in town," Javier tells Rosalie. "I can give you my number — let me know next time you're back in the city."

Tessa smiles as she pulls on her coat. Surprisingly Rosalie, like her, didn't have a boyfriend in high school, and she has sworn not to date any military guys.

"I can get a cab for you guys." Ryan hands Tessa her scarf, watching as she winds it around her neck. "It's late, and the trains are slower after midnight."

Tessa grimaces at the thought of the cab fare from Manhattan to Brooklyn. "Don't worry about it. We'll be fine."

Ryan frowns. "All right. Text me when you get back to your place?"

It reminds her of her and Rosalie's nightly check-in by text every night in advanced individual training. Tessa waves to him. "Okay. Good night."

The night feels even more punishingly cold than it was earlier, after the hours of warmth in the bar. Tessa and Rosalie huddle together as they walk, keeping a brisk pace in an attempt to warm themselves. "Javier totally likes you."

Rosalie waves it off, even though she's blushing. "It doesn't matter. He's here, I'm in Maryland. Long-distance relationships don't work."

"It's not that far. It's only two and a half hours drive time, and less if you're flying."

"We'll see." There's a little smile on Rosalie's face. She nudges Tessa. "I heard Ryan asking you to text him goodnight."

"It wasn't like that. It was just a safety check-in. Like you and I used to do."

"Sure." Rosalie loads the single syllable with a magnificent amount of doubt. Tessa distracts her by asking about her plans for tomorrow.

∞∞∞

Tessa, Matt, and Ryan struggle through their college applications together, with ample assistance from Booker, Javier, and Grace. Tessa and Matt share pessimism over their chances of getting into Barnard and Columbia. Ryan approaches it with bullheaded optimism. He never speaks in terms of *if*. *When we get into Columbia,* he says. *When you get into Barnard.*

All three of them receive their acceptance letters within days of one another. (Ryan is so obnoxious over crowing that he was right that Matt and Tessa renew the old threat to kick his ass.) Still, it doesn't sink in for Tessa — not even after the party that Grace, Booker, and Javier throw for them. She gets her hugs from her friends and hugs them in return. Rosalie and Jesy both tell her that she's amazing and incredible.

"An Ivy, girl! You're a genius." Jesy toasts to her. Rosalie sniffs. "With a poli-sci degree from Barnard, you don't have to be an aide to Ryan when he's in Congress. You can be the representative. You can be the Senator."

"Hell, you can be the President," Jesy encourages.

Tessa tries her best to take the compliments. It is still surreal. It is still a challenge to imagine her future. Ryan oozes excitement for the fall semester, and it's rubbing off on Matt. Meanwhile, she lies in bed awake every night, tossing and turning with anxiety instead of anticipation. She has trained as a soldier and served in a war zone. Starting college shouldn't be so intimidating. It shouldn't frighten her. It does anyway.

ooooo

She was right to be apprehensive. Moving into Barnard housing in Manhattan, having some younger girl as her roommate and not Jesy or Alyssa, is a big change in itself. The rigors of college life are challenging in an entirely different way than her time in the military. Tessa spends hours studying with Ryan and Matt at Columbia and Barnard's libraries. She has never studied so hard before, or spent so many consecutive hours reading and writing papers.

It is a comfort that her classes are so fascinating. It is everything Tessa loved in her high school American Government class, dialed up a thousand in intensity. Political Theory makes her consider the definition of justice, and how to justify the coercive power of states. Tessa writes lengthy papers on whether citizens have an obligation to obey the government, and who should make and enforce the law. She considers what basic rights and liberties governments should protect. She thinks through how the American economic system should produce and divide wealth and material resources. She studies the claims of excluded and marginalized groups and writes proposals for how these claims should be addressed.

Matt's classes mirror her own. Political Theory, American Political Parties, the American Presidency. They brainstorm on their assignments together, Ryan often weighing in with his opinions (of which there are many). In turn, they pick Ryan's brain for International Politics and Introduction to Comparative Politics, which cross over with his International Relations major.

Tessa is two pages into a paper questioning whether there is an ideal level of difference in political parties when she looks up, startled out of her focus. Matt glances up from his laptop too. "There you are."

"Sorry I'm late." Ryan slides into his usual spot beside Tessa. He looks even more exhausted than usual today. He was probably up into the early hours of the morning reading deep-dives of election news and analysis. She and Matt are following the upcoming presidential and midterm election closely, considering their major. Ryan's interest in the elections nationwide has tipped into obsession, which is very much on brand for him. He emails both her and Matt at bizarre hours of the night with links to different pieces of analysis. Each link is followed by lengthy paragraphs of his own opinions.

Tessa slides the untouched to-go cup of coffee over to him. She picked one up for him and Matt on her way over here, when she stopped to get herself a bagel sandwich. "Here. It's still warm."

"You're the best. Thanks." Ryan takes a large gulp of coffee, and then flattens a flier on the table in front of them. "Check this out."

Matt eyes the flier while continuing to type. "NY Dems?"

"Democrats in New York State need volunteers." Ryan pulls out another couple of wrinkled brochures from his pocket and sets them down on the table.

Tessa takes both. "Other volunteer opportunities, at Silverman's and Watts' offices."

"Yeah. Let's do it. Silverman's office is closest. It's right in Manhattan."

Matt stops typing. "Dude, we're coming up on midterms."

"Midterms aren't that important–"

"Yes, they are," Tessa cuts in.

Ryan grimaces, and makes a gesture of acknowledgement toward her. "Okay, fine, maybe."

"But I get what you're saying. You want us to start making connections that could help us in the future." She is still getting the hang of her academics, and now there will be a new challenge to face. She is nowhere near as timid as she was in high school, but neither is she as adept at social situations as her friends. Among everyone, only Grace is as shy as she is.

"Exactly!" Ryan's volume level earns him a dirty look from a couple of guys at a nearby table, and he subsides. "Networking is key. I want to hold a public office by the time I'm thirty. That doesn't come out of nowhere. This is a high-impact year locally and nationally, since it's a midterm election year and a presidential election year."

Matt's reply is, "Ugh."

"All right." Even though it makes her nervous, volunteering for the Democratic Party on the statewide level and at Silverman's office will give her precious real-life experience. "You can sign me up too."

○○○○○

Tessa runs herself ragged, between keeping her grades high and volunteering with the Democratic Party alongside Ryan and Matt. She does this while attempting to have a social life, meeting up with Jesy every other weekend, and Rosalie whenever she's in town.

Volunteering with the Democratic Party consists of making phone calls introducing voters to candidates, door-to-door canvassing of campaign materials, voter registration efforts, and volunteer support at events. The phone calls and door-to-door canvassing are the hardest. People are curt or unresponsive at best, and Tessa gets screamed at and cursed at worst.

Voter registration is infinitely more fulfilling, especially when she is helping new voters who have just turned eighteen, or new voters who have just received their US citizenship. The smiles she offers to these new voters are genuine, and their excitement makes her happy. Ryan and Matt, and so many of her classmates, and even her — they are all so jaded about the process, and the many issues with the system, ranging from gerrymandering to low voter turnout, to outright efforts at voter suppression. It's nice to see people who are excited to vote; to have a voice in the nation's political process.

Volunteering at Silverman's office is a lot of the same, except his volunteer base is smaller. At both places, there are shifts where Tessa interacts with dozens of people, and shifts where she interacts with hundreds. It is incredibly draining. She gives a hundred and fifty percent of her effort anyway. She tries her hardest to be personable, despite her exhaustion.

In contrast, Ryan is effortlessly charismatic, no matter how tired he is and how many directions he is pulled in. He has a big, affable smile for everyone, he is kind and polite, and he connects with people well. Old people, young people, men, women. (Women of all ages and backgrounds love him. Many flirt outright, giggling, flipping their hair and standing close and looking up at him through lowered eyelashes, or even touching his arms or shoulders. Tessa finds all of it incredibly annoying, and she doesn't understand why. Ryan is good at being charming with them. He leverages their interest into a donation, or a commitment to volunteer, or a commitment to vote.)

Jesy and Alyssa show up to volunteer when their schedules allow, to support her as much as the Democratic Party. Grace, Booker, and Javier come by whenever they can too. They always bring treats and liberal amounts of encouragement. Being surrounded by her friends makes it feel less like work, even when events and shifts run late into the evening or on weekends.

The silver lining is that her life as a student and volunteer is so over-whelmingly busy, every half-hour block of every day scheduled, that Tessa is too occupied to suffer the way she did when she arrived in New York City at the beginning of the year.

It doesn't mean she's healed. It doesn't mean she's cured. The flash-backs still strike her at the most unpredictable times, leaving her standing paralyzed, staring off into space. She still misses Spencer every single day. She feels best when she's with her friends. When she's alone, exhaustion and sorrow creep in, putting her in a chokehold. This time last year, she was in Iraq. Too much has happened to her in the past two years. She's still struggling to keep up. To process it all. Sometimes she's just walking to class when she is hit with a wave of profound disorientation. It feels like just yesterday she was in basic training with Rosalie, advanced individual training with Spencer, and Iraq with her team. Now she is walking on campus in New York City. Too much has happened, in too short a time.

She tries to explain that on the phone to Rosalie, taking advantage of her roommate's absence on this late Thursday night. "You know…" Rosalie starts. "I know you quit the Zoloft, but did your doctor at the VA ever recommend anything else? Not medications, but like, counseling or something, to help you process everything that happened? My uncle used to go to a PTSD support group. He liked it."

Tessa thinks back to the fog that shrouded her first couple of months back in the States. "I think the doctor mentioned it. But I didn't look into it." She had been in the depths of it, then. It took all of her resolve just to not kill herself. Jesy and Rosalie don't know that, and they never will. "I wasn't up to it."

"I'll get the info and email it to you."

"I'm so busy," Tessa hedges. "The election is so close that volunteering is getting really crazy, and I need to study for finals."

"I know you're busy. But you have to make time for your health. You don't want to have a nervous breakdown or something."

Within minutes of getting off the phone, Tessa's email pings with a notification from Rosalie. Rosalie has attached a flier for a PTSD support group at Fort Hamilton in Brooklyn. The group meets once a week in the evenings, on Thursdays. She could actually get there in time, if she leaves right after her last class of the day. It would eat into her study time with Ryan and Matt, but she could study on the train.

Tessa heads to the library after class the next day. She would normally stop for lunch, but there's no time. She's a little behind on two of her papers. Her phone buzzes with a text from Ryan. *Our usual spot is taken :(4th floor instead*

She finds Ryan at their second choice study spot — a secluded nook on the far east side of the fourth floor. He is sitting on the sofa, feet up on the study table, wearing dark jeans and a Columbia sweatshirt, and typing furiously on his laptop. Ryan looks up when he hears her approach, and his face lights up with a smile. "Hey." He reaches down and grabs a brown paper bag. "I stopped by Absolute and got lunch for you."

"You're the best." Tessa shrugs her backpack off and sits beside him. They talk while she devours her bagel with cream cheese, and she wipes her hands with the napkins at the bottom of the brown bag. Ryan has the habit of using his laptop directly after stuffing down handfuls of chips, buttery popcorn, or egg rolls. She cringes whenever she sees his poor keyboard. "Rosalie sent me something last night."

"Was it another op-ed from the Baltimore Sun?"

"No. It was a flier for this veterans PTSD support group at Fort Hamilton." Tessa hesitates. "It's on Thursday evenings at six. I'm thinking about checking it out. I thought maybe, if you were interested…"

Ryan's fingers go still on his keyboard. He continues typing, but slower. "I want to." He doesn't look away from his laptop screen. Matt has Grace and school, and Curtis has his family and his first semester at Clemson, and they're coping well. It's only the two of them, her and Ryan, that are still struggling this much. Ryan has confided in her and Matt about his persistent feelings of helplessness and anger. *People are still dying in Iraq and Afghanistan, still getting maimed, still having their lives ruined, every damn day. That hasn't changed, even though we're not seeing it firsthand anymore.*

Then he continues. "But I've been thinking about picking up a couple of extra volunteering shifts a week at Silverman's office and with the Democratic Party. I feel like most volunteers are going to fall off after the elections. I want to stand out from the crowd, you know? So I need to step it up. With getting to Brooklyn and back, and the time for the group itself, that would take up all of Thursdays after class."

Tessa conceals her disappointment. She hadn't realized that she assumed that she and Ryan would do this together. They do pretty much everything together. Especially new things, like volunteering, or going to on-campus networking events with the College Democrats. "Yeah, that makes sense."

"You should still definitely go, though. I hope that it helps. Let me know how it is for you, okay?"

She can tell that his concern is genuine. Tessa tries to smile. Maybe it will be good for her to do something without him. She will be able to learn how to get through it herself, without having him — or any of her friends — as a crutch to lean on. "I will."

Chapter Ten

October 2008 – March 2009

Matt and Ryan head to Silverman's office on Thursday after class, and Tessa takes the subway to Brooklyn. She buries her head in a textbook on the trip, and returns texts from her friends. Rosalie, Jesy, and Grace all sent good luck texts, and offer dinner or a phone call if she wants to decompress after group.

Tessa's worry mounts with every subway stop that brings her closer to Fort Hamilton, and as she trudges to the visitor center to show her veterans ID card and get access to the base. This is her first time on a military installation since her discharge in January.

It is strange being back. Seeing so many soldiers brings a bittersweet sorrow. She was one of them, before everything that happened in Iraq left her in pieces. This reminds her of being with her platoons in training, before her deployment. With Spencer and Ryan, Matt and Curtis.

Fort Leonard Wood, and Lackland, and even Camp Victory — all have been home, more so than the home where she grew up. Fort Hamilton doesn't feel like home, because she's not a soldier anymore. The Army broke her, and then cast her out when she became too broken to serve them. She is as much of an alien, as much of an outsider, here as she is in her lecture halls on campus. (Where she is surrounded by young, happy girls, most of whom haven't known the same kind of loss and fear and pain she has. Most of whom aren't orphans, aren't veterans.)

Tessa's heart is heavy, her emotional strength already depleted, by the time she arrives at the medical center. Over the past couple of months, she has found herself able to think of Spencer for courage and comfort —

even if just for brief snatches of time. She imagines him next to her now, lending her his bravery.

Tessa takes a tentative step into Patient Education Room #4. It's a small room with plastic chairs that have been arranged in a half-circle. She is the only woman here. Two men sit in wheelchairs, chatting with another man who has a prosthetic arm. A few other men stand near the front of the room, talking with one another. They are diverse in race, but all of them have the same distinctive look as the soldiers she served with. The same straight, upright posture, the same muscular build, the same haircuts and clean-shaven look.

One of the men turns to her. His name tag reads *Asher*. Asher steps toward her, hand outstretched to shake. "Hi." His soft tone of voice is incongruous with his large frame. "Welcome to the group. Thanks for being here. My name is Asher, and I'm the facilitator. What's your name?"

Tessa manages to introduce herself without stammering. Asher shows her the sign-in sheet and nametags, and the refreshment table, and lets her know that she can take a seat anywhere. "Owen?" He looks toward one of the soldiers at the front of the room. "Can you get an extra chair?"

"Will do." A tall guy with sandy brown hair heads out of the room. He returns a minute later with a chair, and settles it into the half-circle for her. "Here you go, miss."

"Thanks."

A few other people arrive, all men. Two of them have prosthetic legs. They must be new too, because Asher gives them the same mini-orientation he gave her. Over the time she has been out of the military, hanging out with her friends, in the mixed-gender group of political volunteers, and in her classes, surrounded by women, she has forgotten how odd it is to be surrounded exclusively by men.

They all settle into their chairs, and Tessa notes people's body languages. A lot of the guys cross their arms over their chests. They don't make eye contact, staring at fixed spots on the floor at the center of the circle, or on the wall, instead. She has to stop herself from picking at her cuticles.

Asher introduces the group. "This is a reminder that everything you say here is confidential. The only exception to that is if someone poses an imminent danger to themselves or others."

Nods of understanding ripple all around the circle. Tessa wipes her palms against her jeans. It is a saving grace that she doesn't feel bad enough anymore that she wants to disappear or die.

"Thank you. We have some new people here today, and some folks we haven't seen in a while, so let's do a brief round of introductions."

Unsurprisingly, every one of the group has served in Iraq or Afghanistan over the last five years. Owen and four other guys are still active duty. The others, the veterans with prosthetics or the ones using wheelchairs, got honorable discharges, like Tessa. When it's her turn to speak, the group members look at her curiously, assessing her face, her Barnard sweatshirt, probably her limp ponytail, definitely her disfigured hands.

"Tessa Halifax." Tessa tries to project the same quiet confidence she does when she speaks in class; the confidence that makes her professors and the other students alike regard her with respect. "I served in Baghdad from December 2006 to December 2007. I was — was — MOS 31K, a w-working dog handler." Her voice breaks. She never talks about Spencer to anyone who didn't know him. This can't be happening now, in front of all these strangers. Asher, Owen, and a few other guys regard her sympathetically. Tessa rushes on, desperate to finish before she bursts into tears. "I got discharged in January, and I'm going to school for political science now."

Asher nods when he realizes she is finished. "Thank you, Tessa, for sharing that. Thank you, everyone, for sharing your stories with us. I want to give us the opportunity now to talk about what we've been struggling with lately."

The group is very quiet. A few people fidget in their seats. A few more cross their arms over their chests.

"I'll open the discussion." Unlike everyone else, Asher's body language is open, his palms settled lightly on his knees. "I wasn't sleeping well last week. Difficulty getting to sleep, waking up in the middle of the night and not being able to fall asleep again."

That is way too familiar. "Me too," one of the guys says. "It's this phantom limb thing. I can't get comfortable in bed."

People speak up in no particular order. Zach says he's been having the urge to drink again. Mark feels numb even though he should be excited about his wife being pregnant. Luke hasn't been able to bring himself to leave the house at all between last week's meeting and this week's meeting.

Owen can't concentrate at work or at home. Jesús misses being able to run. Brandon is struggling with angry outbursts at work.

Tessa is the last to speak, only after Asher gives her an encouraging prompt. She's still picking at the cuticle on her left thumb. "I'm just… having a hard time coping, in general. I feel overwhelmed. I've been out for almost a year, but I still feel like this can't be my life now, compared to what my life used to be in Iraq. This new life doesn't feel real. It doesn't feel like it's really mine."

Several guys nod. They segue into a discussion about everyone's experiences with their current struggles. There's some problem-solving and sharing suggestions. There are other moments where they just share support. *That sucks, man.* Or *I hate that.* Or *Yeah, I get it. I felt that way too when I first got back.* Conversation flows easier, and Tessa gradually begins to relax into her seat.

"This has been a great discussion. Thank you for your honesty and your openness. On a related note — can we talk now about what's been working for you, in helping you cope with these struggles, since we last met?" Asher asks. "Please feel free to share what's not working as well."

Everyone takes a moment to think that through. "Sure," Owen begins. "I've gone hiking a few times. Not camping. I can't do that yet. But getting back to hiking is a win. It helps me clear my head."

The replies come fast after that. "Reading," Mark says. "Wild fantasy stuff, like, Lord of the Rings type of stuff."

"Video games." Jesús laughs at himself, but Zach nods in agreement. "Yeah, me too."

"Being busy with school and volunteering, and my friends," Tessa ventures to add.

They talk about things that haven't been working. Church. Spending time with family and friends. Drinking. Weed. Yoga. TV. Tessa remains quiet, with nothing to add to the conversation. She doesn't do much, outside of school and volunteering. She hasn't read a book for fun, or watched TV, since the semester started.

Asher asks them all to commit to doing something to care for themselves until they see each other again. Everyone chimes in. They're going to read a few more chapters of their book, or hike, or see family, or go to another Alcoholics Anonymous meeting.

Asher closes the group, reminding them about their next meeting the following week. "I'll stick around for the next hour in case anyone wants to chat one-on-one." He makes his way over to her first. Tessa stands rooted to her spot, half-convinced that he's going to tell her that she performed poorly at the support group and she's not welcome to return.

"How are you feeling?" Asher asks instead. "I know how hard that first group session can be."

"Fine." Tessa is startled to realize it isn't a lie. "It-it was nice to talk about things without having to worry about worrying my friends." It was also nice to see that she isn't alone in this. That other people are struggling too.

"That's what the group is here for — to be a safe space to express your feelings. Are you planning on coming back next week?"

"It's a little hard with my schedule." Tessa cringes inwardly at the thought of all she'll have to do on Monday, Tuesday, and Wednesday night, to make this group on Thursday work. "But I'll shift some things around. I want to be here."

ooooo

She is light with relief during dinner with Jesy, and then on the train ride back to Manhattan. Not only did she get through it on her own — without Ryan or her other friends to rely on — but it was a success.

Rosalie and Grace text her to check in. Tessa is up until one in the morning doing schoolwork, and then she collapses in an exhausted heap in her bed. She wakes at four in the morning, her heart pounding, body flushed with heat, as usual. Tessa reaches for her phone in an attempt to distract herself. There is one new text from Ryan, time-stamped at 2:11 AM. *Thought of you this evening, hope the group went well. See you tomorrow. Or later today I guess lmao. Night.*

ooooo

Regardless of the upheaval it causes in her schedule, especially during Election Week, Tessa attends the support group at Fort Hamilton regularly. It's just a gray-walled, gray-carpeted classroom with a bunch of chairs stuffed into the small space. It is simultaneously an oasis of peace and acceptance. It is safe, unlike Silverman's office, or the NY Dems headquarters where she volunteers with Ryan and Matt. Both of those spaces are crowded, chaotic, brimming with frantic energy. It leaves her on edge, even though she knows it's important work.

Even the Maple Rose, and the Barnard and Columbia campuses, which Tessa often traverses with Ryan or Matt or both by her side, don't feel as safe. (She has talked about this at the support group — she still feels like she has to protect Ryan and Matt. Their safety is still her responsibility. When she walks with them, it is easy to slip back in time, to the streets of Baghdad. She still catches herself automatically looking for Spencer to signal whether they are safe or not.)

Tessa finds herself anticipating group meetings as a high point of her week, alongside time with her friends. She learns everyone's name, and they learn hers. She learns about the traumas they experienced in the war, their struggles, and their successes. With difficulty, she shares hers.

They wish her luck on her finals, and ask whether she has plans for the holidays, and if she's taking any interesting classes for the spring semester. Some of them wrinkle their noses when she mentions that she volunteers for the New York Democratic Party, but they don't treat her any differently for it. Tessa doesn't love their politics, but she won't treat them differently either. They don't talk about details of politics in the group. "Hey, it's cool that you're so involved," Zach says. Luke asks her if she's ever been to DC.

She shows up for the group meeting on the second Thursday of January ravenous. Normally she times it so that she can arrive about fifteen minutes early to chat with the guys and hit up the snack table. One of her trains was delayed, and she showed up just in time to grab her usual seat.

She heads straight to the snack table on break. Asher is leading them through a guided meditation after this, and she doesn't want her gnawing hunger to be a distraction. Tessa pauses. Owen is already at the table, reaching for the last few crackers in the sleeve. He notices her, and then steps away from the crackers. "Go ahead."

"Oh, no, I'm fine." Tessa takes a step back. "I have a granola bar."

Owen looks unimpressed. He takes the sleeve of crackers and extends it to her.

Tessa wavers. "I can split them with you."

"Take them all. I'm having Vietnamese tonight anyway, so I don't need this."

Tessa finally relents. The crackers are wonderfully, mouth-wateringly salty and buttery. She could probably eat an entire sleeve. "Thanks." She covers her mouth while she speaks. "Is there a good Vietnamese place nearby? My friend lives in Brooklyn too, and we get dinner after group sometimes."

"Yeah, it's called Lẩu Phở Gà." Owen pronounces it carefully but still awkwardly, in a very different way than Ryan, Matt, and Grace pronounce the names of the various Vietnamese, Chinese, and Korean spots their friends hit up. "I'm probably not saying it right. Their pho is incredible, though."

"I love pho." Tessa fondly remembers the pho that Ryan ordered for her, Matt, and himself that one night when they had been half-dead with stress and exhaustion during finals. It was so good that she almost cried. The three of them huddled together in the library (where they weren't allowed to have any food), slurping down their soup in companionable silence.

"If you're not busy after group — if you don't have plans with your friend or need to get back — you could come with me," Owen offers.

The invitation takes her by surprise, but she doesn't freeze up, the way she does when she is surprised in class or volunteering. "Yeah, okay. Thanks."

They head back to their seats. She always loves the different techniques Asher leads them through, but Tessa can't focus during this guided meditation. She replays and analyzes Owen's offer and her response at least fifteen times. What *was* that? Was he asking her on a date? Why had she said yes so fast? That's so unlike her.

No way was he asking me on a date. Tessa tries to relax her facial muscles, as Asher prompts them to. He was just asking her to hang out. She goes out to eat with Ryan, Matt, Javier, and Booker all the time. Those definitely aren't dates. It's just a normal thing that friends do.

That banishes her nerves, and Tessa immerses herself in the rest of the meditation exercise.

Lẩu Phở Gà isn't too far from her subway stop. The walk is painfully cold. Owen seems unfazed, even though his coat is much lighter than hers, and he isn't wearing a scarf or gloves. "You have crazy good cold tolerance." Tessa braces herself against the sharp wind, shoving her hands deeper into her pockets.

"I grew up in Alaska. I had a harder time in summer in Kabul and Fort Benning than in this." Owen waves a hand in the frigid air.

"Alaska?" Tessa remembers Julie of the Wolves, and Call of the Wild, and White Fang, with a pang of nostalgia. "I've always wanted to go there. It sounds so wild and gorgeous. The last frontier."

"It's a beautiful place." There is a note of wistfulness in Owen's voice. "It's got a lot of problems, though. A good place to visit. Not to live."

He holds the door open for her when they get to the restaurant. It's a tiny place, a hole in the wall, really. In her time living in the city, she has learned that spots like this have the best food. The walls are painted vibrant mango orange, and the space is lit by paper lanterns. A few framed photos of Vietnamese landscapes hang on the walls, little bamboo plants sit on the tables, and traditional Vietnamese music pipes through the speaker system. Tessa smiles as they settle at a table. She takes a seat facing the exit — she hates having her back to the door. "This place is cute."

Owen shares her dislike of having her back to the door, for obvious reasons. He pulls a chair around to sit at the other side of the square table, diagonal from her. "It's nice that it's so close to base. And they do lunch and dinner buffets on the weekends. It's great to hit up after a hike."

"I was going to ask you how you were still hiking in this weather, but now I know." Every week, Owen mentions another spot he hiked. He has driven as far as to the Mohawk Trail State Forest in Massachusetts. Tessa studies the menu. "What's good here?"

"It's not so bad, with the right gear. Try the 505, it's my favorite."

They both order bowls of the beef pho, and Tessa sips her herbal tea. "It's nice that you hike so much. I used to love being outdoors when I was a kid. I — don't get much time for that anymore."

(She and her mom would go for evening walks in the neighborhood after dinner every day when the weather was nice. They tried to keep it up when her mom was getting treatment. Their walks shrunk from all around the neighborhood, to around the block, to finally just sitting in the backyard together, shoulder-to-shoulder, Tessa cuddled up to her mom's side like she used to when she was just a little kid. She tried to go for those evening walks in the neighborhood, after her mom passed. Walking without her mom felt like a punishment, like a cruel reminder of all she lost. She made it all of two days, and never did that again.)

"Yeah, well, you sound really busy with school and volunteering. Your schedule is pretty hardcore. Are you still thinking about the minor in Human Rights?"

Tessa blows out a sigh so deep that she ruffles her bangs, and nods. "My advisor says that it's going to be about twenty percent more work, but the classes are really fascinating."

"Good luck with it." Owen hesitates, rubbing the back of his neck. "I've been going back and forth about starting to use my education benefits. You're doing it, Zach and Mark and Jesús are doing it. You guys all seem to be doing great."

Yet he's clearly balking. "The education benefits aren't that hard to get set up," Tessa tries to be encouraging, but not pushy. She is blunt with her close friends, but only with them. "There are a ton of good schools around here."

"Yeah. I'm just… I guess I'm afraid I wouldn't be good at it. I didn't do great in high school."

That's a surprise to hear. "You speak three languages, though." Two of them are Arabic and Pashto, which are notoriously hard, and he's in the process of learning Kurdish. That's what keeps Owen in such high demand as an Army linguist. He's Ryan's age, and a Sergeant as well.

"Yeah, well." The self-conscious shrug Owen gives strikes Tessa as oddly familiar. It's the same shrug she gives people at the support group, and at volunteering, when they hear that she's a student at Barnard.

Their pho arrives, steaming and fragrant. It's as good as Owen said it was. After a long, hard day of classes and frantic work on a dozen different assignments, it absolutely hits the spot. "This is perfect." Tessa speaks around a mouthful of noodles, practically melting in gratitude. "Thank you."

Owen smiles. "I'm glad you like it."

They scarf down half their bowls in a hurry before talking again. "So, what got you into the politics stuff?"

"American Government was my favorite class in high school." Tessa squeezes some more lime into her pho. "And one of my best friends has political ambitions. Large-scale, not just City Council. He got a couple of us into it as well. We want to work with him."

"Do you like it? The work, as well as the theory?"

"Yes. I love educating voters on the issues, and signing people up to vote. I hate it sometimes too," Tessa admits. "We had long shifts leading up to Election Week. We had hundreds of people coming through the offices and to events, and dozens of phone calls every few minutes. And so many emails…" She shudders. Matt and Ryan thrive on that. She tolerates it. "But it's a manageable amount of work now that we're past the elections."

Owen looks rattled by the sheer quantity of phone calls and emails. "I don't follow politics much. My dad always watched Fox News at home. I mean, it was *always* on. It turned me off, with all those dudes yelling, throwing fits all the time. It seemed so…mean. Cutthroat."

"Well, that's because it was Fox News." Tessa pauses, self-conscious. She doesn't want him thinking she was being rude to his dad. But Owen smiles, and she relaxes. "It can be like that, but it doesn't have to be. My friends and I — we've talked a lot about how a campaign could be run. How we could focus our message on giving back to our constituents and our community, rather than just attacking the other candidate."

"That would be more constructive, for sure. It sounds like you've done a lot of planning already."

"Yeah. In a few years, we'll see how it goes for real." The thought is exciting and intimidating at the same time. Tessa finishes her pho, and rests her spoon on the side of the bowl. "Thank you for inviting me out. It was so nice to get a break from thinking about school and volunteering." If not for this, she would have just headed straight back to the train and studied during the whole ride back to Manhattan.

"Anytime. It sounds like you don't get a lot of down time to relax."

"No, but that's a good thing." Too much time to think is dangerous for everyone in their group.

"Yeah, but you don't want to crash." Owen twirls his fork around his last few noodles, but rests it against his bowl instead of eating it. "I went a bit crazy after I got back from my tour of duty. Every minute I wasn't at work, I was out with friends, or triathlon training, or studying Kurdish. I made it four months before I crashed. I ended up — well, you know."

Tessa gives him a quiet nod of understanding. It's come up at their support group meetings. When he finally crashed, Owen fell into a months-long depressive episode that only began to abate when his friends brought him to his first support group meeting.

Owen clears his throat, regaining his composure. "So take it easy sometimes. Take care of yourself."

So many of her other friends have told her the same. It's easier said than done. "I'll try," Tessa says anyway. "Maybe I'll study outside or at Riverside Park instead of in the library."

Owen walks her to her subway stop after they wrap up with dinner. "See you next week?"

Tessa waves at him. "See you."

She allows herself a few minutes to relax after boarding her train. That dinner was fun, and a departure from the norm. She normally doesn't hang out with anyone besides her group of friends. She is so involved with volunteering and her classes that she hasn't even tried to make any other friends, outside of acquaintances from class. This was good.

She pulls out her textbook and picks up where she left off with her readings.

∞∞∞∞

She finds Owen at the snack table during break at their next support group meeting. He breaks into a smile when he sees her, and extends the sleeve of Ritz crackers to her. "Hey."

"Hey." Tessa takes a few crackers. There's the same flutter of nervousness in her chest that she felt the first time she walked up to Rosalie. She shelves it. "I was planning to stop by Giuseppina's before heading home tonight. Do you want to come with?"

Owen had been breaking a bite off one of the cookies Jesús's mom sent with him for the group. He almost drops the cookie. "Yeah! Um, I mean, yes, that would be great."

It becomes a little tradition between them. Support group, and then dinner afterward, at one of the many spots in Brooklyn around Fort Hamilton. Sometimes they talk about support group stuff, debriefing from the group. Sometimes they don't. Tessa likes to hear about Owen's work as a linguist and translator. It's so different from what she did. By virtue of his work, he knows a lot about what's happening on the ground in Iraq and Afghanistan.

Owen always asks her about her classes and her volunteering. He is attentive when she talks about the Democratic Party's issues, and he has plenty of questions. Criminal justice reform and taxes aren't issues that resonate with him, but he surprises them both with how into environmental protections and climate change he gets.

Sometimes other things come up. Owen eventually tells her more about his childhood in rural Alaska, in a dead-end town with a rampant drug abuse problem. His mom died from an overdose, leaving him and his brother to be raised by their dad, who was addicted to pills. "I had to get out of there. The Army sent a recruiter to my high school in senior year. I didn't think twice before enlisting. My brother's still mad at me for leaving, but…" Owen shrugs. "He and my dad are still there. Still up to the same old shit they were when I left. Still in and out of jail. I didn't want that to be me."

There's a leaden weight in her chest; the same weight that settles on Tessa whenever someone mentions a mother or father who died. "Do you talk to them much?"

"My brother, sometimes." Owen toys with the pepper shaker next to their plates. "My dad, never. My brother keeps trying to tell me that I should call him, but I don't even know what I'd say to him, at this point. After everything."

"I'm not going to tell you that you should talk to your dad." She has never brought her parents up at the support group. "I didn't talk to mine for a year and a half before he died."

They talk about it until it gets late, and they finally wander out of the restaurant and toward Tessa's subway stop. She still has readings to do tonight, but it's such a relief to talk to Owen about this that Tessa doesn't want to stop. Out of everyone she knows, only Ryan has lost his parents. And she would never say this to him, but at least Ryan had his aunt. As unconventional and eccentric as she is, there's no denying how much Sherry loves her nephew. She's so proud of him. Her dad never showed her a fraction of that warmth. Owen's dad had never, either.

They linger in front of Tessa's subway stop, despite the cold. "Do you have anything going on this weekend?" Owen asks. "With volunteering, or school and stuff?"

Tessa shivers. "I haven't thought any further than my American Urban Politics exam tomorrow, but I'm pretty sure I'm not volunteering on Saturday."

"Well…" Owen's face is flushed, even though it's just about freezing outside. He shifts from foot to foot. "If you're free this Saturday morning, I'm planning on hiking the Ice Caves and Verkeerderkill Falls Trail. You can come if you want."

She hasn't been hiking since she started at Barnard. "That sounds good." Tessa waves at him. "I'll text you tomorrow."

Her phone buzzes as soon as she gets onto the train. She finally caved to pressure from her friends and bought a used iPhone over the semester break. When she bought her first cell phone in 2006, her only two text threads were with Jesy and Rosalie. Now Tessa has several, including various permutations of group chats.

Jesy has texted. *Brunch Sat??*

Tessa winces. *Can we do dinner on Saturday instead?*

Ofc!! Volunteering Sat AM or school :(

Neither. I'm going hiking with Owen.

… Jesy sends. Tessa furrows her brow at her phone. *Like a date?!!?!*

Tessa initially makes several typos in her haste to type a reply. *No. I don't think so. No one used the word "date." Just friends hanging out.*

Omg. U go out to dinner with him literally every week and now he is taking u hiking. It sounds like a date <3

Tessa drops her phone back in her backpack and pulls out her textbook. Her phone buzzes again when she is halfway through her chapter. Tessa ignores it and only allows herself to check her phone when she is finished with the chapter.

This text is from Rosalie. *Jesy says u have a hiking date with Owen saturday?? :O :O :O*

I regret introducing you both, Tessa types.

Whatever. After a moment, *We r not trying to be pushy about the date thing. We just don't want u to be blindsided if he makes a move on u Sat.*

He wouldn't.

Don't have low self esteem. He obviously likes hanging out with u since u go to dinner EVERY WEEK. And u are so pretty and smart and kind!!

Tessa sighs. Jesy and Rosalie mutually decided she had "low self esteem" in 2006. They have been on a two-person mission to turn things around for her since then. *Thanks.*

What would u do if Owen kissed u? Rosalie asks. *Besides fall off the waterfall with surprise.*

Tessa can't suppress a tiny scoff. For some reason, she actually gives the question some thought. She imagines it. Owen stepping closer to her, leaning down to bridge the inches between them. Maybe putting a gentle hand on the small of her back, or on the back of her neck, drawing her even closer into him. Maybe wrapping his arms around her, pulling her into the warmth of his chest. It makes her palms prickle, makes her heart flutter — but not in the anxious way she's painfully familiar with.

She feels safe with Owen. She feels *understood* with him. She has even confided in him about Spencer. They have spent hours and hours together at this point, and she likes his company. There is no denying that he is handsome, either, with his height and his strong arms and shoulders. He keeps his sandy brown hair longer than a lot of military guys, and she likes long hair. He has a nice smile, and a nice voice.

Tessa stares at her phone for a while before replying. *I'd kiss him back.*

Omg, Rosalie texts. And then, *what are u going to wear!! Do u have any cute hiking outfits!*

Tessa rolls her eyes and drops her phone into her backpack again.

Chapter Eleven

March – May 2009

Hiking with Owen is just as nice as their dinners together. He is a thoughtful hiking partner, matching his stride length to Tessa's, despite their difference in height. He packs extra snacks and water for both of them. He holds his hand out to her every time they come across rocky or muddy or slippery terrain, carefully helping her cross over without falling.

After the third time — after she is disappointed when Owen releases her, after she catches herself staring at his forearms — Tessa realizes that she is in trouble. She tries to act normal about it. She tries not to get nervous around him all of a sudden. She tries not to second-guess every word that comes out of her mouth. She mostly succeeds.

The gorgeous landscape is a welcome distraction. They take a break at Sam's Point, admiring the vistas. "It is so nice to get out of the city. This is amazing. It's so…peaceful and quiet." Tessa's eyes relish the break from Manhattan skyscrapers and the rows of tightly compacted apartment buildings. Her mind relaxes, free from the ever-present strain of keeping vigilant in the crowded city.

"I love finding places like this." There is a noticeable looseness in Owen's shoulders and jaw, compared to how he normally carries himself. "It makes me feel like a normal person again."

They go out for a late lunch after, devouring burgers and fries. When the waitress drops off the check, Tessa reaches for her backpack, and the wallet she tucked inside there. Owen clears his throat. "I'll get it, if that's okay with you."

"A-are you sure?"

"Yeah, of course." Owen sets his credit card on top of the check.

Tessa takes a sip of water, hoping that will be enough to calm her down. Jesy and Rosalie had been right. This was a date. "I'll get it next time." She speaks with confidence she doesn't quite feel. What if that was presumptuous, and there won't be a next time? But Owen smiles at her, and his eyes crinkle at the corners when he does. The nervous knot in her stomach begins to unwind.

They meander back to her usual subway stop. Tessa's thoughts race at a mile a minute, even as she and Owen debate the validity of their respective March Madness brackets. Kissing at the end of a first date is totally a thing. But it's going to be in front of her subway stop, and that is not a good place for a first kiss. At least, she doesn't think so. Maybe it's totally normal. What does she know, anyway?

To her complete surprise, when they stop in front of the subway stairs, Tessa catches a fragment of her own panic reflected in Owen's blue eyes. "I had a lot of fun today." He looks down at the sidewalk. "I don't normally go hiking with other people. Thanks for coming with me."

"I loved it," she says, trying to set him at ease. "Thank you."

"See you Thursday?"

"See you Thursday."

Owen hesitates. Then he pats her on the shoulder twice. "Have a good week, okay?"

He turns and speed-walks away before she can reply. Tessa stares after him. Her shoulder tingles. There is absolutely no reason an innocuous shoulder pat should have reduced her to this. She is going to be useless at studying for the rest of the day.

ooooo

The weeks march on, bringing the advent of spring. Midterms and spring break come and go. Tessa keeps her grades high, never misses a volunteer shift with Ryan and Matt, and keeps attending her Thursday support group. Either Saturday or Sunday morning is always spent on a hike with Owen. Tessa is pretty sure they're dating, which is a development of such enormity in her life that she lies awake in bed at night, still unable to believe it. They text every day, have dinner every Thursday night, and hike and go out to eat every weekend. They hug each other goodbye at the subway stop every time. Tessa loves being hugged by Owen. He's so warm and strong.

"We haven't kissed, though," she frets, to Jesy and Rosalie. After three years of service in Maryland, Rosalie's new duty station is at Fort Hamilton, right at home in New York City.

"Don't worry about it." Rosalie refills all of their glasses of wine. "He's just being a gentleman. Taking it slow."

"That's a good thing. A green flag. You can tell that he really likes you." Jesy raises an eyebrow. "But you can always make a move on him, if you're getting impatient."

"No thanks," Tessa says, even though she *is* getting impatient.

ooooo

She is on the phone with Owen at nine on Wednesday night, sitting in the stairwell of her apartment building like a weirdo, because she doesn't want to bother her roommate. "How was your exam earlier?" Owen asks.

"It was fine." Tessa pauses, and then admits the truth. "I think I crushed it."

Owen laughs at her candor. "That's my girl."

Tessa almost drops her phone. She's torn between yelping *What?* into the phone, and asking him to say that again.

"Anyway," Owen coughs and continues, evidently flustered. "I was thinking — and we don't have to do this — but I was wondering if it would be okay if I cooked dinner for us tomorrow night after group. We've tried all of the good spots near the base."

"That sounds great." Tessa's voice comes out way too high pitched. She cringes at herself, burying her face in the hand that isn't holding her phone.

"Okay!" Owen, who was completely unfazed when they encountered a snake during their hike last Saturday (Tessa, meanwhile, just about jumped into his arms, which he teased her about later), sounds downright jumpy. "I mean, okay. All right. See you tomorrow?"

"See you," Tessa manages.

"Good night, Tess."

"Night, Owen."

They hang up. Tessa tilts her head up, staring at the ceiling. Then she pulls up her group chat with Jesy and Rosalie.

ooooo

She spends Thursday on edge. For the first time since her first session, it is hard to relax during the support group, but Tessa enjoys the journaling exercise that Asher leads them through. She and Owen talk about it as they walk back to his apartment on base. "I didn't think I would get into it," Owen says. "I didn't want to start, but once I got something on paper, it just started to flow."

Tessa suppresses a flutter of not-unpleasant nervousness as he unlocks his apartment. "I'm going to get started with dinner. I did some prep ahead of time, so it shouldn't take too long. Make yourself comfortable. We get ESPN *and* ESPN+ here."

"I can help." She hasn't cooked much since her time living with Jesy and Alyssa, but after all her years cooking for herself and her dad, it is second nature. She could never forget.

"No, I got it. You should relax."

Owen proceeds into the kitchen with the air of a man on a mission. Tessa looks around at the small space. She loves catching glimpses of her friends' personalities from their bookshelves, and what they hang on their walls and have laying out on their coffee tables.

Owen's living room is incredibly neat and tidy, and he has several photo prints of the rugged Alaskan wilderness hung up. "Did you take these yourself?" Tessa calls, admiring the lush evergreen forest and snow-capped mountains.

"I wish," Owen calls back. "Someday I'll be able to afford a decent camera."

The bookshelf is filled with language learning textbooks on Arabic, Kurdish, and Pashto. There are books on the history and culture of Afghanistan, and the tribes of Afghanistan, as well as yet more books on the national parks, hiking, survival, and mountaineering. There are a few framed photos tucked onto the shelf, too — Owen with different friends that Tessa recognizes from his descriptions of them. Some friends are still alive, and at Fort Hamilton with him. Some are at different duty stations. A few of them are gone now, lost to suicide or IED explosions in Afghanistan and Iraq. Tessa takes a deep breath, recognizing the tightness gripping her chest, and looks at the photos of the Alaskan wilderness again.

Owen makes steak, roast potatoes, and salad. "The steak is too well done," he says mournfully, as they eat. "And the potatoes are too salty."

Tessa refuses to hear a word of it. "It's perfect." She swallows a huge mouthful of potatoes. Every meal that someone has cooked for her is perfect. The dinners Jesy and Alyssa would make when she lived with them, the home-cooked Mexican meals that Rosalie's parents invite Tessa over for, the macaroni and cheese that Booker makes for them, the Chinese food Grace makes when they come over for dinner. She had so many dinners alone when she was growing up. Now she almost never eats alone. "Thank you so much for this."

"I should be thanking you for trying my food." Owen saws through his steak. "I've never tried to make anything this nice before."

Tessa offers to help Owen clean up, at least, but he just waves it off. "I'll just do it later. Also…" He stops, abashed. "I forgot to get dessert."

"I saw a vending machine downstairs."

They walk to the vending machine, where Owen buys them both chocolate chip cookie ice cream sandwiches. They eat their ice cream on the picnic table outside and become embroiled in a debate about desserts of choice and preferred ice cream varieties. When they're back inside, settling down on Owen's living room sofa, when he puts his arm around her shoulders, it feels like the most natural thing in the world.

Tessa automatically leans into him, snuggling into his side. Owen holds her close. She thought she would be nervous when they got to the after-dinner part of this date. Right now, she feels nothing besides pure contentment. "This is nice," she murmurs.

"It is." Owen strokes his thumb along her upper arm, and Tessa melts. "Tess," he says quietly, and she looks up at him. "Can I kiss you?"

She is very close to twenty-one years old, and she has never been kissed. There are women her age who have had their first kid already, and she's never kissed anyone. When she has reflected on this before, the thought made her sick with anxiety. "What if I suck at kissing?" she vented to Jesy and Rosalie, a few weeks ago.

In this moment, though, she still isn't nervous. She is just happy, so happy, and so excited. Tessa nods, unable to stop herself from smiling. Owen leans in and kisses her very gently. Their first kiss is everything she has hoped it would be, and more.

ooooo

The joy and fulfillment of her new relationship carries Tessa through the subsequent weeks, and her insane and punishing schedule leading up to finals. Her roughly eight dozen worries about the physical parts of a romantic relationship (being bad at kissing, being pressured into sex, being bad at sex) haven't played out. Everything that has happened with Owen has left her feeling safe, comfortable, respected, and loved. She has their daily texts or phone calls to look forward to, and their Thursday night dates. They spend either Saturday or Sunday together, depending on Tessa's volunteering and study schedule. Their hours together go by way too fast.

Rosalie and Jesy tease her, saying that it looks like she's walking on air these days. "Girl, you are flourishing," Jesy marvels.

Ryan and Matt, miserable due to the strain of impending finals, are baffled. Ryan interrogates her. "How are you staying so calm?"

"I'm always calm," Tessa replies serenely. "What?"

This last question is directed at Matt, who is staring at her with a look of dawning realization. He doesn't look happy. "Nothing. I just realized I forgot to add something to my paper outline."

Ryan groans, running a hand through his hair, which is already standing on end. "I haven't made any progress on my micro-ec paper outline. I might die before the end of the week," he reflects.

Tessa doesn't look away from her American Urban Politics paper. "You can't die. You're a future President of the United States."

"Got it." Ryan pulls out his phone and starts texting. "I'm going to get everyone together for dinner and drinks on Friday night to celebrate being done with these goddamn finals."

"Yes, please." Matt takes a long drink of his coffee.

Tessa takes a bite of her apple. "Can I bring my boyfriend?" she asks, her mouth full.

Matt warily lowers his coffee. Ryan stops texting mid-sentence. "Your… what?"

Tessa grimaces, chews her apple some more, and swallows. "Sorry. My boyfriend."

Ryan sets his phone down with a *thud*. "We didn't know you were dating someone," Matt jumps in, with a smile. "That's awesome. How long have you guys been together? Where did you meet?"

"Almost all semester. We took it pretty slow." Tessa glances at Ryan. "We actually met at that PTSD support group I told you about last fall."

"Right." Ryan picks his phone back up and resumes texting, slower this time. "I remember. Yeah, for sure, you should definitely bring him."

ooooo

Owen takes her out for dinner on Thursday night, to their favorite Vietnamese place. Tessa fills him in on the plans for tomorrow. "I'll text you the address. We're not getting together until eight, so you don't have to rush over to Manhattan after work."

"Thanks." Owen refills her cup of tea. "I'm a little nervous about meeting your friends."

"Don't be. I've told you all about them. It'll be fine."

"I feel like I should read the New York Times or The Economist to prepare. They're, like, Ivy League."

"Not all of them, just Ryan and Matt. And do you feel that way about me?"

"At first, yeah, I did. When I first saw you, wearing your Barnard sweatshirt, and when I first heard that you were majoring in political science. Yeah, I was intimidated."

It's baffling to think that anyone could ever be intimidated by her. "Then I got to know you in group," Owen continues. "And I realized you're just like the rest of us, except for the fact that you're smart as hell."

Tessa takes his hand, rubbing her thumb along his knuckles. "Ryan and Matt are just like everyone else too. They are so into playing Dragon Age and League of Legends right now."

Owen perks up. "Do you know if they play Assassin's Creed? Or Silent Hill?"

"I have no idea, but you could ask them tomorrow." Tessa squeezes his hand. "You don't need to be intimidated by anyone. You know four languages. You know more about the Middle East than most people I've met." She won't push Owen toward college, but she has a suspicion that he would absolutely crush a Middle Eastern Studies undergrad program.

Owen smiles at her. "Thanks, Tess."

ooooo

The party on Friday night at the Maple Rose is one of their biggest and liveliest yet. Tessa leans against Owen, content. There was a time when she had no friends, and then just Jesy. It is surreal to think that this is her life now. She has so many friends, a boyfriend who loves her, and a full year of college complete.

If only she had Spencer sitting by her feet, and her mom just a phone call away, her life would be perfect. Tessa acknowledges those painful feelings, as Asher has taught them at her support group, and then gently places them to the side.

Her friends are so nice and welcoming to Owen. She can tell that his reservations have ebbed away — thanks to an ample amount of video game talk with Javier, Matt, and Booker, and a lively discussion of sports among the whole table.

Ryan is the only one who is more quiet than usual, listening more than he talks (for once). He lacks his usual animation tonight. Tessa catches his eye while several others are talking about the NBA Finals. "What's wrong? You're quiet tonight."

"Nothing." Ryan rubs the back of his neck. "Finals just hit me hard, I guess. I'm super worn out from pushing myself this semester."

Ryan does even more than her. He works a total of three more volunteer shifts a week than she does, between Silverman's office and the Democratic Party offices. She and Matt have told him to slow down because he doesn't want to burn out, but telling Ryan to dial down his intensity is hopeless. "Well, it's a good thing we have some time before starting our summer internships."

"Yeah." Ryan attempts a smile. "Yeah, I'm looking forward to the break."

"Tessa," Javier cuts in. "Who do you think the Clippers' first draft pick is going to be?"

"Blake Griffin, obviously."

Chapter Twelve
May 2009 – May 2012

The months fly by, between classes, volunteering, internships, and time with friends and Owen. Tessa gets through her sophomore and junior year, maintaining her 4.0 grade point average semester after semester. She takes internships at the ACLU (American Civil Liberties Union), and she does a few internships alongside Ryan and Matt, at Silverman's DC office, and the New York State Legislature.

She and Owen get through eleven months of long-distance during his second deployment to Afghanistan. Worry for him triggers her PTSD all over again, and she has nightmares almost every night that he is away. She lost Spencer in Iraq. She is both terrified and convinced that she will lose Owen in Afghanistan too.

They get through it. They have long phone calls with one another, working around the time difference. They send one another lengthy emails.

(*You're my lifeline, Tess,* Owen writes to her. *You're keeping me sane. I love you so much.*)

They cling tight to one another during Owen's too-short, two-week leave, which he arranged to coincide with her junior year spring break. They cling tight to one another when he is finally home. They attend their PTSD support group together every week, trying to heal from the impact the deployment had on them. Not *them* as a couple, thankfully, but each of them as individuals.

Some things don't change, from Tessa's freshman year to her senior year of college. Her friends stay close, despite the demands of academics and internships and jobs. They get together for dinner every week. They celebrate birthdays, promotions, new jobs, the completion of internships, and holidays. (Javier and Booker throw one hell of a Super Bowl party every year, which Tessa and Owen appreciate.)

A lot of things do change. Rosalie leaves the Army when her four-year enlistment is up, and starts working for New York City's Department of Emergency Preparedness and Response. Matt and Grace welcome a baby daughter, Alicia. Alicia had been unplanned, but she is very much beloved, and Matt names Ryan Alicia's godfather. Ryan starts dating Vanessa, an interior decorator for Studio Giancarlo Valle, whose parents are wealthy Democratic Party donors. It's kind of an on-again, off-again thing, unlike Javier and Rosalie and Tessa and Owen, but Vanessa does join the group for dinners and parties on occasion.

Vanessa is nice, but Tessa can't deny that she feels a little awkward around her. Vanessa is just so different from everyone else. They talk about sports they see on ESPN, and Vanessa offhandedly mentions she has had courtside seats at NBA games. Rosalie and Jesy enviously eye her monogrammed Yves Saint Laurent purse, her Burberry trench, and her Saks Fifth Avenue wardrobe. Even Grace, who is the most low-key and perpetually content person Tessa knows, glances at Vanessa's impeccable waist-length chestnut curls out of the corner of her eye, and smooths the ends of her own shoulder-length bob.

Tessa, for her part, catches sight of Vanessa's perfect manicure, and she curls her own burn-scarred hands, with their short, unpolished nails, into fists under the table. Owen notices, and places his hand on top of hers.

ooooo

Tessa is sitting at their usual study table in the library with Matt, admiring pictures of Alicia, when she is startled by footfalls behind her. She turns to see Ryan hurrying toward them. "What's up?" Matt slides his phone into his pocket.

Ryan throws himself into his typical seat next to her. "I have news."

He pauses, letting the anticipation build. "What is it?" Tessa asks impatiently. The last time Ryan looked this eager to tell them something was when he got them their great internship opportunity in DC.

"Calcraft is retiring at the end of her term. Her seat in the Fourteenth is going to be up for grabs."

In the November 2012 election, just over a year from now, a matter of months after they graduate in May. Tessa and Matt exchange a look. Ryan doesn't have to elaborate.

"Are you insane?" Matt forgets to keep his voice down.

Tessa stares at Ryan. It makes sense. He'll be eligible to run. He's already twenty-seven, and he'll have graduated by then.

"No." Ryan's eyes glitter with excitement. "I couldn't ask for a better opportunity."

"This is a little fast. What about running in 2016? You can use the next few years to build funds and get to know people."

Ryan dismisses Matt's cautioning with a shrug. "I'm not worried about getting to know people. I've made a ton of connections over the last few years."

"Fundraising, though?" Tessa presses.

"Yeah, that could be a problem. That's why I want to get moving early." Ryan pulls out his beat-up composition notebook and starts scrawling down notes.

Matt takes off his glasses and rubs his eyes.

"If you're serious about this, we should put some feelers out for the mood in Calcraft's office now," Tessa says. "If any one of her people wants to run, you'll be at a disadvantage when she backs them instead."

"I'll reach out to Calcraft. I know you don't think it's a great idea for me to run now, but there's no time to waste."

"There is," Matt counters. "We should wait until 2016. You can get some more experience, get a job in Silverman's office or something, and raise some funds in the meantime. Don't rush into anything now."

"Don't rush?" Ryan repeats incredulously. "We've been out of the Army for four years, and the same wars are still going on. Gun violence at home is getting worse, the deficit and the national debt are out of control, and so are corporate greed and social inequality. I need to get into a position where I can start making change in a meaningful way."

They are at an impasse. Both Ryan and Matt look toward her, as they so often do whenever they butt heads. Tessa weighs their arguments. "You're both right. This isn't going to be easy. A Congressional run never is, but one under these circumstances will be even more challenging. Waiting might make the run easier."

"But–" Ryan starts. He falls silent, realizing she wasn't finished.

"If you wait, you'll be in a position where you have to challenge an incumbent in the Fourteenth. We all know that incumbents usually have the advantage. Besides, you want to aim higher than the House someday. If that's still the case, the sooner you start making a name for yourself, the better."

Ryan's expression softens. "Thanks, Tess." He looks at Matt. "Are you in too?"

"Of course I am."

ooooo

Ryan texts her later that night. *Calcraft said she can meet with me on Thurs at 11 AM. Come with for backup?*

Yes, Tessa texts. He didn't even have to ask.

ooooo

Tessa is a silent spectator during the meeting with Calcraft. She and Ryan have both met her several times over the years, over the course of their political internships. She is down-to-earth and direct, a refreshing change from a lot of politicians.

"I'm not surprised to hear that you're interested in this seat." Calcraft folds her arms on her desk. "You always struck me as ambitious."

Ryan smiles slightly. "What do you think?"

"I have a meeting with one of my legislative assistants at one this afternoon. I think he's going to tell me that he's throwing his hat into the race."

Ryan's shoulders stiffen almost imperceptibly. He keeps a smile on his face. *I'm not worried,* that smile says. "Hoffman, I assume. No offense, Representative, but he's pretty middle-of-the-road. He's not going to offer anything new to your constituents."

"Hoffman is safe. Republicans haven't won this district since '93, but they're going to try moving in anyway. They always do."

It is a weak argument, in Tessa's estimation. Ryan isn't shy about

142

letting Calcraft know that. "You said it yourself — Republicans haven't won here in more than a decade. They're not going to start now, so why play it safe with Hoffman?" He doesn't wait for her to answer. "Are you going to endorse him?"

Calcraft gives Ryan a long look. She remains silent, pressing her lips together, and Tessa's heart leaps. There is potential in her silence. If she had no reservations about Hoffman, she wouldn't hesitate to endorse him. Maybe she agrees with Ryan, deep down, that Hoffman is too middle-of-the-road.

"I'll endorse the candidate with the strongest performance by July."

Ryan leaps out of his seat and extends a hand to Calcraft. "Thank you, Representative."

"Don't thank me yet." Calcraft shakes his hand. "You have your work cut out for you. Let's see if you can even raise the funds to announce by April."

∞∞∞∞∞

They head to Astoria Coffee right after for a debrief. Ryan buys Tessa a tea and a croissant sandwich, while she gets them a table by the window. Tessa interlaces her fingers together and stares at the crowds passing outside, silently processing the meeting.

"What do you think?" Ryan sets her tea and croissant down, sliding into the seat beside her.

"Thanks." Tessa unwraps the sandwich. "It's promising that she's not endorsing Hoffman right out of the gate, but she's right. Fundraising is our biggest barrier. The average cost of winning a House seat is about $1.1 mil. We won't need all of that up front, but we will need at least some money in the coffers by April. That gives us six months."

"We'll figure that out." Ryan meets her gaze. "I need someone to run this campaign for me. What do you think?"

This doesn't come entirely out of the blue. Over the past four years, she and Matt and Ryan have had countless conversations speculating about his first campaign for public office. Ryan always talked about them running his campaign, but neither she or Matt ever thought their moment would come so soon. "I would run it with Matt. Right?"

"Yeah, but I see you as the point person on this, with him as your deputy. I know he'll agree. He and Grace have Alicia now, and you… Matt said it himself. You're a great strategist, you're organized, detail-oriented, and you're driven. You make everything you do look effortless."

"Are you sure?" Tessa presses. "I want you to win this. We *all* want you to win. Matt and I won't hold it against you if you want to seek out a real, experienced campaign manager to help you through your first campaign."

"No. You're the one, Tess. You don't have to give me an answer right now, though," he hastens to add. "I know it's a big commitment."

This means taking on her own Congressional race, her *first* Congressional race. She will be twenty-four in April, by the time Ryan announces his candidacy. She won't even be a college grad yet. It is the largest professional endeavor she has ever committed herself to. It's completely insane.

And it's the right choice. This is what she has been working toward for all these years, after all. The thousands of hours spent studying, volunteering, at her internships — it has all been with this in mind.

Tessa extends a hand to Ryan. He beams, and then shakes it. "Thank you."

"When's your next class?" Tessa pulls her phone out of her bag. "I'm going to text Matt. We need to have a talk about strategy."

ooooo

They meet at Booker, Javier, and Ryan's apartment on Friday night. Matt and Grace are there, as well as Jesy and Rosalie. Owen comes too, to support her. He stared at her, awestruck, when she broke the news to him the previous night. "This is going to be a huge deal for you. It'll get you on that 30 Under 30 list."

"If I pull it off," Tessa replied automatically. "Ryan's going to be the one who ends up on the lists, since he's the candidate — but thank you."

Ryan orders pizza and buys drinks for all of them. He takes the floor, standing in front of the TV in the living room. There are too many people for the small space, and the guys sit on the floor, saving the limited sofa space for Grace, Rosalie, Jesy, and Tessa. (Vanessa isn't present, which Jesy texted Tessa about as soon as she walked in and assessed the crowd.)

"Thanks for being here tonight." Ryan claps his hands together.

"Thanks for being willing to hear me out. I know that it's a long-shot idea."

"You got that right."

Ryan waves Javier off. "I'm not going to bore you by talking about why I want to do this, or what I stand for. You all know why I want this. And I know that this is sooner than you expected to see me take this on. But if anyone can see this long-shot campaign to victory, it's Tessa and Matt. I'll turn it over to them."

Tessa looks at Matt. He stays seated, gesturing that she should take the floor. She clears her throat, replacing Ryan at the front of the room. With any other audience, she would be nervous. They are soft launching a congressional campaign. But with them, her friends, her family, she isn't.

"There are a few different areas we need to tackle in the early stages." Tessa counts them off on her fingers, pacing back and forth in front of the coffee table. "Financing the campaign, and getting a sense for what voters in the Fourteenth need, and what they want to see in a candidate. We want to raise Ryan's profile in the wider community, and get at least a couple of minor endorsements to get our foot in the door by the time he announces in April. I'm confident about three out of four of those things. We have a lot of connections."

"And no money," Matt mutters.

"And no money."

"Can't help you with that, but I know a couple of people at MoveOn and Planned Parenthood." Booker pulls out his phone and starts tapping away, probably composing emails or texts. "I can see if they're willing to have an early meeting with you."

"One of my friends works at Disabled American Veterans," Owen says. "Veterans are usually Republicans, right? But you're a veteran yourself, which gives you cred over the other guy. If you can talk to the DAV about what you can do for soldiers and veterans, and get them to come out and support you, that's a big deal."

"Exactly." Tessa smiles at both of them. "That's exactly what we need."

"And this will all help with the money, right?" Jesy arranges a throw blanket over her lap. "The more people who know about Ryan, the more people who can donate to the campaign."

"Right. We have to go with grassroots mobilization here."

Grace raises her hand politely.

"Oh — you don't have to raise your hand, Grace. Go ahead."

"Can I suggest forming a volunteer base as another early priority? This is going to take a lot of work, and you, Matt, and Ryan can only do so much between the three of you."

"I can help with finance," Javier chimes in. "It was a big part of my degree."

One by one, they all speak up. Booker will help with communications and marketing, Javier with finance, Grace with finding volunteers. "I'll do general support," Rosalie says. "Whatever's needed." Jesy and Owen immediately agree. Tessa knows they are doing it for her sake, and she resolves to give them a hug at the next opportunity.

ooooo

Tessa, Matt, and Ryan have their work cut out for them in balancing their senior year coursework with their regularly scheduled volunteering and internships. That was hard enough without adding the extra demand of new exploratory meetings for Ryan's campaign.

There are meetings to discuss fundraising, strategy, communications, and policy. They squeeze in meetings before and after classes with community leaders in Queens and the Bronx. They schedule meetings with progressive groups like Justice Democrats and Brand New Congress, and with MoveOn and Indivisible. Tessa sits down for lengthy debriefs with Ryan and Matt after each meeting. She spends long hours with Booker and Javier, delving into the nuances of communications and marketing, social media campaigns, and finance. Booker, Jesy, Rosalie, and Owen are tremendously helpful. They find a broad spectrum of potentially helpful contacts for her to reach out to on Ryan's behalf, and Ryan passes them yet more contacts gathered from Vanessa's vast social circle.

Both Tessa and Matt talk to Ryan about boundaries. "Let us think about campaign strategy," she tells him. "We'll handle that. You're the candidate. You focus on policy and how that intersects with the relationships you're building."

Ryan continues to send them lengthy emails at two in the morning delving into campaign strategy. Matt finally loses his temper, balls up a napkin, and throws it at him. "Don't tell us how to do our jobs, idiot!

Focus on yours!"

"Okay, okay," Ryan says, chastened.

Tessa teases him about it later. "I should have just thrown something at you first instead of trying to talk to you like an adult."

Grace leverages her work experience as a volunteer coordinator, and Booker leverages yet more connections, and their network expands. Booker's friend Mari joins their team. Mari brings her best friend, Daniel Bell, and Andrew Abrams, a soldier she met while serving in Iraq. Grace connects them with Kahaan Achari, an eighteen-year-old communications undergrad at NYU who is eager for some internship experience. Andrew connects them with Vasu Farman, a former Army surgeon. It's a relief to have their added manpower on the team.

"We'll have to think about getting a campaign headquarters at some point," Javier comments. "It's getting really crowded in our living room."

Tessa is so busy with preparing to launch the campaign, and spending her limited free time with Owen, that the fall and spring semester fly by. And then it is April, and Ryan makes his announcement. He wrote his speech himself, and submitted it to Booker and Kahaan for revisions. Most of what they did was condense it.

"Dude," Booker said, alarmed. "I know you have a lot of passion and energy and whatever, but this talk really can't be an hour long."

As soon as Ryan announces, Tessa leans on every media and social media contact she has made over the last four years. She and Matt make dozens of calls, arranging for public appearances and outreach for Ryan. It is hell to juggle it all during the lead-up to finals, and during finals week.

No matter how many public appearances or outreach activities she and Matt schedule for Ryan, no matter how full his calendar gets, he remains unfazed, handling it all with aplomb. He thrives on face-to-face contact with prospective voters and other stakeholders. It energizes him, and his energy and enthusiasm is infectious. Even people who were reluctant or unconvinced end up leaving meetings or campaign events with a more positive impression of him. Tessa, Ryan, and Matt are all on the same page politically, but it is undeniable that Ryan is the only one of them with the it factor, with the charisma, that makes him a compelling candidate. His youth and energy levels are a sharp contrast to Hoffman.

Ryan's candidacy causes a stir on the Columbia and Barnard campuses. Both universities' newspapers write lengthy articles on him, with only minimal prompting from Tessa. More and more volunteers come on board, thanks to Tessa and Kahaan's aggressive focus on outreach to young voters, minority voters, and LGBTQ voters. They rent the basement of a boxing gym, owned by a friend of one of Andrew's friends, and turn that into their campaign headquarters.

The campaign overshadows their graduation. At their friends' insistence, they take the day off campaign work to celebrate. Ryan gets them all together for brunch after the ceremony and rents out an entire room at The Blue Dog. His aunt and Vanessa attend, as well as all of their friends across the city. He pays for all their food and drinks, ignoring their protests. "You guys have been so supportive. This is the least I can do."

Later, when they are hanging out at their apartment, Jesy and Rosalie surprise Tessa with an envelope stuffed full of cash. "For... for the campaign?" Tessa squeaks out, after she recovers from her shock at counting it up.

"Oh my god, no." Rosalie rolls her eyes. "For *you*."

"For that new wardrobe!" Jesy enthuses. "You have to look sharp for DC!"

Tessa laughs, folding them into a hug. She has hunted down all of her internship work wear over the years at thrift stores around the city. Her outfits have been professional enough, but she has always felt so much less polished than the other interns and staffers. "Thanks so much, you guys."

When they pull apart, Rosalie checks her phone. "I think we have time for a quick shopping trip."

"Now? I thought we were going to chill and watch The Newsroom."

Jesy takes her arm. "We can do that later. Don't worry, we'll get back before dinner."

Tessa stifles a yawn. She had to be up ungodly early to finish moving out of her campus apartment and to make it to graduation on time. "Sure." She's excited for dinner — she and Owen are going back to their favorite Vietnamese spot in Brooklyn, the one where they went their first time hanging out.

She and Owen aren't big on dressing up. Whenever they're together, they live in athletic clothes. Tessa buys a new coral-colored dress anyway, and she wears the gold stud earrings Owen got her for her birthday. (Her everyday pair is the amber earrings that he bought for an anniversary gift, saying that they matched her eyes.)

"You look incredible," Owen tells her, as they walk to Lẩu Phở Gà, hand-in-hand. "You look even better than you did this morning."

Tessa smiles up at him. He normally hates wearing dress clothes, but he wore a shirt, tie, and jacket to her graduation ceremony. He swapped out the shirt and tie tonight for darker shades of blue. It suits him. "You look pretty good yourself."

Their dinner is delicious, and they talk over plans for their next camping weekend. Tessa takes his hand after they finish eating. "Thank you for everything," she says impulsively. "I know it hasn't been easy, with my schedule being what it was in senior year, and my whole time in college, really. You've been so flexible, and so patient and understanding. I appreciate it so much."

Over the years, so many of her acquaintances' and classmates' relationships have fallen apart because of the long hours associated with working in politics. Owen has borne it all without complaint. He turned to the gym and video games whenever she was busy, and made himself available for phone calls or texts at the odd hours when she was finally free.

"Thank *you* for putting up with me through the deployment last year." Owen squeezes her hand. "I know how hard that was for you. And don't thank me for anything. Being with you is the best thing that's ever happened to me."

Tears well up in her eyes, and Tessa blinks hard. She has had Owen and her friends for years now. She can still never get used to what a luxury it is to be surrounded by love.

Then Owen takes a small velvet box from the pocket of his jacket. He gently places it into her hand. Tessa's fingers are stiff and unresponsive as she stares at the box. Her eyes fill with tears again.

"Owen," she manages to say. They have talked about their future before, in general terms. About how she will split her time between New York City and Washington DC. They have discussed Owen's plans to leave the Army when his contract is up, so he won't have to deal with another deployment, or move duty stations away from New York. *There are defense contractor jobs that I could look into,* he said. *The pay is better than military pay, so, you know — that would be better for buying a townhouse in the city.*

He opens the box for her, revealing the silver ring inside, and the diamond that glitters at the center. "Tessa." She's never seen him smile like this before. "Will you marry me?"

She speaks before he finishes his sentence. This is one of the biggest decisions she will ever make, but there is no need to think about it. Over the years, Owen has become as integral a part of her life as Jesy and Rosalie, Ryan and Matt. Whenever she thinks of her future, she thinks of working alongside Ryan and Matt on Capitol Hill, and coming back home to Owen. "Yes, yes, of course, yes."

Owen slides the ring onto her finger, and says, "Thank God," when it fits. Tessa shoves her chair back from the table and goes to him, throwing her arms around his shoulders and clinging to him. For once, she doesn't even care that there are other people around, and they're probably making a scene at this restaurant. Owen hugs her tight, kissing her forehead. "Should I get us some dessert to celebrate?"

Tessa pulls back, trying to regain her composure, and cups his face in her hands. She gives him a quick kiss. "You can get us the check. Let's get out of here."

ooooo

They stay up very late that night, celebrating their engagement, talking, and making plans. Tessa doesn't get back to campaign headquarters until the next afternoon. Jesy and Rosalie meet her at her subway stop. She texted them both last night, while she and Owen had been waiting for their check at the restaurant. They mob her with hugs, demanding to see her ring.

"Beautiful," Jesy pronounces.

"Very classy," Rosalie agrees.

They walk to campaign headquarters together. "Skeleton crew today," Rosalie informs her, after they have made her relay every detail of Owen's proposal. "Just us, Matt, Ryan, Javi, and Booker. Matt's leaving to join Grace and Alicia in about thirty."

Jesy checks her phone. "And I'm heading out now for my lunch date.

I'll text you later. We need to talk about wedding plans. Oh, I can't believe I just said that! They grow up so fast…"

Tessa finds her friends huddled around a table, hard at work. A large map of New York's Fourteenth congressional district covers the other table, accompanied by pages of notes.

Ryan is the first to look up as they descend the stairs. "There you are." His relief is obvious. "We were just talking about getting some national attention on this campaign."

"Sorry I'm late." Tessa joins them, shrugging her backpack off and taking a seat at the table, pulling her laptop out. "Last night was — a big night."

Booker's gaze zeroes in on her hand, and he breaks into a grin. "Whoa, you're not kidding!"

"I didn't see that at our graduation brunch." Javier whistles in admiration, while Matt hugs her tight. "Congratulations, Tessa."

Ryan waits until everyone else is finished, and he smiles at her. He looks so tired, as though he hadn't slept much last night. "I'm so happy for you." He gives her a one-armed hug.

"So, when's the wedding?" Javier rubs his hands together in anticipation. "How big is this party going to be?"

"As you know, I am one hell of a DJ," Booker adds.

"No wedding, no party." Tessa ignores Rosalie, Javier, and Booker's ashen expressions. "Weddings are expensive. We're just going to go to the courthouse."

"But–" Rosalie groans, sounding like she's in real pain. "But Tessa, oh my God. You only do this once! Treat yourself!"

Matt comes to her rescue. "Weddings don't have to be expensive. Grace and I got married in my uncle's backyard, and she got her dress for like a hundred bucks."

Ryan glances at him, his expression unreadable. "We'll see," Tessa replies, in a quelling tone. "We can talk about it over dinner. Or after we're done with this campaign. Now, let's get to work."

Chapter Thirteen

May 2012 – January 2013

The campaign heats up in tandem with the New York City summer. It is a powerful relief to be done with school, so that she can focus all of her time and attention on the campaign. Tessa and Matt debate whether Ryan needs to move to the center on any issues to attract more prospective voters. "We should let Ryan be Ryan," Tessa decides. "He won't want to compromise by moving center-left, anyway. Let's focus on our youth outreach, and getting 18-34 year-olds on board with our messages."

They wait with bated breath to see if their strategy works. By late June, they pull a hair ahead of Hoffman in the polls. True to her word, Calcraft gives Ryan her endorsement just after the Fourth of July. That helps. As Tessa cautions the team over and over again, it doesn't mean they can grow complacent. Calcraft's endorsement won't necessarily win them the election in November.

After four years of political internships and volunteering during college, Tessa thought she was more than adequately prepared for the chaos of the months leading up to Election Day. She was wrong. She and Matt and Ryan understood the time commitment, sure. They understood making their way home from the office at ten or eleven at night, to fit in a rushed workout at the empty gym before midnight. They understood walking into the office the next morning at seven, their steps slow, clutching a large to-go cup of coffee or tea.

They understood the kind of work a campaign entailed. Spending hours on research, wading through policy papers, newspapers, data, polls, and surveys on dozens of different topics affecting constituents' lives. Public health, mental health, crime and policing, addiction, access to government benefits and public transport, jobs, housing, childcare, schooling, higher education, public safety, regulation… They used all that research, all those hours hunched over notebooks and laptops, to write drafts of policies that would improve constituents' lives. Then they wrote speeches to communicate their work to their constituents.

They understood that they would spend hours making visits with the candidate to important spots in the district. Struggling schools, to hear directly from teachers. Community colleges, to hear from young adults, and middle-aged adults in the process of retraining for a different career. Churches, community centers, senior centers, YMCAs, mental health clinics, and nonprofits, to speak with volunteers and staff there. Sometimes Tessa, Ryan, and Matt manage to fit in five or six visits in a day, taking the commuting time between visits to write notes and takeaway messages and next steps for supporting those constituents.

They understood that they would find yet more hours in the day to write speeches, delve into polling data, prepare for debates, and do opposition research. They understood that they would be tired and stressed, and that their to-do lists every day would be miles long.

What they didn't understand — what Tessa didn't understand — was how intensely personal it would feel on her own campaign. The sense of ownership, of investment, is worlds apart. Working on a campaign is one thing. Running a campaign for her own candidate is another.

The demands on Tessa's schedule, on her time and attention, grow even more acute in the final week leading up to Election Day. The get out the vote efforts are in full swing. "Just three more days," Tessa mumbles on the phone to Owen, calling him from the treadmill at the gym during her before-bed workout.

"Just three more days, honey. I know you can do it."

Election Day falls on the seventh of November this year. Ryan and Matt, and all of their friends and campaign volunteers and staff, overflow with brittle, nervous energy. That nervousness coexists with cautious optimism. Ryan has a slight lead in the polls, but it is too slight for comfort.

Tessa feels ill all day. Her stomach and muscles ache and cramp like she is battling the flu, and her eyelids are heavy. Her appetite vanishes. Her stomach tries to rebel against the bagels Booker and Javier brought into campaign headquarters this morning.

Jesy is unhelpful via text. *Pregnant?? :O* she sends.

NO, Tessa replies. *Just stressed and tired. I've been pushing myself through this whole campaign and it caught up with me.*

:((can u go home after polls close?

No. Event tonight to watch the results come in. Tessa sends Jesy the link to the hotel in Queens. *Dinner and drinks for volunteers, staff, community members, and donors, if you want to come.* She doesn't feel up to it herself, but not going isn't an option. Ryan and her team will need her support tonight.

Everyone else leaves headquarters by 5 PM for the final get out the vote push. Tessa stays in the office, finishing the work that Mari, Daniel, and Andrew started, until the clock strikes 9 PM. Polls have officially closed for the night. Her phone screen lights up with texts from Owen and her friends.

It's over!!

Congratulations, Tessie!

We did it :)

The wait begins…

Tessa wipes her eyes. Win or lose, her first congressional campaign — the first campaign she has ever run, the product of four years of education — is over. She did it. She freshens up, changing into a more formal outfit befitting a campaign manager on what could be an Election Night victory party, and takes the subway over to the hotel. Matt rented the fourth floor ballroom for the party, and Booker and Javier took the lead on organizing and inviting guests.

The ballroom is packed to capacity with campaign volunteers, grassroots fundraisers, a couple dozen members of the New York State Democratic Party, community organizers, and staff at several Queens-based nonprofit organizations and small businesses. Hotel staff have wheeled in several flat screen TVs. Groups of people cluster around them, watching CNN and MSNBC's breathless election night coverage. They chat with one another, sip their drinks, and eat from small plates of appetizers.

It is loud in here, and it is a bit too warm, especially after coming in from the chilly November evening. She doesn't understand how all these party attendees look so cheery and animated, no trace of stress in their demeanors. Tessa forces herself to make the rounds anyway, to shake hands and smile and thank them for coming. As the campaign manager, she has to set a confident, cheerful tone. She gives a safe, stock answer to everyone who asks her if she's relieved that her first campaign has drawn to a close. "It hasn't sunk in yet. I think it will when I'm listening to Ryan's victory speech later."

She finds all of her staff and volunteers, and checks in on them. "How are you feeling?" Tessa has to step close to be heard above the noise. "It's been a long day. Everything okay?" They all affirm that they're fine, even though they have been up since four in the morning and the exhaustion is starting to show in their eyes. "Get some food," she reminds them. "It's going to be a long night."

"Yes, boss." Javier peers at both of her empty hands. "Wait, where's your food?"

"You good?" Booker hands her his own drink. "Here, have this."

"Oh, no, I'm fine." She tries to hand it back, but Booker refuses, and Tessa pats his arm. "I'm good. I just need some air. I'll be out on the terrace if you need anything, okay?"

"Go chill. We'll handle things in here."

Tessa retreats to the terrace, gratefully drawing in a breath of cold, fresh air. The street noise of the city's traffic is a nice break from the loud chatter and cross-talk inside. She crosses her arms over her chest to warm herself, the wind whipping her ponytail and bangs.

She realizes she isn't alone on the large terrace. Ryan stands by the railing, staring out over the lit-up Manhattan skyline. He turns at the sound of her footsteps. "Hey."

"Hi." Tessa joins him. One glance reveals that this isn't the Ryan she has spent months campaigning with. His camera-ready, constituent-ready smile is gone. The energy that normally brims from him is gone, leaving him strangely deflated.

Stupid, Tessa berates herself. She spent all night checking up on her staff, and on everyone else here, and she forgot to check on her candidate. Just because Ryan has been resilient during the campaign doesn't make him immune to the strain of Election Night. "How are you doing? I'm sorry I haven't caught up with you today."

Ryan waves that off. "You have nothing to apologize for. You and Matt have been so busy, doing all this for me."

Tessa waits for his answer until he sighs, resting both hands on the railing. "I'm so scared that it's not going to happen. That I'm going to — that I'm going to fail. That would be bad enough on its own, but that's not it. All this effort you've all put in — all this time — you and Matt, this has been your *life*. If I don't get elected, I wasted that. I let you all down."

"Ryan–"

"Every ambition, every dream I have, hinges on this." The cold has flushed Ryan's cheeks pink. The energy is returning to him, but with the agitated spin she is familiar with. "Taking the first step here, and getting into the House. If I screw this up, I don't know where to go from here."

"Ryan." Tessa speaks more firmly this time, and Ryan stops. "First — we're not stupid. We knew going in that there would be a chance you'd lose this race. We chose to commit ourselves anyway. Win or lose, this hasn't been wasted time. It's been an even more valuable experience than anything we learned in college. And it's time we spent working towards something we all believe in. This isn't just *your* dream and we're going along with you because you're our friend. Everyone believes in your platform. In your stances on the issues, and how you can help people. Even if you lose–"

Ryan flinches. Tessa fixes her gaze on him, willing him to understand her, to believe her. "Even if you lose, you won't let us down. You put your heart and soul into this, for the right reasons. We can all see that."

"Thanks," Ryan says quietly. "But–"

"Even if you don't win tonight, that doesn't tank your ambitions forever. There are plenty of people who have won Senate races without serving in the House first. I know you don't like the idea of taking things slow, but you could also think of City Council, with your eye on running for mayor or governor someday. Those are valid stepping stones to the presidency too."

She can tell these options don't appeal to him, but Ryan doesn't shoot her down. "Thank you for getting me this far. This alone is an accomplishment, for someone just out of college. I couldn't have done any of this without you."

Tessa shrugs off the compliment. "The candidate is the heart of the campaign."

"The heart is nothing without a brain. Your organization, your leadership, has let me focus on being the best candidate I could be. Your advice never led me wrong." Ryan looks at her as if he has never seen her before, or as if he is seeing her in a whole new light.

"It's too soon to say that. I'll take compliments after I know you've won."

"Don't be so modest. You have a good mind for this. Even if I lose tonight, the fact that I got this far… Anyone looking to break into politics will want you on their campaign staff after this. You have a future in this."

Her bosses at her internships through college told her the same thing. Tessa's face still heats up. "I'm not interested in working on anyone else's campaign." She helped Ryan develop his platform, and she has done research on Democratic candidates across the country. There are no candidates who are so aligned with her ideals.

Ryan rests a hand on her shoulder. It reminds Tessa of all the times he did this with her and Matt and Curtis in Iraq, and with her and Matt while walking on campus. He hasn't done that in a while. The three of them haven't hung out for fun and not work in a while. For the first time, she wonders if things will change between the three of them when Ryan is elected. If they will primarily be his staff, and not his best friends. It seems impossible, but…

Ryan looks just as preoccupied as she feels. He glances down at the street beyond the railing. A few cars pull up to the front of the hotel — maybe carrying attendees to their party.

Her engagement ring sparkles, catching the light of the nearby lamp, momentarily distracting her with its beauty. She should get back to the party soon, but maybe she can take a break in an hour to call Owen. He wanted to be here tonight, but he got pulled into working a long-distance translation assignment via video conference. The time difference between New York City and Afghanistan is nine hours and thirty minutes, and a new day is already dawning in Jalalabad.

The glass double door separating the terrace from the ballroom opens. Ryan releases her shoulder and takes a step away from her. "Vanessa."

Vanessa is stunning in a midnight-blue silk slip dress, silver earrings glittering from her earlobes, a diamond pendant necklace hanging over her collarbones. She approaches them, and Tessa raises a hand in greeting, feeling awkward and — nonsensically — underdressed in her black pantsuit.

Vanessa places a hand on Ryan's arm, looking up at him. "Eddie Stafford and his wife just got here, and they're looking for you."

"I'm glad they made it. Have you seen Pak Seungri from the MinKwon Center yet?"

It is amazing how flawlessly and quickly Ryan slips back into his usual demeanor, his effortless smile on his face, his upbeat tone revealing none of the doubt and insecurity he showed her a moment earlier. Tessa watches them. Vanessa updates him on several pertinent tidbits of information she gleaned from conversations inside, and Ryan grills her for more. They really are a beautiful couple.

The three of them head back inside together, Ryan and Vanessa arm-in-arm, Tessa trailing behind.

∞∞∞

This is one thing that never gets old — the mood on Election Night as results begin to roll in nationwide. Kahaan runs around turning half of the TVs to local, New York-area election coverage. He leaves the other half on national coverage, reporting on House and Senate seats across the country and the presidential race. The hundreds of people in attendance gather around the smaller TVs and the large screens projected onto opposite walls of the ballroom. There are exclamations of joy as the Democrats hold onto contested House seats in Pennsylvania and West Verginia, and as they pick up one House seat in Georgia. There are discontented rumblings in the crowd as Gabatino and DiCarlo are projected to win in New York's First and Third Congressional Districts, and as Republicans flip a seat in Connecticut.

Normally, Tessa would stare at the national election coverage on tenterhooks, following close races around the country — not to mention the presidential race. Now, she stands unblinking in front of a local station, watching Stephanie Siang share her updates. "Galanis is leading in the Eleventh, Romano and Martin are still neck-and-neck in the Thirteenth, and Chao is pulling ahead of Diaz in the Fourteenth…"

The crowd around Tessa cheers, drowning out the rest of Stephanie

Siang's sentence. Mari grabs her arm. "Oh my God."

"It's too early to say." Tessa's lips are numb. "Let's wait and see."

The coverage cuts away to other local news. Every time it comes back to Stephanie for an update, her report has changed slightly. "Galanis and Mora are now tied in the Eleventh, and Romano now has a two-point lead over Martin in the Thirteenth. In the Fourteenth, Chao now holds a five-point lead over Diaz…"

The news ripples through the ballroom. Despite the uncertainty about the presidential election, unofficial celebrations start early. People pop bottles, making toasts to Ryan and the Democratic Party. The Columbia Young Democrats start singing the Columbia fight song at the top of their lungs. Matt finds her in the crowd, hair standing on end like he's been gripping it. "Tessa. It's really happening."

"Wait." A five-point lead — there's no way Ryan will lose that, with so many precincts reporting, with this percentage of votes already counted. Still, Tessa can't let her guard down. "Let's just wait a second."

When Stephanie Siang returns to the screen and announces that the Fourteenth has been called for Ryan Chao, the ballroom explodes with noise. Tessa covers her mouth, staring at the scrolling ticker tape on the screen echoing Stephanie's words. Matt hugs her around the shoulders. Kahaan is at her other side, literally jumping with joy. Booker and Javier escort Ryan through the crowd, all of their faces alight with triumph and relief. Ryan holds his arms out to her and Matt. They congratulate him as he hugs them tight. To Tessa's surprise, people she barely knows start coming up to her and congratulating her too. Not just her friends and staff, but other people she recognizes. People from the New York Democratic Party, volunteers, donors.

"What's next, Tessa?" Alison Cole from the New York Democrats asks. A woman wearing a badge hanging on a lanyard around her neck snaps a photo of her. The badge identifies the photographer as part of the New York Magazine. "When did the press get in here?" Tessa mutters to Vasu, dazed.

"They started coming in as soon as the news broke."

Someone — probably Matt — has handed Ryan a microphone. Tessa leans against the wall, exhaustion hitting her anew, her eyes stinging with tears, as she watches him give his speech. He beams from ear to ear, but he grows serious when he thanks the voters for putting their trust in him. He thanks his campaign staff and volunteers with such sincerity that she sees Kahaan, Mari, and Daniel sniffling in the front row of the crowd.

Ryan talks about how excited he is to get to Washington and start working for the people of the Fourteenth, but Tessa's mind wanders. Back to Landstuhl in Germany, and the conversation they had in her hospital room. She thought Ryan was crazy. Here he is now, an elected member of the House of Representatives, just like he said he would be. He has come so far.

So has she.

ooooo

It's a long while before the victory party winds down, and the guests begin to leave in groups. The ballroom empties out, blue confetti and glitter trampled into the carpet, blue crepe streamers on the floors. The music has come to a halt, but the TVs are still playing, and the long food and drink tables at either end of the ballroom are a mess. The only people left in the ballroom are their friends. Javier, Andrew, and Vasu pull campaign posters from the wall, while Kahaan and Daniel vacuum the floors.

Some ill-behaved party guests actually left their empty appetizer plates in a pile on the floor. "Honestly," Tessa grumbles, bending to pick them up. She deposits them on the food table and turns away, with the intention of helping Mari and Booker take down the balloon installations. Instead, she almost crashes into Ryan, who is carrying his own stack of discarded appetizer plates. "Sorry, Representative Chao."

Ryan grins, setting the plates down. "It still doesn't sound real."

They have been so busy dealing with the crowd and making comments to the media that they haven't even properly talked since the results came in. "I'm so proud of you. I remember when you brought up the idea of running. It seemed like such a long shot for someone in their senior year of college, but…" She gestures around them. "You did it."

"I want to be proud of myself. Maybe I will be tomorrow, when this sinks in." Ryan's smile fades. "I'm ready to go to Washington. I want to get started, standing up for what's right."

"Just two more months."

"The sooner, the better. I want to feel like Representative Chao. I don't yet."

"A journey of a thousand miles begins with a single step." Asher, the facilitator of her and Owen's PTSD support group, has that up on a poster on the wall.

"Profound." Ryan sticks his hands into his pocket. He shed his suit coat when they started cleanup, and he looks less formal than he has all night. "Thank you for being here for me. Not just through these last months, but — all of it. Matt is great, but he has Grace and Alicia, and Curtis wants to stay in North Carolina because of family. It would have been a lot harder for me to pursue any of this without you having my back. I know that change — *real* change, institutional change — matters as much to you as it does to me."

He falls silent, rather red in the face. Tessa shifts awkwardly from foot to foot. "I'm the one who should thank you. I had no idea what I was going to do with myself. I didn't know what career, what purpose I was going to make for myself, before you told me what you wanted to do." Now, as frustrating, challenging, and demanding as it is, she can't imagine herself in any other career besides politics.

Ryan lifts his half-empty champagne glass in a toast to her. "Here's to us, and to the future."

She doesn't have a glass, so she just smiles in return. "To us, and the future, and many more nights like this." Her phone vibrates in her pocket, and Tessa pulls it out to check it. "Owen says congratulations."

"Oh — tell him thank you from me." Ryan drains the rest of his champagne glass in a gulp. "I'm sure he's happy that you get your free time, and your life, back."

"I'm happy about that too." Tessa returns Owen's text and slips her phone back into her pocket "Come on, let's get back to cleanup."

"You should get out of here. Me and the guys have it covered." Ryan makes a shoo-ing gesture with his hands. "Go on. My Chief of Staff needs to be well rested for the week ahead."

Tessa blinks, wondering if she's hallucinating from lack of sleep. "What? Are you serious?"

"You organized this campaign. You'll be the perfect person to keep my staff and offices in New York and DC running."

"I…" She can't wrap her mind around the magnitude of this job offer. "We'll talk about it more tomorrow."

ooooo

Reality takes days to set in. Ryan is catapulted to national overnight recognizability as the youngest person elected to Congress since 1964, and the first Asian-American to represent New York's Fourteenth Congressional District. Their staff is bombarded with media requests in the hundreds.

Ryan trends on Twitter daily. "This is wild," Mari reports, eyes wide, as she stares down at her phone screen.

Kahaan, Matt, and Ryan handle the plethora of media attention. Tessa has enough on her plate with settling into her new role as Chief of Staff. She is the highest-ranking staffer in Ryan's new office, and the chief operating officer, reporting directly to him. She will hire and oversee the dozen-plus employees on his staff, and work alongside Ryan on his policy initiatives.

Tessa spends hours meeting with her friends, discussing what roles are right for them. Matt is her Deputy Chief of Staff. Booker becomes the legislative director, and Kahaan the communications director, responsible for Ryan's relationship with the media. Vasu and Javier join the team as legislative correspondents, drafting letters and emails in response to constituents' comments and questions. Rosalie, Mari, Andrew, and Daniel round out the team as constituent service representatives, helping constituents deal with issues related to federal agencies. They will help veterans get their benefits, help older adults and people with disabilities access Social Security, Medicare, and Medicaid, and work to help resolve constituents' immigration issues.

Tessa helps her new staff get grounded in their roles, and connects with other prominent elected Democrats regarding furthering Ryan's legislative agenda. She, Ryan, and Booker make a trip to DC. Tessa meets a dozen new people every day, mostly the chiefs of staff and legislative directors of the other Democrats in the House and Senate. She spends a lot of time with her new peers. They schedule walking meetings along the National Mall or around the Tidal Basin, bundled up against the cold.

They sit in small groups and talk on the steps of the Lincoln Memorial.

Her world expands. Her physical world; her social and professional world. It is a strange and joyous sensation. Being here in DC, setting up the new office on Capitol Hill, reminds her that she is a part of something even bigger than Ryan's ambitions and all the work she and her friends did to get him elected. She is now part, even a small part, of the workings of this nation within the legislative branch.

"It's humbling, being here." She and Ryan are walking from Capitol Hill down to the Tidal Basin, to a meeting scheduled with Booker and a couple of other representatives' legislative directors. Snow started to fall right as they left the Hill. The flakes are stark white against the wool of Ryan's black overcoat, and in his hair.

"This is just the beginning." Ryan looks straight ahead. The weather has kept the tourists off the National Mall today. They have it almost entirely to themselves. "Now that I've made it to the ground level, the only way is up."

"Do you even know the meaning of *humbling?*"

Ryan grins. "We're built different, you and I." They keep walking, drawing their scarves closer against the cold. "I'm one of 435 Representatives now. In a few years, I'll be one of a hundred Senators. And then…"

"We'll see." In college, Tessa would have warned him of being too cocky. After this recent win, getting a Senate seat somewhere down the road doesn't seem too unreasonable. And having a Senate seat certainly opens doors. She picks up her walking pace. "Come on. For now, we don't want to be late."

Chapter Fourteen

January 2013 – April 2023

The next year brings rapid change. Tessa and Booker travel to DC with Ryan when Congress is in session, staying in short-term apartment rentals, and back home to New York City on the weekends. Tessa's weekends are as packed as her work weeks, with house shopping and wedding prep.

She and Owen get married on the last weekend of May, in Matt and Grace's backyard. The small space is packed to bursting with all of their friends. Both of them pay for the food, from a collection of Mexican and Vietnamese restaurants nearby, and the drinks. Their friends bring desserts and flowers galore.

It is the happiest day of her life. She is gaining family in Owen, after both of them have lacked it for so long. She is going to have the happy home full of love she hasn't had since she was a child.

Tessa still cries before the ceremony, remembering the photos of her parents on their wedding day; remembering how beautiful and excited her mom looked. She misses her mom. She even misses her dad, because being without both parents on a day like this is too hard to bear. Jesy and Rosalie comfort her, and Rosalie disappears from Matt and Grace's bedroom and returns with Owen in tow. "I know he's not supposed to see you before the ceremony, but he'll make you feel better."

Owen holds her in his arms and rubs her back, and Tessa buries her head in his chest. She finally draws back, looking into his eyes, at the wordless understanding and empathy there. His parents aren't here either. He cradles her face in one hand, pressing his forehead to hers. "We'll be each other's family, Tessie. We'll always be there for each other."

Tessa cries a little when she makes her vows to him half an hour later, underneath the ceremonial arch. This time, they are tears of happiness and relief.

They move into their little townhouse in Queens the following weekend, after a short honeymoon hiking and camping in the Great Smoky Mountains National Park. It is a humble home, but they make it cozy. They cover the walls with photos from their hiking trips. Tessa adorns every sofa and armchair with throw blankets to cuddle underneath. The bookshelves overflow with Owen's books about languages and the Middle East, and her books about political science. Their home is a precious respite from the demands of her job, and from Owen's new job as a defense contractor with Lockheed Martin.

There are more engagements to celebrate in the months that follow. Javier and Rosalie get engaged, as do Mari and Booker. Jesy's boyfriend Isaiah proposes, and Matt and Grace welcome their second child, a boy they name Oliver.

Ryan and Vanessa get engaged six months after Tessa's wedding. Their wedding, when it comes, definitely stands out among their circle of friends. Everything from Vanessa's two-carat diamond ring, to her Oscar de la Renta wedding dress, to the Plaza Hotel as the venue, is beyond anything Tessa has ever witnessed in real life.

The guest list is vast, composed of Vanessa's high-society family and friends from the New York City art and design world, and Ryan's friends and colleagues on the Hill. "This is C-SPAN meets The Devil Wears Prada," Rosalie whispers to Tessa during the cocktail hour. After she goes off to get a drink, Owen puts a hand on the small of Tessa's back. "I've never watched that movie."

"Let's add it to the list for our movie nights." Tessa takes a bite of her canape and hums her approval. "Here, have a bite."

Owen does, and he looks most impressed by the lobster-and-gouda stuffed mushroom. "I wish I could have done all this for you," he murmurs. "I look at all this, and I remember how the cops crashed our wedding because of that noise complaint, and how people kept elbowing each other on the dance floor — the dance *square* — because it was so tiny. You deserved a princess wedding, just like this."

Tessa touches his arm. "Well, I remember how you won those cops over by offering them cake, and casually mentioning that you and your new wife were veterans. You saved Matt and Grace from getting a noise citation."

"Yeah." Owen's slow grin is like the dawn breaking. "Yeah, I did do that."

"And the repeated accidental close contact on the dance floor was how at least two couples got together that night." Tessa squeezes his hand. "Our wedding was perfect. I didn't need all this fuss."

"You're the best, Tessie."

"What I do need…" Tessa looks around for one of the uniformed waiters. "Is more stuffed mushrooms."

∞∞∞∞

Tessa, Matt, and Booker scheme together to help Ryan make a name for himself in the House. (Ryan himself joins their scheming sessions whenever he can.) All four of them seek out opportunities for Ryan to sponsor and co-sponsor progressive legislation. They help him forge alliances with other Democrats in the House — the ones who don't publicly or privately decry him for being "too far left," anyway. Their combined effort gets Ryan onto two House committees and four subcommittees.

Ryan serves three terms in the House, winning re-election each time with ease. After his third victory, he starts to watch New York's two senators like a hawk. "You two should spend more time with Moreland and Freyer's senior staff," he suggests to Tessa and Booker. "You know, keep your ears to the ground."

"Should we try to get into a room with the Senators?" Tessa asks, straight-faced. "Start showing them pictures of the south of France and talking about how good the weather is there? How the warm winters are so much easier on the joints?"

Ryan makes a face at her. After he heads off for his meeting, Booker turns to Tessa. "I'm surprised he hasn't asked you to poison their lunches yet."

"Let's hope it doesn't come to that."

∞∞∞∞

Ryan waits, not so patiently, for another year. When Senator Bob Moreland announces he won't run for re-election, Ryan pulls a bottle of champagne from his desk drawer and pops the cork, pouring glasses (also pulled out from the drawer) for Tessa, Booker, and himself. "Drink up, my friends. But first, a toast."

"How long have you had that bottle in there?" Booker laughs. "My god, man, have you had it ready since you moved into this office?"

Ryan smirks and tries to look mysterious. "No, he hasn't." Ryan sends her into his desk — which is always in a horrid state of disarray — at least once a week to find something for him. Tessa narrows her eyes. "That wasn't there a week ago. Who on Moreland's staff tipped you off?"

"Wouldn't you like to know?" Ryan raises his glass. "To the future."

Ryan goes to his committee meeting, and Tessa and Booker head to their favorite lunch spot — a halal food truck parked on the National Mall, just a few minutes' walk from Capitol Hill. "This Senate thing, it feels like a formality. A box he's trying to check before running for President." Booker drizzles spicy red sauce over his lamb gyro. "I know he really cares, but…"

Tessa keeps her voice low. "The only question is how many terms he's willing to wait out."

ooooo

The Senate campaign is a good challenge for her, after the past two easy campaigns in New York's Fourteenth. Ryan's challenger for Moreland's seat is a much more moderate Democrat, which gives him broader appeal upstate. He is just a career lawyer, though, and his only political experience is on city council. Tessa emphasizes Ryan's experience and legislative track record in his campaign. She and Kahaan put together some masterful — if she does say so herself — campaign ads, print ads, and radio spots that highlight how Ryan's legislation has helped everyday New Yorkers, from New York City, to Buffalo, Albany, and beyond.

They walk away with a victory in November. Over December and January, they move their offices in New York and DC. Tessa's own Chief of Staff office, in the room adjoining Ryan's, grows bigger. She stands in the center of it after moving all of her things in, and remembers her college internships in DC. Now she supervises the college interns who rotate through their offices.

There is a knock on her door, and Ryan pokes his head in. "Matt's back."

Tessa joins them in Ryan's new office. Matt hands her a to-go mug of tea, and Ryan a mug of coffee. They sip their drinks in comfortable silence. It has been a long morning. They took a 6:30 AM flight from New York.

"You should get comfortable in this office," Matt advises.

"Ryan and *comfortable* don't go together."

Ryan rolls his eyes, but he lets Tessa's comment pass. "Why should I? This country is even worse off than it was when we were in college. I'm not going to keep lurking on the Hill for the next couple of decades, letting Republicans and centrist Democrats get elected to the White House."

He says "centrist Democrats" like a dirty word. "Watch it," Tessa warns, the byproduct of spending a whole Senate campaign trying to win centrist Democrats and moderates over to their side.

Ryan slumps back in his chair, chastened. "The only real restriction we have is waiting until I'm thirty-five."

"Look, you won't be taken seriously as a candidate if you run at that age," Matt says. "Anything under forty-five — fifty even — is a non-starter."

"Roosevelt was forty-two when he got elected," Tessa replies. "JFK was forty-three."

"Right! Thank you, Tessa. And it's not like I'm unqualified. I have a solid legislative record, and — as of May, at least — I'll have a PhD in International Relations."

Both Matt and Ryan turn to her expectantly, their expressions demanding she back one of them up. They have been playing out this dynamic since they first met in Iraq. Some things never change. Tessa sighs, setting her mug down on Ryan's desk. "Ryan's age isn't just a detriment. We've seen from our polls, over and over again, that younger candidates do a lot to mobilize young voters. You saw how he inspired the 18-25s to vote in this Senate election."

"The highest turnout from 18-25s in any New York Senate race. Ever," Ryan cuts in.

"Now imagine that effect on a national scale. If — when — Ryan gets the White House, it'll be thanks to young voters."

Matt throws his hands up in the air. "You always side with him."

"I do not."

"Look, I won't run unless I have a fighting chance. I'll look at the Republican candidates and the rest of the Democratic field, and then I'll decide if it's a fight I want to get into."

"Right. You won't stand out as much if the other people in the primary are Reese, Velez, and Kellen." Tessa names a few of Ryan's friends and allies on the Hill. "You will stand out if the field is crowded with the old guard."

"Speaking of the old guard, I'm sure Gardner's going to run next time. At his age, it's now or never."

Ryan huffs a little at Matt's mention of the senator from California. "Anyway, just one and a half years until I'm thirty-five."

"I was going to say that I'll start the countdown now." Tessa takes a sip of her tea. "But it appears you've already started."

ooooo

Ryan's thirty-fifth birthday comes and goes, without comment from the man himself. "Are we safe?" Matt asks Tessa, a few months later. "It's been months, and he hasn't said the p-word."

"What, the Patriots?"

Matt rolls his eyes, and Tessa pauses in her typing to smirk at him. "Don't let your guard down. I don't think we're safe yet."

"I bet you hope he's going to run."

Tessa resumes her work. "No comment."

ooooo

She is leaning close to her laptop screen, intently proof-reading the text of the Senate Resolution that Ryan is planning to propose, when an Outlook meeting invite pops up on her screen. The notification sound startles Tessa out of her spell of concentration, and she almost jumps in her seat. She clicks on the invite. Twelve to twelve-thirty. She, Matt, and Kahaan are on the invite list. In the "Location" field, instead of a Zoom link or a specific meeting area in the greater Capitol complex, it simply reads "*my office :)*" All in lowercase, to add insult to injury.

Tessa checks the time, shakes her head, and rises from her desk, grabbing her black binder as she leaves. She raps on the door separating Ryan's office from hers. "Come in," he calls.

She finds Ryan at his desk, looking cheerier than he had this morning. His discussion with Bennett and Subramanian must have gone better than he expected. "We've talked about the emojis."

"That wasn't an emoji," Ryan corrects, as she sits across from him. "It's an emoticon. More polished, more mature."

"Is it, though?"

"I had to make sure you all knew that I wasn't summoning you because I'm mad at you."

"Yes, because you're mad at us so often." Ryan reserves his displays of temper for Republicans on Twitter and on the Senate floor. Tessa and Kahaan have threatened to take his phone away and/or send him to anger management, with limited success.

There is another knock on the door. Matt and Kahaan file in with less grace than she had, and flop down into the chairs on either side of her. "Dude, you can't schedule a meeting with five minutes' notice," Matt complains.

"Sorry. It's important, and it can't wait." Ryan steeples his fingers together, gazing at the three of them. There is a low jolt of anticipation in Tessa's stomach. "I'm thinking of running next year."

She thinks first of what this means for Ryan — her best friend, her boss. She can see him taking the oath of office on his inauguration day. In the next breath, she thinks of what this means for her. She has managed all of Ryan's campaigns, and steered him safely to victory each time. She doesn't want to get ahead of herself, but this could give her the chance to take on the greatest of political endeavors. A presidential campaign.

"You're thirty-eight now. You'll be forty, barely, in 2024," Matt muses. "You'll have served almost a full term in the Senate, and six years in the House before that."

"That's better than other presidents we've had." Kahaan's eyes shine with enthusiasm.

"You guys haven't stopped me yet, so I'll keep going." Ryan stands up and paces behind his desk, unable to contain his energy.

There is fondness in Matt's reply. "I don't think there's any shutting this down."

Ryan stops pacing, locking eyes on her. "Tessa?"

Tessa wipes her palms on her skirt. She tries not to think of every off-the-record phone call or lunch or dinner meeting over the last few years. She has hundreds of pages of notes, wisdom gleaned from those conversations with all those past managers of presidential campaigns — successful and unsuccessful. But this isn't about her and what she wants. This is about what is best for Ryan's campaign. That might be a more seasoned political operative. "Yes?"

"I want you to run this for me."

"Are you sure? This isn't another House or a Senate race."

"I'm sure."

Tessa communicates everything she has to in the nod she gives him. *Thank you. I'll do everything I can to win this for you.*

Ryan returns her small nod. *I know you will.*

Matt doesn't need to say a word to her either. He curls his fingers into a fist and offers it to her. Tessa bumps her fist against his. He will be her deputy, as he has been for their entire professional life thus far.

Kahaan smiles at their exchange. "Do you have any ideas on how and when you're going to announce? I have a few thoughts."

"We should talk about that." Ryan sinks down in his chair again and shuffles a few printouts of meeting minutes lying on his desk. "But I need to talk to Vanessa about it first. Let's circle back to this tomorrow."

Matt raises his eyebrows, and Kahaan shoots Tessa a look. Ryan hurries off to his next meeting, leaving the three of them behind. "Um, shouldn't he have told Vanessa first?" Kahaan ventures.

Matt groans. "That man… I swear to God."

"I'm sure everything will be fine." Tessa smoothes a wrinkle from her skirt as she stands. She and Kahaan should set up a meeting with Vanessa as soon as possible. She will need to be prepared for the campaign, and what lies beyond, as well. If all goes as planned, Vanessa Chao will be the next First Lady of the United States.

Kahaan lowers his voice. "What if she's not on board? What if she says no?"

"There's no saying *no* to Ryan when it comes to politics," Matt says.

"Ask me how I know. Besides, who wouldn't want to be First Lady?"

"She already has the grace, the professionalism, the intelligence and talent, the looks." Tessa glances at Kahaan. "Don't worry. All we'll have to do is beef up her foreign policy knowledge a bit, just in case."

She returns to her office and retrieves the small unmarked key zipped into an inner compartment of her purse. The key makes a satisfying click in the lock of her massive black filing cabinet, and Tessa pulls the doors open. It's all here — and backed up in a safe deposit vault at the bank, of course. Hundreds of pages of notes from interviews with past campaign managers. Close to a thousand pages of her own analysis of both parties' presidential campaigns, from 2012 onward. She wrote up the mistepps and successes alike. She printed candidates' speeches and went through them with a red pen.

She has polls in the hundreds, as well as detailed reports of voter data from every demographic, across every state. She has compiled information and strategies on how to reach rural undecided voters among all age groups. Black first-time voters. Native American voters in Montana. Voters with physical disabilities. Retirees in Kansas. Military veterans on the East Coast. Healthcare workers in the Upper Midwest and Great Plains.

She will finally get to use all of this work; this passion project taken on after hours and during slower work days alike. Ryan has trusted her with the goal of a lifetime, and she won't let him down.

Tessa pulls out her phone to call Owen. She thinks better of it. This information is too sensitive to be relayed over phone or email. She heads home at the relatively early hour of six-thirty, grateful that she got her workout in at dawn. If she doesn't get to tell Owen soon, she is going to burst.

90s rap — DMX — greets her when she lets herself in. Owen doesn't call out to greet her, so the music must have drowned out the sound of the door opening. Tessa breathes in deeply, savoring the scent of Kabuli lamb pulao. She makes her way to the kitchen and stops in the doorway, admiring the way Owen's long-sleeved shirt falls on his shoulders, back, and arms. He chops onions, his back to her, bobbing his head a little to the beat.

"Hey, you."

Owen grins when he turns to face her. "I didn't hear you come in. What are you doing lurking around?"

"I wasn't lurking." Owen holds his arms out to her. Tessa goes to him for a hug, burying her face in his chest with a happy sigh. "I was just checking you out, in a not at all creepy, lurking way."

Owen huffs out a laugh and kisses the top of her head. "How's my girl?"

They have been married for more than a decade, and that still makes her feel warm inside. Tessa pulls back a little, resting a hand on his chest. "Well… I think that we should go on that Nova Scotia hiking trip sooner rather than later. This summer or fall. Not next."

Owen stares at her. "No way."

Tessa nods, hardly able to contain her excitement. "Mm-hmm."

Owen grabs her hand, squeezing it between both of his own. "Are you running it?"

Tessa hugs him again, and Owen holds her tight. "I'm so happy for you, Tessie. You're going to win this one too."

"It's too soon to say," Tessa protests automatically. "We have no idea how crowded the Republican field is going to get. Here, can I help you with anything?"

"No — the rice is in the oven. I'm just making the yogurt sauce now. You can go get ready for dinner."

They eschew the dining table and eat their lamb pulao from bowls, cuddled up on the sofa in the living room, as they plan their Nova Scotia hiking trip. It is late by the time they crawl into bed, spooning together as they always do. Tessa's eyelids are heavy, but sleep is slow to come. Her thoughts jump from campaign planning to her vacation with Owen and back again. There is so much to look forward to.

ooooo

The late night means there is less sleep before her alarm goes off in the morning, and Tessa reports to work feeling sluggish. She forgets her own issues when she runs into Ryan on her way into her own office. His skin is sallow, his hair flopping limp over his forehead, as though it hasn't been washed or styled. There are dark circles underneath his eyes.

"Oh my–" Tessa rummages in her purse and finds the emergency bottle of antacids she keeps for such occasions. Ryan, Javier, and Booker all eat like they did in college. "You have got to quit with the burgers and fries right before bed."

Ryan waves the antacids away. "No, I'm fine. Hold on a second. Kahaan and Matt will be in soon."

Matt and Kahaan come into Ryan's office, and both regard Ryan with mingled horror and concern. "Are you okay?"

Ryan indicates the chairs across from him. "Sit."

They do. "There's been a little hiccup in my plans." Ryan regards them from atop his steepled fingers, as he did just yesterday. "I told Vanessa that I want to run for president. She told me that she's filing for divorce."

Tessa blinks, uncomprehending. She thought — she thought that Ryan would say that he and Vanessa had a fight. Or that Vanessa told Ryan not to run. She hadn't expected this.

"I'm-I'm so sorry," Kahaan stammers.

"Why?" Matt asks, baffled. "I mean — *why?*"

"She's tired of taking a backseat to my career." The flatness in Ryan's tone fades, hints of irritation and disbelief creeping in. "She knew my ambitions when we got engaged, none of this was kept secret from her, but… Anyway. She said that all the *neglect* would just be worse if I became president."

"What did you do? Did you tell her you would change?"

"I don't want to change." There's a distinct edge to his voice. "I want to be President."

A heavy silence falls over the four of them. Maybe this isn't coming out of nowhere. Now that Tessa thinks about it, she has noticed a little bit of strain in Vanessa's smile over the last few years. Ryan's messages and emails come in on late nights, on weekends, even on the rare vacations that he takes with Vanessa. His workaholic tendencies are no secret. That kind of behavior must take a toll on a marriage. She works long hours too, but when she is at home with Owen, she is fully present with him.

"How are you doing?" It is a stupid question, but that is all Tessa can come up with. There have been several divorces in her extended social circle, but she hadn't known any of their partners — any of those relationships — well enough to be truly shocked.

"I feel like the ground's been pulled out from underneath me." Ryan leans closer to them, his expression grim. "How much does this hurt my chances of running?"

It is a cold question, but unsurprising, coming from him. "The media and the public still love the "family man" image in a politician." Kahaan throws air quotes around the term. "It's unusual enough that you and Vanessa don't have kids. A divorce now isn't a death sentence, but it does hurt you."

Tessa considers the other Democrats who will announce their candidacies for 2024 soon, according to the rumor mill. "Walgren and Leath are both on their second marriages."

"Yeah — the key is that they're both remarried," Matt says. "And they both have two kids each and a dog."

"It's about the messaging around the divorce. There are going to be questions. We could go with the "we just grew apart" angle, if that works for you," Kahaan suggests. "No one's at fault. It won't be messy."

"At least there's no cheating scandal." Matt straightens in his chair as a thought occurs to him. "We need to get ahead of any rumors, anything ugly. Cheating, money problems, whatever. But especially cheating. That's going to be the first thing most people's minds jump to."

Ryan shakes his head. "No. There was none of that. We've always been faithful to each other."

"We'll be honest but tactful in our messaging. Don't mention the word *neglect* in any interviews or statements. Don't say that you made mistakes or that you wish that you could have been a better husband. That screams cheater or abuser at worst, and inept at best. Just be matter-of-fact. Say that you're sad, but grateful for the years you spent with Vanessa, and that you wish her the best." Tessa looks at Ryan. "Does that work?"

"Sure. Sounds about right." Ryan's reply comes with no small amount of bitterness, and he sighs. "Thanks, you guys. I know I just made your job harder."

"Don't apologize," Matt says. "We're all here for you."

Tessa lingers after Matt and Kahaan have left. Ryan checks his cell phone — maybe waiting on a call or text from Vanessa? — and glances at her. "What's up?"

"What you said earlier… Are you sure about this?" Maybe she is overstepping. But she remembers visiting dozens of different hotel conference centers and ballrooms and restaurants with Ryan. She remembers him fishing his phone out of his pocket to snap a photo of a particular light fixture, a piece of artwork, a rug. *Vanessa would love that,* he muttered to himself, sometimes. Sometimes he smirked, saying, *Vanessa would hate that.* Ryan arranged for Lady Gaga to meet Vanessa at a campaign event. *She's always been a fan,* he said to her and Matt, with a laugh. *She's always singing Lady Gaga in the morning when she gets ready...* "You can patch it up, Ryan. It's not too late."

Ryan shakes his head, averting his eyes. "I think it is."

He doesn't elaborate. Silence stretches between them. There is something he isn't telling her, but she can't force him to say it.

Chapter Fifteen
October 2025

Tessa dreams of being back in the hospital with Owen. "I want to go back home, Tess." Owen's eyelids droop closed. His speech is slurred. "Why won't they let me go home with you?"

In her dream, Tessa packs up her husband's things, and helps him get dressed and up from his hospital bed. "It's all right. We'll find the doctor and we'll talk to her. I want you to come home too." She puts Owen's arm around her shoulders for support. They walk the hallways, searching for Owen's doctor, for the nurses, for anyone. The hospital is deserted, save for the two of them. The exits lead only to a maze of other hallways, and the elevator spits them out everywhere but the ground floor lobby. Owen grows more and more agitated. Tessa keeps trying to be brave; to assure him that they will find a way out. She's frightened too, frightened of what will come next.

Leo's cold nose against her cheek jolts her awake with a gasp. Tessa blearily blinks around her room. It has been a year now, but she still expects to be greeted by her and Owen's bedroom in their old townhouse. The wedding photo on the wall, and the collage of framed photos from their hiking trips over the years. Acadia National Park for their five-year anniversary trip, a long weekend in Stowe, Vermont for Owen's thirty-fifth birthday, and photos from a dozen more weekend hikes around New York State, just because.

Her bedroom walls are blank, here. Tessa turns to Leo, stroking his fur. He woke her up when he sensed her mounting distress. "I should put up a photo of you. How does that sound?" Leo presses his nose against her cheek again.

After that dream, all she wants to do is curl up in bed and put the pillow over her face. This is the only time she gets to see Owen now. Dreams. But she hates seeing him because of how it makes her feel afterward. Her chest and stomach hurt so badly that she could cry like a child if she let herself.

That is one of the million good things about having Leo. Lying in bed brooding isn't an option. She has a dog to take outside. Leo hops down to the floor as soon as Tessa gets up, allowing her to make the bed. She pulls the curtains open, studying the sky. Slate-gray, cloudy and overcast. A typical October day in DC.

She gets ready for her morning, and checks on Leo. "Will you be okay if I do a fifteen-minute yoga video?"

Leo wags his tail, but doesn't move otherwise. If he urgently has to go, he stands by the front door. Tessa rolls out her yoga mat, before folding herself into a series of poses. Leo observes her yoga practice, and at one point does a puppy stretch of his own. She rises from her mat with her stiffness gone. The two of them run the length of the National Mall and back to their apartment, four and a half miles total, and the energy from the run carries her through the rest of the morning. Tessa checks her texts as she eats breakfast. Jesy messaged her while she was running. *OMG*, her text reads. *New ep of beyond the blinds was so good!!*

Tessa smiles, thinking back to their days of watching E! News while on shift at Fundamental Fitness. Twenty years later, both of them still have the same taste for celebrity gossip. She stands in the middle of the living room after her chores and getting ready, at a loss for what to do with herself until she and Leo have to leave for dinner. She has two hours. She could get a good amount of work done.

She is almost at her laptop when her better judgment kicks in. Tessa changes course, joins Leo on the sofa instead, and pulls up a library book on her tablet until it is time to head out. The Del Sur Cafe is just under four miles from her apartment, but with DC traffic, it takes half an hour to get there. P Street is already filling up with Georgetown students and neighborhood residents out for the night. Tessa spots Rosalie from a good distance away, standing in front of the cafe. She cuts a dramatic figure in her crimson wool overcoat, matching her signature red lipstick and her black Coach tote. Her dark, curly hair cascades down her back.

Rosalie garners more than a few glances of envy and admiration from passersby, but she ignores the attention she receives, instead gazing into the window of the boutique across the street. She catches sight of Tessa, and her face lights up. "Hi, Tess!"

Tessa hugs her when she gets in range. Rosalie smells of a delightfully spicy perfume. "I hope I haven't kept you waiting long."

They step into the warmly lit eatery, with its unique hanging lights. Tessa's mouth waters at the scent of Argentinian barbecue, yuca frita, and arepas. They get settled at a cozy table near a window, and place orders for drinks and appetizers. The server departs, and Tessa leans back against her seat with a sigh of contentment. It has started to drizzle outside. It's good to be here, inside, in the golden warmth with her best friend. "How are you? How's your day been?"

"Crazy. It was my turn to host book club and brunch this morning, and thank God it all went well, but I had no time to chill after. This kid in Ruby's class had a birthday party at some adventure park. Javi and I were stressing just watching her fly down those zipline things." Rosalie shudders. "She was totally fearless about it. I don't know where she gets it."

Tessa recalls Rosalie's grim-faced determination as she tackled the obstacle courses in basic training. "Oh, I'm sure you have no idea."

"Hold on." Rosalie ducks under the table, retrieving her purse from where she set it down, near Leo. "That reminds me — I have something for you."

She hands Tessa a folded piece of paper, and Tessa smiles at the drawing before her. "That's you, with Ruby and Leo." Tessa in the drawing has yellow-crayon hair in a high ponytail, and is impossibly, disproportionately tall. She holds hands with a small girl smiling so widely her mouth exceeds the diameter of her face. In lieu of his service dog vest, Leo wears a pink bow tie.

Tessa admires her goddaughter's drawing. She hasn't put any of her old framed photographs up in her room, but she has several pieces of Ruby and Zahra's original artwork stuck on her fridge. "Please tell Ruby thank you for me. I especially like Leo's bow tie."

"Come over for dinner next weekend and tell her yourself. How have you been today?"

They are interrupted by the arrival of their drinks. "Fine. I've just been cleaning and catching up on chores. I started reading this thriller novel before I got here, and I'm already disturbed by it."

Rosalie takes a sip of her wine, her dark eyes not leaving Tessa's face. "Are you feeling okay? I got a news alert this morning about you and Ryan visiting Walter Reed."

Tessa's first instinct is the kind of evasive reply she mastered last year. A perfect, polite brush-off and redirect so subtle that the other person might not even realize she isn't being a hundred percent truthful. *Oh, I'm fine. The hospital visit went all right. We got so caught up in working on the clean energy initiative afterward that I didn't get home until almost midnight.*

She isn't supposed to do that anymore, though. She has discussed that with Taliyah, her therapist. And after last October, Rosalie and Jesy made it clear that they expected more transparency from her.

"The visit was…" Tessa toys with the string and paper tag on her tea sachet. "It wasn't easy. Being there. It brought up a lot of–"

She trails off. *Pain, grief, loss.* The corners of Rosalie's mouth turn down. "I don't know why he didn't take someone else with him instead."

"It's all right."

The waiter arrives with their yuca fritas, empanadas, and arepas, and they tackle their dishes. Tessa hopes that Rosalie will leave it at that, but her hopes are unfounded. Rosalie cuts off a chunk of her arepa with her fork. "You being forced to confront those memories isn't all right."

"I'm surrounded by those memories." She hasn't set foot in Fiola Mare since moving to DC. She and Owen celebrated their anniversaries there, when their anniversaries coincided with time spent in DC rather than New York. She flinches inwardly whenever she hears someone mention hiking, or any of the national parks she and Owen visited. "I need to deal with it. I'm not going to shirk my job because of my own personal issues."

She can tell Rosalie doesn't think much of this argument. "You have never, *would* never, not do your job. But someone else should have gone yesterday. It didn't have to be you."

"Thinking about me and how I might react to something isn't Ryan's job. He has enough on his mind."

"That is his job. As your friend."

"Well, he did that later." Tessa divulges the rest of what happened that night, her speech halting, but at least she doesn't stutter. "I fell asleep in his office last night. I woke up — well, Leo woke me up. I was… shaken up." She leans down and pets Leo to calm herself. He immediately moves to sit upright, making it easier for her to reach his head. "Ryan tried so hard to make me feel better."

"Good." Rosalie lifts her hands in apology for interrupting. "Sorry. Go on."

"He hugged me." She remembers how Ryan wrapped his arms around her, drawing her into his chest, holding her close. His solid, warm embrace grounded her; held her together. "And I just — I don't know — I remember wanting to go right back to him for a second there, after I pulled back. It was weird." Tessa picks up her cloth napkin, twisting it in her hands. "Never mind. I was just really distraught."

"Right." Rosalie studies her. "Tess, do you think you're…"

She trails off, her expression a closed book, for once. Tessa prompts her to continue. "What?"

Rosalie takes a sip of her wine. "I meant to say — do you think you've been working too hard? Maybe we should do a spa day in the city with Jesy soon."

ooooo

Tessa and Leo are among the first to arrive at the Eisenhower Executive Office Building on Monday morning. The massive building is quiet at five-thirty in the morning. In one or two hours, the elevators will be full, fifteen-hundred footfalls will land on the two miles of black-and-white hallway floors, and the halls will buzz with chatter. The EEOB houses the Office of the Vice President, the Office of Management and Budget, and the National Security Council. It is also home to the Department of Defense and the Department of the Treasury.

Right now, though, Tessa has the grandeur of the EEOB almost to herself. She has reported to work here every day for almost a year. The lavish surroundings — the stained glass rotundas, the monumental curving granite staircases, the four skylight domes — still leave her in awe.

Tessa's office is in the antechamber of the Vice President's. Ryan hasn't arrived yet, and neither has anyone else. She is greeted by new emails in the triple digits, half of which are marked urgent. She scans her inbox and double-clicks on one from Ernesto Ortega, her counterpart in President Gardner's office, first. *President requests VP to travel to Japan November 14-16 to attend Quad.*

Tessa blinks at Ernesto's email and then looks down at Leo. "Am I reading this right?"

Leo gazes up at her with his soulful eyes. Tessa types up a quick response. *November 14-16 — 2025 or 2026?*

Ernesto's reply comes even faster. *25. If all goes well, we can plan on 26 too.*

Tessa growls with frustration. She is no stranger to navigating last-minute changes in Ryan's schedule. But this is ridiculous. *You're giving us two weeks of prep time for the Quadrilateral Security Dialogue?* She considers calling Ernesto and giving him a piece of her mind. This is a major event. Australia, India, and Japan will all be at the table.

At least Ernesto has the grace to apologize. *Sorry. The President planned to attend this one, but he has his plate full right now. We'll send over the material we have.*

ooooo

The day passes in a whirlwind of meetings. Ryan calls Tessa and Matt in to help him begin prep for the Quad. The three of them also devote the evening to discussing whether Ryan wants to encourage the President to invest in nuclear power as a clean energy source versus wind and solar.

"I get the environmentalists' concerns, I really do," Ryan muses. "But nuclear energy has a few real advantages over renewables."

"Lean into the higher capacity factor. That's the most salient point. But the President might push back on cost as well as the environmental concerns," Tessa points out. "In terms of construction and installation, nuclear power is more costly than renewables."

"How much more?" Ryan looks at Matt. "Do you have any numbers on that?"

Matt consults his folder of notes again. "The WISNR says that nuclear energy costs between $112 and $189 per megawatt hour. Solar is $36-$44, and onshore wind power is $29-$56."

"There are ways to make nuclear energy cheaper, though. Environmental Progress wrote a good report on it a few years ago. Hold on, I have notes on that somewhere."

Ryan heads over to his desk to retrieve his laptop, and Tessa checks her phone. "I'm sorry, but I have to head out. Matt, can you let me know where we land on this?"

"Don't apologize." Ryan knows why Monday nights are the one time of the week she has to leave before nine PM. "Good night."

Matt gives her a small smile. "I'll send you notes before I leave tonight. See you tomorrow."

Tessa settles on the sofa at home with her laptop and headphones a few minutes before seven PM. Leo comes to sit beside her, and she opens up the secure video chat portal offered by Taliyah's clinic. She has been doing these therapy sessions every week for almost a year. It isn't as painful as it once was. It still isn't easy.

There is a small sound effect as Taliyah appears on screen. Her therapist smiles in greeting. The artificial lighting in Taliyah's Georgetown office is much kinder to her than the dim yellow lamp in Tessa's living room. "Hello, Tessa."

Just the sight of her therapist, with her long, braided hair, and large, dark eyes, helps Tessa relax a bit. It's good to see a friendly face. "Hi, Taliyah."

"How are you doing?"

There are some weeks where Tessa can answer this question better than others. *It's been a bad week,* she says sometimes. Sometimes, she can honestly answer, *I'm okay.* At least she doesn't automatically deflect to *I'm fine* anymore. "I'm... I was all right until Friday."

"You were scheduled to visit the hospital that day." They discussed the impending visit at their session the previous Monday.

"Yeah. It didn't go very well."

"I'm sorry to hear that," Taliyah replies gently. "Do you want to talk about what happened?"

Tessa rests a hand on Leo to comfort herself first. Only then can she start recounting the experience of visiting the veterans on the traumatic brain injury ward. She is slow and halting, disjointed in a way that she never is with anyone besides her therapist. Taliyah understands her nevertheless. "I-I've visited some difficult places with Ryan over the years. Grieving families, funerals, disaster zones, nursing homes, homeless shelters, domestic violence shelters. It was all sad, it all weighed me down, but none of them made me feel like I needed to get out of there as soon as possible. I wanted to run out of this place. I was *desperate* to get out."

"This was intensely personal for you, in a way many of the other places weren't."

Tessa describes the rest of her night. Her lingering discomfort and unease, and the fear of returning to her empty apartment. Succumbing to her exhaustion, and the nightmare, and the terror and pain that greeted her upon waking.

"I was so messed up that I wasn't even able to use my grounding technique correctly. I couldn't keep myself in the present. I kept remembering Owen's voice instead. Leo helped. If I hadn't had him to touch and look at, I don't know what would have happened."

"I'm so glad you had him with you. Did Leo help bring you out of the episode too?"

"Not quite. It was Ryan, actually. I was so upset that I started crying, and he comforted me."

Taliyah's expression betrays some surprise. She knows how hard it is for Tessa to open up. "You allowed yourself to be vulnerable with him. How did that feel in the moment, and afterward?"

"It was awful and embarrassing. I couldn't believe I was doing it. But then..." Tessa pets Leo. "It actually felt good to let it all out and to lean on him, and let him be there for me."

Taliyah nods encouragingly. "This is important progress. I'm happy that you got to experience receiving support in that way."

"Yeah, well." The rest of what she has to stay sticks in her throat.

"You don't look happy," Taliyah observes.

"I felt–" Tessa shrugs, unable to dance around it any longer. "It's bothered me all weekend. After Ryan and I hugged, I wanted to go right back to him and hug him again."

Taliyah pauses, waiting to see if Tessa will continue. When it is clear that she has clammed up again, she speaks. "That makes sense to me. Outside of Leo and a couple of your friends, you don't experience a lot of physical touch. A desire to be held by a dear friend is normal and doesn't have to be romantic or sexual."

Tessa nods, relieved. When Taliyah says it like that, it makes sense to her too. She loves hugging Jesy, Rosalie, and her goddaughters. "Okay."

"We could talk about some ways to get more physical touch into your life. What do you think?"

There was a time when she didn't have to think about this at all. When she could reach over and hold Owen's hand or hug him in a matter of seconds, without thinking twice about it. What a luxury that had been. And she hadn't known that luxury was temporary. "That sounds good to me," Tessa says quietly.

Chapter Sixteen
April 2023 – January 2024

Tessa works with Kahaan, and Kahaan works his magic with the media. The news of Ryan and Vanessa's divorce breaks as quietly as possible. They arranged for the news to drop on the same day as the Tauke murder trial began, and Mike Frenzel, the controversial Republican governor, announced his run for president. The items perfectly overshadow Ryan's news.

After that is dealt with, Tessa's work days fill up with planning. She and Kahaan plan for Ryan's announcement, and she plans campaign financing alongside Javier. Tessa plans campaign strategy and voter outreach, alone and with the rest of the senior staff. She meets with Booker regarding holding the fort down in New York and on Capitol Hill while Ryan is on the campaign trail.

The campaign launch, at home in Queens, is a dream come true. Tessa helped Ryan and Kahaan write the announcement speech. She proofread it a dozen times. She still tears up at hearing Ryan deliver his announcement to a cheering crowd of hundreds at Astoria Park. The same spot he announced he was running for Congress, more than a decade ago.

They have all come so far together. They have already had a tangible impact on their constituents and the nation. If this long shot works out, they could be under two years away from leading the country. She could be under two years out from being the first woman to ever serve as White House Chief of Staff. It is a daring, audacious dream. Still, Owen and her friends have encouraged her at every turn.

Donations from the public pour in, in the minutes and hours after

Ryan's announcement. Social media lights up like wildfire. "We're getting celebrity endorsements, influencer endorsements, without even asking for them." Kahaan pops his head into Tessa's office, wide-eyed. "He's trending on Twitter, TikTok, Tumblr, and Reddit. Twitter's a mixed bag, but everything else is crazy positive."

Mari follows him in, her phone in hand. "It looks like our 18-34s are thrilled that he's running. They're already calling Ryan their candidate. This is exactly what we wanted."

Tessa calls a senior staff meeting the next morning. Spirits are high all around; everyone is all smiles. This won't last. It never does, in a campaign, so she savors it while it does. "Javier, what do you have for our finance report?"

Javier, normally so relaxed, has been sitting on the edge of his seat since they came to the conference room. "Want to guess how much we raised in the first 24? Go on, all of you, guess."

Booker balls up his napkin and lobs it at him. "Just tell us, you clown."

Javier spreads his arms wide in celebration. "9 mil. Average donation is 20 bucks. You've got a lot of supporters already, my man."

Tessa smiles. "We could break Sanders' one-month, 42-million record."

Javier salutes her. "On it, boss."

"Kahaan?"

"Ryan has about 200 interview requests. I'm pacing them out. Let's start planning today for Rachel Maddow's show on Monday."

Ryan nods. "Got it."

Booker provides a report on the polls they have out in the field, and Matt gives an update on next steps on the campaign trail. Tessa closes her laptop and opens her black binder. "We all know which Republicans have announced so far. On our side, our competitors are Walgren, Leath, Stoyer, Silva, Gardner, Flores, Haase, and Backstrom."

"Who are these guys?" Javier looks to Booker.

"Mayors, governors, Senators. I'm sure Tess has background checks on all of them, and their resumes and transcripts dating back to high school. Aside from Gardner and Flores, though, none of them have name recognition."

"That's right." Tessa flips to Gardner and Flores's section in her binder.

Ryan furrows his brow, leaning closer to her. "Does that heading really say *Threats?*"

"Keep your eyes to yourself, Senator. Gardner and Flores are the ones to watch. They have the experience, the legislative history, and the name recognition, on both sides of the aisle."

"Gardner's too old and too moderate," Ryan argues. "Flores is just too moderate. The good thing is that those two will have to fight for the same voters in the primaries."

"Exactly," Booker says. "Ryan is by far the most liberal of the candidates, and the youngest."

Matt chimes in. "The others are going to dogpile you in the primaries. Gardner and Flores will say that you're too far left to have any chance in the general. They're going to make a case where, if we make you the nominee, we're handing the Republicans the election."

Javier shakes his head. "Can't have that, after the eight years this country has just been through."

"They're going to hit you on your youth and lack of experience — because you *do* lack experience, compared to Gardner and Flores." Tessa ignores Ryan's attempted protest. "The name recognition will be a double-edged sword as soon as the general election comes around. Fox News and Congressional Republicans have been roasting you for the past ten years."

"You're polarizing," Kahaan agrees. "People who love you *really* love you. People who hate you… well."

Tessa prepares to address the elephant in the room. Or, rather, the donkey. "It's likely that the DNC*—" Groans all around. She rolls her eyes and continues. "It's likely the DNC will throw their weight behind an establishment candidate like Gardner. Without their backing, we have an uphill battle."

"All right. If we can't count on the DNC's support, who can we count on?"

"The College Democrats, the Young Democrats of America, and the Progressive Democrats of America," Tessa says. "Luckily, we have a few more reliable sources of support…"

ooooo

*Democratic National Committee

Unsurprisingly, Ryan does well at his first several national campaign rallies. "His appeal isn't limited to New York, thankfully," Tessa reports to her staff. She, Matt, and Booker join Ryan on the campaign trail, and everyone else holds down the fort at home and in DC.

"His appeal isn't limited to the country," Rosalie says. "Taiwanese and South Korean Twitter are going crazy for him."

"Oh, God. If he hears that, he'll be unbearable."

The weeks roll on, and poll result after poll result comes in. Ryan's performance is solidly in the top three among the Democratic primary candidates, along with Gardner and Flores. "There are others in the field who have longer careers, others who are more moderate, but nobody knows who they are." Booker glows with excitement during Tessa's morning strategy meeting. "No one knows their legislative history. No one knows what they've done. Ryan, Kahaan — all you guys' work with social media all these years has paid off."

Matt holds up a finger for clarification. "By *work,* are we talking about the relentless self-promotion, or the Twitter fights with Congressional Republicans?"

"I had nothing to do with the Twitter fights," Kahaan maintains.

∞∞∞∞∞

The first primary debate among the Democratic candidates is scheduled for late August 2023. Tessa and Matt spend hours every day in debate prep with Ryan. She and Matt have comparably high stress levels over their candidate's debut on a national stage. Their candidate, on the other hand, chomps at the bit at the prospect of setting himself apart from his competitors.

There are six primary debates before the Iowa caucus in late January 2024. Ryan acquits himself well in all of them. A few Democratic candidates drop out in the first two weeks of January, thinning the field of competitors. The mood among the staff in January is focused, brimming with quiet optimism as the Iowa caucus approaches. It is still a long shot, but it's not as long as it seemed in summer of 2023. Ryan's message resonates with Democrats around the country.

"By this time next year, we could be preparing for the inauguration."

Tessa doesn't dare speak those words aloud to anyone besides Owen. Even then, she speaks quietly, as she hands him a sweater. "Here, take an extra. It's going to be really cold."

"Thanks, Tessie." Owen tucks it into his duffel bag. He comes over to her, placing a hand on her back and rubbing it affectionately. "Have you ever lost an election? Have you ever not celebrated an inauguration in January?"

"No." Tessa gives him a hug. "But this is different."

"I don't think so." He kisses the top of her head. "I'm sorry I can't spend the caucus with you."

"I wish you didn't have to go at all." Tessa picks at the skin around her cuticle, even as she holds Owen. "Poland, with everything that's been going on — I don't like it."

"It's only a week and a half, honey."

"Still." Tessa draws back, wrapping her arms around herself.

"You were worried about the trips to the Middle East and the DMZ too, and I got through those okay," Owen reminds her.

Those had been miserably tense weeks for her too. She doesn't like Owen's job for a lot of different reasons, and the travel to high-conflict parts of the world is one of them. But he has always been so supportive of her job, so encouraging of her career and ambitions, that Tessa has hesitated to voice her reservations about his. He is good at what he does. Lockheed Martin had been eager to hire a veteran, and the flexibility of his remote work has helped them accommodate her career. The money had been a draw for Owen too, even though her salary is more than respectable on its own.

Owen tucks a stray strand of hair behind her ear. "Don't look so sad. You're going to win this thing in Iowa, and I'll be back in time to watch you crush it in New Hampshire too."

Tessa steps close, tilting her face up to his. Owen responds to the wordless request the way he always does, wrapping his arms around her and kissing her with such slow, lingering warmth that it makes her melt. They hold each other close, sighing their satisfaction, nuzzling their noses together and pressing their foreheads together. Tessa slips her hands underneath Owen's sweater, and he cradles the back of her neck in his hand. "I'm done packing for tonight, aren't I?" he asks, in between kisses.

"Yes. You are."

ooooo

Owen is in Poland when they lose the Iowa caucus. Tessa keeps a brave face. That is what she has to do, as campaign manager. For the sake of her staff, the campaign volunteers, the voters, and for her candidate. Ryan is undeterred, after all.

She holds it together all night. Afterward, she cries alone in her hotel room, doubting herself and reconsidering her entire campaign strategy. She ignores the comforting texts pouring in from Jesy, Rosalie, Grace, and her other friends. After the tears stop, Tessa sits cross-legged on the bed, staring blankly at the wall. The doubt and fear recede, replaced by resolve. She can do better in New Hampshire. She will do better in New Hampshire.

They return home. The one silver lining to Owen's absence is that Tessa can fling work-life balance out the window. She works from dawn until close to midnight, comes home, crawls into bed, and then does it all over again the following day.

She's tired, sure. But she would rather be tired now than crying in New Hampshire later.

Tessa falls into bed at one in the morning. The last thing she thinks of before drifting into sleep is how much she misses Owen holding her at night.

Her cell phone vibrating on the nightstand jolts her awake. Tessa blinks, bleary-eyed, at the digital clock. It is two in the morning. Her chest constricts, the way it always does when she receives a call on her personal cell when Owen is away.

A long international number, one she doesn't recognize, flashes across her home screen. Tessa snatches her phone up, pushing herself upright. "Hello?"

Her heart pounds. A couple of long beats of silence. Tessa knows. She knows, the same way she knew that Spencer was killed during the firefight in Baghdad. The same way she knew when her mom and dad came back from that last visit to the oncologist.

"Is this Teresa Halifax?" The speaker's voice is male, trying to be gentle.

Tessa nods shakily, gripping one hand in her hair. Their bedroom is very dark, and she feels very alone. "Y-yes."

"Teresa, I'm so sorry to tell you this, but there's been an incident…"

Tessa gets off the phone and stares at it for a while, numb. *Move, you idiot,* she orders herself. *Move.* It's like moving through molasses, turning the bedroom light on, stumbling through finding clothes. She bumps into the wall. She staggers and almost falls on her face putting her jeans on. She can't remember where she left her purse.

Should she buy a ticket online or should she buy it at the airport? Ticket counters won't be open now. When is the next flight out to Warsaw? She has to get herself to the airport. She can't drive in this state. She could call Jesy or Rosalie for help. Something clicks in her mind. Had she really been about to go to another country without calling–

She picks up her phone. The line is ringing before she realizes she should have emailed or texted. It's past two in the morning.

Ryan still answers. "Tess? What is it?"

"I'm sorry, but I have to go. Emergency leave. To Poland. I don't know when I'll be back." Tessa is out of breath even though she's just on the phone, one arm wrapped tightly around her middle. "I'm so sorry. Matt can come by and pick up my work files. He has passwords to all my secure files and documents, and a key to the filing cabinet."

"Wait, wait, slow down. Where are you? Are you home?"

"Yes." She heads for her laptop, distracted. She has to buy a plane ticket.

"Stay there. Don't leave. I'll be right there, okay?"

"Okay. I need to buy a plane ticket." She tries to remember the flight time from New York City to Poland. Eleven hours? Eight hours? "I need to go."

"We'll get you there. I'll be right over." Ryan's voice is calm, tightly controlled. He hangs up.

She can't see the laptop screen correctly when she tries to make her purchase. That, or the words and the date and time on the screen just don't make sense. A key clicks in the lock downstairs. Owen's home. No — it's just Ryan with the spare key, Ryan calling her name. "Tessa?"

"I'm here."

Footsteps hurry up the stairs. Ryan comes through the doorway, black overcoat pulled on over pajama pants. He takes one look at her. "Owen?"

Tessa presses the heels of her hands to her eyes. "They just called.

They said there's been an incident and he's in the hospital. He's not — not conscious."

Ryan curses under his breath. "I'll talk to them. Did you get your ticket yet?"

"No, I–" Tessa gestures at the screen uselessly. "It wasn't making sense."

Ryan takes the laptop from her. "Do you want me to come with you?"

"What? No." She shakes her head, dazed. "You have the campaign. New Hampshire."

"I'm not sure you should travel alone. I'll get a direct flight, anyway. I'll talk to Lockheed Martin, get them to pick you up at the airport and take you to Owen." Ryan stops typing. His expression crumples when he looks at her. "It's going to be alright."

ooooo

Ryan gets her a first-class nonstop flight to Warsaw, on the first flight out in the morning. He calls Owen's boss, and their contacts at the site visit in Poland. He texts Jesy, Rosalie, and Matt for her. He packs a duffel bag for her and drives her to the airport. He brushes off her disjointed attempts to talk to him about the campaign, and her apologies for leaving before the New Hampshire primary. He gives her a long hug, standing in the departures area of JFK, in the predawn darkness. Tessa leans into him. "Thank you."

"It's nothing. There's Wi-Fi on the flight. Text me or email me, let me know how you are. And call me once you land if you need anything. At the airport with immigration, at the hospital. Anything."

His eyes are red. Tessa raises a hand in farewell. "Go get some sleep before work." She walks into JFK, her chest aching with every step. She hasn't received any more calls from Lockheed Martin. She isn't sure if her husband is still alive.

She checks her phone compulsively as she waits at the airport and as she boards her flight. She could get a call with the news she is dreading at any minute. There is nothing except texts from her friends, as they wake up to Ryan's message. *Anything you need, okay? We're always here for you. Let me know if you want us to fly out. We'll be there.*

She can't be a widow. She is too young to be a widow. It is agony, to not know what faces her when this plane lands. And yet, to know enough to understand it's nothing good.

The hours drag on. Tessa can't sleep. She tries to work instead, letting politics be the escape it has been since she was a college student. One of Owen's colleagues meets her at the airport, which is swarming with police. A byproduct of the incident, apparently. Normally she would be examining the implications of an attack like this on Polish soil. How Europe would react, how the US would react. How a developing conflict could affect the election. Normally, she would want to know the details of everything that happened, so that she could analyze how it could have been prevented. She would search for any red flags that local security forces had missed.

She doesn't care about the political implications right now. There are other people in the hospital, a couple dead. It's terrible, but she doesn't care about anything besides Owen's well-being.

Owen's colleague drives her to the hospital and takes her up to the ward. He has her wait in a small, private lobby while he talks to the nurses about getting Owen's doctors here to speak with her. Tessa waits, clutching her bag at her side. Her eyes throb. Her muscles ache with fatigue. She hasn't waited in a hospital since those days when she and her dad came in for her mom's CT scans and MRIs. The imaging tests that should have shown her cancer shrinking showed the opposite instead. There is nowhere worse than a hospital. So many people, sick and dying.

Footsteps on the floor again. A woman in a white coat and scrubs approaches. "Ms. Halifax?"

Tessa stands up so quickly she almost stumbles. "Yes. Dr. Wojcik?"

The doctor puts a steadying hand on her shoulder. "Yes. My team and I have been caring for your husband since he arrived in the morning. Please, sit."

Tessa does, and the doctor sits beside her. Her eyes sting, and she swipes her tears away. "His coworker said that Owen woke up a couple of times today, but he didn't have a lot of information for me. Just that there was a car accident caused by an explosion."

She can't continue. She has heard of so many terrorist attacks since she left the Army. The Boston marathon bombing in 2013. The bombings in France in 2015. The 2016 bombings in Istanbul, and Brussels, and

Germany. Once, a lifetime ago, she and Spencer used to detect weapons just like that.

"Your husband suffered a head trauma during the accident and lost consciousness. Upon his arrival here, we did a CT scan to check for a traumatic brain injury and to assess the extent of the bleeding, bruising, and swelling in the brain."

Tessa can't stop picking at her cuticles. They are red and raw. She has seen what improvised explosive devices do to human heads. Skulls fragmented, bits of brain leaking out. "How — how was it?"

"There was bleeding in the brain, but we stopped that with surgery," Dr. Wojcik explains. "And he has regained consciousness, which is promising."

"Okay." Her breathing is still shallow, but hope begins to take root. They stopped the bleeding, and Owen is conscious again. "You mentioned the injuries to the brain. How long does that take to heal?" Her hands had been a burned, useless ruin after Iraq. Now, they are perfectly functional. Ugly, scarred, but functional.

"That depends on the patient. We will begin assessing Owen's functioning tomorrow, if he is up to it. I always recommend rehabilitation. Cognitive, physical, speech, and occupational therapy, to help address any deficits."

Deficits is a frightening, loaded word. But that's okay. That's what rehabilitation is for. She couldn't even hold a toothbrush with her injured hands after leaving Iraq. Within weeks of starting physical therapy, she was typing again. Her movements were slow and laborious, but they worked. "Okay. We'll do everything we have to."

"I would like to monitor him and keep him in inpatient therapy here for at least two weeks. Once Owen is medically stable, I will clear him to return home with you for outpatient follow-up. He will need a team of specialists in the States. I will send his medical records from here with you, so the doctors in the States know about his history and situation."

Tessa wipes her eyes. "Thank you. Can I see him?"

Dr. Wojcik leads her to Owen's room. There is nothing more disturbing than seeing Owen, her Owen, lying motionless in the hospital bed, his head swathed in bandages, hooked up to an IV pole and vitals monitoring system that illuminates his heart rate and blood oxygen levels. But it is better than the alternative — Owen lying here, not hooked up to any machines, draped in a white sheet.

Tessa hugs him gently, fighting the urge to weep. She wants to kiss him, to cradle his face in her hands, but she's worried about jostling his head. She takes his hand instead, holding it and pressing a kiss to his palm. She is taking stock of the cuts and scrapes on his face and his black eye when his eyelids flutter. "Tessie?"

Tessa has never heard his voice so weak. "I'm here."

He blinks, and the movement dislodges a few tears. "I thought I wouldn't see you again."

Tessa carefully puts his hand to her cheek, leaning into his touch like she always does. "I'm here. I'll always be here with you."

It isn't long before Owen lapses back into sleep. The nurse assures her that is normal. Tessa drags a chair over to Owen's bedside and settles there with him. She gazes at him, struggling to process the past twenty-four hours. When she finally checks her phone again, it is flooded with texts. Her email inbox has two hundred and fifty new messages. For once, the impulse to dive into work is gone. Ryan and the campaign are in good hands with Matt. She can focus on Owen now.

"Ms. Halifax?" The nurse has returned, speaking softly so she doesn't disturb Owen. Tessa turns, and the nurse holds out a business card. "Your husband's company has arranged a hotel nearby, and a car service, for you."

"Thanks." Tessa takes the card. "I'll stay for a while." She will stay until night falls and she has to leave. She doesn't like the thought of Owen waking up without her. She takes a deep breath, pulls up her search engine, and types out *traumatic brain injury.*

Chapter Seventeen

January 2024

They meet with Owen's doctor the following afternoon to discuss his rehabilitation and treatment plan. He has been more alert today, but the speech difficulties Tessa attributed to sedation yesterday are still present. It's nothing major, though. Not like some of the case videos she saw online. Owen's speech is just a little slurred, and it takes him longer to find his words. There is speech therapy for that. It is jarring to hear Owen not sounding like himself, but she will get used to it. At least he can speak.

"We are going to keep you in inpatient care and rehabilitation for the next two weeks." Dr. Wojcik catches Owen's grimace. "You have just had brain surgery, and it's not safe to fly at this time. I would like to keep you out of the air until your six-week post-op scans, but I know that you are eager to return home."

"How long until I'm healed? Until I'm back from — back to normal?" Owen had been baffled to find himself struggling with balance while getting dressed, and during his short walks to and from the bathroom. Tessa provided a steadying arm around his waist.

"It is hard to pinpoint the length of recovery from moderate to severe TBI, but the range is typically months to years. Rehabilitation helps with the process," Dr. Wojcik adds. "It really does. It's crucial."

Owen's thumb taps out an anxious rhythm against the armrest of the chair. Tessa rests her hand atop his. "Can I keep working? I'm a…" The words escape him, and he finally settles on, "I work in security consulting."

The reports that Owen reviews and writes are long and dense, even by Tessa's standards. She saw the information online about cognitive impairments after brain injury. Difficulty concentrating, difficulty organizing thoughts, becoming confused and forgetful. None of those align with a high-level job.

Her worry must show on her face, because Dr. Wojcik glances at her. "I recommend taking a medical leave and focusing on your recovery," she says tactfully. "You may resume light duty in some months, if you feel up to it."

Owen frowns. "What about other work, then? It's not fair for my wife to be the sole provider, especially with medical bills."

"Don't worry," Tessa reassures. "It's all right. That doesn't matter at all."

Dr. Wojcik adds a word of encouragement. "Career outcomes can be positive with cognitive rehabilitation and occupational therapy."

Owen's grip on her fingers tightens. "I know three languages besides English. I'm — I *was* — fluent. I could think in them if I wanted to. I can't remember my words. They're getting all mixed up."

"That's normal with multilingual TBI patients, unfortunately. Continue practicing those skills, and you may regain fluency. That will help with your cognitive rehabilitation as well."

Dr. Wojcik leaves, and Owen slumps in his seat, staring at the floor. "You know how they talk here? Everything is *may* or *might*. Not — I *will* get better."

"Yeah. I noticed." Tessa rubs his arm. She found the same thing, as she stayed up until one in the morning doing online searches with endless permutations of "TBI outcomes" and "TBI recovery."

"It *could* take me months or years to get back to where I was. If I do. I hate this," Owen bursts out. "I don't want to be a burden to you. I can't even walk across the room by myself."

Tessa's shoulders stiffen. "You're not a burden. Please don't say that."

"I don't know. I'm just — not thinking right."

The distress in his voice, the note of helpless confusion, cuts to her core. "I felt the same way when I was in the hospital after Iraq, dealing with my injuries and with…" The aftermath of the firefight. What happened to Spencer. "This environment is awful. You'll feel more like yourself when you're home. And you were just attacked, on top of the injury. It's probably PTSD, just like you felt when you came back from Iraq."

"This feels different. Physically." Owen swipes irritably at the tears welling up in his eyes. "I can't just get up and go for a run. And I'm not — I don't remember being so scared, before. About not being able to work. About being half brain-dead forever."

Tessa flinches. "You're not brain-dead. That's being unresponsive, comatose. That's not you."

"I don't *recognize* me." Owen is talking faster, and it takes her a beat longer to understand him now. "It's - it's scary."

"I know. It must be." Tessa keeps a brave face for him. This isn't about her, and how frightening this uncertainty is. What matters is making the person who is sick or hurt feel better. She remembers that much from witnessing her mom's years with cancer. "I'm here for you."

ooooo

Tessa works as best as she can, when Owen is resting or at his rehabilitation sessions. She replies to every email, and has frequent calls with Ryan, Matt, and Kahaan. "I'm so sorry about this," Tessa tells Ryan, after one of their strategy calls.

"If you apologize to me again, I'll fire you. How are you doing?"

"I'm hanging in there."

"And Owen?"

"Making progress with physical therapy. His balance is getting better. The dizziness is still a problem, but there might be medications that can help with that." Tessa stops herself from picking at her cuticles again. They have started bleeding. Dr. Wojcik mentioned a long string of medications — for the dizziness and vertigo, the headaches, and antidepressants to help with the anxiety and insomnia. Owen refused the antidepressants.

"Okay. That's good." Ryan is quiet for a few moments. "Remember to take care of yourself too. I've seen the timestamps on your emails. Are you sleeping?"

She spends her nights wracked with worry about Owen and the campaign, and then wracked with guilt for thinking about work when she should be thinking about Owen. Then a new layer of guilt sets in, about abandoning her candidate and staff when they need her. Then she starts the whole cycle of anxiety over again. Tessa sidesteps Ryan's question. "Don't waste your energy worrying about me. Focus on yourself. You have a nomination to win."

"I'll worry about whatever I want to." With that, Ryan hangs up.

Typical. Tessa sighs and checks the clock. Owen should be back from the rehab gym soon. She attended his first few sessions, remembering the ordeal of her own physical and occupational therapy after her burn injuries. She offered the occasional quiet words of encouragement she would have loved to hear. Still, after the first few sessions, Owen told her that she should stay back and use that time to get caught up on work.

Owen enters, cane in hand, a physical therapy assistant at his side. Tessa joins him, putting her arm around his waist for support. Owen leans against her with a sigh of relief. He hands the cane off to the therapy assistant at once, as if eager to put some space between him and the mobility aid. "Thanks."

"See you tomorrow, Owen. You have speech therapy in an hour."

Owen looks at her. "Is that enough time to get some sleep?" Until this hospital stay, the last time her husband napped was when he was a toddler.

"It is." She sits beside him on the bed. "What did you work on today?"

"Holding stuff." Owen frowns, dissatisfied with his own description. "Handwriting, chopping, shaving. Some memory stuff."

Fine motor skills. "I could come with you to speech therapy," Tessa offers, even though she knows what his answer will be.

Owen shakes his head before she even finishes speaking. "No, that's fine."

Tessa hesitates, unsure of whether to press the issue or not. It's his choice. It's also her job to support him. "It's fine," Owen repeats. "I don't… Look, Tessie, I know you care, but I don't want you seeing me like that. Struggling to do what a kid could do, and being so weak."

His words are loaded with bitterness and self-loathing. "It's not weak to struggle or have difficulties. Remember our support group?" The cognitive rehabilitation specialist warned them that there could be memory loss after a TBI, but Owen's cognitive assessment revealed no major gaps in long-term memory.

"It's different," Owen mumbles. "I can say that all I want. It's true for my friends. But it's not true for me."

That doesn't make sense, but Tessa stops short of pointing it out. She tells her friends to rest, to sleep, to take care of themselves. She doesn't always take her own advice. She leans her head against Owen's shoulder.

"We vowed to be with each other, to support each other, in sickness and in health. When I leave you to deal with all of this rehab alone, it feels like I'm not holding up to those vows."

"But you are. I'm not alone. You're here." Owen rubs her back. "I feel so stupid when I'm doing all of this. I'll feel even more like a fool if you're there. You can just be here for me. You're already doing enough."

Post-injury, it's rare that he speaks that much at one time. Tessa kisses him on the cheek. She still doesn't feel right about it, but she doesn't want to argue. "Thank you. Now get some rest."

ooooo

They fly back home two weeks to the day of Tessa's flight to Poland. She is anxious about Owen's safety in the air, despite him receiving medical clearance to fly. Owen is withdrawn for his own reasons. "When I flew out here last month, I was fine," he says, an hour after takeoff. "I spent the whole flight working. Now I can't read half through a stupid news article." He gestures to the New York Times website, open on Tessa's laptop.

Tessa tilts her laptop screen half shut. She is too familiar with those times in life that delineate a clear *before* and *after*. Nothing is the same after. She rests a hand on Owen's arm in an attempt to comfort him.

"And I feel bad for making you miss work." Owen covers his face with his free hand. The pressure of the flight may be worsening his ever-present headache. "You never miss work, especially not during a campaign."

"I didn't miss any work," Tessa replies bracingly. "I've been working remotely. We're in good shape ahead of New Hampshire. I'm going to keep working remotely when we get back. It'll be easier, since I'll be in the same timezone as everyone else."

"What? Why? Don't you need your stuff, and to go places?" Owen scowls at his own perceived lapses. *I'm writing and talking like a first grader,* he said, frustrated, after returning from a therapy session earlier this week.

She does, but Ryan and Matt have been so accommodating. Ryan has turned down all her offers to resign. "I thought I could help you with what you need around the house, and drive you to your appointments."

Owen's shoulders hunch as if he's protecting himself from a blow.

"You don't have to do that. I'll be fine on my own."

Around the house, maybe. But driving — the cognitive assessment made it clear he shouldn't be behind the wheel yet. "Getting to your appointments–"

"I'll just take the subway. You don't have to babysit me."

"I'm not..." But there's an edge in Owen's voice, one that has never, ever been directed at her. Tessa falls silent, and reminds herself not to feel wounded. Dr. Wojcik came to talk to her once, while Owen had been at rehab. *A lot of TBI patients struggle with regulating their emotions, and how they feel and express emotions. You may notice rapid mood swings, irritability, or that he feels depressed or tearful. Don't take it personally. It's nothing to do with you or your relationship.* She gave Tessa a pamphlet, which she reviewed later that night, alone in her hotel room.

"Okay," Tessa says, and she leaves it alone.

Chapter Eighteen
January 2024 - July 2024

It is so good to be back to the familiarity of the office, her home away from home. Even with the New Hampshire primary just a couple of days away, Tessa's friends and staff organize a welcome-back party for her. Rosalie orders cake from her favorite bakery, and Booker and Javier show her the photo they taped to the conference room wall. "It felt like you were with us during the morning meetings," Matt says fondly. "What would Tessa do?"

"Oh my god." Tessa peers at her photo, snapped by a photographer during their campaign kickoff event. "Why did you pick this one? I look so… stern."

"Well, we were going for accuracy." Presidential candidate or not, Tessa shoves Ryan in the arm.

She immerses herself in work, looking forward to the primaries ahead, the debates, and Super Tuesday. She checks in with Javier twice a day to follow the progress of the campaign's fundraising. Unfortunately, carrying out campaign strategy requires a *lot* of money.

Many of the other Democratic candidates have a personal net worth north of 20 million. Many others are solidly in the pockets of big donors and have close relationships with powerful political lobbies. Ryan has spent his career keeping a distance from lobbyists and ultra-wealthy special interest donors. He is proud of his grassroots support, and always emphasizes how he hasn't been bought and paid for like other candidates. That means Javier and his team have to work twenty times as hard to collect the donations that other Democratic candidates secure with one lunch meeting.

Their win in New Hampshire helps with fundraising — and more importantly, morale. It lets them hit the ground running for Super Tuesday. Tessa revels in the victory, relishing every moment of her friends' joy and optimism. She leaves her usual caution on the shelf for once. When Matt and Ryan toast to her, and to the future President Chao, she doesn't immediately brush them off.

It is good to feel effective. Capable. It is a sharp contrast to her helplessness at home. Tessa pores over TBI treatment and rehabilitation protocols every day. Her findings are the same. There is no strategy that she can implement to help Owen. The work of his rehabilitation, treatment, and recovery is out of her hands.

Physical, occupational, cognitive, and speech therapy are his new jobs. Owen never misses an appointment. He does his cognitive exercises at home, even when they leave him growling with frustration, tossing his tablet or workbooks aside, burying his face in his hands.

"It's not working," he says. Sometimes fighting back tears, sometimes with his hands balled into fists, his voice tight with anger. "Why isn't it working?"

Tessa places her hand on his shoulder. His muscles are tense beneath her palm. "It is working. I can see the difference."

"Well, I can't." Sometimes he snaps at her. Sometimes his voice is barely audible, the slur coming back into his speech the way it does when he is exhausted or emotional. Sometimes he cries. Owen always walks away, unable to face her anymore, until the moment passes and he finds some equilibrium again. Then he returns, and he gives her a hug, and Tessa holds him close.

There are some things she could help Owen with. Paying the medical bills (that are pouring in, and piling up on the counter). Refilling and picking up his prescriptions. Doing the laundry, and grocery shopping, and cooking — the chores he used to take on around the house. Owen flatly refuses her offers. "I'm not a kid. I can handle that myself."

(Except that he has panic attacks at the grocery store. Or he forgets something, or several things. He gets angry at himself for forgetting when he gets home, and he paces in the kitchen, unable to think through the recipe substitutions he used to make without hesitation. Owen goes upstairs to get the laundry and forgets why he went upstairs. He paces, as he waits for his memory to return, or he starts another chore entirely. Which he leaves half-finished, by no fault of his own, as he remembers another chore he wanted to get done before she returned home.)

Tessa learns, after the fact, that Owen got lost on the subway a few times. She insists that he either take an Uber or go out with her. Owen says she's overreacting. She argues that she isn't. She's justifiably worried about what could happen. Owen says that this is why he didn't tell her what happened — because he knew she would think he was too incompetent to ride the subway on his own.

It sparks their first real argument, their first fight, ever. They raise their voices at one another, which would have been unfathomable just a few months ago.

Tessa cries, and Owen does too.

He says he will take an Uber or walk to where he needs to go. Tessa starts texting him from work more often, and calling to check in, between meetings or on her short lunch break. Owen rarely replies to her texts or calls. Worry for him lingers at the back of her mind, pushing through to the forefront, for the rest of her work day.

Thankfully, when she gets back home, he is fine. She finds him lifting weights in their small weight room, or sitting with his rehab workbooks, or trying to make his way through a dinner recipe. Tessa goes back and forth about whether to broach the topic, their fight last week still fresh in her mind.

Finally, tentatively, she brings it up over dinner. "I noticed that you haven't been replying to my texts or calls during the day. Are they getting in the way of your focus when you're out, or doing things around the house?" *Are they annoying you?* Tessa wants to ask. *Am I annoying you?* These days, Owen is irritated by things that never used to bother him. Noise on the street, crowds in grocery stores.

"No." Owen rubs the back of his neck. On top of everything else, he has had neck pain since the accident. Tessa reaches out, massaging his neck. He sighs, his head dropping forward. "I'm losing my phone a lot. Just — in the house. That and other stuff like my keys and my workbook, and my headphones. Things just disappear as soon as I put them down. It's so goddamn frustrating to lose my stuff ten times an hour."

"I bet." Tessa bites back a suggestion to leave things in the same place each time. He doesn't need cognitive strategies right now. He just needs to vent.

"I don't mean to ignore you."

"I know." There was a time she would say anything on her mind to Owen. Now she has to stop and think about how he'll take it. "What do you think about going back to a support group? I could come with you. I think it would be good for me too."

Owen glances at her, startled. "For PTSD?"

"There's actually a brain injury support group at your rehab clinic. It's Tuesday evenings from seven to eight-thirty."

Owen is quiet for a long moment. "Yeah. Okay. We'll try it."

Tessa takes his hand, giving it a squeeze. Owen studies her, and his lips quirk up in a small smile. "You look happy."

"I was just remembering how we met."

Owen puts his arm around her shoulders, drawing her close. He presses a kiss to her forehead. Tessa leans into him, enjoying the now-rare moment of pure contentment.

∞∞∞∞∞

It is impossible not to reminisce about their long-ago PTSD support group as they drive to Owen's rehabilitation clinic on Tuesday evening. "I'm nervous," Owen confesses.

"Me too. But we've done this before. We can do it again."

Attending the support group at the clinic gives Tessa an odd sense of deja vu. The facilitators are soft-spoken, calm, and kind, like Asher was. The chairs are arranged in the same circle. Most of the group's twenty participants are men. Almost all are attending with a partner. The group begins with a reminder of the ground rules, including confidentiality and respect for one another, and a round of introductions.

"Let's start today's group by thinking about self-esteem." Drayton, the group's facilitator, looks around the room.

"That's how you think about yourself," his co-facilitator chimes in. "Your relationship with yourself."

The group takes a while to mull that over. The responses, when they eventually come, make Tessa's heart hurt. Owen echoes everyone else's sentiments. "I feel stupid. Physically, I'm getting better, but my memory is shot. I forget things all the time. I don't remember that my wife tells me what time she's going to be home, and then I get worried about her when she's not back yet. Then I get mad at her for not telling me what time she'd be back. Even though she did. She always does."

Tessa looks down at her hands. The anecdote triggers several nods around the circle. Group members start talking about other ways their self-esteem has taken a hit since their injuries. "I got put on a performance improvement plan at work," one man admits. Someone else comments that they can't focus on board games and leading tabletop role-playing games anymore.

That opens the floodgates for Owen. He speaks more in one stretch than he has since his injury. "I loved reading. Now I lose my place on the page every few paragraphs, or my attention goes. I'm trying audiobooks, but it's hard to focus on them, and I always forget what I listened to last time. It's the same with the news and TV. I just can't follow what's happening anymore, especially with all the side plots and different characters and stuff." He gestures unhappily, and Tessa rests a hand on his arm. (They haven't cuddled up together to watch a TV drama in a long time. They had been four seasons into Justified when Owen left for Poland.)

The ninety minutes fly by. After the slow start, everyone seems eager to unburden themselves, releasing pent-up anger and frustration. And, underlying it all, sorrow and grief over their multiple losses.

After the group concludes, Drayton approaches Owen to check in on how he's doing. Tessa walks up to his co-facilitator, who is gathering TBI pamphlets from the literature table. The heating in here doesn't work too well, and she crosses her arms over her chest to keep her warmth close. "Thank you for doing this. It was really helpful."

He turns to look at her, and Tessa is suddenly self-conscious of whether the dark circles and bags under her eyes are visible. Worry has kept her up at night since Owen's injury. She tries to cover the telltale marks with makeup, but she isn't that skillful, despite all the YouTube videos she has watched. He takes a brochure from his stack and holds it out to her. "We do a care-partner support group too. Thursday night at the same time, on Zoom."

"Oh." That throws her for a loop. She hadn't thought she might need some help of her own. Tessa takes the flier and raises her hand in farewell. "See you next time."

She and Owen walk back to the car arm-in-arm. They haven't done this in a while. They don't go out for their weekend run-and-brunch dates anymore, since crowds wear on Owen's nerves. "How was it?"

"Good." They settle into the car, and they are pulling out of the parking garage when he speaks again. "I actually wish it was longer. Or that they had another one this week."

"I'm glad you liked it so much. And you don't have to wait until next week. You can talk to me."

She half expects him to brush her off. Maybe being in the moving car helps, or he's still in sharing mode from the group. "I still don't want to get on pills. But this goddamn anxiety — it hurts."

Tessa stays silent. Owen's mother had been addicted to opioids, eventually leading to her fatal overdose. His father is still an addict. Owen's distrust of medication runs deep, and it isn't limited to opioids.

"I keep getting up at night, hearing things, thinking someone's breaking into the house. I can never remember if I turned the stove off or not, or if I locked the front door. And you… Well, you know."

She does. She is the focal point of so much of Owen's anxiety. When he has his phone, he will triple or quadruple text, or call multiple times. If she doesn't answer — because she's in a meeting, or working — he assumes she is hurt or dead. When she finally can reply, his relief turns into sadness or fear, anxiety or anger, at a moment's notice. (*You* know *that I get anxious,* he snapped at her earlier in the week, wringing his hands. *So why can't you just keep the sound on your phone on? Or check it more often, or something?*

I'm trying, Tessa replied, trying her best to keep the stress from her voice. *I really am. But I'm in more meetings than I ever used to be because of the campaign, and —*

The campaign — I'm so sick *of this damn campaign. Every time I go online, every time I turn on the news, every time I talk to you, it's this damn campaign. I wish it was next November already.*)

Tessa takes one hand off the wheel to rest it on Owen's. "I'm sorry. That sounds so hard."

"I'm just… I know I'm not thinking or feeling right. It reminds me of my grandma, with her dementia, and I fucking *hate* that."

His voice has risen. Stress courses through her, as it always does when his voice gets this edge to it. *De-escalate, de-escalate.* She talks Ryan down when he is worked up over the election, which is often. She talks Owen down when he's upset, which is often. This is her life now. De-escalation. Tessa reads articles about effective de-escalation and redirection strategies during her ten-minute lunch breaks.

"I've been to visit memory care centers and nursing homes for work," she says carefully. "Those poor people — they can't function. They can't dress themselves, can't shower on their own, can't brush their teeth. They can barely feed themselves. They can't speak. That's not you, Owen."

Thankfully, that sinks in. Owen reaches over to rub her shoulder. "Thanks."

ooooo

The support group is helpful, but it isn't a panacea. There are things Owen doesn't share because they are too embarrassing. Like the time Tessa comes home from work to find him watching the most recent Democratic primary debate on MSNBC, his cognitive rehabilitation workbook open on his lap. "Look at these guys," he murmurs, unable to tear his attention from the TV. He watches as Ryan and Gardner spar over universal basic income. "They have to remember all this stuff. Come up with answers to everything on the spot. And follow everyone talking over each other."

Tessa comes to sit beside him. "First, they have notes. Also, it's not as on-the-spot as it seems." She nudges him, trying to cheer him up. "The cross-talk is annoying, though."

Owen doesn't reply, still watching Ryan and Gardner duke it out. He doesn't have to say anything. The envy is written clear on his face.

ooooo

There are things that Owen — and Tessa — don't share, because they are too personal. They have always had a happy, healthy intimate relationship. Ever since the injury, that's just gone. They have tried. They have cuddled and kissed, and touched each other. It always ends with them pulling apart from one another, looking each other in the eyes, Tessa worried and trying not to be hurt, and Owen ashamed. "I'm so sorry, honey," he says to her every time, stroking her hair. "It's not you. I just don't… I'm not feeling like myself in my head, and I think that's affecting things."

She kisses him, every time. "Don't worry about it."

It is keenly frustrating. They both want to be with one another, but they can't. Late that night, Tessa turns to Google, as she so often does these days. *About half of people with a traumatic brain injury experience a drop in sex drive,* she reads. *Between forty and sixty percent of men have either temporary or permanent impotence following their injury.* She swallows over her suddenly dry throat, and hopes that Owen doesn't decide to look this particular symptom up online.

ooooo

Rosalie comes to find her in her office the following day, bearing a mug of tea as a gift. "Thank you." Tessa takes it gratefully. She needed another caffeine fix.

"Anytime." Rosalie takes a sip of her own coffee. "Is there anything we can do to make Friday night work for you?"

Guilt slices through her. She hasn't been to a single one of the twice-monthly dinners with Jesy and Rosalie since early January, before Owen's injury. After returning from Poland, she felt too guilty to leave him for a night. She works too much as it is. But that isn't fair to Jesy or Rosalie, either. Tessa tries to ignore the persistent inner voice that decries her for being a bad friend, a bad wife, and a bad campaign manager.

"I'll be there." She holds her hand out. "I'm sorry I've been such a bad friend lately." The only way she has really connected with her two best friends of late has been over text.

Rosalie squeezes her hand. "You're not a bad friend. You're just being pulled in a million different directions, and we're worried about you."

On the drive home, Tessa rehearses how she will tell Owen that she'll be out on Friday night. She can compensate by going on a hike with him on Saturday, though. He takes it okay. Eight o' clock on Friday night finds Tessa at a Mexican place in Queens with her friends. Before long, she feels oddly emotional, struck with the urge to cry. She puts one hand on Jesy's arm and one on Rosalie's. "I'm so glad that we could do this."

"You should come out more," Jesy encourages. "You're pushing yourself too hard. You need a break."

Tessa takes a sip of her wine. She swallows all the things she can't say, because they have families of their own, and she doesn't want to worry them. "I will."

(She doesn't say that this is the first time she has felt light, unburdened, in months. The office is her second home, but the contest between Ryan and Gardner over who will earn the Democratic nomination is past the point of exhilaration. It has turned into a bitter, miserable slog for delegate votes in the primaries.

As for her real home — she is hypervigilant there, always so aware of how Owen is doing and what kind of mood he is in. Sometimes he is fine. Sometimes he is a storm cloud on the verge of bursting, and she doesn't know whether to soothe him or just lie low and wait until the storm passes.)

ᴏᴏᴏᴏᴏ

"I'm home," Tessa calls. She shuts and locks the door behind her. (She startled Owen in the kitchen a few times, and he asked her to call out when she returned home.)

She follows the sound of Owen's greeting and finds him on the sofa in the living room, one of his Arabic-language textbooks in hand. "How was your night — oh." Tessa stops dead, noticing the bottle of Jack Daniels on the coffee table. It's about a fourth empty. Four shots worth of liquor?

Owen follows her gaze. "It's fine."

"The doctor said–" *Drinking makes cognitive problems worse and increases the risk of emotional problems.*

"I know what she said. But it helps quiet things, you know?"

Tessa comes to sit beside him. "Ryan used to say the same thing. It just created a whole new set of problems for him."

"Well, I'm not Ryan," Owen snaps.

Her reaction is visceral; she recoils. "I-I know you're not."

"What's that supposed to mean?"

She's so wrongfooted, stumbling through this conversation. She hadn't spoken with anything acerbic or bitter in her tone, had she? This could easily devolve into a fight. "It didn't mean anything." Tessa speaks as calmly and evenly as she can. "You're two different people, just like Jesy and I are different."

Owen smooths his palm over a page of his book. "I just need to take the edge off a little. That's all."

There is so much she wants to say, but she can't say it now and keep the peace. Maybe tomorrow during their hike, when he's in a better mood. "Okay."

∞∞∞∞

Two of her meetings are canceled on Thursday, which gives her two hours back in her day to actually work. She begins a focused work session, catching up on everything on her to-do list. Tessa heads home for the day feeling better about her productivity than she has all week.

That alleviated some of her anxiety, but it comes roaring back with dinner. She can tell from the way Owen handles his silverware that he is irritated. "It's missing something," he says, of the Thai green curry he made for dinner. "I don't know if I forgot to add the fish sauce or the ginger and garlic. I definitely forgot something. It doesn't taste right."

Tessa spears a slice of bell pepper with her fork. "It tastes good to me."

"Yeah, but you've barely had anything."

"Ryan, Matt, and I had some snacks at the office, since we worked through lunch today."

"Oh."

The silence hangs over them. There is something moody about it, along with Owen's expression. He shakes some salt over his rice and curry. Tessa takes another bite of her dinner, but her mind isn't focusing on the flavors. "Is everything okay?"

"It's fine," Owen says shortly.

It's clearly not, but she doesn't want to push him. Tessa keeps eating, guilt lodging in her stomach, heavy as a stone. She has arranged her work hours so that she is home almost every evening in time for dinner, but she should do more than that. She spends the bulk of each day away from her chronically ill husband. That makes her a bad wife, by any definition.

Her father stopped working when her mom got sick. He devoted his days and nights to taking care of her. Through round after round of chemo, through the too-brief periods of remission, through hospice and through her end of life. He did that for his wife. It had been the best thing — the only truly, deeply good thing — her father ever did. And she hadn't learned from that.

(Can they afford for her to scale back her work, though? She is their sole income earner for the time being, as they wait for Owen's application for disability to be processed. The medical bills keep coming. All of Owen's physical, speech, cognitive, and occupational therapy isn't free.)

"I'll do the dishes," Tessa offers, once they have finished. It is something tangible she can do, to make up for working so much. To make up for having too many snacks with her friends. To make up for Owen feeling like she didn't enjoy the dinner he worked so hard to make.

"I can do it." Owen takes her empty bowl. "You were at work all day."

Tessa tries not to flinch. She helps him with the dishes so that he won't feel alone.

ᴏᴏᴏᴏᴏ

After that, she is even more dedicated to getting home earlier on the weekdays. It means that she has to work from home later in the night, after dinner, exchanging emails and Slack messages with Ryan, Kahaan, and Booker. Tessa sits besides Owen while he works on cognitive rehab tasks, reads, or revisits his Arabic textbooks.

"Who are you texting?" he asks, sometimes. Or, "Who are you emailing?"

That is a departure from the norm. He always used to assume — correctly — that she was either talking to her staff, or Jesy and Rosalie. "The guys at work," Tessa answers absentmindedly, typing out a response to Booker. Once, she answers, "Ryan. Flores just dropped out of the race, and he wants to know what he has to do to get Flores to endorse him."

Owen turns the page of his Arabic textbook. "Why is he bothering you so late at night? Doesn't he have anyone else he can go to with this stuff?"

Flores will want nothing short of you making him your running mate, which has its pros and– Tessa stops typing, and glances at Owen out of the corner of her eye. "It's my job. I'm the best qualified to help him with questions like this."

"I know that. It's just — it's late at night. That's all. He thinks he's entitled to your time."

"He kind of is," Tessa points out. Her mild tone conceals how weird this is. Owen used to work late all the time, especially when taking meetings with clients in different time zones. He understood when she did the same during campaign season. "He's my boss."

"Right," Owen says quietly. He returns to his textbook, and Tessa returns to her work.

ooooo

Owen doesn't have to get up early for work anymore, but old habits die hard. The brain injury and the anxiety lead to insomnia, worsening the issue. He is often up when Tessa rises at four-thirty or five. He takes the opportunity to make her a thermos of tea and pack her lunch. It is so very helpful, especially on mornings like this, with a high-stakes day ahead.

Owen walks into their bedroom, thermos in hand. Tessa smiles at him as she takes it. "Thank you so much. That smells amazing."

"It's that new jasmine green tea." Owen takes her in — her black pencil skirt, tawny silk blouse, and black blazer. "You look good, Tessie."

Tessa finishes braiding her hair, and sweeps her bangs out of her eyes. "Thanks. I'm trying something new with my hair. This style looks so good on Rosalie, so I thought…"

Owen studies her. "Are you wearing makeup?"

The question throws her for a loop. He doesn't normally pay attention to what she wears. He compliments her the same whether she's wearing a hiking outfit, no makeup, hair in a bun, or an evening gown for a campaign event.

"Yes. I have a meeting with Flores' campaign manager today, and I haven't caught up with her in a few years." She has one item on her agenda for this meeting: get Senator Flores to endorse Ryan over Gardner.

"Okay." Owen doesn't seem reassured. "As long as you're not trying to…"

Tessa pauses in twisting and pinning her braid into an updo, letting it fall back down over her shoulder. "What?"

"Nothing." Owen turns to leave the bathroom.

She reaches out, snagging the back of his sleeve, her heart beating faster. "Wait. What do you mean?"

"Nothing. Forget I said anything." Owen moves his arm, and Tessa's hand falls limp to her side.

She follows him out of the bathroom and into their bedroom. "No. Owen–"

He turns to face her. He doesn't look her in the eye, instead fixing his gaze on a point above her head. "As long as you're not dressing up for someone. That's all."

His voice is too loud, and he flinches. Tessa finds it difficult to breathe. "What — what do you mean by that?"

Owen doesn't look happy to be having this conversation, but he doesn't back down. "I remember that Ryan and Vanessa got divorced."

This cannot be happening. This just doesn't compute. "What does that have to do with anything?" She has the creeping suspicion she knows where he's going with this. It makes her stomach hurt with confusion. Owen has never been jealous. And — of *Ryan*? And her?

"Come on, Tess." There's a note of exasperation in Owen's voice. He takes a step toward her. Without knowing why, Tessa takes a small step backward. "I've seen how he looks at you."

She couldn't have been more bewildered if he started talking to her in a different language. Tessa shakes her head. "No. Ryan and I are just friends. We've always been just friends."

"Look, I know what I've seen, all right?"

Suddenly, it all makes sense. Owen being upset about the time she spends with Ryan, and Ryan texting or emailing her in the evenings. "It's not like that between us at all. You can read our emails and texts if you want." The confusion had been a shield. Now that it has passed, the hurt sinks its claws in. "Do you — do you really think I'm cheating on you?" She can barely get the words out.

"What am I supposed to think?" Owen gestures, frustrated. "My wife spends almost all of her waking hours with another man. You guys travel around the country together. You've spent your whole adult life with Ryan, trying to build him up, help him live his dream."

"I've spent my whole adult life with *you*. You were my first kiss, my first everything." Tessa rakes her fingers through her bangs. "I'm not helping Ryan get to the presidency because I'm in love with him. I'm doing it because he has the right platform — a platform *I* helped write. You've always known this is what I wanted to do. I told you about it before we even got engaged. Have you always felt this way?"

Owen doesn't answer her question. "Is it really just about the ideals?" he shoots back. "I've seen how you look when he talks. So — so *proud*, so invested, so committed."

"Yes, I am proud and invested and committed. Because he's my candidate. He's my boss. And he's one of my oldest friends. That's it." Tessa takes a deep breath, fighting to keep her tears at bay. "I need to go to work."

She flees the house, barely remembering to grab her things before leaving. She normally uses her commute as precious time to begin mentally preparing for the work day. As hard as she tries, she can't stop replaying their fight. Owen's accusations — his anger, his jealousy– Tessa grips the steering wheel tight, her breaths still shallow, her chest still aching, shoulders rigid. She's reeling, she's — afraid. She is Ryan's campaign manager, during the most important campaign of all of their careers. She has to get him the Democratic nomination by summer and a win in the general election in November. She has enough to worry about without her husband being jealous of her candidate. She has to fix this.

Can she fix this? Maybe the best thing to do for her marriage, for Owen, would be to step back. Tessa flinches from the thought. The last thing the campaign needs at this pivotal stage is upheaval.

Besides, as humble as she is, as she tries to be — she does have her pride. She is the best equipped to help this campaign succeed. After that first stumbling block in Iowa, she has done well. She has gotten her candidate to be one of the final two. If she pulls this off, if she gets Ryan elected, she will be the first woman in history to be a White House Chief of Staff.

Tessa parks at campaign headquarters. She rests her forehead on the steering wheel, releasing a shuddering exhale. When she gets out of this car, she will leave what happened this morning behind.

She fully immerses herself in work all day, locking her personal cell in her desk drawer and leaving it there. She is as on-point, as competent, as ever. Her meeting with Flores' campaign manager is a success. On behalf of her candidate, Tessa offers Flores a spot on Ryan's ticket, in exchange for the Senator's endorsement. On behalf of her candidate, Isabella Ramirez accepts.

It's a win. Tessa's body still feels the impact of all the stress she's trying to quell. Her stomach is tied up in knots, and her shoulders and neck are miserably tight. She is restless, pacing up and down her office while on the phone with representatives from the DNC.

This isn't the first fight she and Owen have had, but it's the worst. It is the only one that hasn't been resolved. For the first time ever, she is nervous to go home and face him. She doesn't know how these things go. Will they continue where they left off? Will they act like none of it happened? The best case scenario is that Owen apologizes and says he wasn't in his right mind…

She has a quick lunch with Rosalie and Mari that afternoon. Tessa briefly considers turning to them for advice, or texting Jesy. She can't bring herself to do it. Booker and Isaiah, Jesy's husband, are so mild-mannered. They never fight. Rosalie and Javier's "fights" are really just them butting heads about money, with Javier trying to convince Rosalie that they don't need the most expensive vacations and cars on the market.

Five-thirty comes and goes. One by one, Tessa's friends and staff leave for the day. Tessa sits at her desk in front of her laptop, a dozen different documents about strategy pulled up. She is effectively paralyzed. She has thirty minutes until her and Owen's usual dinnertime. She should leave soon. She should have left already.

A knock sounds on her office door, startling her. "Come in," Tessa calls.

Ryan pops his head in. "I was going to order dinner. Since you're still here, do you want–"

Tessa shakes her head before he even finishes his sentence, shutting her laptop. "No thanks. I need to get home."

"Alright." Instead of heading back to his office, Ryan lingers in the doorway. "You've seemed… on edge today. Is everything okay?"

Tessa wipes her palms on her skirt and stands, trying to muster a smile. "It's just the campaign getting to me."

Ryan gives her a searching look, but then he appears to accept her answer. "Try to relax. You're supposed to be the calm one around here."

"Right." Tessa is aware she sounds anything but relaxed, as she packs up her things. "Good night."

She puts a podcast on during her drive, in an attempt to distract herself. Instead, she remembers a conversation she had with Kahaan, way back during Ryan's years in the House of Representatives. *We need to determine the tone of the conversation,* Kahaan said. *That puts us in a position of power.*

Tessa arrives home, and she is greeted by the aroma of a pasta bake in the oven. A good sign. She doesn't stop to over-analyze it, and she doesn't call out a hello to Owen. She proceeds directly to the kitchen, and finds him chopping basil. She stops in front of him. "You have to believe that there is nothing going on between Ryan and I," Tessa says, without preamble. "You are the only person I have ever loved in that way. Look at me, and you'll see — you have to see — that."

Owen does, and his expression crumples. "I do. I'm so sorry, Tessie. I'm just — I'm just afraid of losing you."

She can see what the admission costs him. Tessa sighs, her eyes filling up with tears for the first time since that morning. She steps forward, wrapping her arms around him. "You're not going to lose me."

ooooo

She puts that incident behind her, as best as she can. She doesn't have the time or energy to dwell on that unpleasant episode. Under normal circumstances, by this point in early summer, the Democratic Party should have had their nominee. The Republicans have theirs. Both Gardner and Ryan refuse to concede, clearing the path for the other to win the nomination. It is getting contentious. Both the DNC Chair and Gardner's campaign manager yelled at her over the phone just this week, saying Ryan's stubbornness was hurting the party.

"There is no way your guy wins in the general," Ernesto Ortega told her. "No way. The country just isn't where he's at on his platform. Maybe in 2032 or 2036, but not now. Not this year. Don't ruin our chances at the White House over this. It would be selfish."

Tessa relays this to Ryan. "Gardner and his people are underestimating the country," he responds. Then he asks her if she will accompany him on his campaign trail stop to Arizona tomorrow. "Matt wants to sit this one out. Grace is pretty sick, and he doesn't want to leave her alone with the kids."

"Sure," Tessa says, as easily as she can, betraying nothing of the apprehension that floods through her. She momentarily considers lying to Owen, telling him that she and Jesy are taking a spur-of-the-moment trip together. She is so appalled at herself that she's nearly breathless. Lying to her spouse? That's unconscionable.

But it would only be to save yourself from the consequences of telling the truth. Tessa refuses to engage any further with that thought.

"I'm so sorry for the short notice, but I have to fly to Arizona for the campaign tomorrow," she tells Owen over dinner, projecting a calmness she doesn't really feel. "Matt can't go because Grace is sick. I'll be back Friday evening."

He hears what she doesn't say. That *for the campaign* translates to *with the candidate.* With Ryan. Owen's brows knit together in a frown, but he just nods.

ooooo

Tessa tries not to fret when she misses a couple of Owen's texts during dinner and an evening work session with Ryan. She makes it a point to video call him when she's back in her hotel room for the night. Alone, in her pajamas, under the covers. Her mind is split in two. One half, ruminating on Ortega's accusation that Ryan — and by extension, she — are being selfish, acting against the party's best interests. One half, begging Owen to see — *I'm a good wife. I'm not cheating on you.*

ooooo

She is unpacking after her trip, listening to the latest episode of her celebrity gossip podcast, when Owen comes up to their bedroom. "Dinner's in the oven. It'll be ready in thirty minutes."

Tessa pauses her podcast. "Thanks. The food at the airport wasn't great."

"How was your trip?" Owen hands her one of her packing cubes, and Tessa unzips its contents directly into her laundry hamper.

"It was fine. Arizona is a tough crowd. And I hate these whirlwind trips where we're in and out in twenty-four hours."

She is setting her things back in the bathroom when Owen speaks again. "How was Ryan?"

Tessa freezes, and then shuts her drawer. There is definitely something off in his voice. Like he is trying too hard to sound casual, but it doesn't quite hide the hard edge of resentment. She is struck with the urge to remain in the bathroom, but she returns to the bedroom, pulling her laptop and charger out from her duffel bag. "Stressed about the campaign, but hanging in there." She chooses her words carefully.

Owen looks like he is having an equally difficult time. He shifts from foot to foot. "He didn't say anything to you? Do anything?"

Her heart plummets. This again. "No. Never. It's not like that. I told you." Exasperation mingles with desperation. *Please believe me.*

"It's not like that for *you*. He's a politician. They have a reputation. And the whole #MeToo thing, with all these sleazy guys hitting on women who work for them —"

"That's not Ryan," Tessa replies sharply. "He would never. He has never."

"Not yet, maybe. Like I said, I've seen the way he looks at you. And he invites you on these overnight trips —"

The way he says that makes her bristle. "There is nothing salacious about it. It's work. And the way he *looks* at me?" Tessa tries to be gentle, but she is so rattled that it's a struggle. "Owen, I'm so sorry, but I think you're seeing something that isn't there."

Owen blinks at her. "Are you — are you trying to gaslight me?"

His voice rises with incredulity, and Tessa's does the same. *Gaslight? What the fuck?* "No! How could you even–"

Her phone buzzes with a text, from where it's charging on the nightstand. It's probably Jesy or Rosalie checking in. She breaks off with an impatient sigh, turning to pick her phone up.

"Tessa–"

Owen's grip on her forearm stops her in place, and it's so tight that she yelps in pain. It is a sound she doesn't recognize as something that could come out of her. It is the sound of an injured animal. He lets go of her at once, raising both hands and stepping away. "I'm sorry, Tessie. I didn't mean to hurt you."

Tessa stalks over to her phone. Jesy's name is lit up on her Messages app. *Did u get home safe from phoenix??*

She types a quick reply. *Yes. Lunch tomorrow?* Tessa ignores — suppresses — how shaken she is. Her arm still throbs. Should she tell Owen not to do that again? Should she tell him that scared her? She has never read an instruction manual for this.

As soon as she sets her phone back down, Owen takes one small, tentative step toward her. "I'm sorry. I didn't mean to — I didn't mean to do that."

He looks so crestfallen, so genuinely remorseful. Tessa nods once, slowly. "It's okay."

Owen's cell phone timer goes off downstairs. Dinner is ready.

∞∞∞

Tessa has a hard time falling asleep that night, despite the long, exhausting travel day. Owen tosses and turns beside her. This time last year, she would have snuggled close to him until sleep claimed them both.

It is a strange, painful feeling, to miss Owen, even though he is right beside her.

∞∞∞

Tessa notices the bruises on her arm the following morning. She stares, unable to believe it.

When she emerges from her daze, she returns to her closet and hangs up the short-sleeved top she selected to wear today. She picks out a light-weight, long-sleeved blouse instead. She tells herself that last night was a fluke, a mistake. It won't happen again.

Chapter Nineteen

July 2024 – October 2024

It does happen again. Through the summer, there are a few more accidents, a few more instances. Always, Owen's hand closes around her wrist, her shoulder, her forearm, when she's trying to walk away from what could turn into a fight. Always, when she comes home late from work, or after Ryan calls or texts at night with campaign business.

Her work is an escape, but she is being punished for exactly that. Her work. The only way to salvage this situation is to quit and put as much distance between her and Ryan as she can. But she can't bear that. She loves her job. To leave it now would be a crushing blow, especially on the heels of this other loss; the loss of Owen's old gentleness.

She is with Owen at home. She is surrounded by people all day at work. Tessa still hasn't felt this alone since she was a girl who lived in an almost-empty house with her father. She hasn't felt this frightened since her time living and working in a war zone. Owen is fine most of the time, except when something sets him off, and those triggers are inevitable.

At least once a day, Tessa considers telling Jesy and Rosalie. Matt. Kahaan. Booker. Javier. Ryan. All of her friends — any of them — would be willing to listen. To tell her, *Tessa, it's okay, it's not your fault.* But she can't. She just can't, as definitively as she can't quit her job. They all have their own lives and families to worry about.

Besides, everyone has their hands full with the campaign. With recalibrating. Switching gears. With crafting and delivering the announcement that Ryan is suspending his presidential campaign, and will be honored to serve as Gardner's Vice President.

The choice hadn't come easily — to say nothing of the maneuvering Tessa had to do to get Ryan on Gardner's ticket. It had been a personal crisis for Ryan. The biggest, the *only,* setback of his entire career. She and Matt spent hours consoling him. "Being Gardner's VP will give you one-of-a-kind qualifications and experience," Tessa pointed out. "It'll prepare you for a successful run in 2028 or 2032."

Ryan agreed, resentfully. He is all smiles in public and with the press. In private, he chafes at playing second fiddle to Gardner. An establishment Democrat, a centrist Democrat, everything he has railed against for the last decade.

The transition from working for a presidential candidate to working for the Vice Presidential nominee is a tough one. Tessa shelves her dream of being White House Chief of Staff. She is almost as haunted by her own failure to get Ryan the nomination as she is by the changes in Owen.

Ryan makes it clear that he doesn't blame her. "We had the DNC blatantly favoring Gardner from day one. You did everything right. But without establishment backing… I got as far as I did because of you. You'll still be my Chief of Staff in January."

That helps a little bit. It is still difficult for all of them to stop being the masters of their own destiny. They take orders from Gardner's staff and the DNC on where to go to campaign, and when. They take orders on what their campaign strategy and their talking points should be. Every day becomes even busier as they hurtle toward November's general election.

So there isn't a lot of time — truly — for Tessa to sit with herself and examine the situation with Owen. She thinks of calling his doctor or his rehabilitation therapists to seek advice. To tell them about the personality changes, this irrational jealousy and paranoia, and the uncharacteristic aggression. Tessa cringes at the thought. The longer she goes without speaking about this to anyone, the more impossible it is to break that silence. Besides, it would be a betrayal to go behind Owen's back like that. It would be a gross violation of his privacy.

(And part of her is afraid of how he would react, if he knew she told them about this.)

That fear makes Tessa's skin prickle with shame. She shouldn't be afraid of Owen. She shouldn't complain about him to other people or expose his difficulties with emotional regulation. None of this is his fault. All of this is happening as a direct result of the brain injury. He isn't well. She made vows to support him in sickness and in health, and this is sickness.

Owen has recovered from the physical challenges brought on by the brain injury. Maybe in a few months, he will start to recover from these issues too. The anxiety, the insecurity, the anger. Maybe a couple of years from now, this will be nothing but a distant memory. A rough patch. Lots of marriages go through rough patches. Her closest friends happen to have pretty idyllic marriages, but that isn't the case for everyone in her extended network. She has seen marriages that have survived alcoholism, addiction, disability, infidelity, loss and grief… It can be done. She can put the same hard work, patience, and resilience that she puts into her job, into her marriage. She — *they* — will get through this.

∞∞∞∞∞

Maintaining her resolve takes a toll. Continuing to function at a high level at work takes a toll. It is early October, and Tessa has been under months of stress ever since Owen's injury in January. Ten months, now. All with a presidential campaign as a backdrop. All while not breathing a word to anybody about what is going on. All while making the best effort she can with her marriage, going on hikes and to quiet bookstores with Owen every weekend, appreciating those moments when he is the old Owen.

Tessa's body starts to break down. She is cold all the time, even when swathed in a cardigan and a scarf. Her exhaustion is bone-deep. For the first time since high school, she stops running and lifting weights. She trudges on the treadmill, gaze fixed straight ahead, on the TVs mounted to the opposite wall, playing CNN, MSNBC, Fox News.

She has to apply light makeup every morning just to look like her old self. She applies some color to her cheeks and lips, and conceals the dark shadows under her eyes. Her appetite fluctuates between completely absent and painfully ravenous. Tessa struggles with sleep every night, thanks to her worries. Owen hates the idea of moving to DC full-time, which they will have to do if they win the election and Ryan becomes Vice President.

At the same time, even he can see that her quitting isn't an option.

The amount of disability he had been awarded was paltry. Tessa inevitably ends up on her phone late at night, huddled under the covers, compulsively checking her usual rotation of news and political websites.

ooooo

The mood in the office on the fifth of October is grim. The Vice Presidential debate is in three days, and it will bring Ryan face-to-face with the Republican governor Tom Barnes. Barnes is the Republican Party's answer to Ryan. Young, charismatic, ultra-conservative. It's going to be contentious. The stakes are high, with Gardner's staff putting the pressure on. Gardner and Thompson's first debate had been considered a tie.

Tessa spends half her day reviewing Ryan's campaign speeches for the next week, and key messages for every campaign stop on the way to and from each rally. She sends the documents back to Kahaan with her changes. She spends the rest of her day helping her candidate with debate prep.

She hates to do it, she really, *really* does, but Tessa heads back into her office for a quick break at five-thirty. She grabs her cell phone out of her purse. *Honey, I'm so sorry, but I'm going to have to miss dinner tonight. All of the senior staff are working late on debate prep.*

Her heart flutters in her chest. Her stomach hurts. He's going to be mad. He's already been melancholy about how this will be their last fall in New York City. The *thanks to Ryan* is left unsaid.

Three dots flicker underneath her message for a few moments, and then vanish. Tessa stares at the screen. Finally, the dots reappear, soon followed by a text. *Okay. I'll miss you.*

Tessa exhales, wrapping her cardigan closer around herself. Maybe it will be fine. He seems fine. *I'll miss you too,* she sends.

It is past nine when they finally wrap up, after a lengthy Zoom call with Gardner's people, who want to review all of Ryan's messaging in excruciating detail. Tessa hurriedly packs up her things, back in her office, her chest pain back in full force. She checked her phone after their meeting to find her usual end-of-day check-in texts with Jesy and Rosalie — and two from Owen. *Hope everything's going okay,* at eight-thirty. At nine, *Where are you?* She fired off a quick text — *just finished, home soon, so sorry* — she's always apologizing — but there had been no answer.

She told him she would be back late. She should be fine.

Tessa forces a smile as she waves to Ryan, Kahaan, Booker, and Matt on her way out.

She drives home on autopilot, throwing repeated glances at the clock, biting back the uncharacteristic curses that come to her lips every time she hits a red light. And she hits every single fucking red light there is. Her heart hammers. Her stomach roils like she is about to be sick. Of all the times to have a panic attack. She hasn't had one like this since the night it became clear Ryan wouldn't get the Democratic nomination.

Tessa is already on the verge of tears when she arrives home. She parks. She takes a second to press her fingertips underneath her eyes and steel herself for whatever reaction Owen is going to have. Then she hurries inside.

ooooo

That one second is so pathetically inadequate to prepare for what comes next.

ooooo

She locks herself into the bedroom, and she has her phone in her hand, still — she picked it up from the ground. Jesy and Rosalie are just a text or call away. Tessa can't reach out. She can't do anything but wrap herself up under the covers and weep, the kind of wrenching, helpless sobbing she hasn't done since that last night in Iraq. She curls up into a ball and cries until she can't breathe. She ignores Owen's knocks on the door, his pleas for her to let him in, his tearful apologies. She ignores the eventual, distant sound of the front door opening and slamming shut.

She worked so hard at building a good life, a beautiful life, after losing her parents. After Iraq. She found friends, a fulfilling career, a husband who loved her. Who would be her family, to replace the one she lost.

In less than a year, it has fallen apart. She hadn't been good enough to get her candidate the Democratic nomination. She cost him his chance at the presidency. And worst of all, her marriage — her marriage has imploded. She has lost what she valued most, and it is all her own fault.

What does she have now? Without Owen, she has lost her family. Again. She can't be alone again. Maybe it had been foolish and naive of her, but she never thought this would happen. She never thought it would get this bad. She can't stop reliving it, over and over again. The fall. The blinding pain.

The tears don't stop. Sleep doesn't come. Four-thirty comes around, and then five. Tessa staggers to the bathroom. The realization that there is no way she can go to work like this — so close to the debate — almost sends her to her knees. Her eyes are swollen near shut from weeping, dark circles pronounced underneath them. Her skin is red and blotchy. There is a bruise forming.

Tessa gingerly brushes her teeth and takes a hot shower, in the futile hope that she can salvage this. She dresses in fresh clothes. It's no use. She can't go out like this. She doesn't know if she can keep it together in front of everyone.

It is already past the time she would be at the office. Tessa paces in a tight circle in the bedroom, and then calls Booker. Matt will be busy getting Alicia and Oliver off to school.

"Hey, Tess," Booker greets.

"Hi. I'm so sorry, but I have to work from home today." She tries to speak as normally as she can. Her voice is still too brittle for her liking, and she's congested, after the long hours of crying. "Matt can use the keys to my office. I'll be available by phone, Slack, and email if anyone needs anything."

"Sure." A pause. "Is everything okay?"

"I'm fine. Just — sick. I'll be there tomorrow as planned." Will she? Everything is so uncertain now. Owen hasn't come home. She has no idea where he is. She has no idea what will happen when he comes home.

Booker hesitates. "Okay. Feel better soon."

"Thanks." Tessa hangs up. She tosses her phone on the bed, gripping her hair with both hands. No texts or calls from Owen. What does she do now? What do they do now? Her mind has stuttered to a hard stop, non-functional, the way it did after she learned of Owen's injury. Then, she called for help. She can't now.

Tessa unlocks the bedroom door. She makes her way downstairs and sits at the kitchen table. She stares at the wall, numb.

A hard knock at the door jolts her out of her — not thoughts. There had been no thoughts. Tessa looks belatedly at the door. Owen. But why would he knock? Unless he forgot his keys in his haste to leave.

Another hard knock on the door. A familiar voice, muffled by the distance. "Tessa?"

Booker. He would only show up unannounced at her door if there was some sort of emergency. She stumbles as she gets to her feet, and she hurries down the hallway, wrenching open the door. "Come in — what is it? What's wrong?"

Booker stares at her, his jaw falling open, his expression one of undisguised horror. "I was worried about you. I wanted to check in. Tessa —"

There is that sick, swooping feeling again, of losing the bare modicum of control she has over a situation. Over her life. She felt exactly that last night. Tessa stutters uselessly and tries to shut the door. She isn't ready for this. Booker pushes his way in, but he moves slowly, non-threateningly. "Is Owen here?"

His tone is gentle. Tessa manages to shake her head.

"Good. Come on. I'm going to make you some tea, okay?"

Tessa follows, her movements slow and mechanical. Booker shouldn't be here when Owen gets back, but she doesn't know what to do about that right now. She is vaguely aware of Booker pulling out a chair for her at the kitchen table, getting a throw blanket from the back of the sofa, draping it around her shoulders. He doesn't need to ask where she keeps her electric kettle and her tea. He and Mari have been over here for dinner with her and Owen often enough over the years.

Booker returns with a mug of steaming chamomile tea. "Drink this. I'll be right back, all right?"

Tessa wraps her hands around the mug, letting its warmth seep into her. She hasn't eaten or drank anything since last night at the office. "Thanks," she mumbles. She sips her tea. She should be thinking about what to do when Owen gets back. She should be coming up with a plan.

Slow sip by slow sip, she empties her mug. Nothing comes to mind except the endlessly repeating, incessant thought of, is there anything, *anything,* she could have done differently last night, to prevent things from escalating the way they did? If she had said something different, done something differently, maybe it wouldn't have happened. Or maybe last night was too late. She should have made changes months ago. Instead, she changed nothing. She buried her head in the sand and expected things to get better on their own. Like an idiot.

The front door opens. Tessa looks up from her empty mug so fast that she almost pulls a muscle in her neck, already thinking about what she should say to explain Booker's presence. She recognizes the other low murmur that has joined Booker's, and dismay floods through her. This is getting so much worse. Of all people, he shouldn't be here.

Ryan stops dead upon crossing the threshold into her kitchen. Tessa rises, setting her hand down on the table to steady herself. "You should be at work. You have a meeting with the national advisory board right now."

"I'm where I need to be." Ryan doesn't take his eyes off her, even though it is clear how disturbed he is. "Tessa — what happened?"

She just looks at him. She can't form the words, because that would make it real. Last night, when it happened, she had wanted to cry out for help. Now help is here. Her secret is finally out. She is as paralyzed, as unable to speak, as she was all summer. Tears fill her eyes. She opens her mouth, and nothing comes out. Tessa shakes her head wordlessly.

Ryan approaches her, moving slowly, non-threateningly, the same way Booker did. He holds his arms out, making his intention clear. When she doesn't move, he wraps his arms around her, hugging her very gently. It is so tender, so warm. Tessa crumbles, pressing her face against his shoulder, muffling a sob. "It's going to be okay," Ryan says quietly. "It's going to be okay. I promise."

Her system floods with cold fear, despite his reassurances. Owen could come back and see this, and both of them will suffer the consequences. She steps away from him. "You need to go. You need to get back to your schedule for the day."

Ryan ignores her. He moves toward the kitchen table, pulls her chair out, and gestures to it, indicating that she should sit. This time, Tessa ignores him. "The debate is in two days."

"I will get back to my schedule for the day." Ryan speaks slowly, patiently. Normally there is an authoritative edge to his voice when he gives commands. That edge is gone now, but the expression on his face is tense. "But I need to talk to you first."

Tessa sinks down into the chair. Ryan pulls one of the other chairs close and sits in front of her, so close their knees are almost touching. She can't look him in the eye. She takes in fragments of him instead. Black suit pants and coat, matching shoes, silver-gray dress shirt and black tie.

"Tell me what's been going on."

She doesn't know where to begin. She remains silent.

That isn't true. She does know where to begin. Her throat aches, and Tessa reaches up to massage it. "The brain injury."

Ryan listens with the utmost patience to every disjointed sentence as the floodgates break, and it all comes out. Every incident that she hasn't spoken of to anybody. The only thing she holds back is the details of Owen's accusations. The specific cause of his jealousy. Ryan doesn't need to know that.

In spite of Ryan's struggles with anger management over the years, he isn't anything but quiet and calm now. The pity, the concern, the sorrow as he looks at her makes Tessa feel all of an inch tall. How did she, of all people, ever get reduced to this?

(During Ryan's tenure with New York's Fourteenth, and then as New York's junior senator, they visited crisis centers serving domestic abuse survivors. Ryan co-sponsored House Bill 4471, Kara's Law, for survivors of domestic violence. She had never thought, back then — never in a million years — that one day, she would be —)

"I know you don't want to leave." Ryan still sounds so patient. "But if you stay, this will happen again. Or something worse."

"No," Tessa says automatically. "No, I can't leave, I–"

The argument that *no, it won't happen, no, this doesn't have to happen again, no, we can change things*, or even, *no, I can deal with this, it isn't that bad*, dies in her throat. She listened to those presentations at the crisis centers. She knows the statistics about domestic violence. She knows how it escalates. *It's just a slap*, and *he'll never do it again*, giving way to more violent assaults. To choking. To *cause of death: strangulation* listed on the coroner's report.

"I can't support you staying in this situation, Tessa. None of us would. We need to know that you're safe."

Ryan remains calm and quiet. He is making an effort, for her sake. Under normal circumstances, he would be on his feet, a muscle twitching in his jaw as he ordered her to pack her things and get out.

"I made vows. In sickness and in health. And this — this is a sickness."

Her face crumples again. It hurts so badly. She knows he's right. All women know this. Should know it, at least. The first time he hits you, you leave. You don't allow a second time. But this isn't like other domestic abuse situations. Owen didn't just drink too much and lose his temper with her. This is just because of the injury. It isn't his fault.

"Yes, it is a sickness," Ryan says tersely. "But that sickness could hurt you. It could kill you. I can't let that happen."

Tessa can't speak. Ryan leans close, his voice low. "Do you trust me?"

"Yes," she whispers. She has, since the day they met in Iraq.

"I've always — I've always tried to look out for you." Ryan's voice cracks. To her astonishment, he blinks rapidly, as if he is holding back tears. "I'm trying to do that now. Let's get you out of here, and somewhere safe. Let me give you my lawyer's number."

The *yes* is on the tip of her tongue. He's right. Her mind still screams at her to stop. The pain and guilt that floods through her is even more acute than the agony of the previous night. This is abandonment. She would be abandoning Owen.

But if she says no… Ryan won't back down on this. He will call Rosalie, Jesy, and Matt. He'll have them all come here and talk sense into her. She can't withstand replaying this conversation again with the three of them.

"Okay." Her tone is so wooden she doesn't recognize it. "You need to get back to work." It is very important that Ryan gets back to work. She will never be able to forgive herself if this ends up distracting him and derailing his performance at the debate. She has cost him enough already. "You said you would get back to work."

Ryan's shoulders relax, ever so slightly. "I will. I'm going to call Rosalie. I figure it'll be easier for her to get out of work than Jesy. Is that all right?"

Tessa's stomach turns. The thought of explaining herself to Rosalie — and soon, Jesy — makes her insides roil. She has hidden so many things from her best friends this year.

"I'm going to ask Vasu to come too." Ryan steps out of the kitchen to make the call. She wraps her arms around herself. Earlier, she wanted a plan. The plan Ryan gave her is nearly as frightening as the orders she was handed as a soldier. She can't imagine packing her things and leaving her home — the home she and Owen have shared since they got married. And she has to call a divorce lawyer.

She remembers the afternoon she married Owen, in their simple backyard ceremony. It was the happiest day of her life.

I want to die, Tessa thinks, with sudden clarity. *I wish I were dead.* Being dead would be preferable to this. It is the same thought that crossed her mind, over and over again, last night.

Ryan chooses that moment to re-enter the kitchen, and he sits with her at the table. Tessa has to clear her throat before speaking. "Are you going to go back to work?"

"I will, when Rosalie and Vasu get here. There are things more important than work."

Tessa shakes her head mutely, rejecting that idea. She is halfway through her second mug of tea when the front door opens and closes, and she hears the low murmur of Booker and Vasu's voices. Booker has stayed in the front room the entire time, guarding the front door, making and taking phone calls in a hushed voice.

Vasu enters, a nondescript army green duffel bag slung over his shoulder. The duffel appears like nothing more than a nondescript weekender bag. Only their staff is aware of the wealth of medical equipment and supplies inside.

"Thank you for coming." Ryan pulls over another chair for Vasu.

Vasu is unusually pale. Tessa can't bring herself to greet him as she normally would. "You are welcome. Rosalie should be here shortly. Her car was just a few behind mine in traffic."

He sits in front of her. "May I?" he asks, with his typical careful manner. He may no longer be practicing, but for as long as she has known him, Tessa has wished that all doctors were as respectful in their demeanor. She nods.

Vasu tries to be gentle. His touch still sends agony lancing through her face. Tessa rears back, a tiny hiss of pain escaping her clenched teeth. He apologizes, his mouth turning down in utter misery. "It's all right," she manages. "I'll stay still. Try again."

He examines the left side of her face with the utmost caution, and Tessa tries not to whimper. "No facial fractures," he declares at last, pulling away.

Tessa realizes belatedly that the fingers of her right hand curled around the sleeve of Ryan's suit coat. He hadn't dislodged her, and she lets go of him. "When will it heal?" The bruises on her arms were one thing, but this is much worse. She can't go out in public like this, let alone to work in her public- and media-facing job.

Vasu hesitates. "It could take ten to fourteen days."

The front door slams so loudly that they all jump. "That will be Rosalie," Vasu announces unnecessarily.

Rosalie hurries into the kitchen. Booker or Ryan must have warned her on the phone. She still halts in her path before continuing forward. She doesn't say anything, for once. She just bends and hugs Tessa very tenderly. Tessa bites the inside of her cheek to keep herself from crying. If she starts to cry again, she won't stop.

Rosalie finally releases her, and looks at Ryan. "Stuff, lawyer, apartment," she recites.

"That's right. I can stay to make sure–"

"No," Tessa interrupts, more forcefully than she has all day. "I've kept you long enough."

"Booker and I have this under control." Rosalie gives him an encouraging nod.

Ryan doesn't move. "Call me if you need anything. Anything," he emphasizes.

"We will." Tessa stands up. "Now go. Tell everyone that I'm sorry for being absent today and pulling Booker and Rosalie off duty."

"I'm not going to do that. Don't worry about work. Don't think about work at all." Ryan rests a hand on her shoulder. His purposeful stride is slowed as he leaves the kitchen, his shoulders slumped, like he carries the weight of the world on them.

He stops at the threshold and looks back at her. Tessa summons all of her strength and gives him a resolute nod. She doesn't want him worrying about her. She doesn't want to be a distraction.

Chapter Twenty
October 2024

Ryan makes it to the living room before bracing his back against the wall and dropping his throbbing head into his hands. He wants to get into his car and search every inch of the city until he finds where Owen Shepherd is hiding.

He hasn't punched anyone in years. His hands almost tremble with how badly he needs to slam his fists into Owen's face. He needs to strike Owen until his face is bruised black and blue, until he's just as much of a mess as Tessa.

He needs a drink.

He quells that last thought. Booker comes up to him, touching him lightly on the arm. "Do you need anything?"

Ryan lets his hands fall uselessly to his sides. "No. Just stick with Tessa and Rosalie." The statistic runs a merciless loop in his mind. *The most dangerous time for a victim of domestic abuse is when she leaves the relationship.* "If Owen shows up at the house... "

"I know what to do."

Ryan rests a hand on his shoulder. "Thank you."

"They're safe with me."

Vasu emerges from the hallway. "I will return with you. Tessa was very insistent that there should be minimal disruption to our operations."

"Of course." Ryan used to tease her about it. *The world could be ending, and you would make sure that our operations kept running smoothly.* Tessa would stare back at him in that unruffled way she had. *That's right. If the world is ending, we're still serving our constituents.*

In a way, Tessa's world — the life that she built with Owen over the past fourteen years — is ending now.

ooooo

It has been over an hour of sustained tension. It would be nice to take a moment to clear his head, but he has no such luxury. Ryan turned off his phone before walking into Tessa's house. He switches it back on. Over a hundred notifications — email, calendar, news, Slack — flood the screen of his smartphone, each one demanding his attention.

Matt and Mari clearly had their hands full with trying to clear and rearrange his schedule during the unexpected time away. Ryan texts both of them. *Vasu and I are heading back to HQ now. Booker, Tessa, and Rosalie are out for the rest of the day. Booker might be accessible by phone/ email.* He accepts his new calendar invites on autopilot.

Vasu finally pulls the car up in front of campaign headquarters. Traffic in the city had been as oppressive as always. "Ready?"

Ryan shoves his phone into the pocket of his overcoat. It's time for him to pull it together. To get his head back in the game. "Yeah."

Headquarters is a mess of activity, as it has been since Gardner tapped him for VP. The perfect ecosystem of his staff was disrupted after Gardner sent over ten new staff members from his own team. Ryan was tempted to refuse them. *Is he implying that my own staff isn't up to par?* Matt and Tessa had to talk him down. *Take the offer. You don't want to get on Gardner's bad side so soon,* Tessa ordered.

Tessa keeps the chaos in perfect order when she is here. Ryan misses her as soon as he walks in. He proceeds quickly down the halls, automatically replying to the greetings that Kahaan, Mari, Andrew, and Daniel call out. He doesn't make eye contact with them. He doesn't stop to talk. They will ask about Tessa, who has never unexpectedly missed a day of work.

Ryan finds Matt in his office. His Deputy Chief of Staff has his phone tucked between his ear and shoulder, as he types rapidly on his laptop. "Yeah, we can do all three events on the fifteenth. Phoenix, Tucson, and Albuquerque. That's — what, a three-hour flight between Phoenix and Albuquerque?" In his pocket, Ryan's phone vibrates three times with new calendar invites.

Javier sits beside him, hunched over a thick report with a red pen in hand, elbows braced on the desk. His sleeves are rolled up to his elbows and his tie is undone, hair standing on end as if he has run a hand through it several times. It has clearly been a rough morning. His staff, as competent as they are, are used to having Tessa around to call the shots.

Matt catches sight of Ryan. Ryan jerks his head in the direction of his own office. "I'll call you back in fifteen." Matt hangs up the phone. Both of them rise, following Ryan to his office.

His desk is in a bad state, overflowing with speech drafts, other paperwork, and reports. Some of the overflow has landed on the two chairs in front of his desk. Ryan clears some space for Matt and Javier to sit, and he collapses onto his own seat. "Thanks for covering for me this morning."

"No problem." Matt's face is tight with strain, the lines around his eyes more pronounced than usual. "What's going on?"

He doesn't know how to answer that question. Ryan lowers his gaze to the paperwork on his desk. Yesterday's responses to potential debate questions about climate change and the war in eastern Europe. Tessa's notes are written in red pen, in her meticulous script. She wrote these notes last night before going home. It was that late night that set Owen off. "Tessa's…not well."

Javier and Matt exchange an uneasy look. "Is she all right?"

She isn't, but he understands how lucky they were. It could have been so much worse. "She will be."

"Is she taking a leave of absence?"

"Is she going to be back by the debate tomorrow?"

"I didn't ask about either. I think it'll be no to the first question, and yes to the second." It probably isn't a wise choice, but he has worked alongside Tessa for long enough to know that she won't be deterred.

"Thank God," Javier sighs. Matt studies him the way he sometimes does, like he can read everything that Ryan isn't saying as clearly as a book.

"Thank you for handling everything," Ryan repeats. "Really."

"Don't make a habit of bailing in the middle of important meetings. I might have a heart attack." Javier stands up. "I'm going to get back to it."

"I'll be here, working on this." Ryan gestures to his debate answers.

"We'll talk later," Matt says, before heading back to his own office.

The door clicks shut behind him. He really needs to make up for lost time. Ryan pulls out his phone anyway and checks his messages. One from Rosalie, ten minutes ago. *Tessa and I called your lawyer. She's meeting with Tessa after the debate. Clearing Tessa's stuff out now. She's staying with me tonight.*

Martina Lopez made sure his divorce was handled quickly, cleanly, privately, just before he announced his presidential candidacy. Ryan scribbles a note in his planner to send Martina a thank-you for accommodating Tessa so quickly. He opens up a new tab on his phone. A few minutes' search provides him with three apartment buildings in Tribeca with solid security features. The statistic creeps back into his mind. *The most dangerous time for a victim of domestic abuse is when she leaves the relationship.* He sends the links to Rosalie.

You need to focus. Ryan hears Tessa's directive as clearly as if she were standing in the doorway of her office, regarding him in that stern way she often does. She would give him an earful if he let his attention lapse on the day before the debate.

Ryan sets his phone face down on the desk and massages the back of his neck, trying to loosen some of the knots of tension there. He opens his laptop and begins his work.

∞∞∞

Matt walks into Ryan's office at nine that night, a bag of Chinese take-out in hand. The order from Queens High Pearl is substantially reduced from its usual size, as the two of them are the only ones left in the office at this hour. Normally, Matt would be at home with his family.

Matt sets a white carton and a pair of chopsticks in front of Ryan. The aroma of the beef chow fun hits him before he even opens the carton. His appetite, withered away to nothing since this morning, hits him like a truck. Ryan mutters his thanks before grabbing his chopsticks and diving in. Some sauce lands on a first draft for his speech in Tucson, and he wipes it away with his thumb.

"Did you eat at all today?" Matt asks, around a mouthful of his Szechuan shrimp with rice.

"I had a sandwich this morning." More than twelve hours ago.

They finish their meals in a matter of minutes, and Ryan clears the empty cartons away. "Sorry to keep you here so late. I'm sure you'd rather be eating Grace's cooking."

"It's fine. She wanted me to ask you to come over for dinner sometime. It would do you some good to eat something besides takeout." Matt removes his glasses, cleans the lenses, and puts them back on. "Now, what's going on? You look worse than you did in July."

It has been only four months since the worst defeat of his career. It feels like four years.

After today, July feels more like a setback than a death blow. Ryan stares down at his speech draft for a couple of moments before he can face Matt. "Tessa is filing for divorce."

Matt's expression registers shock, and then confusion. "What? What the hell?"

"Owen hit her." He can barely get the words out.

Matt's mouth opens, but speech fails him. "What?" he finally croaks. "He wouldn't. What?"

"She said that he's been different since coming back. Since the — injury."

"That was in January! How could this have been going on for so long? How did we not notice?" Matt demands. "She never seemed…"

He trails off. Ryan has been doing the same thing since the morning. Wracking his mind over every interaction he has had with Tessa over the past several months, looking for signs that something was amiss. She kept her fear and her struggles locked away, devoting herself to the campaign while her life crumbled around her.

"I know." Ryan's throat is tight, all of a sudden. "I would be lying to you if I said I didn't want her single. But not like this. Never with her in pain like this." Humiliatingly, his voice breaks, for the second time that day.

He hadn't meant to confess that, and he regrets it in the next instant. But Matt doesn't react with shock or disgust. There isn't anything about him that his best friend doesn't know. "I know. I get it, Ryan."

He can't continue. If he keeps talking, he might weep in earnest at the memory of seeing Tessa like that. He failed her. She is one of his two closest friends, his right hand, and he failed her. Tessa has been so devoted to him, and to their goals, for so long. When she suffered, he hadn't even noticed. He should have seen something. He should have commented on the long-sleeved blouses in summer. *You've seemed preoccupied lately,* he remarked to her several times over spring and summer. Tessa brushed it off. *It's the campaign.*

He should have pressed her. He should have asked her if everything was really all right. He had been ignorant, and self-absorbed in his own ambitions, all while the woman he loves was suffering.

Matt leans across the desk and grips his arm. The touch is warm and reassuring. "I get it," he repeats.

Ryan still can't talk, so Matt continues. "This is a terrible thing, but Tessa has survived terrible things before. She's strong. She'll get through this. She has all of us to help her through it."

"I failed her," Ryan whispers.

Matt's reply is gentle, and infinitely compassionate. "You didn't know. If you had known, if you'd had any idea, you would have stepped in to help her as quickly as you did today."

"Thanks." A few tears escaped his eyes. Ryan wipes at them with the sleeve of his coat, a quick, embarrassed swipe.

Chapter Twenty-One
October 2024

Rosalie kneels in front of Tessa's chair and takes her hands in hers, stroking her thumbs over Tessa's knuckles. The tenderness of the touch brings tears to her eyes. "Booker's going to stay in the front room and keep an eye on things. I'll help pack up your stuff. Does that sound okay?"

Tessa leads Rosalie upstairs, her steps slow, one hand gripping the banister tightly for support. She hadn't even made the bed this morning. That's so unlike her. Her luggage is where she left it in the closet. Rosalie helps her haul it out. She thought the next time she would use the carry-on was for flying out to the Vice Presidential debate tomorrow.

Rosalie rests a hand on her shoulder. "Where do you want to start with packing?"

"Work clothes," Tessa mumbles. "Gym clothes."

She is normally so neat with packing. She folds her clothes precisely, even her underwear. She puts everything into her packing cubes for optimal organization and usage of space.

Today, Tessa folds and rolls her clothes clumsily, emptying her shelves in the dresser and in the closet. She is moving in reverse of the way she did over a decade ago, when she and Owen moved in. Their realtor called the little townhouse a "starter home." People generally upgrade their townhouses as they get older, trading them in for a larger house in the suburbs. She and Owen never wanted to do that. They joked that they would get old in this house, and struggle up and down the stairs well into their eighties.

She never imagined she would leave.

It doesn't take them long to pack her clothes. Rosalie rubs her back as Tessa stares down at her bags. "We still have some space. Is there anything else we should grab? Your books, or anything?"

"No. We should focus on important things first." Tessa checks her phone. Nothing. No calls. No texts. "What's he going to do when he comes back and sees that my stuff is gone? That I'm gone?" Her voice breaks at the thought of Owen alone, Owen facing the realization that his worst fear has been realized. That she has left him. "He's going to be — he's going to be devastated–"

"I know it's hard, but what Owen does — what he's thinking or doing — isn't your priority anymore. You have to think about your own safety first."

There's a hard edge of anger, barely concealed, in Rosalie's voice. Tessa flinches before the realization hits. Rosalie isn't angry at her. She's angry at Owen.

"I — I probably have to tell him. Right?" Tessa wipes at her face. "I can't just leave him hanging. He'll worry about me." (He's so anxious. He worries about her even when she's a few minutes late getting home at night. She agreed to leave and she can't back out now, but it feels evil to do this to Owen.)

"Fuck him," Rosalie hisses. The words overflow with a venom that Tessa has never heard from her best friend. She shakes her head, releasing Tessa's arm. "I'm sorry. I just — ugh. My God."

She stares at the ceiling, trying to gather herself. Tessa pulls one of her notebooks from her suitcase and finds a pen. She gets that far before her hand starts shaking. There is so much she wants to say, but she can't. The note she comes up with is short and impersonal; horrible and lacking. *Please be safe. Please don't come looking for me.*

She sets the note atop the dresser. Her breathing is jagged. She knows what comes next. She just can't bear it.

Tessa twists her rings off her finger. Her engagement and wedding ring, always worn as a set. The ring Owen gave her on the night of her college graduation, over dinner at their favorite Vietnamese restaurant.

There is a pronounced tan line on her ring finger. She has almost never removed her rings, for all the years since Owen gave them to her. Her left hand feels light, feels wrong, without their weight.

Tessa bends double with grief, unable to stand up straight, unable to even breathe through her sobs. Rosalie is at her side in an instant, holding her up. "It's going to be okay," she promises. Tessa can't stop weeping, covering her face with her hands. "Not now. Not even in a few weeks or months. But it will be, I promise. You'll be with me and Ruby and Javier. We've got you."

○○○○○

Rosalie drives Tessa over to her house, Booker following in Tessa's car. She takes Tessa's phone and blocks Owen's number, ignoring her protests. "He'll worry about me if he can't reach me. And I'm worried about him hurting himself."

Rosalie keeps her eyes trained straight ahead. "You're his emergency contact, so EMTs can get in touch with you if they have to."

As soon as they get to Rosalie's, she gets Tessa set up in the spare bedroom, ignoring all of her protests. "I don't want to impose–"

Rosalie fixes her with such a glare that the rest of the sentence dies in Tessa's throat. "You're not imposing. This is what friends are for. Let us help you." Her phone vibrates, and she pulls it from her pocket. "Ryan sent over his lawyer's info. We don't want to pressure you, but we think you should call today."

They think she will reconsider her decision if she doesn't act soon. Tessa makes the call, just to assuage their nerves. Her speech is halting, and she can barely get the words out. *I would like to file for divorce from my husband.*

After that, texting Jesy shouldn't be difficult, but it is. Between every word, every line, lies the ugly truth that she and Rosalie and now Jesy can see. *I've been lying to you and Rosalie every day for the better part of a year. Every day, every time, you asked me how I was doing, how Owen was doing, I lied.*

Tessa's phone vibrates at the same time Rosalie's does, with a text from Jesy. *Told M there's been a family emergency. Coming over now.*

Jesy makes it over from Brooklyn to Forest Hills in record time, before Rosalie has even finished reheating last night's lasagna. The three of them settle down on the sofa with their plates, an unusual, heavy silence hanging over them. Tessa's chest hurts. She can tell what's coming.

Jesy is the one to speak first. "Tessa?"

"Yes?" Her stomach cramps with anxiety. She knows that they're not going to yell at her, that they're not going to hate her. Still, she is terrified.

"You know how much you mean to both of us."

She knows. She has known since they both chose her to be the godmother to their daughters — and the legal guardian, in case anything ever happened to either Javier and Rosalie, or Jesy and Isaiah. Even though Jesy has a sister of her own. Even though Isaiah and Javier have sisters. "I do." Tessa fights to keep her voice steady.

"Why didn't you ever say anything?" There is no judgment in Jesy's question. Only sorrow.

"Was there something that made you think you couldn't?" Rosalie asks tentatively.

Not for the first time, Tessa reflects on the unique dynamics of a best friendship between three people. She was the one who brought Jesy and Rosalie together. Over the years, they forged their own bond. Rosalie lived with Jesy for more than two years, before they both got married. They got pregnant at the same time, and their daughters are the same age. They commiserate with one another, exchange advice, and relate to one another in a way that Tessa can't. They both have a keen sense of work-life balance that she doesn't. All that aside, they have always been so careful to never make her feel like the odd one out.

Tessa blinks back tears again. "That wasn't it. I knew I could — I thought about it so many times — every day — but I just *couldn't*. Not because of either of you. Because it just hurt so much to say it out loud. I couldn't — I didn't know where to start. I didn't know how to say it."

(There are some things that hurt too much to talk about. Like her mother. It has been so many years since her mother died, and Tessa can't say more about it, even to Jesy and Rosalie, than *she died from cancer*. Four short words that don't come close to capturing the horror of what her mother suffered in those last several weeks.)

Jesy takes her arm, resting her head on Tessa's shoulder. Rosalie takes her hand. "It's over now," she says bracingly. "No more secrets, okay? We're here for you. Please let us be there."

ooooo

After lunch, Tessa takes a nap in the guest room, sleeping for the first time since what happened the previous night. Jesy and Rosalie are there when she wakes up, quietly working on their laptops. Her normal fear of being a burden wars with her relief that she wasn't alone when she awoke. Rosalie carefully applies makeup to conceal the bruise on her face, and Tessa gets to spend the afternoon and evening with her goddaughters after they are finished with school. The distraction of playing with Ruby and Zahra at the park is bliss, much-needed respite, after the last several days.

Guilt sets in when Javier returns from the office. The day before the debate, and she spent it not only off work, but dragging Rosalie, Booker, and Ryan away for part of it, too. "I'm so sorry," Tessa blurts, as soon as Ruby has run off to retrieve her arts and crafts project from her room to show to him. "I've been offline all day. I'm going to get back to work as soon as I can tonight."

"Don't apologize, Tessa. Jesus." Tessa flinches, but there is no hostility or irritation in Javier's demeanor — just concern, as he looks at her. "Listen. Stay with us for as long as you need. You're not alone in this, okay?"

After dinner and a bedtime story for Ruby, Tessa goes to the guest bedroom, settles at her desk, and opens her laptop. Ninety unread messages sit at the top of her email inbox. That's fine. It is easier to catch up on all the work she has missed than it is to begin to process the ending of her marriage.

Tessa works in the dark until she has caught up with half her emails. She presses her fingertips underneath her aching eyes, mindful of the injured side of her face. Nine-thirty at night.

She hasn't checked her phone in hours, not since she made the call to Martina Lopez and put their appointment in her calendar. All of her friends have texted to check in. *We miss you!! Feel better soon!!* The messages are peppered with emojis, gifs of cute dogs, and memes.

Ryan's cell rings just twice before he answers. "Hello?"

"It's me. Am I interrupting anything?"

"No. I was just about to call you. Is everything alright?"

Ryan's voice is roughened with stress. "Everything is fine." Tessa shuts her laptop and sits there in the dark. "I'm sorry for missing work today, and for derailing your schedule."

"Don't apologize for that."

The sharpness in his voice makes her eyes sting. Tessa hugs the stuffed dog Ruby gave her with her free arm. "I'll be back tomorrow morning. I'll join you and the others at the office before we head over to the airport."

"Are you sure you want to come back to work? I don't expect that of you. Matt can cover for you while you're dealing with all of this."

"I need to come back to work. I can't just… I can't just sit here with this." That will rob her of her sanity. That will kill her. "I need to work."

"All right. I thought you would want to come back by the debate."

"I wouldn't miss it. Thank you for everything today." The words are painfully inadequate. She can't find anything better, not after the day she has had.

"Of course. Tell me if there's anything else I can do. If you need help with any of Martina's fees, or with a deposit for an apartment, I can send–"

"No." Tessa's palms grow warm at the mention of the legal fees. Ryan confided more to Matt than her about his divorce, but even she knew how expensive it had been. "It's fine. We — I have savings." She and Owen have also had a frightening amount of medical bills since his injury. But she can't think of that now. She will find a way to deal with this.

"All right." Ryan's skepticism is evident, but he doesn't push her.

"I'll see you tomorrow."

"Good night," Ryan says gently. "Try and get some sleep."

"Good night." Tessa curls up in bed, staring at her phone as the display dims and switches off. Her phone's lock screen image is her and Owen, hiking at Kaaterskill Falls last autumn. She should change that. It hurts to look at him hugging her close; at her smile as she leaned against his side.

She moves slowly, as though there is a weight tied to her wrist. She saves the dog photo that Mari sent her — a Samoyed sitting in the snow — and sets it as her phone's wallpaper. The photo of her and Owen disappears.

ooooo

Getting ready for work the following morning takes longer than usual. She applies makeup until the bruising on the left side of her face is concealed by foundation and powder.

Tessa doesn't let herself dwell on the previous day. She doesn't let herself wonder about what Owen is doing and where he is, and how often he has tried to get in touch with her. She doesn't let herself miss home, *her* home, the little townhouse. She drives to campaign headquarters. From now until the inauguration in January, this is her new home.

ooooo

She sticks to Ryan and Matt, Kahaan and Booker, and Vasu and Mari, during the morning in the office — the flurry of last-minute preparations — and the flight to Texas. Their presence is a comfort. A steady, reliable constant, in the face of everything else that is going on.

They work on the plane, up until thirty minutes before landing. As if it had been mutually agreed upon, all six of them lapse into silent reflection, phones face down on their seats, laptops shut, eyes closed, or staring out the window. Tessa doesn't let herself dwell on the previous day. Instead, she remembers every one of the debates during the Democratic primaries. She remembers everything she and Kahaan had to do on the ground, at the venue, to get their candidate prepped and ready to go.

When the plane touches down, she is ready.

ooooo

The ninety-minute debate is as contentious as they expected. Ryan doesn't falter. He performs even more brilliantly than he did in the debates between the Democratic candidates. He shines. It is Ryan at his very best.

The six of them huddle together backstage, watching the debate play out on one of the television screens that UT Austin provided for that purpose. They divide their attention between metrics and the debate as it unfolds, checking the metrics reports on their phones and laptops, the images streaming to the other several TV screens in the staging area.

The debate finally comes to a close. Ryan strides back to them immediately after, stopping only to unclip his mic and hand it to an assistant with a word of thanks. "Well? How did I do?"

"Exactly what we hoped for." Kahaan's face shines with excitement,

249

as he gestures to one of the screens. "Your performance is exceptionally strong in the eighteen- to thirty-four age group — across almost all racial, religious, educational, and socioeconomic backgrounds."

Mari pauses her cell phone conversation with their polling division. "It's looking promising with independent voters, too."

They have an impromptu team meeting in Ryan's dressing room to review the stats from the polls out in the field as they come in. They linger for over an hour as they discuss the results. Matt orders pizza for the whole staff. The mood is high, and Tessa perches on one of the stools with Ryan on one side of her and Mari on the other. She knows a sensation of intense, profound gratitude. At least she still has this.

ooooo

Tessa holds tight to the memory of that joy on Friday morning. It is an effort to keep her attention on the road.

She should have asked Ryan what to expect from an appointment with a divorce lawyer. She should have Googled it, at least. She had been too wrapped up in work to do either. Will she have to disclose the details of what happened? Will she have to see Owen again during the process?

Tessa is briefly tempted to ignore the directions from her phone's Maps app. She could take a left turn instead of a right, and drive in the opposite direction of Martina Lopez's office. Only the knowledge that Rosalie is following, and will undoubtedly hunt her down and drag her to Martina's office by the hair, keeps her on track.

After all these years of working in politics, she is no stranger to spacious, elaborately decorated offices. Martina's office still gives Tessa pause. The reception area alone is larger than the average Brooklyn studio apartment, the walls are adorned with enormous watercolors that wouldn't look out of place at the Met, and a glimmering chandelier hangs from the ceiling. They only have a short wait before the receptionist escorts them back to the client consultation room. Martina greets them at the door, and the three of them settle at the polished mahogany table at the center of the room. "It's nice to meet you both, though I wish it was under different circumstances. What can I help you with, Ms. Halifax?"

"Tessa. I — I need to divorce my husband." She wipes her palms on her skirt. At least there is one thing she remembers from Ryan's divorce. "I understand that there's fault-based divorce and no-fault divorce, for irreconcilable differences or incompatibility. I'm — I'm looking for a no-fault divorce."

Rosalie's expression must have betrayed something. Martina's gaze flickers over to her, before returning to Tessa. "I understand how difficult this is for my clients. I want everyone who works with me to know that this office is a safe space to share about what happened, and why they are seeking a divorce."

Tessa takes a sip from her mug of tea. She doesn't want to say, *god,* she doesn't want to say — but Rosalie is here, and Martina must have heard it all before, anyway. "There was–" She stammers. *Physical abuse* and *domestic violence* sound so harsh. "He hit me."

Martina's expression softens. "I'm very sorry that happened to you, Tessa. It's good that you came here today. This is one of the hardest steps to take, in domestic violence cases."

"Does that mean it has to be a fault-based divorce?" Tessa catches herself picking at the skin around her cuticles, but she can't stop herself. "I don't — I don't want anything contentious."

"It doesn't have to be fault-based if you don't want that. That may be less arduous, emotionally speaking. In a fault-based divorce, you would allege in your divorce paperwork that your spouse's abuse caused your marriage's breakdown. You'll need to prove your claim of abuse by presenting evidence — such as witness testimony, telephone records, police records, or photos — in court. The judge might require you to testify or file an affidavit swearing that you've experienced spousal abuse."

Tessa shakes her head emphatically. It is a cold morning, but she has started to sweat underneath her blouse. "No. I don't want to do any of that. I don't want to drag my husband's — Owen's — name through the mud. I don't want any public attention. I want this to be as private as possible. I don't want anyone outside of my friends to know what's happened. Just like what you did for Ryan and Vanessa."

"That should be possible. Do you want to pursue a protection order from the court during the divorce proceedings? That would go into the public record."

"No, I don't," Tessa says hastily. She doesn't want that in the public records, for Owen's sake, and for hers.

"Tess," Rosalie interrupts. "Please don't think about the campaign or, I don't know, political scandal or whatever, right now. You need to think about your own safety. Owen could be unstable."

"He wouldn't hurt me." Tessa pretends she doesn't see Martina and Rosalie's pity. She turns back to Martina. "He doesn't own a gun, or anything like that."

"That's good. That's very important, in cases like these."

"I'll find an apartment with good security, and I'll change all my passwords."

"What about if Owen shows up at work?" Rosalie presses.

Tessa tries to relax her shoulders. She hates that thought, but he definitely wouldn't do that. "If he does, then I'll handle it."

She can tell that Rosalie doesn't like that answer. "Look," Tessa says, trying to placate her. "If he does anything, I'll pursue a protection order. I can do that anytime, right?"

"You can, yes." Martina regards her seriously. "Do you think Owen will contest a no-fault divorce?"

"I don't — I don't know." She really can't stop herself from picking at her skin, even though it is starting to hurt. "He won't want to lose me."

Martina hums thoughtfully. "What about any property and debt distribution? Custody of any children?"

"We only own our townhouse, which is paid off. We don't have any debt, just medical bills that are coming in. And we don't have children."

They get into the details of that, with Martina delving into questions about Owen's employment history, brain injury, and current disability status, for spousal support. Rosalie sits bolt upright in her chair. "He hit her. She shouldn't have to pay him spousal support. Temporary, permanent, nothing."

"I'm going to ask for that to be waived." Martina directs her attention back to Tessa. "What do you think?"

"I don't care. But I don't like the idea of him struggling." During her months of unceasing TBI research, Tessa became all too familiar with the stats around underemployment and unemployment, poverty, and traumatic brain injury. "I just want this to be over. I want to move on with my life and focus on my work."

"I understand. I felt the same way after my own divorce. I'll do everything I can to facilitate that process for you," Martina promises. "Let's talk about next steps."

∞∞∞

Martina gives Tessa two referral lists. One for high-security apartments, and one for therapists in New York City, DC, and Philadelphia, specializing in working with survivors of domestic abuse.

Tessa reads over both lists. She prioritizes one over the other, ignoring Rosalie and Javier's protests that she doesn't have to be in such a hurry to leave. "Just stay with us until we move to DC," Javier says. "It's safer for you to not be alone, anyway."

She brushes off their protests. "It's fine. I need to get used to — to living on my own." She hasn't ever lived alone. She went from living with her parents, then her father, to Army basic training and then the Army. After that, there were shared apartments and dorm rooms, and then living with Owen.

Javier and Rosalie make her promise to look at apartments in Forest Hills, so that she can be close enough to come over whenever she wants. October passes in a nightmarish haze of the busiest work days that Tessa has ever experienced, as the general election is just weeks, and then just days, away. She gets maybe thirty minutes of free time to herself every day after finishing up work at the office, and maybe five hours of fragmented sleep a night.

Her limited free time is no respite. Tessa moves into a little studio apartment in Forest Hills. It is such a departure from her beloved home she shared with Owen that it makes her sick. It has her things, taken from the townhouse during a second visit with Booker and Rosalie, during a morning when they knew that Owen would be out of the house at an appointment. It is a nice apartment, objectively.

She hates it. Walking through the door sets her nerves alight with a bone-deep discomfort. It's wrong. It isn't *home.* It is a reminder that she no longer has a shared home, a shared life, with Owen. Moving around that little apartment all alone makes her feel like she is a ghost. Like she is a dead woman walking.

Her personal email inbox offers no respite. There are emails from Martina, and forwarded emails from Owen's lawyer, letting them know that Owen has recently left the state and returned to Alaska. He is living with his brother. He isn't contesting the divorce, and he has waived any right to spousal support.

This is a win for you, Martina writes. *My client expresses deep regret and sorrow over the current circumstances, and a desire to reconcile, if possible,* Owen's lawyer writes. That makes Tessa put her head into her hands at her desk.

The hardest thing, the worst thing, is that she doesn't hate him. She isn't furious at him. She misses him like she misses her mother, like she misses Spencer. She worries about him every day. Every night. The only thing that keeps her from unblocking Owen on her phone and email, from reaching out to him, is the distraction that work and the campaign provide. That scares her. Because the campaign will be over in seven short days, and all that it will take is one moment of weakness for her to call Owen.

Tessa pulls out the list of domestic abuse therapists that Martina provided for her. She takes time she doesn't really have to research therapists who are cross-licensed in New York City and DC. She finds a promising lead. Taliyah Harris, based in DC. Masters degree in social work; licensed social worker. Taliyah's photo on her profile on Psychology Today reveals that she looks about the same age as Tessa herself. She has gentle dark brown eyes, and a sweet smile. Before she can second-guess herself, Tessa sends a quick inquiry email.

Chapter Twenty-Two
November 2024 – January 2025

It is two-thirty in the morning on November 5 when the election is called for the Gardner-Chao ticket.

The room explodes with shouts of joy and relief. Andrew picks up Daniel and Mari in an embrace and spins them around, all three of them laughing. Kahaan jumps up and down with delight. Matt, Javier, Booker, and Vasu surround a dazed Ryan, hugging him, clapping him on the back.

Tessa stands at the side of the ballroom and soaks up all of the joy, unable to tear her eyes away. This joy is such sweet relief after the hell on earth that the last month has been. This is the moment she wants to revisit late at night, when she is unable to find the sanctuary of a peaceful night's sleep.

Her phone vibrates, undoubtedly with texts from Jesy, Rosalie, and Grace. Mari and Javier wave her over. Tessa lifts a hand in acknowledgement and ducks out of the ballroom through a side door that won't take her anywhere near the press.

She finds the antechamber. The TV is on here as well, turned to CNN. Tessa leans against the wall and gives in to her tears. She has wept so much over the past month. She has cried every day. Every night. This is the first time she has shed tears of happiness.

Ryan would say that this is just one step closer; that his journey is far from complete. But it is a momentous step. He will gain valuable experience as the Vice President, and this will perfectly position him to run for President in 2028. He will get the Democratic Party's nomination this time, and she and the rest of their staff will get him the White House. For four years, and then four more.

"Tessa? What's wrong?"

Tessa hastily wipes at her face. Ryan stands at the threshold to the antechamber. "Nothing," she tries to assure him. "I'm just so happy." She hasn't felt more than a fleeting moment of happiness in months. She forgot what it felt like to experience joy.

They meet each other halfway, and Ryan hugs her tight. "Thank you. I couldn't have come this far without you at my back. I couldn't have done any of this without you."

It is amazing how he doesn't see that her failures prevented him from being at the top of the ticket. He's grateful to her anyway. Tessa leans into him. "Congratulations, Vice President Chao."

Someone clears their throat. Tessa backs away from Ryan so quickly that she almost stumbles. The first, irrational thought that comes to mind is that it's Owen. But it's just Matt, looking like he wishes he were anywhere else. "Sorry. You're going to need to make your statement to the press soon."

"I'll be right there." Ryan straightens his tie. Tessa follows him out of the antechamber.

∞∞∞

The relief at the campaign being over is all-encompassing, and short-lived. The White House, Gardner, and Ryan begin work on the transition immediately. Ryan names her his Chief of Staff less than an hour after the election results come in, meaning that Tessa is his point person regarding the transition of power in January.

There is also the matter of moving. Their entire staff has to uproot themselves and their families to move to DC and the surrounding suburbs. They frantically look for available houses, apartments, and townhomes, blowing up the group chat with Zillow links. Daniel, Mari, and Vasu start a shared document of the best neighborhoods, restaurants, child-care resources, schools, physicians, and veterinarians in DC. Over the years of Ryan's tenure in Congress, they have all spent chunks of time in the nation's capital, staying in short-term rentals, but that's nothing compared to living there full-time.

So even though the campaign is over, there is plenty to keep her busy, and keep thoughts of Owen at bay. It is past eleven at night, but Tessa is still ensconced in her office, working on her and Ernesto Ortega's joint proposal for how Ryan can support the President's legislative agenda during his first ninety days in office. She doesn't notice the Vice President-elect standing in the doorway of her office until he clears his throat.

Tessa jumps in her seat with an uncharacteristic yelp of fright. "Oh my god, why are you just standing there in the dark? Don't do that."

"Sorry. I didn't mean to startle you. I just wanted to come by to see why you're, you know, working in the dark."

"That's all right." Tessa lowers the lid of her laptop, giving him her full attention. "I just got in the zone, I guess, and I didn't get up to turn on the light. What can I help you with?"

"Nothing, right now. It's almost midnight. We should call it a night."

"There are a few more things I need to take care of." Tessa opens her laptop again, making it clear that he is dismissed. "You go on without me."

Ryan doesn't budge. "You know I'm not going to do that."

Tessa's fingers go still on her keyboard. She knows what's on his mind. "You don't need to worry. His brother emailed me. He's planning to stay in Alaska permanently."

"Good." Ryan winces apologetically. "But it's still late, and I don't want you walking to your car alone."

Tessa takes a deep breath, trying to conceal her unhappiness, as she gathers her things. She was fine here. She was in the zone. "Alright."

She evidently hadn't been good enough at hiding her irritation, because Ryan looks troubled. "I'm sure you're not behind on work. It can wait until tomorrow."

"I just..." Her exhaustion chooses that moment to make itself felt. Tessa sinks down into her office chair again, unable to face the thought of the drive to her apartment and the ordeal of getting ready for bed, alone. She and Owen used to get ready for bed together. For more than ten years, whenever neither of them were traveling for work, they used to floss and brush their teeth together, milling about in the bathroom and talking to one another around their toothbrushes. Sometimes Owen would pour a cup of mouthwash for her, or she would do that for him. It is all the little things that she misses most.

Ryan crosses the distance between the threshold of her office and her desk in a few quick strides. "Tess?"

"Sorry. I'm fine." Tessa sits up straight again, embarrassed by her lapse.

Ryan pulls out the chair in front of her desk and takes a seat there. "Talk to me."

He won't budge until she does. She is picking at the skin near her fingernails again, and Tessa folds her hands atop her desk, staring down at them. "I wish I could stay here all night." She can't believe she is saying this out loud, but after what happened last month, Rosalie and Jesy have been insistent that she open up to her friends more. "It's like home, a bit. I can practically feel everyone else running around, talking, even when they're not here."

It is a weird thing to say about an office, but it's true. Even when they aren't here, everyone has left their mark on the space. There are plenty of family and pet photos hung up. Rosalie's cubicle is an explosion of rose gold. Mari's and Daniel's are covered in sports memorabilia. Vasu has a couple of beautiful small statuettes of Brahma and Saraswati tucked behind his computer monitor. Andrew has his prized collection of mini potted succulents. The office space is a reflection of everyone who works here. It is truly a shared space.

Ryan's expression reflects understanding. "Yeah. I feel the same way."

"I don't-" Tessa can't make eye contact with him. "I just don't like going back to that apartment."

"I feel the same way," Ryan repeats. Tessa looks up at him, and they share a silent moment of understanding. Now they both have this in common. The cleaving of one shared life into two. Losing a life partner, a home, and everything they built together. Starting afresh.

Ryan finally breaks the silence. "It won't be for long. We'll find you somewhere better in DC." He speaks to her in the encouraging way she and Matt often speak to him, when he is in a bad mood. Under different circumstances, Tessa would find that amusing. "The change of scenery — getting out of the city — will help you."

Tessa tries to smile. "I hope so."

∞∞∞∞∞

She gets a text from Ryan at almost one in the morning, after she has returned home and gotten ready for bed. Tessa expects that it's just something random he forgot to tell her earlier. Instead, it is a link to the webpage of an organization she vaguely recognizes. Service Dogs for America.

Service dogs for PTSD, the page title reads. Ryan's text is short. *It might help to have some company at home.*

She stares at the page. Three dots appear under Ryan's text, and then disappear. They reappear again, and are soon replaced by a message. *Sorry if that's overstepping!*

It's not, Tessa texts back. *Thank you for thinking of me. Good night.*

Good night, Ryan replies. For some reason, he sends her two emojis, of a crescent moon and a star.

It is late, and she should try to get some rest. She reopens the page that Ryan sent instead.

∞∞∞∞∞

Tessa rubs her temple with her thumb as she reviews the latest version of her and Ernesto's proposal. All of this sounds reasonable. Ryan made it clear to Gardner that he wanted to have an active role in the White House. This proposal does give Ryan ample opportunity to drum up public support for Gardner's climate initiatives.

Tessa sends the document over to Ryan. She crosses over to the door that separates their offices, knocks once, and enters when Ryan calls out for her to come in. "He handed me his climate bill," Ryan says, by way of greeting. "His most unpopular initiative."

"Handed to someone who has the charisma to sell it to the nation. Think of it like that instead."

Ryan grumbles something under his breath. "Thanks for working on this for me. I'm glad I'm not being pushed into a corner and forgotten, anyway."

"What's the quote from that movie? Nobody puts Baby in a corner?"

Ryan laughs. "Yeah, but why am I Jennifer Grey?"

"It seemed appropriate." Tessa hesitates. "I have news."

"What is it?"

"The link you sent me earlier this week." She can't even remember the last time she felt excitement for anything in her personal life. She has been almost dead inside, lost in a sea of fear and pain and anxiety, for so long. "I did a lot of research into the kinds of things their dogs can help with. Companionship, of course — and providing support through flashbacks and p-panic attacks." Tessa stammers on that; it's so embarrassing to admit out loud.

"I'm glad that the link was helpful." Ryan's smile and tone are gentle, encouraging her to elaborate. Tessa approaches, taking a seat across from him at his desk.

"They have profiles of their dogs available online, and there was one dog… He just — his eyes reminded me of Spencer. I sent the staff an inquiry and filled out an application."

"Tessa, that's amazing. Have they gotten back to you yet?"

"They've scheduled a Zoom interview with me for Monday of next week. They mentioned that the dog I noticed — Leo — will be finished with his training and ready to be picked up right before New Year's." The staff also asked for three testimonial letters to accompany her application paperwork. Ryan would have written one, but he has enough on his plate already. Matt, Jesy, and Booker have already agreed to write her letters.

"Leo," Ryan muses. "A good, strong name. Do you have a picture?"

Tessa pulls up the screenshot she took of Leo's profile on her phone. "Here."

Ryan studies the picture, and then nods his approval. "He's cute. What kind of dog is that?"

"A border collie." Tessa had been struck by Leo's face — by his good-natured dog smile, paired with the empathy and alertness in his eyes. "They're known for being intelligent and loyal."

Ryan smiles at her. "The perfect fit for you, then."

"I know that you're busy. But I wanted to ask if you would be interested in coming with me to pick him up. The training center is upstate, just outside of Albany. You don't have to," Tessa adds, suddenly afraid that it's an inappropriate or boring request. "I could go alone, or I'm sure Jesy, Rosalie, and the girls would enjoy coming."

"I'll be there." Ryan adopts a mock-serious expression. "I would like to meet and interview your new Deputy Chief of Staff, after all."

ooooo

Tessa places a sticker of a small gold star on December 23, 2024, on her calendar. Her Zoom interview, and the review of her testimonial letters, went well. The match director called her just a few hours after her interview to let her know that she would be able to pick Leo up from the service dog training center before the end of the year.

For the first time in months, she has something to look forward to that isn't related to work. Her anticipation isn't marred by anxiety, the way it was when she considered the election. There is no shadow of worry, the way there is when she considers starting her new job in January. There is just excitement and relief. She won't have to be alone in her apartment at night anymore. She will be able to walk and play with Leo, like she used to with Spencer. Giving him enrichment and stimulation will help temper the compulsion to be on her phone during every moment of her time alone in her apartment.

Leo will give her a reason to find the parks in the Capitol Hill neighborhood of DC, which will be their new home, as of January 10. He will give her a reason to take breaks during the work day, so that she can take him out to stretch his legs.

More than anything else, Tessa is excited to have him live with her. She misses sharing her home with someone she loves. She misses carrying out the dozens of little acts every day of caring for someone, spending time with them, and making them happy. She will be able to do that for Leo.

Tessa leaves work early and goes shopping at the pet store before it closes. She lingers in the aisles, taking her time to pick out the most plush dog bed, and the sturdiest food and water bowls. She selects the highest-quality food and treats. She fills her cart with other essentials. Leashes and harnesses, snow boots, blankets, a raincoat, a first-aid kit, a good brush for grooming, and toys for enrichment. She stands in the empty aisle, her eyes filling with tears, as she remembers the last time she did this. Outfitting Spencer, before their deployment to Iraq.

Leo will have a longer, safer, happier life. He might be her service dog, but she will care for him, as much as he cares for her. She will give him the best of everything.

∞∞∞∞∞

At the office holiday party, her friends and staff surprise her with a gift basket full of dog treats and squeaky toys. Matt signs the card on their behalf. *For your new BFF and partner.* Tessa rests the card atop her desk, beside the framed photo of her, Jesy, Rosalie, Ruby, and Zahra. A knock sounds on her office door, and she glances up to see Ryan. "Hey," he greets, around a mouthful of cake. "Are we still on to pick Leo up tomorrow?"

"You remembered," Tessa replies, surprised. She didn't send him a calendar invite, and she is pretty sure no one on staff did either. They have to send calendar invites to remind Ryan to do anything. He's terrible at remembering his own doctors' appointments.

"Of course I did." Ryan sounds affronted. "I put it in my calendar. Look." He pulls out his phone and approaches her desk, calendar app open, to show her the proof. He has noted the event down simply as "tessa" — all lower case, of course — alongside a dog emoji.

Tessa can't hold back a tiny huff of laughter. "Sorry for doubting you. But are you sure you're not too busy?"

"No, I'm looking forward to it. And as the passenger seat driver, I'll get to pick what we listen to, right?"

"We'll see."

"I'm going to make a playlist," Ryan declares, before returning to his office.

∞∞∞∞∞

Tessa drives to the training center with Ryan in the passenger seat. One pair of Ryan's Secret Service protection detail follows them, while the other black SUV leads the way. They chat as she drives, talking about their impending move to DC. "It's going to feel wrong to not come back to the city whenever Congress isn't in session."

"Tell me about it." Ryan's ties to the city are even stronger than hers. He has lived in Queens for his entire life, barring his deployments to Iraq. "We'll come back to visit whenever we can."

"I would like that." Everyone seems to assume she wants a fresh start in DC, after her divorce — to live somewhere she never settled down with Owen. But she has thousands of wonderful memories of New York City. Alongside her friends, alongside her goddaughters, and on her own. Leaving New York is just the latest of all the losses she has weathered this year.

When they arrive, the sight of the center takes Tessa's breath away. Aside from the Secret Service vehicles and three other cars — probably belonging to the staff — they are alone in the parking lot. The grounds of the training center are even more vast than they appeared online. It looks idyllic, covered in a blanket of fresh snow, woods bordering the large fields.

She hasn't been upstate since her last hiking trip with Owen. She hasn't even thought about getting out into nature again. That experience is so inextricable from memories of Owen. Maybe, in time, she will be able to take Leo out hiking and camping instead.

Inside, the center runs on a bare-bones staff, thanks to the proximity to the holidays. Tessa is grateful for that, for Ryan's sake. She doesn't want this visit to leak to the press. The walls of the reception area are covered with framed photos of people with their service dogs at their side. A lot of the people are visibly disabled. There are men and women in wheelchairs, or using walkers or canes. There are people with missing or prosthetic limbs. Many of the people in the photographs don't have a visible disability.

They get a call from the chief handler, directing them out to the grounds. Their boots crunch on the snow as they leave the building, and light flurries have begun to fall again. The Secret Service agents follow at a distance. "How are you feeling?" Ryan asks.

"I'm–" Tessa wipes her palms on her wool coat. "I'm nervous. I'm excited. I have *butterflies*." Positive feelings are so rare for her, after this past year. She can barely recognize herself when feeling something that isn't work-related focus, stress, or pain.

"You look so happy." Ryan's comment is so quiet that she almost can't hear him over the wind.

"I'm not going to be alone anymore."

Ryan rests a hand on her shoulder briefly. He looks like he wants to say something, but he doesn't. "Ah, there they are."

Tessa turns in the direction he indicates. Leo cuts a picture-perfect silhouette in his red service dog harness as he emerges from the kennel building, the chief handler at his side. His gait is springy and lively, his expression focused but friendly. Other dogs might have been excited by the snow, but Leo keeps perfect pace with the handler.

It's Cassie, the chief handler who Tessa had spoken with during her Zoom interview. Her face breaks into a smile as she approaches. "It's so nice to meet you in person, Tessa. And here's Leo. Ready to say hi?"

"Yes," Tessa says, at once.

Leo proceeds straight to her without sparing a glance back at Cassie, or looking at Ryan and the Secret Service agents. He sits politely at her feet, looking up at her. His face breaks into the smiling expression that some dogs seem to have.

That expression melts her in the same way her goddaughters' smiles do. Tessa sinks to her knees, heedless of the snow. She removes the glove from her right hand, and offers her hand to Leo, who sniffs it. He licks her palm once, with gentle restraint. She nearly laughs at how decorous he is. "Can I pet him?"

"Of course! He's a companion as well as a service dog. Some of our dogs are more reserved by nature, but Leo likes being petted and hugged."

Tessa carefully scratches Leo behind the ear, overwhelmed with gratitude for the ability to deliver a gentle touch. She used to be hugged and held every day. Now she doesn't touch or get touched much anymore, save for her hugs with her girlfriends and goddaughters. Leo leans into her hand, enjoying her scratches. "Hi," Tessa whispers. "I'm so glad to meet you."

Maybe he picks up on the emotion in her voice. He edges closer to her, as if already trying to provide support. Tessa hugs her dog for the first time, resting her forehead against him. She takes in the softness of his fur and listens to his breathing. Leo leans into her in turn. This is everything she missed. Everything she wanted.

When they finally break apart, Cassie gives her an orientation to working with Leo, recapping the handbook she emailed earlier in the week. She hands over a folder filled with information. "I'm going to go in and prepare the rest of your adoption paperwork. I should be done in about thirty or forty minutes. Feel free to come in, or you can stay and hang out outside."

"I'd like to stay outside with him." Tessa pets Leo. "I want to give him a good walk and tire him out a little before the drive back down to the city."

"Take your time." Cassie heads inside, leaving them (and the Secret Service agents) outside with Leo.

Light snow continues to fall. Leo looks up at the sky, licking the flakes off his nose. It's an adorable sight, and Tessa realizes that she's beaming. "Do you like that, Leo?" They set out on a walk, and her dog wags his tail. "I hope his paws don't get cold," she frets. "I should have bought his boots today."

"He has boots? I hope they match his vest." Ryan frowns. "On second thought, you should get him a blue outfit. He's a Democrat, after all."

"Oh, that would be cute." Tessa looks up at him. The snowflakes are piling up on his hair and on the black wool of his overcoat. He is the future Vice President of the United States. He could be doing a dozen more important things with his time, but he's out here in Albany with her. "Thank you for coming with me today, and for — caring. And for suggesting this. I would have never thought about it on my own. I'm actually looking forward to going back to my apartment and showing Leo around."

Ryan waves that off. "Don't thank me. It's enough to see you happy."

∞∞∞∞

Leo becomes her constant companion. He comes to work with Tessa every day. He sits quietly by her feet when everything is calm. He nudges her leg, encouraging her to pet him, whenever anxiety sets in, or when her mood plummets.

He sticks by her side at night, curling up beside her on the sofa. He sleeps beside her when she goes to bed. It is incredibly comforting to not be alone; to have Leo's steady, reassuring presence within arm's reach. He wakes her by nosing against her hand whenever she has a nightmare. He snuggles up beside her when she needs comfort afterward. He readily allows himself to be hugged.

Leo helps her rediscover the outdoors. She used to spend her outdoor time exclusively with Owen, or with her goddaughters. Between work, the gym, and various restaurants and cafes with her friends, Tessa spent the rest of her time indoors. Now she walks Leo in the morning, at lunch, and in the evening, with a quick trip outside at night as well. It's so unusual for her to experience the sunrise or sunset outside, and not through her car or office window. She is always swathed in a coat and scarf, the brisk winter wind flushing her skin, but it is invigorating.

She rediscovers moments of joy with Leo, at the park. Tessa marvels at how fast he can run to catch his red ball, and how much air he clears in a vertical leap to grab a stick from midair. She snaps pictures of the look in his eyes as he runs back to her, tail wagging, stick in his mouth, and sets them as the wallpaper on her phone. Seeing Leo happy makes her happy. Fleeting but genuine sparks of joy.

He helps with her phone and Internet compulsion, too. Tessa doesn't have to look at her phone for immediate distraction whenever isn't at work. She looks at Leo instead — at the alert, upright posture of his ears, or how he's carrying his tail, or the expression in his eyes. She pets him while she is brushing her teeth.

Tessa keeps him close. When they are alone in her apartment, she keeps one hand on Leo. He anchors her to the present moment, and keeps her from slipping back into memories that only cause her pain.

∞∞∞

They move into her new apartment in DC together. Leo sits beside her during her first video appointment with her new therapist. Tessa keeps her hand on him for the whole appointment as she tries to open up, halting word by halting word. He stays beside her during every weekly appointment afterward.

Leo sits at her side silently at the presidential inauguration ceremony. Tessa watches Ryan take his oath, his head held high, his voice strong and proud. The youngest Vice President in modern history. The first Asian-American and first member of the Democratic Socialists of America to hold the office. She surreptitiously dabs at the corner of her eyes.

Ryan's gaze finds her in the crowd. She and his aunt, along with Matt, Grace, Alicia, and Oliver, are seated in the row reserved for his family. He smiles at her. Tessa can read his thoughts as easily as if he sat beside her and spoke them aloud. *Four more years.*

She returns his smile, and she knows that Ryan understands how proud of him she is. He always does.

Chapter Twenty-Three

November 2025

The week leading up to the Quadrilateral Security Dialogue is even more frantic than usual. Tessa doesn't have any work days shorter than sixteen hours. She even has to cancel her Monday therapy appointment for the first time since she started seeing Taliyah. On Monday night, she packs a duffel bag full of Leo's things, and both of them drive over to Rosalie and Javier's house. It is past Ruby's bedtime, but her goddaughter is the one who flings the door open for both of them, her expression alight with joy. "Auntie Tessa! Leo!"

"Hi, Ruby." Tessa embraces her, pressing a kiss to the top of her head. "It's late for you to be up."

Tessa gives Javier, Rosalie, and Ruby a brief orientation on caring for Leo. Ruby nods very seriously and writes each instruction down in her pink composition notebook. "We'll take great care of him."

"And we won't feed him human food and let him get fat," Javier promises. Rosalie whacks him on the arm.

Tessa tries to smile. "I know he's in great hands with all of you." She kneels, hugging Leo, who cuddles close. A stab of fear lances through her. She hasn't been apart from Leo since she got him.

Rosalie touches her on the shoulder. "Are you sure about this?"

Tessa stands, discreetly wiping her eyes. Thankfully, Javier is distracting Ruby, showing her where she can hang up Leo's leash and harness. "I'm sure. I just — I can't bear to take him on a long plane ride. Not after Spencer." Not after she sat through that long plane ride to Iraq with Spencer, and then had to come home without him. She has talked through her fears with Taliyah. Even though it is irrational, she can't shake the conviction that she could take Leo to Japan and have something terrible happen to him there, just like what happened to Spencer.

Her own unhappiness is mirrored on Rosalie's face. "Okay. How will you get through tonight, though?"

The prospect of a night without Leo is grim. "I'll handle it," Tessa says, with confidence she doesn't feel. "It'll be good practice for Japan."

∞∞∞∞

Tessa paces in her apartment after returning. She checks her phone and her packing list in an attempt to distract herself. Everything is packed and ready. She checks her work phone, email, and Slack, still pacing. Everything has been squared away for tomorrow. Matt will hold down the fort here while she and Ryan are gone.

Leo is at home with Ruby, Javier, and Rosalie, probably curled up at the foot of Ruby's bed. He's *fine*. She just saw him. All of this still takes her back almost twenty years, to the intense bereavement after losing Spencer. That empty space at her side. Tessa's heart hurts, as it still does, as it always does, when she thinks of her first dog.

Her personal cell vibrates, startling her so much that she drops it. Tessa picks it up clumsily. Ryan's name lights up her Caller ID. She misses the green "Accept Call" button the first time, and then her thumb lands on it. "Hello?"

"Hi."

Tessa navigates to her Notes app and pulls out her packing list for Ryan. He is notorious for forgetting things. She carries backups of everything he could possibly need, including charging cables for all of his devices, Chapstick, floss, mints, Ibuprofen, and antacids. "What's up?"

"Nothing. I just wanted to check on you. You mentioned you were dropping Leo off with Javier and Rosalie today. I thought it might be hard for you, considering…"

Tessa sinks down on her sofa. "Thanks." Her throat is tight. He knows her so well.

"Anytime." Ryan's voice is gentle. She never hears him like this in the office. He is so brisk there, always desperate to move the needle forward on a dozen different projects and initiatives. "Do you want to tell me about that book that you've been listening to? The Silk Roads?"

Tessa runs a hand through her hair as she attempts to calm herself. "I just finished the third chapter. This one was called The Road to the Christian East…"

∞∞∞

She and Ryan spend over an hour on the phone together. Tessa has to end the conversation in the middle of their discussion about the current situation in Syria when she notices the time. "But Tessa–" Ryan argues.

"We have an early flight to catch. A *fourteen-hour* flight. We can talk then."

"Fine," Ryan grumbles. "Good night. I hope you sleep well."

"You too. Good night." Tessa hangs up, and the smile slips from her face. She shouldn't be so rattled by the sense of warmth the impromptu phone call left her with. But she is. *I would have been just as happy if Rosalie or Jesy called me to talk,* she tells herself.

She can't fully convince herself of that. Tessa wipes her palms on the blanket lying across her lap. All of this is too reminiscent of her most recent session with Taliyah. She mentioned that she didn't mind all the late nights in the office that she and Ryan had pulled while prepping for the Quadrilateral Security Dialogue. That she actually enjoyed it, and that enjoyment left her with a horrible, twisting sense of guilt and anxiety.

Taliyah prodded that, as she always did. "Why do you feel guilty about enjoying working late with Ryan? You're doing work you love, with someone you work well with. You aren't neglecting any responsibilities to yourself or other people you love, like your friends and Leo."

Tessa stuck her hand underneath Leo to keep herself from picking at her cuticles. "B-because that's what—" It takes an effort to speak up, to not mumble. "Owen said when we would fight. That I liked working late with Ryan. That I was choosing to do it because — I enjoyed spending time with him. It wasn't true. Not in the way he meant it. Not then."

She flinched, and Taliyah watched her carefully. "It wasn't true then, in the way he meant it. What about now?"

There was so much wrong with that that she didn't even know where

269

to begin. Tessa shook her head, speechless. She finally landed on, "I can't have that kind of interest in Ryan."

"Why not?" As if Taliyah didn't know that Ryan was the Vice President of the United States and also Tessa's boss. But those reasons were further down her list.

"Not him, of all people. He was the one person Owen was — so suspicious of. The one person he didn't trust." Tessa's chest started to ache. Leo cuddled close to her, and she put an arm around him. "Right up until the end, I swore to Owen that it wasn't like that between Ryan and I. I can't — I can't have lied to him like that."

"*Was* it like that between you and Ryan at the time?"

"No," Tessa said, at once.

"Then you weren't lying to Owen."

"Still. I feel like it would be cheating on him, by having any kind of feelings for Ryan. I just *can't*."

"Tessa." There was such kindness, such infinite compassion, on Taliyah's face. "You're no longer married. It isn't cheating."

Tessa flinched again, hugging Leo. "N-no. I'm not." It has been a year since their divorce. It still feels wrong to not be married to Owen.

"You're not doing anything wrong," Taliyah emphasized. "You are no longer married, and neither is Ryan. There are other issues that could be present with the two of you having a relationship, but infidelity is not one of those issues."

Tessa tried to allow that to sink in. Taliyah was right. She was physically and emotionally faithful to Owen for the entire length of their marriage, and during their relationship prior to getting married. This desire to spend more time with Ryan has only recently become an issue.

Taliyah tilted her head to the side a little, studying Tessa. "How does Ryan make you feel?"

The question came out of the blue. Tessa replied without hesitation, which was unusual for her. "Safe," she said. "He makes me feel safe."

Now, Tessa sits and stares at the wall. She should get up and get ready for bed. She grabs her phone and navigates to her podcast app instead. She can't be alone with her thoughts right now. Especially without Leo.

∞∞∞∞∞

The flight from DC to Tokyo is fourteen hours nonstop. It has been a long time since she was on such a lengthy flight. It is inevitable that the memory of her last flight with Owen, the return from Poland, surfaces. The memory makes her queasy. Tessa forces it away, but then she remembers another intercontinental flight. To Iraq, in December 2006. Packed in with her fellow soldiers like sardines, Spencer at her feet.

Tessa leans back against her seat and makes herself take a deep breath in, to the count of eight, and a long breath out, to the count of six. She curls her hands into fists — her palms are damp — to keep from picking at her cuticles. The last thing she needs right now is to think about Owen or Spencer. She drags herself back to the present by focusing on the spaciousness and comfort of her surroundings.

Air Force Two is enormous. Ryan could sit anywhere he wants, but he sits right next to her. "What are you thinking?"

Tessa clears her throat, keeping her voice from wavering. "I'm thinking that a long flight is a lot more comfortable on this than on a C-17."

Ryan takes in their surroundings. The front segment of the plane houses a communications center, galley, ten business-class seats, and a bathroom so large that Tessa's jaw dropped when she saw it. There is a fully-enclosed stateroom in the second section, a dressing room, and a sofa that folds out into a bed. The other two sections of the plane have more seating, closets, and galleys. "You know that Air Force One has its own medical room, operating room, and doctor. There are full-sized office spaces on the plane for senior staff members — like you — too."

"Oh," Tessa says, in an undertone. "So we still have that chip on our shoulder."

A frown furrows Ryan's brow. "How could I not? I was…" He sighs. "Not cheated. I lost, fair and square. That hurts worse than if I was cheated out of the nomination."

"I know." Tessa looks out the window. They have reached their cruising altitude of 38,000 feet. "At least Gardner won, thanks to you convincing the progressives and the younger voters to not sit out the election."

"Yeah." Ryan takes a sip of his coffee and grimaces in a wordless complaint about the quality of the food and drink on Air Force Two compared to Air Force One. "I've been thinking about 2028."

"Me too." Tessa takes a sip of her tea. "This is good." She offers her cup, fragrant with the scent of Harney & Sons hot cinnamon spice, to Ryan.

"No, you keep it. The lead-up to 2024 was…challenging."

"The lead-up to 2024 was a nightmare." For more reasons than one.

"It wasn't easy," Ryan says, with unusual diplomacy. "Are you ready to be with me on another campaign?"

"Yes, in whatever capacity you want me." Her efforts as campaign manager hadn't been enough to secure him the nomination in 2024, after all.

Ryan looks at her, an unreadable expression on his face. He glances away, and the moment passes. "Then we'll finally get to upgrade to Air Force One for trips like these."

"Don't get ahead of yourself."

Ryan gives her a wry smile. "Too late."

"I will keep you in the present moment if it kills me." Tessa reaches for the binder containing their notes for the Quadrilateral Security Dialogue. "Let's do some more prep before we get to Tokyo."

ooooo

Tessa has all of two hours to decompress between landing in Tokyo and the beginning of the welcome dinner. The decor is lavish and the menu is extensive, incorporating traditional dishes and innovative fusion dishes melding all the member nations' cuisines — Australia, India, Japan, and the United States.

The dinner stretches late, despite the early start to the talks tomorrow. Tessa keeps an eye on Ryan, observing how easily he interacts with the other world leaders. His signature charm is on full display tonight. He displays no sign of weariness after the long flight, or nervousness about tomorrow's meetings. His developing rapport with these Prime Ministers is a good thing. Some of them may still be serving as leaders of their nations when Ryan takes the presidency in January 2029. *If,* Tessa reminds herself. His optimism is infectious. *If.*

She worried about jet lag, and about being away from Leo, and the troubling thoughts she has been having of late. The long hours of work on the plane and the exhaustion after the lengthy dinner sends her right to sleep. Tessa remains by Ryan's side at every discussion the following day, and the two days that follow. Vasu and Mari round out the Vice President's contingent. The long hours of research and preparation served them well. There is nothing that comes up during the discussions that throws them for a loop.

How's he doing? Matt asks, in a Slack message.

He's amazing, Tessa types back. *He's the youngest out of the group and the least experienced on the global stage, but he's the best communicator out of the four leaders. They like him, and I think they respect him now too. He's measured and reasonable and fair, even when the discussion becomes charged.*

Tessa blinks, rereading what she wrote. She backspaces all of it. *He's doing well.* She presses Send.

News on the development of the dialogue makes its way back to DC. By the end of the last day's discussion, all of their inboxes fill up with congratulatory messages from her friends, and Gardner's staff.

"The President is going to love you for this," Tessa remarks, as she and Ryan walk back to their neighboring suites after the final day's discussion wraps up. Mari and Vasu headed straight out for sightseeing in Tokyo. She is going to join them after she changes into more comfortable clothes.

Ryan grins. "More like, he's kicking himself for not coming here himself."

"He already rescheduled his knee surgery three times. It couldn't wait any longer."

Ryan steps closer to her — close enough that the Secret Service agents following them at a discreet distance won't overhear. "These are the drawbacks of being a president in your late seventies, I suppose."

"You don't have to sound so happy about it."

Ryan laughs, unfazed by her chastising. They stop in front of her door, and Tessa rests a hand on the doorknob. "I'll see you tomorrow morning. Sorry you have to miss out on tonight."

"Actually." Ryan clears his throat. "Do you want to come to tonight's dinner with me?"

The welcome dinner on their first night was a large, elaborate affair. Every one of the world leaders' staffers had been invited, as well as the leaders' families. The invite list for the farewell dinner is significantly more exclusive. "I — I don't think that would be appropriate. Besides, I haven't been included on the guest list, so the catering team wouldn't have planned for my presence tonight."

"I don't think that would be a problem. I've worked catering before. We always prepped enough extra food to cover an extra plate or two."

"This dinner is supposed to be for the leaders and their spouses, Ryan." She doesn't even want to think about how this would be spun if the press at home gets hold of it.

"I know." Ryan's face falls. "I just don't want to be the only single guy at the table. Not at this event. I thought it would make me stand out too much."

The stigma against politicians who are divorced and single is regrettable. Attitudes are significantly different for men who have been divorced and are now remarried — even on their second, third, or fourth wife. But for men and women who are divorced and single? The message is entirely different. *It's a glaring red flag,* a Fox News commentator said about Ryan during the election. *Not only did his wife divorce him after more than a decade of marriage, but he still doesn't have any serious partners. You have to wonder, why are women staying away from this guy?* The conversation devolved further from there, veering into baseless speculation about Ryan's "personality flaws," coupled with "analysis" of why Vanessa sought a divorce from him.

Tessa sighs. "Fine. Okay. I get it."

Ryan perks up. "So you'll come with me?"

"Yes." Tessa mentally evaluates the outfits she brought with her. She always brings a nice dress when she travels, in case of any unexpected dinners with potential campaign donors. It's not an evening gown, but it will do. "I'll text Vasu and Mari."

"You're a lifesaver."

Tessa waves a hand at him in dismissal. "Go away. I need to get ready."

∞∞∞

Tessa is in the last few minutes of double-checking her outfit, hair, and makeup, when panic slams into her like a wave crashing over the shore. Nausea makes her stomach twist, and she doubles over. She can't breathe. Tessa places her hands flat on the dressing table, forcing herself to inhale. She needs Leo, but isn't here.

Who are you trying to dress up for? Who are you trying to impress? Are you trying to get his attention?

How could she? How could she step into a role, even for a night, as Ryan's wife? It is a betrayal of Owen. Tessa blindly reaches for her hairbrush. She curls her fingers around the handle, holding it in a white-knuckled grip, and begins to tap the bristles against the dresser. She thinks of Leo. The look in his eyes. His expression when he gazes up at her. The way he leans against her when she pets him.

Taliyah's voice sounds in her head, a compassionately spoken but firm reminder. *You're no longer married, Tessa.*

The voice of reason sinks in. Tessa manages to draw in an inhale to the count of four.

ooooo

She is so on edge as she and Ryan arrive that she barely even takes in the elegance of the private dining room. The indoor Zen garden adjacent to the room, the graceful flower arrangements as table centerpieces, the silk prints hung on the wall.

The Prime Ministers of Japan, India, and Australia are too well-mannered to comment on the fact that she is definitely not Ryan's wife. Their wives notice that the Prime Ministers greet her with some familiarity, referencing her presence at their meetings. They are just as diplomatic.

She is seated at Ryan's right side. They handle the conversation at dinner as adeptly as they navigated the previous days' meetings. Sometimes they both converse with a couple. Sometimes Tessa talks to a few people on her own, and sometimes Ryan gets drawn into his own conversations. Ryan engages with the Prime Ministers' spouses with as much courtesy, respect, and genuine interest he showed to the other heads of state. Tessa forcefully reminds herself not to be intimidated by her company. She discusses a safe topic with the Japanese, Indian, and Australian Prime Ministers — sports.

She had worried about not fitting in with the spouses present. The various cultural differences didn't faze her. People always have common ground. She was more concerned that she is at least a decade younger than the other women, and she doesn't have children. To say nothing of the fact that she is Ryan's Chief of Staff, not his wife.

To her surprise, Tessa manages. She relies on the lessons she learned as a twenty-year-old student in her first political internship. She listens more than she talks. She keeps her body language open and polite. She asks the right questions to convey her interest and understanding.

Everyone is so gracious, devoted to being good company. It is still a relief when they finally bid farewell and exchange wishes for safe travels to their respective home countries. Ryan checks his watch as they depart the dining room. "It's not too late. Do you want to go to the garden?"

He always gets restless after sitting for long periods of time. "Sure."

She, Ryan, Vasu, and Mari would take their breaks during the day's discussions out here. This is the first time Tessa has been to the garden after dark. The garden is even more serene now, bathed in the glow of the full moon and the hanging lanterns. The light from both are reflected in the large koi pond. They walk over the bridges and along the paths, under the shelter of Japanese maple, cherry blossom, and pine trees, along with precisely manicured shrubs and ferns. Tessa catches the scent of pine every time she breathes in. A couple of Secret Service agents fan out around them, as quiet and unobtrusive as ever.

"So? How was it?"

"It was all right. Not as bad as I worried."

"I knew you would be a natural."

They walk in silence. For some reason, Tessa thinks of Vanessa. She often talked about incorporating other cultural influences into her interior design. She would have loved those flower arrangements inside, and the refinement of this garden.

If things had worked out differently, Vanessa would have been the one sitting at Ryan's side tonight, while Tessa enjoyed Tokyo with Vasu and Mari. Vanessa would be the one walking with him right now.

Tessa shies away from the thought. The vehemence of her reaction — the possessive, jealous distaste for the mental image of Vanessa beside Ryan at the dinner, or walking arm-in-arm with him here — takes her by surprise. She had never been jealous of Vanessa in years past, when she had still been married to Ryan. She never envied Vanessa anything besides her beauty.

Tessa tentatively attempts replacing Vanessa with someone else. Some nameless, faceless other woman, sitting beside Ryan at a state dinner a year from now, resting her hand on his arm as they talk. She bristles just like she did before. The thought of someone else with Ryan makes her want to shove something hard, with both hands.

It is awful of her to want this, but she doesn't want anyone else to take the place she has now. Not her spot as Ryan's Chief of Staff, one of his best friends and most trusted confidants. She is irreplaceable there. But she doesn't want to lose this place, at his side after the work day is done. This place — that isn't even hers. That can't ever be hers, for so many reasons.

This is a mess. How could this have happened, after all these years? How could things have changed so much in a matter of twelve months? Her conversation with Taliyah replays in her head, answering her question. *He makes me feel safe.*

"What's on your mind?"

The question jolts her out of her reverie. Tessa looks up at Ryan, startled. "You look upset," he says, by way of explanation.

"Oh, it's — it's nothing." They come to a stop in front of another koi pond. Tessa draws her wrap closer over her shoulders. "I'm just not looking forward to the long flight back."

"Hmm." Ryan sounds unconvinced. He lets it pass, which is unlike him.

Tessa stares at the moonlight rippling on the surface of the pond. She shifts from foot to foot, slightly off balance in her high heels. She should just be quiet. For some reason, she speaks up anyway. "This has been nice."

"Tonight?" Ryan is standing close enough beside her that her shoulder brushes his upper arm.

"This whole trip. Working together to prepare for it, and watching you at work. You were incredible. And tonight, yes."

Normally, Ryan would tease her about being called incredible. He would draw himself up to his full height, run a hand through his hair, and preen like a peacock. He displays unusual self-restraint. "We were a good team, for all of it. From the early stages of prep, when we were just figuring out what the goals of this summit were, to tonight. I couldn't have done it without you."

He speaks to her as gently as he did on the phone, the night before they came to Tokyo. She has only heard him like this a couple of times before, in the years since they returned from Iraq. It soothes her as much as it always has.

"I was happy to–" Tessa breaks off. It is a strange sensation, to feel that she has somehow brought herself to a pivotal moment. She didn't wake up today with that intention. She didn't even enter the garden with that intention. Yet, here she is.

She should let the moment pass. She should go home, and go back to her therapist, and talk about all of the reasons why she should let this go. Developing feelings for someone after a divorce is one thing, but this situation — this situation is a thousand times more loaded than that.

For some reason, her usual caution doesn't set in. For the first time in her life, her gut instinct warns her against silence. It makes her speak out. "I've always been happy to be there with you, Ryan."

These are some of the truest words she has ever spoken. Nostalgia wraps itself around her like a blanket, and Tessa is transported seventeen years back in time. To the Maple Rose with Ryan on one side of her and Jesy on the other, laughing with their friends. To their study spots in Butler Library. To the subway, making their way to their endless internship and volunteer shifts. To all the campaign events across New York City and New York State. To all the campaign buses and all the red-eye flights. To the drive to pick up Leo, and the chaos of moving to DC. To the long days and late nights at this office and all the ones that have preceded it.

Ryan moves, and Tessa almost jumps away from him. "Sorry," he says, in a rush. "Sorry."

"It's fine." She takes a moment to settle herself, to calm her fight-or-flight response. She remains still.

Ryan rests a hand on her back, right between her shoulder blades. It is a gentle touch. Respectful, almost hesitant. "I've always been…" Ryan, who always knows the right thing to say, no matter what, no matter when, even in the most harrowing of situations, seems to be struggling to find words. "I've always been happy to be with *you*."

Realization sinks in. Even she can't pass this kind of lingering touch off as platonic affection. Her first reaction to this development should be horror or dismay or guilt. It isn't. It is disbelief and awe and, unbelievably, tentative hope.

She doesn't look at him yet. He doesn't move his hand from her back. Tessa summons her courage, and looks him in the eye.

She has seen a thousand expressions on Ryan over the years. She can read every single one with a single glance. She knows his different frowns, from faintly concerned to thoughtful to truly burdened with worry. She recognizes his different smiles, from the camera-ready one, to the smug one, the self-satisfied smirk, or the mischievous smile that comes out around their friends. Or that smaller, softer one that, now that Tessa thinks of it, seems reserved for her.

This is one expression that is new to her. This kind of vulnerability, mixed with tentative hope. Ryan hasn't looked like this at any of the election nights they have weathered together.

"Tessa," Ryan says. "Can I kiss you?"

She should say no. This is a terrible idea. The Secret Service agents are nearby. Ryan is her boss. The last thing a future president needs is a sex scandal. She has always been Ryan's voice of reason. (She has always tried to be, at least.) She should say no.

Tessa steps forward and curls a hand around the nape of Ryan's neck. She draws him closer, kissing him on the lips. It isn't strange, kissing someone she has loved as a best friend for so long. Ryan gently kisses her back, resting his hands on her waist.

She has known more than her share of brutality and agony and heartbreak. Losing her mother, her relationship with her father, losing Spencer. Everything she saw in the war and everything she did. The nightmarish pain following her burn injury. The terrible PTSD from Iraq, and that last firefight. Owen. A thousand times, Owen. Her life has been full of shattered, jagged edges.

Ryan kisses her, and Tessa knows softness and warmth, care and safety and trust. She makes a sound, involuntary, unconscious, almost a sob. Ryan pulls back at once. "Are you all right?"

Tessa manages to nod. She can't find the words, so she kisses Ryan again, cupping his face in both of her hands, drawing him close to her. Ryan places one hand between her shoulder blades, the other at the small of her back. He returns her kiss with such thoroughness and attentiveness, and Tessa clings to him. They trade kisses, nuzzling their noses against one another's, pulling each other closer. Ryan's hands slide down to rest on her waist, her hips, the small of her back. She runs her fingers through his hair, caressing his shoulders and his neck. With every kiss, her mind is wiped clear of fear and pain and sorrow. It is astonishing how right this feels. Ryan has been an integral part of her life for so long. A backbone, a constant, her North Star.

She fought this so hard, but now, she doesn't want to stop. There is equal desperation and eagerness in the way Ryan kisses her, holding her tight to him. It is as though now he has her in his arms, he can't bear to let her go.

Reason finally comes creeping back in, and her hands go still on Ryan's shoulders. Tessa breaks their kiss, breathing hard. Ryan doesn't release his hold on her, and he searches her face. "What are you thinking?" There is that vulnerability, again. She hasn't seen him like this since Iraq. He looks almost afraid.

Tessa places her hand on his chest, over his heart. She can't bring herself to look around the gardens for the Secret Service. "This is a problem."

Ryan rests his hand over hers, holding it in his own. "Is it?"

"I work for you." The obvious solution is that she takes a different job, but the thought is anathema. "I don't want to leave. Not now. Not before I can finally see you win the Presidency."

"Of course not." Ryan rubs his thumb over the back of her hand, trying to soothe her. "I don't want that either."

"Then what?"

"I don't know." Ryan's resolve doesn't waver. "We can think about it later."

Normally, she would never take that for an answer. Ryan offers her his arm. "It's been a long day. Do you want to head inside?"

It is late enough that there should be very few other people around, so Tessa takes it. They return inside and take the elevator up to their neighboring suites in silence. Two Secret Service agents ride with them. This is the most embarrassing experience she has ever had. Of course the agents sign nondisclosure agreements, but still. They know something about her that she would rather nobody know, save for her best friends.

Tessa's stomach tightens with nerves as soon as they approach her room. She hasn't had such a momentous night since–

She breaks off from that train of thought. She doesn't want to revisit that memory. Not tonight. Not after what just happened.

She would benefit from Leo's calming presence. She misses him so much that she could cry from it. Her steps must falter, because Ryan slows his pace to match hers. "If you want, you can stay with me tonight," he murmurs. "Just to sleep."

She should say no. She should be brave and strong, and cope with whatever difficulties this night will bring on her own.

"Yes," Tessa replies, against her better judgment. It is reckless, but she has already done so many things she shouldn't have tonight. Being this far from home and without the typical media circus contributes to this sense of freedom. They will be back in DC within the next forty-eight hours. Once there, they will have to act accordingly.

One of the agents does a safety check on Ryan's suite, making sure the space is free of any threats. Both of them wait outside with another agent. Ryan has been receiving Secret Service protection for a year, since he became the Vice President-elect. Tessa still isn't used to their presence, but unsurprisingly, Ryan has struck up a great rapport with every one of his protection detail.

"Clear," the agent reports, emerging from the suite. He echoes the report into his radio and nods at Ryan and Tessa, the picture of professionalism. "Good night, Mr. Vice President, Ms. Halifax."

"Thank you, Agent Decker," Ryan replies easily, as if this isn't awkward at all. "Good night."

They enter Ryan's suite, and he locks the door behind them. His suite is even larger and more sumptuously decorated than hers. Tessa steps out of her heels, following Ryan from the sitting room into the bedroom, passing the small study on the way. She should feel out of place, coming here with Ryan. She should feel nervous. She hasn't done anything like this since her first time going to Owen's apartment. But this feels just as natural as attending the dinner with Ryan, and kissing him in the garden.

Ryan removes his suit coat, throwing it over the dresser. "Hold on. I'll get you something to change into."

He has only been here for a few days, but his entire suite looks like a hurricane swept through it — which is how almost all offices, meeting rooms, and living spaces look, after more than a few hours' exposure to

Ryan Chao. Books, binders, notebooks, and charging cables are scattered all over the coffee table in the sitting room, the desk in the study, and the dresser in the bedroom. Discarded ties and dress shirts lie on the sofa. Bafflingly, there is a sole dress shoe in the middle of the floor, its partner nowhere to be seen.

Tessa leans against the wall, torn between amusement and the desire to shake her head in disapproval. "It's going to take you a while to pack all this up."

"Oh, this is nothing. I can get it cleaned up in ten minutes or less." Ryan ceases his rummaging in his dresser. He returns to her, a pair of men's gym shorts and a dark blue t-shirt in hand. "Here you go. There are extra toiletries in the second bathroom."

Tessa falters, and then takes the clothing, holding it to her chest. She used to sleep in Owen's t-shirts. Over the last year, it has been a painful adjustment to sleep in women's pajama sets. One of a thousand painful adjustments she has had to make. "Thank you."

Owen would loathe this. He would be furious, disappointed, vindicated. *Him, of all people? It had to be him?* Or, *I knew it,* punctuated by an angry stab of his finger. *I fucking knew it.*

She and Taliyah have talked about these appearances that Owen makes in her mind, and how to address them. Tessa remembers that, as she retreats to the bathroom and gets ready for bed. She faces her reflection in the mirror, and she can see Owen's reflection there too. Shoulders tense, jaw clenched, one hand balled into a fist.

The memory of his anger has a physical impact on her. Tessa imagines Leo at her side, and continues to face the mirror. *I never lied to Owen,* she reminds herself. *I never dishonored my marriage. It was never like that with Ryan and I, until now. Until this past year.*

The tension seeps from her shoulders, allowing her to take a deep, calming breath.

Ryan is already in bed when she returns. He sits leaning against the headboard, wearing a matching t-shirt, scrolling on his phone. He sets it down, and Tessa sees he was surfing the NYC subreddit. "I can sleep on the couch, if you want."

"No, that's fine." Tessa tentatively joins him in bed, the stiffness in the way she pulls back the covers reminding her that she hasn't done this in more than a year. Not since her last night with Owen. She never thought she would get into bed with another man ever again. Even to sleep. She knew that other women in her situation moved on. That they were capable of finding joy and love again. That was fine, even wonderful, for them. She still never imagined that would be her.

Tessa gestures to Ryan's phone in an attempt to distract herself. "Homesick?"

"Always. But I checked a couple of others too. India, Nova Scotia, Brazil."

"I don't think any other world leader spends as much time lurking on Reddit as you do."

"What can I say? I like to hear directly from the people. I keep my finger on the pulse of what's happening." Ryan brandishes his scrolling thumb at her. Tessa can't help but laugh, leaning away from him.

"Besides, you'd be surprised." He sets his phone down on the nightstand. "I saw a few others on Reddit during a break at the last NATO summit."

Tessa readjusts her pillows, settling on her back. "Can you get the light too?"

"What, so we're not going to stay up all night talking?"

"Only during election season."

Ryan switches off the lamp, plunging them into darkness. They remain quiet. The joke hit too close to home. There are things they need to talk about, but she can't bring herself to have that conversation. She isn't ready. She hasn't been thinking with her usual clarity tonight. She has been too emotional. Too reckless.

"Tess." Ryan holds his arm out to her.

They are already in bed together, already crossing almost every line there is, so Tessa moves close to him. She nestles against Ryan's chest, letting him wrap an arm around her, stroking the hair at her temples with the lightest touch. She can hear his heart beating. She closes her eyes, immersed in a sensation of safety and ease. The riot inside her ceases, for the first time since they pulled apart from their kiss in the garden.

The smart thing would be to go back to DC tomorrow and never do this again. They have three years of Ryan's vice presidency left, and hopefully eight years of his presidency ahead. They can't take the risk of any scandal getting in the way of that, and compromising everything they have worked toward since 2009.

That would mean she won't get this again.

Maybe that is for the best. Maybe she can find love again, in someone who isn't Ryan. Owen would find that easier to accept. Her own conscience would rest easier with that.

It would be impossible. She doesn't truly want anything besides this. She could try to go back to the way things were — but how could she? She has made herself withstand a dozen traumas and horrors, but she doesn't want to forget this.

"We're in trouble," she whispers, her voice muffled by Ryan's shirt.

"Yeah." Ryan sounds undaunted. "It's not new to me."

Chapter Twenty-Four

November 2025

Ryan Chao wakes with a start, gasping for breath. It isn't unusual for him. More than twenty years have passed since his first deployment to Iraq, but he still has nightmares of firefights, and the aftermath of suicide bombings.

Working in American politics doesn't help. He spoke with first responders to the Uvalde school shooting, asking them to describe everything they were able. With their permission, he put every painful detail of their stories into an address to Congress pleading for Second Amendment reform. The plea for reform went nowhere. Now the images of the firefights in Iraq — the remembered terror — are interposed with images of high schools and elementary schools in America.

Ryan reaches for Tessa. He finds nothing but empty space.

Her half of the bed is neatly made, and there is a note resting atop the covers. Ryan grabs it. The digital clock at the bedside table tells him it is eight in the morning. Air Force Two is scheduled to leave in less than an hour.

It's seven in the morning — sleeping in, by Tessa's standards — *and I don't want to take the chance of running into anyone going back to my room. Thank you for keeping me company last night.*

The note is written in Tessa's usual perfect script. Ryan stares at the blank space on the rest of the page. He turns the paper over, in case she added anything there. There is nothing.

He goes weeks, sometimes months, without thinking about Vanessa. That is a trigger for guilt in itself. She gave him more than a decade of her life, and she only occasionally crosses his mind. It is always small, unexpected things. *Vanessa would have appreciated the decor at this gala. Sometimes, Vanessa would have hated the decor at this gala. Vanessa wouldn't have liked this pasta — she thought Alfredo sauce was too rich.* Or, *Oh, I'm meeting Pedro Pascal. Vanessa loved him in Narcos.*

Vanessa always signed her notes with *xx. Going to brunch with the girls. I'll see you this afternoon, xx.*

(When they first started dating, Ryan had no idea what that meant. He asked Matt. "Two kisses," Matt said, and then gave him a nonplussed look. "You're such an idiot.")

Tessa writes the same way she texts. Formally, with proper grammar, without so much as a single emoji or an *xx* to be seen. All their friends tease her for it. He used to tease her for it too, back in college. *Weirdo,* he called her, and Tessa balled up her napkin and threw it at him.

He found it endearing, even back then. Ryan isn't sure why he does it — Tessa's handwriting, in the form of various annotations, are all over his own notebooks and binders, after all. He folds up the note and sticks it in the pocket of his gym shorts anyway. He should really get out of bed, get dressed, and pack. He sinks back into bed instead and presses the heels of his palms to his eyes.

The note betrayed no sense of unease. If Tessa was really rattled, she would have left without taking the time to write that. There is nothing to indicate that she regrets last night, but that doesn't mean much. She can be inscrutable sometimes, even to him. Even to Rosalie and Jesy, who share a special bond with her.

His phone vibrates on the nightstand, and Ryan reaches for it. Between Slack, email, news alerts, and texts, he has notifications in the triple digits. The latest is from Tessa. He scrambles to open it, and almost drops his phone.

Wake up, if you haven't already. You don't want to delay takeoff again.

Ryan groans at the memory of what happened when Fox News learned about his last delayed takeoff. He gets up, gets ready, and begins packing up his things. He should focus on the work he needs to do on the flight, and the debrief that he has scheduled with the President later this week. He keeps coming back to Tessa instead. It felt so right to have her with him last night. Is that what things could have been like, for all these years?

Ryan stops himself. That way madness lies. His aunt always used to tell him to look forward, not back. So he looks forward. He imagines coming here as President someday, in the not too distant future, with Tessa.

Tessa's admonition on the plane drifts back to him. *Don't get ahead of yourself.* Apprehension curls in the pit of his stomach. No matter what she said or felt last night, there is a real chance that she sees things differently in the cold light of day. She is rational to a fault. That whole encounter in the gardens had been borderline out of character for her.

He has his work cut out for him, trying to act normal when he meets up with Tessa, Vasu, and Mari at the elevators. Vasu and Mari greet him enthusiastically, and Ryan doesn't have to fake a smile for them. "How was your sightseeing last night? Sorry I stole Tessa."

The four of them chat on the way to the airfield. "We're going to put on The Expanse for our work session," Mari points toward the back section of Air Force Two as they board the plane. "You're welcome to come hang out."

"I'll stick around up here for now." Tessa settles into a seat.

Ryan hesitates, and takes the seat next to her. "I'll join you guys in a bit."

Tessa opens up her laptop, pulling up her email and Slack. There is nothing unusual about that. She does more work in one morning than most people manage all day. Her focus is easily slipped on and iron-clad, nearly impossible to break. He has always envied that. Ryan tries to follow her lead. After an hour reading the news while procrastinating on getting started with his work for the day, he finally draws up the strength to wade through his email.

He is wrapped up in a Google Doc, writing down a list of bullet points he wants to address in his speech in Ghana next month, when he notices that Tessa has finally stopped typing. He pauses his own work. "What's up?"

"We should talk." Tessa's voice is barely audible over the hum of the engines. "Not now. Not here. Just — we need to find the time, after we get back."

"Right." It is actually quite tricky to get privacy, in his position. Not only is the Secret Service always around, but Booker and Javier have gotten him more than a little paranoid about bugs. Surveillance bugs, not the insects — although Vasu gave him an ominous warning about tropical insects as soon as he heard about the impending trip to Ghana.

His shoulders are stiff with tension, and not just from the several days of meetings and the short hours of sleep. *We should talk.* The last time he heard that, Vanessa told him she was filing for divorce.

Ryan glances at Tessa, and she returns his gaze. There is silent reassurance there, a softness in her beautiful doe-colored eyes, rather than the guarded, professional look she almost always has. He nods once. "Okay."

Tessa resumes working, and Ryan follows her example.

∞∞∞

Being patient isn't his strong point, but Ryan tries his best. He focuses on catching up with everything he has missed in DC and around the country. Tessa does the same. They get back to their fourteen-hour work days. Before he knows it, a week has gone by.

Days are bearable, thanks to the distraction provided by work. Nights are not. Ryan gets even less sleep than he normally does. He runs laps at midnight, around the huge backyard at Number One Observatory Circle. (His backyard. A nine-thousand square foot house, for one man who lives alone. It is phenomenally wasteful.) He lifts weights in his home gym at one in the morning. He paces in front of the fireplace with his phone on the other side of the room, so he can't text or call Tessa. When he finally settles into bed, his arms ache with the lack of her.

He has been "unbalanced" — as Matt so kindly puts it — about Tessa before. After he found out she was dating Owen. After his divorce. After he lost the nomination to Gardner. After everything that happened with Owen, just a year ago. It was never like this. That longing for her had been the frustrated, futile hope devoted to something impossible. This is entirely different.

∞∞∞

"Are you going to ask Tess to meet up with you?"

They sit at the breakfast bar in Matt and Grace's kitchen, the remnants of the bagel breakfast that Ryan bought for the family scattered around them. Grace and Alicia have just headed out shopping for Alicia's Winter

288

Formal dress. Oliver lies sprawled out on the living room floor with the dog, reading The Hobbit.

"I'm going to let her decide when she wants to." Ryan takes a sip of his coffee. Matt winces. "What?"

"Nothing. I just haven't seen you look so down in a while."

"I thought it would be best. She's the one with more… baggage to resolve. It takes time. I'm not going to rush her."

"It's good that you're giving her the time she needs." Matt gives him a sidelong look. "I'm proud of you, man. I know that it must be hard for you to wait, considering everything."

If it was anyone else, he would brush it off. *It's fine.* But Matt has been with him longer than anyone else. Since they were in middle school, lab partners in their chemistry class. Just kids, just a little bit older than Oliver is now. "It is hard." Ryan cups his hands around his mug. "I had it all, everything I wanted with her, for one night."

Matt sums up his emptiness concisely. "Now you know exactly what you're missing."

∞∞∞∞∞

The following week, Ryan receives an invite to Javier and Rosalie's Friendsgiving dinner. Everyone has taken turns hosting over the years, and they all take the responsibility seriously. Matt and Grace offer a traditional Chinese feast. Vasu and his wife prepare tandoori chicken and fish, while Kahaan supplies the sides of samosas, naan, aloo gobi, and palak paneer. Booker and Mari cook soul food to die for. Tessa and Owen put an Alaskan spin on their menu, in a nod to Owen's home state. Rosalie and Javier plied them with arepas, empanadas, elote, and chipotle-spiced smoked turkey. For their part, he and Vanessa always had the meal catered.

The dinner at Javier and Rosalie's is as informal and chaotic as their first Friendsgiving dinners were, so many years ago. Before politics, marriage, and kids. The party overflows from the dining room to the kitchen and living room. The kids and the dogs have taken over the backyard. Jesy had put on some music, but the music is drowned out by all the chatter.

Ryan catches snatches of conversations. Kahaan and Daniel's

boyfriend are talking about the recording equipment one would need to start up a podcast. Vasu and his wife are telling Booker and Mari about the travel plans they have just made to visit their family in Kerala. Matt and Grace share home renovation horror stories with Jesy and her husband.

Ryan's gaze finds Tessa. She leans against the kitchen island, taking it all in, listening to all the activity around her. This is her second Thanksgiving, after Owen. Last year, as could be expected, she was pale, drawn, and quiet. She tried to smile and participate in conversation, but it was clear how much of a toll the night took on her.

There is a marked improvement this year, thankfully. Her posture and expression are soft and relaxed, in contrast to how she carries herself at work. Tessa catches sight of him, and gives him a small wave.

It is a little mortifying to be caught staring at her from across the kitchen like a lovesick idiot. Ryan makes his way over to her anyway. "Hey. Want an extra jalapeno popper or two? I figure I don't really have to eat an entire dozen."

Tessa rolls her eyes affectionately, and slides her plate over to him. "Sure. Try a piece of this pumpkin arepa instead. It's Rosalie's mom's recipe."

Ryan does so. "Oh my god," he says, his mouth full.

"Right?" Tessa takes a bite of her jalapeno popper. "I love this. These family dinners. Being together with everyone like this, outside of work."

It is implicit in the way she treats all of them, but he doesn't think he has ever heard Tessa speak the words aloud. She lost her parents first, and then Owen. She has lost more family than anyone ever should. She is still surrounded by love, though. She still has family in all of their friends, and she is the godmother to Rosalie and Jesy's daughters.

"I do too." His detractors never get tired of talking about how he has no wife, no kids. *No family,* they point out gleefully. They say it as though his aunt means nothing to him. As though his friends mean nothing to him.

Javier keeps trying to get everyone's attention by waving a dish towel in the air like a cowboy swinging a lasso. "Hey!" Everyone is too wrapped up in their conversations to listen. He finally stops swinging the dish towel and then looks to Rosalie, rubbing his bicep in mock exhaustion. "A little help, here?"

Rosalie whistles like a drill sergeant, and silence falls. The conditioning from basic training is strong. Ryan has to stifle the impulse to drop to the ground and do fifty push-ups. He can tell from their grimaces that Matt, Andrew, Mari, and Tessa have the same reaction.

Mari boos her. Rosalie lifts her hands up apologetically. "Sorry, sorry! I had to get your attention somehow!"

"Now that we've all taken the edge off our hunger, we thought it would be a good time for toasts." Javier raises his glass, and a cheer goes up among their friends as everyone finds their glasses.

To Ryan's alarm, Javier raises a glass to him. "To our fearless leader, the reason why we're all gathered here in DC today."

That was unexpected, and surprisingly moving. Tessa smiles at him, and everyone echoes the well wishes.

Ryan toasts Javier and Rosalie. "To our hosts, Rosalie and Javier — and Ruby — for their warmth and hospitality. And to all of you, for walking along this path with me. It's been a long, difficult journey, but I've never felt alone in it."

They all take turns, their toasts ranging from humorous to sincere. Tessa toasts Leo, which earns a chorus of *awws* from everyone. "I know Ryan said it already, but I want to recognize all of you, as well." She looks into her glass shyly, and then back up at them. "I couldn't ask for better friends."

It is a simple statement, but Ryan sees how it makes everyone's faces shine. They value kind words from Tessa as much — or more — than they value his encouragement. He may be the Vice President, but Tessa is the true day-to-day leader of his staff. Her office door is always open to them, and she effortlessly guides them through any problems they can't solve on their own.

The party is a precious respite from the daily stresses and struggles of their work. It is such a relief to forget about deadlines, to-do list items, and priorities, and just laugh and talk with his friends. Tessa remains by his side for much of the night, and that definitely helps with his good mood. Hope stirs in him, even though he tries to avoid stoking that fire.

Javier starts up a bonfire in the backyard for the kids and the dogs, the warm orange glow visible through the glass double doors separating the kitchen from the backyard. A cold draft sweeps over the kitchen, and Ryan turns to see the kids piling inside, earnestly discussing Fortnite as they make a beeline to the dessert table.

"Javi, can you put the fire out?" Rosalie calls, as she pulls out a pie from the oven.

Javier looks over from the living room, where he is explaining the rules for a game of Avalon. Ryan gestures for him to stay put. "I'll get it."

The chill outside bites right through his sweater. No wonder the kids headed inside. Leo and Frodo, Matt and Grace's family dog, are still lying out by the fire, the picture of contentment. "You guys are going to hate me if I put this fire out," Ryan mutters. He can't bring himself to do that to them yet. He sticks his hands into his pockets, standing close to the fire, and sighs his relief at the warmth.

"It's nice, isn't it?"

Ryan turns, startled. Tessa approaches him, the breeze stirring her hair, which she left loose tonight. Leo springs to his feet and trots over to her. She smiles, bending to scratch behind his ears.

"It is. I'm starting to get why you liked to go camping so much."

He curses himself as soon as the words leave his mouth. She used to go on those camping trips with Owen. Tessa's smile wavers, but it doesn't fade. "Yeah. I taught Ruby how to build a fire the last time I came over for dinner. We made s'mores together. A little slice of the camping experience that she can do on a school night."

It is good to hear that Tessa has been able to build some new, positive memories of something that was such a big part of her life. Ryan smiles at her. "I bet she loved that."

She comes to stand next to him, her shoulder brushing his upper arm. They haven't been in such close proximity since that night in Tokyo. "We were all talking earlier about the things we're grateful for." Tessa speaks so softly that he can hardly hear her over the crackle of the flames. "Thank you for being so patient with me these past couple of weeks. I know I said that we should talk, and I haven't followed through until now."

"It's no problem." It isn't as eloquent as he would have liked to be, but it is the truth. All the agitation and the anxiety of waiting– It hadn't been easy, but Roosevelt was right. Nothing worth having comes easy.

"It's been a hard question to think through." Tessa's gaze doesn't leave the fire. The light is reflected in her eyes, and the heat brings a warm glow to her cheekbones. "I've always been driven to do what's best for you, as your friend, and as your Chief of Staff."

He can see where this is going, and he doesn't like it. Ryan remains silent, committing to let her speak.

"With that in mind, I should give you my resignation." Tessa looks up at him. He understands her meaning. If she were to resign, she wouldn't be working for him anymore. That one barrier to their relationship, at least, would be gone. "Or I should tell you that we can't allow what happened in Tokyo to happen again."

"I don't want–" Ryan breaks off. "I can't imagine you not being by my side. I've worked with you for my entire career." Tessa helped him build everything he has. She helped him develop and refine his political platform, and many of his stances. She talked through the nuances of every issue with him, from domestic to foreign policy. She helped him figure out where he stood, and how to back up his stances.

Tessa takes a steadying breath. "Then the decision is made for us. We forget what happened in Tokyo."

Ryan speaks before she even finishes her sentence. "No. I can't do that."

"Then what?" Tessa retorts.

"There's a third option."

Realization dawns on her, and her lips part slightly with shock. "I can't. I'm not going to open you up to scandal."

"It's only a scandal if we get caught." Ryan dares a glance at her. Predictably, Tessa looks appalled. "Neither of us is stupid or careless. We're more than capable of keeping this discreet. It wouldn't even be political suicide if it did come out. It would be a scandal, but not a career-ending one. Neither of us is married, after all."

Tessa huffs out a tiny, disbelieving laugh. "Well, you've thought this through."

"Yeah, I have. A hundred times over the last couple of weeks. I don't want to — I *can't* lose you."

"You're being greedy." Tessa crosses her arms over her chest and looks off to the side.

"Guilty as charged." Ryan studies the set of her mouth and her shoulders, searching for and finding her tells. "You don't really want to resign."

"Of course I don't." Tessa shrugs irritably. "You've shaped my whole career. I could go my own way, if I wanted. Emily's List or the National Organization of Women would want me, but…" Her shoulders sag. "I would hate to leave everything we've built. I would hate to leave my friends. Seeing you get elected to the Presidency without me would hurt."

Ryan dares reaching out, placing a hand on her back. Tessa doesn't pull away. "I think my option is workable. I think my option is the best option we have."

Tessa doesn't say anything, but she doesn't move away from him.

"What do you think?"

Tessa's reply is soft but resolute. "Yes."

Chapter Twenty-Five
November 2025

The rest of the party goes by fast. Tessa wants to stay by Ryan's side out by the fire, or slip into the shadowed far reaches of the backyard with him. Far from the warm lights of Javier and Rosalie's house, and the neighbors' houses. Far from the Secret Service agents patrolling the perimeter.

Ryan shows no sign of wanting to leave the fire, making her have to take on her usual role as voice of reason. "We should go in. We've been out here for way too long."

"Right." Ryan follows reluctantly.

They haven't been missed. Half their friends are embroiled in a game of Avalon. The other half are talking in front of the TV, a football game on. The only ones who took notice of her absence are Jesy and Rosalie. Only three people know about what happened in Tokyo — her best friends, and her therapist.

The party winds down, and their friends begin to leave. Almost all of them are heading out of DC and back to New York City to spend Thanksgiving with family. (All of them except for Ryan and Tessa herself. Ryan's aunt is arriving in DC on Thursday, and Tessa… Well, this was her Thanksgiving. Both Rosalie and Jesy invited her to join their extended families, in New York and New Jersey, but she hadn't wanted to intrude.)

Tessa gives Rosalie and Jesy a whispered promise when she hugs them goodbye. "We'll talk after Thanksgiving."

She and Ryan are the last to leave, Leo trotting by her side. The chill in the late November night air makes Tessa's eyes water. Two Secret Service agents wait by Ryan's car. Not his beloved old Prius, but the black Vice

Presidential SUV. "It must be nice to not have to worry about driving." Tessa fishes out her car keys from her purse.

"I actually miss it. I dream about it sometimes."

Tessa remembers the occasional trips upstate in college with their friends, and the road trips with Ryan and Matt from New York to DC for their college internships. She can't hold back a smile. "It's probably good that you're off the roads."

"What?" Ryan is the picture of indignation. "Is this about…"

"It's about the road rage incident, yes."

"It wasn't that bad. I would hardly call it an incident."

Tessa hums skeptically. "People from nearby cars were filming it. I think that qualifies as an incident."

"Whatever." Ryan's feigned nonchalance slips, and he grins. "I'm surprised it didn't come out during the election."

"Thank God it didn't." They linger in front of their cars, and the Secret Service looks nervous. They hate when Ryan lingers, which is unfortunate for them. Ryan can't say a concise goodbye to save his life. She can't blame him for it tonight, though. She doesn't want to get into her car with Leo and drive away either.

"Do you want to…" Ryan looks over her head, into the night. "Do you want to come over?"

The question isn't unexpected. This is one of dozens of hypotheticals she has dissected in her mind over and over again since Tokyo. Tessa nods. "Yes."

There is such relief in Ryan's smile. He touches her shoulder. "Drive safe. I'll let the agents know that you'll follow us."

Tessa lets Leo into the backseat and pets him to calm her nerves. Her hands are steady as she buckles herself in. Therapy has taught her how to check in with herself and be attentive to her true thoughts and feelings, not just the surface-level ones. The drive at night, the roads free of the traffic that snarls them during the day, gives her the perfect opportunity to do that.

Tessa checks for fear, which has shadowed her for so long. There is none. She marvels at its absence. Its companions, panic and dread, don't cast their shadow over her. She checks for sadness. There is the sadness that she has carried for more than a year, but it isn't at the forefront of her mind. It is manageable. The same is true for guilt.

It is a massive relief to know that she has made this amount of progress in the last month. The weekly sessions with Taliyah, and the talks with Jesy and Rosalie, have made an impact. *There's no point in denying yourself a second chance at love,* Jesy told her heatedly. *Life has been hard enough for you, especially over these past couple of years. Don't rob yourself of a good thing.*

What is your vision for your future? Taliyah asked her, when she had been nearly paralyzed with guilt during a session. *For the rest of your life, without Owen in it?*

Those questions hit like a slap. Tessa choked out a reply that focused on work and helping Ryan attain the presidency. *What about life outside of work?* Taliyah pressed.

That took more effort, to the point where she stuttered over several words. She wanted to be there for Jesy and Rosalie, and for her goddaughters. She wanted to get back to hiking again, and share that with Leo. She wanted to travel and see more of the world.

When it came, mid-sentence, the breakthrough left her speechless. She didn't envision herself on her own for the rest of her life. That was what she originally intended after Owen, but that wasn't true anymore. In her vision of her future life, she imagined Ryan there with her. At her side at family get-togethers with Rosalie and Javier, Jesy and Isaiah, Matt and Grace, watching their godchildren grow into adulthood. She imagined Ryan hiking with her and Leo, complaining about mosquitos and being paranoid about bears. She imagined traveling with Ryan, seeing all the great cities of the world.

She confessed it all to Taliyah. They sat there quietly with that realization for a while.

Tessa sighs, pressing down on the gas pedal as a traffic light turns green. It would have been smart to give Ryan her resignation tonight, allowing them to proceed with a relationship on safe ground. She accused him of being greedy, simultaneously wanting her as a partner and unwilling to give her up as his Chief of Staff. She is just as bad as he is. The path they have chosen is risky and unwise.

A memory of Javier talking about finance some years ago comes back to her. *High risk, high reward.*

Tessa pulls up in front of Number One Observatory Circle. Ryan got here first, unsurprisingly. Instead of waiting inside in the warmth, he stands on his front porch, hands tucked into the pockets of his black overcoat, bathed in the golden glow of the porchlight.

Her memory is acute, the envy of her friends. There are certain images that have emblazoned themselves indelibly into her mind. Spencer and Leo, on the days she first met them. Meeting her goddaughters for the first time, shortly after both were born. The jubilant crowd at the Democratic National Convention roaring their approval on the night that Gardner and Ryan accepted the presidential and vice-presidential nomination. The sunrise over the Grand Canyon, with Owen at her side. There are other images that have imprinted themselves onto Tessa's memory, but she tries to avoid revisiting them.

This sight — Ryan in the golden light, his hair tousled by the wind — is something that will stay in her mind for a long time.

Leo hops out of the car and shakes himself before they go to join Ryan. Tessa waves awkwardly at the Secret Service agents posted near the front entrance. She is going to see a lot more of them than she used to. A cynical voice that sounds like Matt points out that if she is on good terms with them, they will be more likely to protect her privacy. "Good night."

"Good night, Ms. Halifax."

"Thank you," Ryan calls to them. "Have a good night."

"You could have waited inside." Tessa ducks her head against the wind. "It's cold out."

"It's fine." Ryan opens the door for her, and they step into the warm interior of the Vice Presidential residence, the spacious entryway softly illuminated by the chandelier above them. He eases her coat off her shoulders, hanging it up in the closet along with his own. Even that brief, innocuous touch makes her remember Tokyo.

(She talked about this in therapy as well. It has been weeks, but Tessa has been unable to ignore or forget about how good it felt to kiss Ryan, and the way she melted under his hands. The memory returns to her when she lies down in bed at night, and when she wakes up in the morning. It triggers a craving she has almost forgotten.)

Tessa distracts herself by unfastening Leo's leash and service dog vest for the night. He looks up at her curiously, and she pats him on the head.

"You can relax, Leo."

Upon being given permission to leave her side, Leo goes to sniff around the expansive downstairs. Ryan rests a hand at the small of her back. "Can I get you anything to drink?"

"No." In the past, Ryan and her other friends have teased her about her tendency to skip over the social niceties. *Straight to the point, as always.* She holds her hand out to Ryan.

He takes it at once, looking at her as if he can't really believe this is happening. Tessa is sure she is gazing at him in the same way. All of this, after so many years?

"Come here," Ryan says softly. Tessa steps forward without a second thought. This is a step she has wanted to take for the past weeks, every time they have stood in proximity to one another. She relaxes as soon as she is in his arms, tilting her face up to his for a kiss.

The kiss is all the relief and sweet familiarity of coming home. Of years of mutual support and reassurances, of shared laughter and struggle and tears. Of being with the person who has been her constant companion for the past seventeen years. Tessa savors the comfort of it, along with the slow, steady heat that builds in her with every moment that passes.

It is the same as what she felt in Tokyo. The sensation of never wanting this to stop. That is just as intoxicating as the scent of Ryan's aftershave and cologne, the same warm, spicy bergamot-and-pepper he has worn for years. Tessa cradles Ryan's face in her hands, and he wraps his arms around her. The growing intensity of their kisses leaves him bending her backwards, supporting her with his hand on her back, his other hand in her hair. Tessa makes soft sounds of satisfaction with every kiss as she nestles closer to him, gripping his shoulders. Every time she makes a sound, Ryan holds her a little tighter, kisses her a little harder.

This time, the only reason she pulls away is to catch her breath. Ryan is just as breathless as she is. He hugs her, kissing her forehead, her temple, the top of her head. Tessa rests her head against the crook of his shoulder, returning his embrace. "Wow."

Ryan laughs, hugging her tighter. "That's the reaction I was going for."

Tessa deliberately steps on his foot. The sound of his laugh is infectious. It makes her smile, as it always has. She stands on the tips of her toes and kisses his cheek, before glancing up the stairs. She recognizes her nervousness, and she can identify it as being born out of anticipation rather than anxiety.

Ryan follows the movement of her eyes. "Do you want to go up?"

Tessa places her hand in his, and she looks around as they approach the staircase. This isn't the first time she has been here. Ryan has had their friends over for dinner a few times over the past year. Number One Observatory Circle, as grand as it is, still feels unfamiliar to her. She was better acquainted with his old townhouse in Astoria. (The townhouse Ryan shared with Vanessa.)

The second floor is a little less imposing than the main floor. It is closer to a normal house, with Ryan's study, a den, the guest bedroom his aunt stays in when she visits, and the main bedroom suite. The guest bedroom is the only space remotely approaching neatness. Ryan's bedroom looks like a small bomb exploded there. There are books, magazines, newspapers, paperwork, and charging cables everywhere. He clears his throat, abashed. "Sorry. I, uh, I didn't expect that you would be over here tonight."

Tessa's attention is drawn to the framed photograph on his bedside table. It is all of them on the night that Ryan won his House seat. Their friends stand in a tight cluster in the middle of the hotel ballroom, their expressions alight with joy. Vasu is beaming so hard that his eyes are almost completely shut. Kahaan has two thumbs up and a wide grin. Javier has one arm slung around her shoulders, and one arm around Booker's. Booker brandishes a large, navy blue *Ryan Chao, Democrat for Congress, NY-14* sign, and Tessa is laughing. Ryan stands in between her and Matt, so proud that he is practically glowing.

She looks back at him now. She was so young in that photo, engaged to Owen, soon to be married. Tessa chooses to focus instead on Ryan, and how far he has come. How far *they* have come. She smiles. "I don't care what your bedroom looks like."

Tessa takes a step toward him. Ryan meets her halfway, folding her into his arms. Their kisses are hungrier than they were downstairs, both of them aware of their mutual physical chemistry, and matched in the desire to explore that to the fullest. She caresses Ryan's chest, running her hands over his upper arms. When he traces the curve of her waist and hips, pulling her flush against him, her knees go weak.

She forgot what this kind of passion was like. She forgot how it impeded her ability to think clearly. How it drove every other thought from her mind. She hasn't had an iota of desire for physical intimacy until very recently. She thought that part of her was dead. She hasn't even touched herself in well over a year and a half, since months before Owen–

Ryan rekindled that desire, and now it threatens to blaze out of control. They step toward the bed in unison. Tessa sinks down first, pulling Ryan down on top of her. He places a careful hand on her waist, and she snuggles closer to him. They trade kiss after kiss, pressing kisses down each other's jawbones and necks, and back up to their lips. They nuzzle their noses against one another's, and against the column of each other's throats. They murmur each other's names, interspersed with sighs of contentment. It is so new to interact with Ryan like this. It is also very easy to get used to.

She could slide her hands underneath the hem of Ryan's sweater and trace the muscles in his back. She could pull his sweater off and change positions so that she is straddling him. She could remove his belt and touch him. She could take off her own sweater. It would be so easy.

She could do any of those things. She doesn't. She loves kissing Ryan, and she would do more with him. A strange confusion still roils inside Tessa at the thought of experiencing all of that tonight. She has never felt this mismatch, this lack of alignment, before. This sensation of her body being ready to go further, even though her mind isn't.

Ryan picks up on her unspoken hesitation. Their kisses grow slower, and he finally breaks away, stroking her hair. Tessa leans into him, resting her forehead against his shoulder. "I want to do more." He would never react in this way, but she hates the thought of disappointing him. (Maybe it isn't Ryan she has disappointed, but herself.) "But — I haven't been with anyone since–"

Ryan rubs her back and kisses the tears away from her eyes. The tenderness of the gesture almost makes her weep. It isn't the physical act of taking her clothes off that is the barrier. It is the fear that even though kissing Ryan doesn't feel like cheating, maybe it will feel like cheating to have sex with someone besides Owen.

"We can take things slow. We'll wait until you're ready." Ryan's hand goes still, before he resumes rubbing her back. "I'm nervous too. I haven't been with anyone since Vanessa."

Tessa wipes at her eyes self-consciously. "I don't think I've ever heard you say that before."

"What, that I'm nervous?"

Tessa manages a smile. "No, that you'll take things slow. Being willing to wait doesn't sound like the Ryan I know."

Ryan kisses the top of her head. "I've always been willing to wait for the things that matter most."

Chapter Twenty-Six

November – December 2025

The days and weeks following Thanksgiving are surreal. Tessa felt the same in college. She used to lie awake in bed at night, struggling to wrap her mind around the fact that she had a boyfriend. "Similar," she amends, in therapy with Taliyah. "It's similar to what I felt in college. My boyfriend wasn't also the Vice President then."

It is easy to maintain the same working relationship when she and Ryan are surrounded by their staff and friends. It is harder when the two of them are alone, reviewing everything that has to be accomplished that day. Occasionally Tessa looks up from her binder and catches him gazing at her instead of taking notes. She directs a meaningful look at his notepad, and Ryan remembers to be Vice President Chao and not just Ryan.

It helps that they have developed the ability to communicate nonverbally over the years, and to read between the lines when they speak with one another. Even when they are alone, they talk to each other in the same casual, platonic way they always have. They never touch. They don't need to.

"Go eat lunch," Ryan says, and Tessa hears the caring in it.

"I'll take these meetings so that you don't have to," Tessa tells him, and he smiles at her.

It is all business during the week. There is no time for anything else, with their long work days. They travel outside of DC on a weekly basis. Ryan speaks at the University of Nevada about abortion rights, visits a clean-energy nonprofit in Los Angeles, and delivers a climate change talk in Miami in the span of a single week.

Weekends are the only times they can carve out for one another. Tessa and Leo accompany Ryan back to Number One Observatory Circle late on Friday nights, and she parks her car in the hidden underground lot. The enormous Vice Presidential residence becomes comfortable. It is the only place they can be together as Ryan and Tessa, and not the Vice President and his Chief of Staff.

They linger over homemade brunches and dinners with one another. "Remember when we used to heat up MREs to eat together?" Ryan asks, as he slices green onions.

Tessa pours teriyaki sauce over their crispy tofu. Her chest aches at the memory. Spencer used to eat his rations, of course, but all four of them used to give him scraps from their MREs. "I remember." It is a fragment from an entirely different life from the one she has now. The pain still lingers.

The stir-fry turned out beautifully. "Wow." Ryan takes another enormous bite. He has picture-perfect table manners in public. In private, he still wolfs down food in record time, ending up with crumbs everywhere and sauce on his chin.

Tessa savors her first bite. "This turned out well." She catches Ryan gazing at her, and she dabs at the corner of her lips with her napkin. "What? Do I have something on my face?"

Ryan's expression softens. "It's nothing. You just looked so happy."

"It's just — you know how it is, since…" Tessa leaves the rest unsaid. Since they both lost their spouses. They work through lunch and dinner during the week, but they eat alone on the weekends. She had been worried about the intimacy of sex. She found that preparing meals together and sharing them is surprisingly intimate too.

Ryan refills her glass of water. "I get it. It's nice to have company. It's nice to have *you* for company."

"We haven't eaten together without talking shop since college."

"Yeah."

There is something rueful in the way Ryan looks at her. Tessa takes another bite of her food, giving him a wordless prompt to elaborate.

"I was thinking about college. You and me, in college, and all the time we used to spend together. I've always wondered how differently things could have turned out, if I had just wised up sooner."

Tessa remembers what Rosalie said to her. *I always did get the vibe that you were his favorite person. Even when Vanessa was in the picture.* She quells her nerves, and sets her fork down. "How long have you…?" There should be no right or wrong answer. Life isn't that simple. But there are answers that will be easier or harder to hear.

"I think that I started to have feelings for you in Iraq." Ryan rests his free hand on top of hers. "I didn't get it then. I didn't understand that I loved you differently than I loved Matt and Curtis. Then we got back home, and I couldn't think about anything besides–"

"Getting into Congress before thirty." Tessa squeezes his hand, speaking in unison with him.

"Exactly. And you were always with me. I got used to you being there. You and Matt, my right hand and my left. I didn't realize how much I screwed up until you told us that you were dating Owen."

Tessa tries to keep the dismay from her voice. Owen was right about Ryan having feelings for her, and she had dismissed him entirely. "That was such a long time ago."

"I know." Ryan looks down at their interlaced fingers. "But I knew you were happy with Owen. I tried to make the best of things, with my career, with Vanessa. I was fine. Everything was fine."

Until Vanessa filed for divorce. Until Owen– Until everything fell apart.

Tessa tries to put a name to her emotions. She lands on sorrow and regret. She lifts Ryan's hand to her lips and presses a kiss to his knuckles. "We're here now," she reminds herself aloud.

"We are," Ryan echoes.

ooooo

They sit close together on the sofa in front of the fireplace on Saturdays, Ryan's arm around her shoulders. Tessa leans against him, Leo at their feet. This is the only place where their privacy is completely guaranteed. They take the opportunity to talk, uncensored, as they can't anywhere else.

"I thought things were bad back in 2007. In 2009." Ryan stares at the ceiling, resting with his head on her lap. "They definitely were. But the way things are now… We've gotten so off track as a nation. Gun violence

305

is worse than ever. Each school shooting and mass shooting isn't even in the news for longer than a day anymore. Women's rights are under attack. Income inequality is worse now than it was a decade ago. 2009 was just the beginning. Now, we've almost completely lost our way."

Tessa cards her fingers through his hair. "Yes, but we can't afford to be so pessimistic and lose hope in the possibility of a better future. I still believe that back-to-back terms for Gardner and you will get our country back on track."

"You have such faith in me."

"Well, you haven't proved me wrong yet."

ooooo

They walk Leo together and play with him in the enormous back-yard, tossing toys for him to fetch. "He reminds me of Spencer," Ryan comments. Leo trots back to her, red ball in his mouth, tail wagging. "Is that all right to say?"

"It is." Tessa takes the red ball, feints, smiles as Leo leaps, and then tosses the ball for him. He goes bounding off after it, tail wagging. Healing is being able to remember Spencer and appreciate the similarities between him and Leo without being crippled by pain. "He watches out for me, just like Spencer did."

(She wonders if she will ever be able to remember Owen in the same way. With appreciation for all that was good, without the pain of the end.)

ooooo

They work out together, competing to see who can run longer or faster (always Tessa), or lift heavier weights (always Ryan). He still boasts about his lifts as much as he did when he was a young soldier. Tessa humbles him by getting him to stretch with her. "You can't touch your toes?" She bends over, placing her palms flat on the floor, keeping her legs straight. Meanwhile, Ryan hinges at the hips, and his fingertips dangle a good several inches off the floor. "How sad for you."

Ryan retaliates by straightening and sweeping her off her feet. "What do you mean, you can't pick me up? How sad for you."

"Who said I couldn't pick you up? I'm just as prepared to carry your ass out of danger as I was back in the Army."

"I have the Secret Service for that now." Ryan gathers her close, smirking down at her. "Haven't you heard?"

∞∞∞∞∞

They watch TV together, pulling up old episodes of The Wire or The Newsroom. Sometimes they read together, and chat about their books. Ryan suggests they start a podcast, and Tessa nudges his foot with hers. "I don't think that the VP is allowed to have a podcast."

"My freedom of expression is being limited," Ryan complains. Tessa rolls her eyes.

∞∞∞∞∞

Another intimacy that Tessa has to get used to is sleeping together. Just sleeping. Leo stays nearby, settled into his dog bed by the fireplace. Settling into bed is always a combination of comforting and interesting. She and Ryan cuddle and sometimes get distracted by warm, increasingly long spells of good-night kisses and caresses.

Falling asleep like that is bliss. It doesn't always translate to a peaceful night.

Her old fears resurge in her dreams and nightmares. She dreams of cancer diagnoses and hospice care. Her two oldest, most deeply-held fears. Just hearing the word *cancer*, just hearing the word *hospice*, fills her with fear and dread and pain, with a primal plea of *no, no, no, please, no.*

She dreams of firefights, mass shootings, and attempted coups in the Capitol. She dreams of car accidents on rainy roads late at night. She dreams of assassin's bullets, of IEDs, of the gruesome aftermath of suicide bomb detonations. She dreams of dead dogs.

She dreams of Owen. Not in the early days, but as he was at the end.

It is one of those nightmares that Ryan wakes her from. His hand is tight on her arm, gripping it hard. "Tessa. Tessa, sweetheart, you have to wake up."

Leo nudges her side insistently. Tessa fixates on Ryan's grip instead. She wrests free of him, crying out in terror. She covers her arms to protect her face, curling up in a ball underneath the covers.

"Tessa–" Ryan's voice breaks. He settles himself near her, stroking her back through the covers. "It's just me. Leo's here too. It's okay. You're okay."

Tessa's breath comes in ragged gasps. She untangles the past from the present, the nightmare from reality. When she is back in the realm of reason, she dissolves into tears. Leo snuffles around, desperate to get under the covers with her. She gropes blindly at the blankets, letting him in, wrapping an arm around him and hugging him close. She tries to remember what she learned when she first got Leo. To steady her breaths along with his.

The tears don't stop. The memory of her pain and fright is too much. Ryan's hands are gentle on her back. Tessa clings to that, and to the comfort of Leo's presence right against her side. She remembers the fear as though it happened yesterday, but that's not real. That's not real. Right now, in the present, she isn't terrified and alone. She has Ryan and Leo.

Tessa finally emerges from the covers, breathing hard, wiping her tears away. To her shock, Ryan's face is wet too. She hasn't seen him cry since that last night in Iraq. She holds out her arms to him. Ryan hugs her tight, whispering soothing words, kissing the top of her head.

"I'm sorry I disturbed your sleep," Tessa finally whispers. Their usual roles are reversed. She lies down with her head in Ryan's lap, as he strokes her hair. All of that sobbing left her voice hoarse.

"Don't apologize to me." Ryan's fingers brush her temple. He is silent for a while. "Does it — does it happen often? During the week?"

She can tell from his sudden tension that he is bracing himself for her answer. He is afraid that this happens when he isn't there to comfort her. "Sometimes." Tessa wipes her face again. "Not as often as it used to, thankfully."

"You know that there's EMDR therapy for this kind of PTSD. Eye-movement desensitization and reprocessing. I don't know if Taliyah does it. I can find some resources for you, if she doesn't."

"No." Tessa startles herself with the vehemence of her refusal. Leo lifts his head from where he is nestled against her side. "I looked into it. Part of that therapy has the client focus on the traumatic memory or nightmare. I can't do that. I can't."

"Okay," Ryan assures her, at once. "Okay. I understand."

Tessa settles into his lap again. She closes her eyes, focusing on his touch. She is safe and loved. Tomorrow she will be safe and loved with Ryan and Leo too. "This is enough," she murmurs. "This is enough."

ooooo

"I'm worried that you'll get sick of me," Ryan teases, as they work on a thousand-piece jigsaw puzzle together. The puzzle depicts Central Park in fall, a little slice of home.

"Me? Never." Tessa holds up a finger, and then feigns a mini-coughing fit.

It is Ryan's turn to roll his eyes. "You don't get any breaks anymore. You work with me. You spend weekends with me."

Tessa fishes out a corner piece from the pile of puzzle pieces and hands it to him. "This isn't much different than it was in college." (Before she started spending part of her weekends with Owen.)

"Yes, but you don't have Matt as a buffer."

"It's been almost twenty years, and I haven't gotten sick of you once. I'm not going to start now. Why do you think I've stuck around for all this time?"

"Commitment to our ideals? Because I'm the future of the Democratic Party?" Ryan completes a row, and surveys it with satisfaction.

"Humble," Tessa replies dryly. "That's just a small part of it."

"So, back to college — if I was still your friend, but a hopeless case politically, you would have stuck with me anyway?"

Tessa considers this. "Matt and I would have whipped you into shape."

Ryan laughs. "The Tessa Halifax and Matt Han Reform School for Hopeless Politicians." He blocks an imaginary headline with his hands. "The ideal students — losers with no charisma and/or no intellect."

Tessa takes her phone and opens her Notes app. Ryan rests his chin on her shoulder. "What are you doing?" In moments like this, he is the same hyperactive young man she met in 2006.

"Writing that down. It's my new idea for what I'm going to do with my life when you're finally out of office."

They go on a tangent with talking about retirement plans, and then lapse into a comfortable silence as they work on the puzzle together. It is relaxing, but Tessa is too aware of the time. It is already eleven in the morning on Sunday. She will have to head home in just a few hours. Tomorrow morning, she and Ryan will be back in their professional roles. Her work as Chief of Staff is satisfying, and she wouldn't trade it for the world. She will still count down the hours until they can be together like this again.

∞∞∞

It is a slow, awe-inspiring transition, falling in romantic love with someone she has loved as her best friend for almost twenty years. She loves Ryan's sense of humor, his sharp mind, his unique quirks and mannerisms, in the same way.

He still brings her joy and comfort, as he always has — but in a different way. Tessa holds his hand and sits close by his side, and nestles into his arm around her shoulder. She gives and gets hugs, burying her face in the crook of Ryan's neck, as he kisses her forehead and the top of her head. It is pure bliss she hasn't felt in so long. They trade long kisses in the living room, in the gym, in the kitchen, in the backyard. Each kiss brings with it an unmistakable certainty.

"It isn't just a rebound," Tessa confides to Jesy, as they sit together in Jesy's living room. She took advantage of Ryan's speech at his alma mater to return to New York City with him. "I thought it might be that, at first. After Tokyo. I thought I was just reacting to being alone, and missing the love and affection I used to get from Owen. I thought I was just projecting that onto the closest available man, someone who I already cared so much for."

"Not to be a brat, but I knew you weren't just on the rebound. I'm so happy for you, Tess. I know Ryan loves you just as much. Everyone can see it."

Tessa shudders. "Don't say that. We don't want anyone to see it."

"No, I just meant our friends — the people who are closest to you guys. I have news alerts on both of you. I haven't seen any rumors or anything. Lots of talking shit about Ryan from the right, and lots of speculation about 2028 from the left and the right, but nothing linking him romantically to his gorgeous Chief of Staff."

Tessa smooths down her beige sweater. "Please."

"You know what you need to really protect you against any kind of allegations?" Jesy muses. "You need a fake boyfriend. Maybe even a fake fiancé."

"Absolutely not." Tessa pats Leo, who is curled up by her side. "This is the only other man I need."

ooooo

Tessa noticed Ryan's looks before, in the same matter-of-fact, objective way she noticed everyone's looks. Jesy and Rosalie's beauty, Grace's delicate features, Matt's strong jaw, Javier's broad shoulders, Booker's great smile, Vasu's height, Kahaan's thoughtful deep brown eyes, and Mari's flawless complexion. Tessa recognized Ryan's nice hair, his smooth, deep voice, his smile and the way it made his eyes crinkle at the corners. All the pieces fit together to form an undeniably handsome picture.

That worked wonderfully for her and Matt. Attractive politicians always did better than those who weren't perceived as good-looking. Looks mattered, even if voters and prospective voters would never admit it. Ryan Chao was objectively handsome. Everyone could see that. It was just another thing that worked in Ryan's favor.

Her assessment of Ryan physically is no longer the detached, objective thing it once was. Tessa has a new awareness of his hands. She has a brand-new awareness of the way he sheds his suit jacket between meetings at work and rolls the sleeves of his shirt up to his elbows, exposing his forearms. Every day at work brings its challenges, and Ryan's hair stands on end by midday, as he digs his fingers into it in frustration.

When Tessa sees that telltale sign of a tough work day, she still advises Ryan to breathe and take five, as she always has. She also fights to shelve all thoughts of pressing against him, distracting him with a kiss or several, letting him lean her back over his office desk.

"He looks too good in those stupid suits," Tessa vents to Leo, while she walks him one night after work. "How hard would it be for him to come to work in sweatpants and a t-shirt?"

Leo looks over his shoulder at her sympathetically and wags his tail.

Unfortunately, Tessa knows that sweatpants and a t-shirt don't hurt Ryan's attractiveness at all. She heaves a sigh.

Her growing awareness of her attraction to Ryan is difficult. It is strange to catch herself admiring a man who isn't Owen. Tessa has to remind herself daily that she isn't doing anything wrong in finding her own boyfriend attractive.

It is also strange to have Ryan, and their relationship, and their increasing forays into physicality, resurrect a part of her that she thought was dead. She really forgot what it was like. The restlessness, the sense of being on edge, the frustration, the drive, the literal ache that came with the need for intimate touch. For deep, eager kisses, fingers threading through one another's hair as they pulled each other closer. For hands on her back, bending her backwards, caressing the curve of her hips, squeezing her ass, cupping her breasts in strong hands. For words of praise whispered against her neck or in her ear. *You feel so good, baby.* She forgot what it was like to melt against someone, unable to form real words, unable to do anything besides moan and whimper and sigh with pleasure, and pull them closer into her.

Tessa mulls this over for some time before summoning the courage to bring it up to Taliyah during their next therapy session. "I want to talk about sex." Her face burns, even though she has confided much more painful, intimate things to her therapist over the past year.

"We can talk about that." Taliyah nods, and Tessa knows that she is checking her notes from previous sessions. "Last time we discussed sexuality, you mentioned that it felt "awkward" and "weird" to have sexual feelings. Has anything changed?"

"Yes. Well, yes and no." Taliyah patiently waits for more, and she elaborates. "Ryan and I haven't had sex yet. That hasn't changed. But I'm reacting differently to these sexual feelings."

"How so?"

"It doesn't feel awkward or strange to have those feelings of desire anymore. It feels… It's starting to feel familiar. It feels good, and exciting. Not just in a physical way," Tessa hastens to add. "Not just as it relates to Ryan. It's like meeting an old friend again, except that old friend is part of me. Does that make sense?"

"It absolutely makes sense. You're reconnecting with a part of yourself that has been buried for a long time now. It makes sense that you would feel joy, and maybe relief, too."

After they wrap up their session, Tessa heads to the kitchen to make some tea. Her face and neck are still warm, after her conversation with Taliyah. It reminded her of the way Ryan makes her feel, and the things did last weekend. They haven't had sex, but they have gotten more intimate. They have had more than a few lengthy makeout sessions that have involved her experimenting with touching Ryan. She wrapped her hand around him, stroking him until he came apart underneath her touch, his voice rough with strain as he told her how good she was.

She pushed the envelope this past weekend. Less than ten minutes after they made it through the door on Friday night, she was overcome by a dizzying, dangerous mixture of boldness and lust. She ended up on her knees, Ryan's fingers gently gripping her hair, cradling the back of her head. Thank God it hadn't felt like cheating.

Ryan held her in his arms afterward, rubbing her back as she rested against his chest. "Are you sure you don't want me to do anything for you?"

"I'm sure." Tessa lifted her head, making eye contact. "This is good for me, for now. I like having control over the situation." She hasn't had to stop at any point, but it has been a solution to her anxiety to know that she could do so easily. If things start to feel wrong, if she feels guilty, she can just withdraw her hand or mouth, as simple as that. It is easier than stopping sex. Her clothes have (mostly) stayed on during all their forays into intimacy too. Ryan and Taliyah have reminded her that taking small steps back toward expressing her sexuality is okay.

Ryan kissed her forehead. "Whatever makes you feel comfortable."

Tessa curls her hands around her mug of peppermint tea, breathing in the fragrant steam. The home screen on her personal cell lights up, distracting her. Jesy has sent a picture of Margot Robbie in a golden evening gown. *Do u have your outfit for the WH Christmas party yet?? This would look soooo good on u. Margot Robbie who??*

Tessa does a quick image search for the dress. *This is Balmain,* she texts back. *$6,800 price tag. No thanks. I got a dress from Nordstrom.*

Pics?? Jesy texts.

Tessa heads to her closet, mug in one hand, phone in the other, Leo following behind.

Chapter Twenty-Seven

December 2025

"Oh my God." Rosalie releases Javier's arm and makes a beeline to Tessa. She waves a quick hello at Ryan, who goes to greet Javier.

"I know." Tessa eyes their surroundings. She is no stranger to extravagant holiday parties. Ryan and Vanessa hosted lavish New Year's parties every year, and Vanessa brought her full expertise as a luxury interior designer to bear at each event. "It's gorgeous."

The White House tonight makes Ryan and Vanessa's parties look shabby. Each room is exquisitely decorated to align with its own theme. Faith and light in the Red Room, nature in the Green Room, kindness and gratitude in the Vermeil Room. Tessa has never been sentimental about Christmas, but even she can see that the White House decorators have transformed the space into a scene right out of her childhood storybooks.

Rosalie shakes her head impatiently. She left her beautiful curly hair loose tonight, cascading down her back, in striking contrast to her saffron-colored evening gown. "I was talking about you. You look gorgeous."

"Oh, I–" Tessa shrugs, smoothing her palms over the satin skirt of her ballgown. "Thank you. I wasn't sure if it was too over the top." She scrutinized her reflection in the dressing room at Nordstrom's, twisting back and forth to study herself at every angle. The swirling full skirt and the train pooling at her feet would have made it difficult to move if not for the thigh-high slit in the skirt.

"That emerald really suits you. See! Colors besides neutrals work for you!" Rosalie pronounces *neutrals* in the same tone that some people would pronounce *biohazard.*

"Maybe," Tessa says quellingly.

"The necklace and earrings — are those new? I haven't seen you wear them before."

Tessa reaches up to brush her fingers over the necklace revealed by her strapless sweetheart neckline. A Tiffany Knot pendant in yellow gold with diamonds, paired with diamond stud earrings. It is the first set of jewelry that she has received since Owen. Accepting the gift felt like more of a betrayal than anything physical that she has done. With effort, she talked herself down from her hesitation. She is in a new relationship, after all. A fresh start. Accepting the gift symbolized that. It is undeniably comforting to have a tangible reminder of Ryan and his love for her so close at hand. "They were a gift."

Rosalie's mouth falls open. "Nice."

"It was too much," Tessa protests, as Rosalie leads them over to a passing waiter bearing a tray of canapes. "Thirty-seven isn't a milestone birthday."

Rosalie waves a hand to hush her. "You need to let people spoil you when we can."

"Hmm." Tessa munches on her canape, unconvinced.

"Think about it this way. It makes us happy to do something for you, after all that you do for us."

Tessa relents. "Thank you." Across the room, Javier and Ryan have been joined by a few members of Gardner's senior staff, as well as Andrew and Booker.

"What is it?" Rosalie follows her gaze. "Worried that Gardner's people are bullying ours?"

"No." Tessa sighs, thinking back to how happy Ryan had been last night. They made a bonfire in the backyard, and made s'mores. "I can tell he's on edge tonight."

"Why?" Rosalie speaks as softly as she does. "Because it's cutting into your weekend together?"

"That's part of it. Being here tonight is salt in the wound, again. Look at all of this."

The crowd mills around them, moving from one room to the next, chatting and laughing, enjoying the food, drink, and festivities. There are hundreds of people here, key figures in the political landscape of DC, the nation, and the media. All of this could have been Ryan's. It chafes at him to see Gardner at the center of it. Ryan is acknowledged by the party itself and by the media as the future of the Democratic Party. Still, at events like this, etiquette demands that he play second fiddle to the President. He does so with a facade of good grace, but it takes a toll.

"I can't really blame him," Rosalie whispers. "Three more years."

"Hopefully." The Republican Party is already mobilizing everything they have to take back the White House in 2028.

They find Grace, Mari, and Daniel in the Blue Room, chatting with a few staffers from Senator Padilla's office. The Blue Room is the most magnificent of them all. Renderings of the official birds from all fifty-seven states, territories, and DC adorn the official White House Christmas tree. Each trimming would have shone on its own. Woven together, the collection transforms the eighteen-foot fir tree into a work of art.

Almost everyone in the Blue Room comes to cut in on Tessa's conversation. She pastes a smile on her face and engages with them as politely as she can. Everyone knows that the Chief of Staff is the key to getting any face time with the VP. She and Matt have to deal with an ungodly amount of transparent smiles and artificial politeness from every lobbyist, Representative, or Senator who wants to get in front of Ryan.

"Was he trying to get to you or to Ryan?" Grace comes up beside Tessa, who has just dispatched an Amazon lobbyist.

"Ryan." Tessa turns to face Grace in an attempt to deter the woman who is approaching her. At any given time, she has to dodge at least a dozen meeting requests from lobbyists and special interest groups who are trying to poach her from Ryan.

The woman steps right up to her, undeterred. "Ms. Halifax? I'm Jessica Lopour, from Telluria Inc."

Tessa's patience frays. "Jessica, I'm so sorry, but I have someone I need to connect with." She makes a quick exit, throwing Grace an apologetic look as she goes.

The party has grown yet more crowded since she arrived. An unexpected stab of fear lances through her. An IED placed here would have devastating results. She misses Leo — but Leo is safe, curled up in his dog bed in her office at the EEOB*. She doesn't often bring him to events hosted at the White House, like state dinners. Guests always gawk at him, and at her by extension. Tessa can practically see the wheels turning in their heads. It grates on her. She doesn't look like she would need a service dog, after all. She doesn't look like she has a disability.

"Tessa!"

Tessa looks up sharply at the familiar voice. She smiles with relief as she catches sight of Matt and Ryan making their way toward her. She hadn't seen Matt yet tonight, but she knew he was here. "Did you two plan the matching suits?"

"No," Matt and Ryan say in unison, rather defensively.

"Are you okay?" Ryan almost reaches over to put a hand on the small of her back, like he would if they were in private. Thankfully, he catches himself in time.

"Yeah. I just needed to get away from a lobbyist. The Blue Room is swarming with them right now."

Matt jerks his thumb over his shoulder. "Booker, Andrew, and Kahaan are in the Green Room, if you want some saner conversation."

"That sounds good. Where are you two headed?"

"I'm going to find Grace," Matt says brightly.

"She's in the Blue Room," Tessa says, and Matt heads in that direction.

"The President suggested that I have a little chat with Monroe and Shaw, so I'm going to do that. They're supposed to be in the library."

Tessa raises an eyebrow. Ryan just named the two most problematic members of the House Democratic Caucus. "Isn't that the Whip's job?"

"Well, Gardner said he couldn't get it done." Ryan speaks the words through a smile, so quietly that none of the people around them would be able to hear. The Whip, Ueland, has been a thorn in Ryan's side since his own days in Congress.

"Good luck."

"Thanks. See you later?"

Tessa picks up on the question in Ryan's eyes. She headed back to her apartment around midafternoon to get ready today. She can go home with him tonight — making a discreet exit from the White House, of

Eisenhower Executive Office Building

course — and they can enjoy the little that remains of the weekend together. The way Ryan looked at her when she arrived…

Tessa nods, almost imperceptibly. "Later."

She finds Booker, Andrew, and Kahaan chatting in front of the fireplace in the Green Room. Kahaan notices her first. He waves, a smile lighting up his face. "Hi, Tessa!"

Tessa joins them. "I'm so relieved to see you guys."

"You look wonderful," Andrew compliments. "Very regal."

"Please. I saw your sister earlier. *She* looks like a queen." Olivia Abrams, R-MT*, is one of the only power players in DC who still intimidates her. She, Ryan, and Matt have been courting Olivia for years, trying to get her to switch parties, to no avail. Olivia is staunchly pro-choice, pro-gay marriage, and anti-racist. Unfortunately, she disagrees with Ryan's platform, and the Democratic Party, on every other domestic and international issue.

Andrew blanches. "Olivia's here?"

The last time the Abrams siblings were in the same room did not end well. Andrew's family is obscenely wealthy, with a lengthy history of close involvement with the Republican Party. They weren't receptive to their son choosing a different path.

"Don't worry. There are hundreds of people here. You probably won't run into each other."

Andrew looks unconvinced, and Tessa touches his arm briefly. "We'll run interference." Olivia might be an imposing figure, but no one is going to harass one of her friends in front of her.

Andrew smiles weakly. "Thanks."

Booker starts to say something, but Tessa's back stiffens. She picks up on footsteps in the hallway outside. Multiple footsteps, walking fast, forceful footfalls. Male. A distinctly different sound from the typical slow, leisurely milling about at parties like this. She holds a hand up, and her friends fall silent at once. Tessa whirls toward the door just in time to see two Secret Service agents burst into the room, radios in hand. She recognizes both as agents assigned to protect the White House.

"The White House is entering lockdown." The agent ignores the

Republican—Montana

shocked gasps that ripple through the room. "For your safety, we ask you to remain in this room until the lockdown is lifted."

Tessa shuts out everything she hears around her. Every exclamation of *oh my god,* or *holy shit,* or *is everything okay? What happened?* She is nineteen years younger, an Army soldier again. Is the threat internal or external? It has to be external. Every guest who entered the White House tonight went through an extensive background check prior to receiving their invitation, and a security screening upon arrival.

She hadn't heard a detonation or shots fired. A gunshot or a detonation would have sliced through the ambient noise of the party. The present threat must be more insidious. Perhaps some sort of exposure to an airborne hazard? Or it is a different kind of external threat. The shadow of January 6, 2021 still looms over all of them.

Ryan has to be protected. When the terrorists stormed the Capitol in 2021, they called for the execution of the Vice President. Ryan has his protection detail with him tonight, but still. Tessa strides toward the Secret Service agents, pushing through the rest of the crowd, her friends close at her heels. "Is the Vice President in the library?" Had Ryan made it there to meet with Monroe and Shaw, or had he gotten sidetracked with someone else who wanted to talk to him?

Recognition clicks in the agent's face as he realizes who she is. "The Vice President is secure in the library, Ms. Halifax."

"Can I– Can we–" Tessa knows, even as she speaks, that it is impossible. The agent is already shaking his head.

"No, ma'am. Everyone's staying put where they are until the situation is resolved."

"What's going on?" Booker's tone is low, so that they won't be overheard by the crowd around them. Andrew and Kahaan stay at either side of her.

"I'm not at liberty to say anything at this time, sir." The agent steps away, consulting his radio again.

Tessa fights to control her breathing, pressing the heel of her hand to her forehead. Tonight, of all nights, to be separated from Leo. Why the fuck had she let Ryan go to the library alone? She should have gone with him. Is it domestic terrorists storming the White House gates? Anthrax particles released through the vents? The Secret Service won't be able to do anything to protect Ryan from exposure to a bioterrorism agent.

Kahaan rapidly scrolls on his phone. "It doesn't look like this is in response to another 9/11 or nuke strike or anything like that. Nothing alarming on major US news networks and international sources. #WHChristmasLockdown is already trending on Twitter, but there's no real info there."

"Okay, that's something, at least." Booker places a gentle hand on her shoulder. "Try to breathe, Tess. Every room here has at least two Secret Service agents posted in it. I bet there are dozens more in the halls now. I know it doesn't feel like it, but we're safe. Ryan is safe."

She needs to know if Ryan is okay. Andrew takes off his suit jacket and drapes it across her shoulders, and she realizes she is shivering with fear. Rosalie and Javier are here too, Matt and Grace, Mari, Daniel — all their friends. They are all exposed to whatever this risk is. Her phone vibrates in the pocket of her skirt, and she almost jumps.

Tessa fumbles to retrieve it, and her friends do the same with their phones. Ryan's name lights up their home screens. He has sent a group text to all of their friends at the party tonight. *Everyone check in here.*

Everyone texts back in rapid succession, accounted for. The text thread quickly dissolves into speculation. *Where are the Pres and First Lady?* Javier texts.

Overheard an agent saying they were in the East Colonnade when it went down. I'm sure that they've been taken somewhere more secure, Ryan texts back.

Tessa exhales slowly, resting a hand on her stomach. Nausea swells in her, as it always does during times of intense stress. The minutes tick by, slowly, interminably. The four of them stay huddled in a tight knot, drawing strength from one another. On the other side of the room, a White House staffer cries quietly. Another Gardner staffer pulls out a prescription bottle of pills from his pocket and takes a couple. The two Secret Service agents remain guarding the room. One of them steps out every so often to listen to and give reports on his radio. Tessa strains to listen, but his words are inaudible.

One of the agents is gone for a longer spell than usual. Tessa can't tear her eyes away from the door, waiting for him to return. When he finally steps in, she recognizes that some of the tension has left his face. "We have the all-clear, ladies and gentlemen," he calls. Thank you for your patience."

"What happened?" someone shouts, from the back of the room.

The agent is evasive. "The White House is secure, and the President and First Lady invite their guests to continue with the night's festivities."

"It probably wasn't anything major, then. I need to find Mari." Booker heads for the exit.

"I'm going to call my family. They sent about thirty texts." Kahaan pulls out his phone again. "It's only been forty-five minutes. It feels like it was hours."

"I want to make sure my sister's okay." Alex moves to follow Booker.

"Wait." Tessa gives him back his suit jacket. "I saw her in the East Colonnade earlier, so head over there first."

The Secret Service mentioned the President and First Lady, but Tessa doesn't give a damn about Gardner and his wife right now. She hurries over to the closest agent. "The VP?"

"The VP is fine, Ms. Halifax."

Tessa leaves the room before he even finishes speaking. The halls of the White House bustle with activity, the party guests apparently none the worse for wear for the ordeal, their voices raised in excitement and speculation. She makes her way through the crowd, proceeding to the library.

Ryan strides around the corner of the long hallway ahead, outpacing his Secret Service agents. His hair stands on end from where he must have gripped onto it during the lockdown. His eyes lock onto her. It is all Tessa can do to prevent herself from breaking into a run toward him. Ryan quickens his pace further, his agents trailing him.

They come to an abrupt stop just an arm's length away from one another. He doesn't embrace her. She doesn't throw her arms around him and cup his face in her hands to look him over and make sure that he is safe. There are people around. They stand an arm's length away from one another, only able to search each other's faces for any sign of distress.

"Are you okay?" They speak in unison. At any other time, Ryan would have laughed at that. He is much paler than usual, and anxiety is written all over his face.

"I'm fine. I was just worried about you."

It is a gross understatement, when she says it aloud. She quietly panicked in the Green Room, fingers clutched around handfuls of her skirt. She had been unable to stop thinking about crowds of furious terrorists breaking into the library, frantic for the blood of the progressive Democrat who is a convenient scapegoat of all their racist hatred. She had been unable to stop thinking about Ryan struggling for breath after inhaling a lungful of anthrax. Ryan alone, hurt or in pain, without her for support or protection. The thought of losing Ryan, of Ryan hurt, dragged her as low as she was in the months after Owen.

"There's no need to worry. I'm always the second safest guy in this building." Ryan flexes his hands, as though resisting the temptation to take her into his arms. "Come on. Let's get together to regroup."

Their friends meet up in the Blue Room. Tessa stays by Ryan's side, and she barely listens to his explanation of what happened. A young man with a gun attacked a White House security checkpoint. One Secret Service agent sustained non-life threatening injuries, and the other agent shot at and hospitalized the attacker. Their friends pepper Ryan with questions, trying to figure out details about whether the person was acting alone, and the shooter's background and motivations. Ryan shrugs. "This is all I know so far. We'll all know more by Monday morning. I'm just glad you guys are okay."

Their friends all leave early, justifiably rattled by the night's events. Booker and Mari are the last to depart. They hug Ryan and Tessa goodbye. "Be careful out there," Booker warns Ryan.

"I'm going to buy you some Mace," Mari promises Tessa. "You never know. There are so many crazy people out there now."

Tessa and Ryan stand in the East Room at a respectable distance, watching their friends walk out into the night. She told them all to text when they got home. She hates these periodic reminders that DC is far from safe. Home — New York City — had its issues, but they didn't have to worry about politically motivated violence there.

"We shouldn't leave together," Ryan says quietly.

"No. I need to pick up Leo, anyway."

"You head out now, if you want. I'll wait about half an hour and then follow."

"All right." Tessa dares a glance at Ryan, and he does the same. "Be safe."

"You too. I'm going to have a couple of my plainclothes detail escort you to our office and through the security checkpoints. Don't be alarmed if you see them following you."

The EEOB is a short walk from the White House. Tessa finds Leo where she left him, in her office. He darts over to her, picking up on her distress. Tessa kneels, hugging her dog around the neck. "Oh, Leo." She clings to him, filled with indescribable comfort at his presence. She had been so scared. Anything could have happened to Ryan tonight, or to the rest of their friends.

Leo edges closer to her, and Tessa presses her forehead against his. "Thank you. I love you."

Leo gives her a small, polite lick on the cheek. Tessa laughs for the first time in hours. "Let's go home." She catches the slip. *To Ryan's,* she amends mentally.

She is tempted to put Leo in the front passenger seat, just so she can have him closer to her, but his safety is the priority. Dogs and children aren't safe in the front seat if an airbag deploys. Tessa begins the now-familiar drive over to Number One Observatory Circle. The area surrounding the White House is choked with traffic thanks to the enhanced security and police presence after tonight's incident. Media vans, Secret Service vehicles, and the DC Police line every street.

Her shoulders are rigid with tension. Alternating waves of remembered terror and dizzying relief wash over her. Tessa throws an impatient glance at the clock on the dashboard. All she wants to do is get home and hug Ryan tight.

It takes twice as long for her to get to his place as it normally does. The Secret Service agents check her license plates and the underside of her car, before waving her into the well-concealed entrance to the secret underground lot. Ryan's beloved old silver Prius is parked here, as well as two backup Secret Service SUVs, a trailer containing a fully-equipped mobile hospital unit, and a small armored tank. Another trailer is stuffed to the brim with emergency supplies — drums of filtered water, canned food, MREs, and more medical equipment.

Tessa and Leo climb up the two flights of stairs separating the lot from the residence. She keys in the ten-digit code, and the access door opens into Ryan's kitchen. A guest would think it is just a door to a second pantry. She unhooks Leo's leash and harness. "Good boy. You were wonderful tonight."

The front door opens, and she hears the distant sound of Ryan thanking his agents for all they did to keep him safe tonight. The door clicks shut. "Tess?" Ryan calls.

Now, in private, she doesn't have to hold back. Tessa kicks her heels off and rushes through the darkened kitchen, the train of her skirt dragging behind her. Ryan meets her right at the entrance. He hadn't bothered to take off his shoes or overcoat. She throws her arms around him, and he holds her close, cradling the back of her head. He kisses her forehead, her nose, her lips.

Tessa cups his face in her hands. "I'm so glad you're all right. I thought–"

Ryan hugs her. "I know. I couldn't stand just waiting there for them to call the all-clear. I just wanted you with me."

"I can't lose you, Ryan. I can't ever lose you." She has lost so much already. Her mother, even her father, Spencer, Owen. Somehow she managed to continue on, loss after shattering loss, but Ryan — Ryan is her North Star. Her intellectual match, her best friend, who gave her the ability to dream and love again.

"You won't." Ryan grips her shoulders, letting her see his absolute sincerity. "I promise you, Tess. I'll always be with you."

Tessa stands on the tips of her toes, kissing him hard. It takes Ryan by surprise, and he stumbles back from the force of it. He recovers swiftly, wrapping her in his arms. She moans against his lips, caressing his shoulders. They fall against the doorframe, kissing one another with helpless abandon, tugging each other closer. Ryan's hands are on her waist, and then they are warm on the bare shoulder blades exposed by her dress. Tessa breathes in the scent of him as she nuzzles and kisses his neck. She shoves off his overcoat and suit coat so she can run her hands over his back. It is unlike her to be so heedless of his things, but she just wants to be as close to him as possible.

Ryan doesn't seem to mind. He sweeps her loose hair over one shoulder and bends to press kisses along her shoulder, her collarbone, the hollow of her neck. His nose brushes the chain of her necklace, and Tessa sighs with delight.

"This looks so good on you. And you looked so gorgeous tonight that I couldn't keep my eyes off you." Ryan touches the pendant of her necklace.

It falls right at the middle of her chest, close enough to the neckline of her dress that Tessa bites her lip. It is that little gesture that settles it for her. She is ready to make every one of the fantasies that she has had over the last month a reality.

"I like having something that reminds me of you," she says, a little breathlessly. She takes his hand, intertwining their fingers together. Ryan kisses her on the forehead, and she places his hand on her breast.

They are so close that she feels his breath stutter in his chest. Tessa would have chided herself for being too forward if this didn't feel so good. She arches her back into his touch. Ryan doesn't need further prompting. He wraps one arm around her, leaning her against the doorway. The combination of his kisses and his fingertips skimming the tops of her breasts, gently squeezing her through the bodice of her dress, leaves her weak at the knees, gasping for breath. He lowers his head and starts kissing down her neck, past her collarbone, toward the neckline of her dress. "God," he murmurs against her skin. "I love being with you like this."

She loves it too. She is getting carried away as she does when she thinks about this alone in her apartment at night. One of Ryan's hands cups the back of her head, keeping her from hitting against the wall. Tessa takes the other, guiding it to the slit of her dress. They both breathe a ragged exhale as Ryan strokes her leg, dragging his knuckles down the inside of her thigh.

She tugs lightly on his hair, prompting him to look up at her. The raw, unconcealed desire on his face leaves her momentarily speechless. "We should go upstairs." Tessa runs her hands over his shoulders. "More privacy."

"Good idea." Ryan lifts her into his arms, one arm underneath her knees and one arm supporting her back.

Tessa yelps in surprise and delight. "Careful. I don't want you to hurt your back." She has solid muscle through her arms, legs, and core. She isn't exactly light.

Ryan rolls his eyes. "I'm not going to hurt my back." To demonstrate his point, he hefts her a little higher in his arms, and grins down at her. "I've been training for this."

Tessa laughs, leaning her head against his shoulder. Ryan takes the stairs two at a time and opens their bedroom door, revealing that he left a lamp on and that he actually cleaned up since she left this morning. He deposits her on the bed with care. Tessa tugs him down with her, catching his lips with hers. Ryan pulls her on top of him with some difficulty, thanks to the volume of her skirt. He frowns against her lips, and she giggles. "You can't find the slit in the skirt, can you?"

"No," Ryan replies grumpily.

Tessa kisses the line of his jaw, undoing his tie. "You can just take it off."

Ryan cranes his neck, allowing him to make eye contact with her. "Are you sure?"

"Yes." All this time, she had been wary of escalating intimacy, frightened that she would feel Owen's presence in the room with them. She had been scared that getting intimate with Ryan would feel like cheating.

But now, she doesn't feel Owen in the room with them. All there is is Ryan, and her. Ryan, who has been by her side for so long. Looking out for her and keeping her safe in Iraq. Comforting her when she had been horrified at the things she saw and did there. Ryan, who sat with her after she learned about her father's death, and wiped the tears from her cheeks after Spencer's. She still remembers that first sight of him in the hospital in Landstuhl, holding a bouquet of sunflowers for her. A bright spot, after weeks of all-encompassing darkness.

All there is is Ryan, and her. Working on their college applications together, studying together in Butler Library. Sitting side-by-side on the subway on their way to their internships. Ryan asking her to manage his very first campaign. Standing on the balcony together on the night of his first victory. Being by his side at every victory over the next decade and a half, campaign after campaign.

Now, there is just them, as they have been over the past month. In Tokyo. Standing side-by-side in front of the bonfire at Javier and Rosalie's Thanksgiving party. Every weekend spent here at this house, discovering a different kind of love than the one they have shared for so long. The two of them are alone in this room, and Tessa is ready to move forward.

Ryan moves toward her at the same time she leans in. They share a long kiss, and Tessa savors the joy of it. She has had so little of that in the past year and a half. But steadily more, over the past month, thanks to him. Ryan finally finds the zipper at the back of her dress. He tugs it down with surprising patience, tracing his fingers down her spine, over every inch of newly revealed skin. Tessa squirms free of the voluminous dress, discarding it to the floor with a kick of her leg. That leaves her in just her lacy underwear, and the necklace Ryan gave her.

He stares at her, speechless. A flush creeps up his neck, over his collar, flooding his face with color. "What?" Tessa places her hands on his chest and straddles him. She removes his tie and begins to unbutton his shirt, slipping her hands underneath the shirt to caress him.

"I can't believe this is real." Ryan places his hands on her hips. The rest of his meaning is visible on his face, and Tessa remembers their conversation over dinner a few weeks ago. He has wanted this for so long.

"I can't believe it either." It has been a long, painful road here.

Whatever Ryan was about to say dissolves into a moan as she bends down and kisses him, pressing and dragging her chest against his. The skin-to-skin contact is divine, and it makes her want to pin Ryan's arms up above his head and grind against him until she can sate the increasingly demanding need inside her. Ryan wraps his arms around her, trying to turn them so that he is on top. Tessa digs her knees into the mattress, resisting. "I'm not done with you like this yet." She runs one hand through Ryan's hair, and uses the other to take one of his free hands, pressing it down onto the pillow and intertwining their fingers together.

Ryan beams, settling back against the pillow, enjoying his view of her. "I'm glad to hear it."

It is the most fun she has had in a long time. Unrestrained, eager, openmouthed kisses, tentative and then increasingly bold experiments with tongues and teeth. An ample amount of touching that makes Tessa grateful for the soundproofed walls. They roll around on the bed, trading the opportunity to be on top, until Ryan has shed the rest of his clothes and so has she.

Earlier in the night, she entertained thoughts of riding him, but the orgasm he gives her leaves her too limp. Tessa collapses against the bed, holding her arms out to Ryan. "I want you inside me." The orgasm took the edge off her physical need, but this desire for closeness with him transcends that.

Ryan caresses her flushed face, gently smoothing her bangs out of her eyes. He kisses her. Tessa wraps her arms and legs around him, holding him close, digging her fingers into his back. He whispers her name, and Tessa closes her eyes, reveling in this.

They hold each other afterward, her head pillowed on Ryan's chest, both of them trying to catch their breath. Ryan pulls the blanket over her, making sure that she is tucked in. "How are you feeling?"

Tessa snuggles closer. "So good." That is an understatement. Not only did she get to experience something she wanted to with Ryan — but the fact that she was able to do this means something tremendous. It is a successful step forward after Owen. Toward healing and recovery.

Ryan kisses her forehead. "I'm glad."

She opens her eyes, glancing up at him. "What about you? I hope it wasn't a letdown."

There is a kernel of truth underneath the dry joke. Ryan strokes her hair, and Tessa expects him to make a joke in return. "No way," he says softly, instead. "This was the best night of my life."

Tessa hugs Ryan tighter.

Chapter Twenty-Eight
January – February 2026

The New Year begins. The midterm elections, still ten months away, become a hot topic of discussion. Tessa accompanies Ryan on his domestic and international travels when necessary. She remains in DC, holding down the fort, at other times. She settles into a new routine. Work Monday through Friday, and devoting time to her new relationship on the weekends.

She has even less time than she used to, thanks to that new addition to her schedule. She doesn't realize that Valentine's Day is approaching until the talk among her friends and staff turns to Valentine's plans — dinner reservations, weekend trips, gift ideas.

"Toronto is just one and a half hours from DC, and they have some great museums and shopping," she tells Daniel. "Check out the Wintergreen Resort for skiing," she suggests to Mari and Booker. She recommends a few DC-area restaurants to Matt and Javier.

She returns to her office, sinks down into her chair, and presses her fingers to her temples. Then she reaches down to pet Leo.

○○○○○

The Lunar New Year falls in early February this year. Matt and Grace commemorate the occasion as they always do, with an elaborate home-cooked Chinese dinner at their place.

The menu hasn't changed much over the years. Egg rolls stuffed with shredded pork loin, shiitake mushrooms, Napa cabbage, and carrots, and

329

deep-fried until golden brown. Pan-fried shrimp and vegetable dumplings folded into the shape of gold ingots, to symbolize wealth and good fortune. Whole sea bass steamed with ginger, scallions, cilantro, soy sauce, and freshly ground white pepper. For dessert, Nian Gao, sticky rice cakes flavored with ginger, dark brown sugar, oranges, and dates.

It takes two days of prep work from Matt and Grace, and Alicia and Oliver, once both children were old enough to participate. They have always dismissed Ryan's suggestions of having the meal catered, with all of their friends pitching in to cover the cost. "This is tradition," Grace maintained. "But you're welcome to help prep if you want."

Year after year, Ryan shows up in their kitchen, dons one of Matt's spare aprons, and laboriously rolls out uneven rectangles of flour for the dozens of dumplings. The kitchen is full, and everyone trades off picking whatever music, podcast, or TV show they listen to while prepping. There was an era of Chinese martial arts movies (Ryan and Grace's influence), and a decade of dubbed Chinese dramas (Matt's contribution). Now, Alicia and Oliver make them listen to C-pop while they work.

Ryan's sole contribution to the prep is the dumplings. The ugly dumplings never fail to cause him shame. "Don't beat yourself up, Uncle," Alicia assures him. "They still taste good."

No matter how busy he is, Ryan always sets aside a few hours to come and contribute. Matt and Grace's celebration of Chinese culture is the only real connection he has to that side of his own heritage, after all.

Lunar New Year falls the weekend before Valentine's Day. Matt and Grace's downstairs is crowded with their friends, who never pass up an opportunity to get together, eat, and play board games. Booker and Vasu play a game of Chinese chess, spectated (and coached) by Mari, Grace, and Ryan. Matt, Javier, Daniel, and Andrew brave the cold to kick around a soccer ball in the backyard. The kids run around in the backyard with the dogs. Rosalie, Tessa, and Kahaan sit in the living room with Alicia, answering her questions about colleges and majors. Tessa very unsubtly encourages Alicia to visit Barnard.

A timer on Grace's phone goes off. "The dumplings are ready. I'll be right back."

"No, you stay." Ryan gets up from the floor, gesturing for Grace to stay seated. "I'll take care of it. I'll get another batch going too."

Twenty-four dumplings sizzle in hot oil, spread across two pans on the stove. Ryan inhales deeply when he enters the kitchen, delighting in the aroma. He grabs two pairs of tongs off the counter and clicks them like a crab clicking its claws, something that never fails to make Oliver burst out laughing.

"That would go viral on social media. Lunar New Year prep, Veep-style."

Ryan turns to see Rosalie enter the kitchen, looking amused. He gives the tongs one final click. "Better clear it with Kahaan first." The young communications director had not been happy when a shot of Ryan looking bored and unimpressed at the DNC convention a decade ago did major numbers on Twitter, ultimately reaching meme status.

"I can help." Rosalie grabs a fresh plate from the counter and takes one pair of tongs from him. They transfer the dumplings from the pan to the plate, lightly shaking each dumpling to drain it of excess oil. "So. I've been meaning to talk to you."

There is no question about what Rosalie wanted to talk to him about. Of course she, Jesy, and Taliyah know, just like Matt knows. "Of course. What's on your mind?"

"A lot, actually," Rosalie replies carefully. "I'm surprised, and not surprised, at the same time. I'm happy for Tessa, and scared for her."

That last part throws him for a loop. "Why would you feel–" Ryan shakes his head. "I would never hurt Tessa." But Rosalie never thought Owen would hurt Tessa, either. What happened blindsided them all.

"I know you wouldn't. I'm just…" Rosalie sighs, placing one of the new batch of raw dumplings onto the pan. "This is so far out of character for her. You know her. There's never been anyone as straight-laced."

It is a serious conversation, but the comment still makes Ryan smile. "True."

"I'm just afraid that the one time she breaks the rules and does something wild, it's going to come back and bite her."

"You're afraid that we're going to get caught."

"Yeah. And if it comes out, Tess is going to take the brunt of the fallout, because she's a woman." There is a bitter twist to Rosalie's lips. "She's been through enough. She can't handle — she shouldn't *have* to handle getting blasted on a national scale."

"She won't. It won't happen."

Rosalie scowls. "How can you guarantee that?"

"There's a lot of institutional power and privilege that comes with this role." Ryan gestures to the front door and then the back door, where Secret Service agents patrol the perimeter. They have the whole street on lockdown, the same way they do whenever he comes to visit the Hans. "I know you see it. You're surrounded by it every day at work. I swear to you that I will, that I *do*, use every bit of that to protect Tessa."

"You could make a story go away?" Rosalie counters.

Ryan shrugs. "Vice Presidents have gotten away with a lot more."

"You would do that?" Rosalie's expression is unreadable. "That's not very on brand for you."

"It's not. But I would do it for her."

Rosalie's shoulders slump in the manner of someone who has accepted defeat. "Don't think I hate you or I'm mad at you, okay? I'm just worried about her. Tessa comes first."

"That's why I appreciate you and Jesy so much." Tessa has no fiercer advocates than the two of them, her oldest and best friends.

"Thanks." Rosalie's tone becomes brisk, businesslike, as they put the rest of the raw dumplings into the pan. "If you're going to be with her, there are some things that you should know. You know her history. You can't raise your voice around her. You can't make her think you're mad at her."

The words are a harsh reminder of the trauma that Tessa keeps so well concealed. "Right."

"May twenty-fifth is a really bad day for Tessa. Her and Owen's anniversary," Rosalie explains, in a whisper. "October first is rough — Owen's birthday. Valentine's Day too."

The first and second dates aren't news to him. Tessa had been noticeably quieter than usual on May twenty-fifth and on the first of October. She was truthful on both occasions when he asked her what was wrong. The third comes as a surprise. Ryan frowns, thinking of the gifts tucked into his closet. "Valentine's Day?"

"She and Owen always did something for Valentine's. Nothing big or extravagant, but they were into it. Also, just the celebration of romantic love, after you lose your own like that… It was hard for her last year. It was like the holiday was rubbing her face in all that she didn't have anymore."

He had no reaction to Valentine's Day after he and Vanessa divorced. "Thanks for warning me."

"No problem." Rosalie picks up one of the plates, laden with dumplings. Ryan follows her lead. "Thank you, too. For treating her right. I never thought that I… I worried that I would never see her like this again."

He had shared the same worry. Tessa after Owen had been like a ghost, like a dead woman walking. "I hope that I can always make her this happy."

ooooo

The fourteenth of February falls on a Friday this year. Ryan and Tessa dismiss their staff from work by early afternoon. "Go have fun," Tessa says.

Ryan gives them cheery smiles. "Don't do anything I wouldn't do."

He and Tessa leave the office at nine-thirty that night. They drive separately, and he is the first one to get home. Ryan is in the midst of hanging his coat up when the door in the kitchen creaks open. He shoves the coat and hanger hastily back into the closet. "Tess?"

After fifteen hours at work, battling through endless meetings with his staff, Gardner's staff, and over on the Hill, he doesn't recognize his own voice. He sounds like a happy, excited kid, the way he was, a long time ago.

"Ryan?" There is a touch of the same hope and joy in Tessa's voice too, so different from her sharp, decisive way of speaking in the office.

Leo barks, as if announcing himself too. Tessa laughs, and so does Ryan, as he strides toward the kitchen. On some Friday nights, he and Tessa greet each other with hungry kisses, desperate to get their hands on each other after five days of professional behavior.

This isn't one of those nights. Ryan holds his arms out to Tessa. She comes right to him, hugging him tightly. He treasures the feel of her in his arms; this precious slice of peace and sanity amidst the tumult of his life. He misses this so much during the week. Ryan breathes in the scent of her hair, and then kisses her on the forehead. Tessa makes a small, contented sound. She hugs him again, burying her face in his shoulder.

If he could only have this, if they could have this, every single day, instead of once a week–

Don't be so greedy, Ryan chastises himself. It is remarkable that he can be with Tessa like this at all. He should be grateful for what he has.

Tessa finally releases him, and she presses a soft kiss to his cheek. "Hold on."

She goes to her leather tote bag. Ryan smiles at Leo, who sniffs around the kitchen, investigating the space to ensure that there have been no changes since Sunday.

"Here." Tessa returns, holding a package wrapped in nondescript gray wrapping paper. "Happy Valentine's Day."

Ryan looks at her, taken aback. The smile she gives him is small, but genuine. "You didn't have to."

"I wanted to." It is obvious what this gesture meant to her.

Ryan hugs her again. "Thank you, sweetheart."

"Don't thank me yet." Tessa speaks with her usual pragmatism, her voice muffled by the collar of his shirt. "You haven't even opened it. You may hate it."

Ryan laughs. Tessa is famous amongst their friends for her gift-giving. She has keen observational skills, and a talent for selecting presents perfectly aligned with what people want and need. "I doubt it."

He tugs at the gray wrapping paper, revealing a monogrammed leather notebook with a royal blue cover. "Wow — is this Columbia blue?"

"Yep." Tessa smirks. She once did an inventory of his closet and found that a good half of his leisure clothes are relics from his college days.

"It's perfect." He works with a half-dozen different notebooks and journals at any given time. Of course Tessa noticed that he was getting close to the end of his domestic policy notebook. "Just like you."

Tessa scoffs, giving him a reproving nudge in the ribs, the way she does whenever he says something unacceptably corny. "Oh, stop it."

"I have something for you too, upstairs." Ryan holds out his hand to her. After what Rosalie shared, he thought he would have to hold off on giving this to Tessa until her next birthday.

They go upstairs together. Ryan heads straight into their closet and carries the gift bag back to Tessa. "For you." He kisses her on the head, setting the bag at her feet.

Tessa looks at him warily. "This better not have been expensive."

"It wasn't." The earful she gave him when she realized how much her birthday necklace cost scared him off any more jewelry. For now.

"Hmm." The skepticism in Tessa's expression is replaced with wonder, as she lifts a framed photo from the bag.

"From Ghana in December," Ryan explains unnecessarily. Tessa breaks into a smile. Their trip had been a whirlwind one, intended to show support for Ghana amidst their economic crisis and security concerns. They still managed to snag an hour and a half to visit the National Museum in Accra, accompanied by Andrew and Booker. Ryan took a selfie of the four of them huddled in front of a magnificent batik wall hanging.

"Remember that banku and fried tilapia we had afterward? I hope we can go back someday, for a longer visit."

"I'll put it on my agenda for when I'm President."

Ryan has the pleasure of seeing Tessa beam as she pulls out the next photo, a selfie taken by Jesy, of her, Rosalie, and Tessa at their most recent Friendsgiving. There are several more photos, all framed. One of Leo sitting loyally at Tessa's side while she works. One of Tessa and Leo together on the Barnard campus, the last time they visited New York City. A group photo of their friends from their Tokyo visit, in the garden during a meeting break — the same garden where he and Tessa shared their first kiss. There are a few photos that Rosalie and Jesy contributed, of Tessa with Zahra and Ruby through the years.

She is smiling so hard by the time she gets through them all. Ryan can't take his eyes off her. It is so rare to see her like this. Even in better days, Tessa has never been an outwardly expressive person.

"These are wonderful." She gently places the last photo back in the bag and then hugs him tight. "Thank you."

"You mentioned once that you didn't have photos up at your apartment, so I thought you'd like these." He doesn't like thinking of her alone in that little apartment at night. At least she has Leo.

"Ryan." Tessa looks up at him. She wavers, seeming to lose her nerve. Then a softer version of her legendary resolve crosses her face. "I love you."

Ryan cups her face with a hand, and she leans into his touch. "I know." He has never had a happier moment than this. He has known dizzying exultation at victory, and the joy of belonging with his friends, with his family, but this — this is the pinnacle of everything he has experienced before. This sensation of being loved by the woman he loves. "I love you too, Tess."

Tessa stands up on the tips of her toes, and kisses him on the lips.

Chapter Twenty-Nine
February 2026 – January 2027

Leo is, as always, Tessa's constant companion. They sit together on the sofa every night after work, no matter how late it is. Leo settles down atop her feet to keep them warm, and Tessa shares her soft pink throw blanket with him. She methodically checks tabloid websites, random political blogs, and celebrity gossip subreddits. She runs Ryan's name and her own — together and separately — through every search engine she can think of.

Night after night, nothing out of the ordinary comes up. Tessa shuts her laptop, a little bit of the tension easing from her neck. "Safe, for now."

Leo looks back at her with sympathetic eyes. It would be so much easier if this wasn't just her and Ryan's secret to keep. Kahaan is their communications director, and he has his eagle eyes on every source out there, conventional or unconventional. He is aware of every developing story around Ryan, even if the story is in the embryonic stages. But Kahaan doesn't know to keep an eye out for this.

Leo moves, settling himself on her lap. "That's my good boy." Tessa hugs him, her sigh ruffling his fur. The risk of her relationship with Ryan being exposed is a constant source of anxiety. That anxiety is as ever-present as her grief and pain were. It is almost as exhausting and draining to cope with. Every text or news alert that pops up on her phone, every phone call that comes in on her office line, always sparks a moment of stomach-clenching fear. Maybe this is the text or call that could ruin everything for her and Ryan.

("Ruin everything?" Ryan frowned when she shared this fear with him. "This isn't the '90s. This isn't Bill Clinton and Monica Lewinsky. It isn't John Edwards. If this comes out, it'll be a story, sure. But it won't be a career-killing scandal.")

He is partially right. The excoriation of Bill Clinton and John Edwards came because they were married. They broke their vows. Tessa still doesn't share Ryan's confident attitude.

("If this story comes out, it's not going to stop with the here and now." Tessa paced up and down the length of the kitchen, picking at her cuticles. Leo rose from his spot by the window and came to stand by her side, nudging her leg. "I'm worried that the media is going to conjecture that this has always been going on — even when we were married to other people."

Ryan's frown grew deeper. "Well, they have no proof of that, so that's all it'll be. Baseless conjecture.")

The political fallout of that is one thing. The personal fallout is another. Tessa lies in bed awake at night, imagining Vanessa's reaction to that story breaking. Imagining Vanessa turning on the news, forced to see innocuous photos of Ryan alongside Tessa at campaign events, cast in a new light. It makes bile rise in her throat. She knew how jealous Owen could be. As far as she knows, Vanessa hadn't carried that same burden. Tessa doesn't ever want her to.

Sometimes she catastrophizes, imagining what the headlines and articles would say about Ryan, about her, about them, if the news broke. She hates the thought of Ryan's reputation getting dragged through the mud. Of him being lumped in with all the other politicians and creeps who have sexually coerced an employee. She hates the thought of anyone perceiving her as someone who would cheat on her husband. She had never been unfaithful to Owen, in thought or deed.

The anxiety even flavors Tessa's nightmares. She hasn't lived with this kind of prolonged anxiety since that last year with Owen. It takes a toll on her now, as it did then. The recurring fear consistently comes up in her therapy appointments. She and Taliyah talk through strategies to help her cope. Tessa dedicates ten minutes every day to deep breathing exercises. She comes up with plans to address every *what if* situation she can think of.

Sometimes she wonders if everything that she is putting herself through is worth it. She is putting her privacy, her professional and personal life, her entire reputation, at risk.

Those questions only last a split second. That is how long it takes for her to remember the security and joy of being in love again, of loving and being loved. The love she shares with Ryan, and their quiet moments together, are worth the risk.

ooooo

The months roll on. The worst doesn't happen. Tessa never sees anything untoward on her news alerts. The only calls she receives from journalists are for reputable articles about the Vice President's political initiatives and efforts. Ryan remains free of scandal, and so does she.

In May, Tessa and Matt help Ryan prep for a meeting with the CEOs of four major companies developing artificial intelligence technologies. (Later that month, on the twenty-fifth of May, Tessa walks with Leo around the enormous backyard of Number One Observatory Circle. She can't stop thinking about where she was fourteen years ago today, and tears come to her eyes. Ryan takes her hand and squeezes it lightly, without a word, and releases it. After a few minutes, Tessa reaches out and takes his hand. They keep walking in silence.)

In July, Ryan gives a speech at the Disability Pride Parade in Chicago. He visits a few other spots in the city, and delivers speeches at the University of Chicago, UnitedHealth Group headquarters, and Boeing headquarters. Tessa accompanies him to each event, and to a visit of the Barack Obama Presidential Library. They enjoy seeing Chicago, even though it is with their entourage. They sit side-by-side at Bonci Pizzeria and try Chicago-style deep-dish pizza, which is very, very strange. "This isn't a pizza," Ryan mutters to her. "This is a casserole."

September and October, leading up to the midterms, are hectic. Ryan goes out to campaign for dozens of Democrats in tight races around the country. Gardner sends Ryan out to campaign on his behalf for even more candidates. Campaign events eat into the evenings, nights, and late nights. They tear chunks out of the weekends, the sacred time that Tessa has to share with Ryan. It leaves him irritable. Not at her, but irritable nonetheless. It leaves Tessa off-balance, alone in bed with Leo on Friday and Saturday nights. Their level of discretion means that there can be no affectionate phone calls, texts, or emails. If they aren't together at Number

One Observatory Circle, they are nothing more than the Vice President and Chief of Staff.

November brings a modicum of victory. They hold off the Republicans' promised "red wave." They hold onto the House by the skin of their teeth, but they fail to secure the Senate. There is a lot of talk in Ryan's office, and in the West Wing, and in the Oval Office, about what this means for 2028.

Ryan insists on hosting their friends' Thanksgiving that November, and he places a jaw-droppingly huge sushi order for them from Sushi Nakazawa. Tessa notes the choice of cuisine and raises an eyebrow. "Any particular reason for the Japanese theme?" she asks, when their friends have left for the night.

"A shout-out to our visit in Tokyo this time last year." Ryan places a hand on her back. "I have no idea what possessed you to kiss me in that garden–"

"Neither do I," Tessa cuts in, straight-faced.

"—But I'm grateful you did, every day," Ryan continues doggedly.

Tessa rests her head on his shoulder. "I can't believe it's been a year."

"What are you thinking?" Ryan peers down at her.

"I never thought I would get into another relationship. I could never imagine myself going on a coffee date with someone else, let alone..." Their relationship has blossomed, deepened, despite the limited time they can devote to one another. It is hard to admit, even to herself, but she thinks of Ryan in the same way that she thought of Owen. She thinks of him as almost her husband, her family. "I never saw all of this coming."

"I hope it's not too much of an unpleasant surprise," Ryan jokes.

"It's not unpleasant at all. It's just a strange feeling, to surprise yourself." Tessa kisses him on the cheek. "Happy anniversary."

Ryan's smile lights up the whole room. "Happy anniversary, Tess."

ooooo

Ryan allows himself to spend Thanksgiving weekend relaxing with her. He returns to his regularly scheduled anxiety on Monday. His anxious energy infects the entire staff, save for Tessa. "How are you being so chill about this?" Booker asks, while he and Mari accompany her on Leo's daily lunchtime walk. "You're probably going to run the campaign again, right?"

"I can't think about that now." Tessa takes a sip from her thermos of tea, flavored richly with cinnamon, ginger, and cardamom. "I have to focus on the day-to-day running of this office, until I get confirmation that I need to do otherwise."

The question leaves her unsettled, though she doesn't show it. Running Ryan's campaign the first time around was hard enough, and she still failed. She stands by that harsh assessment, even though Ryan and Matt have argued with her about this for hours. She could let Matt manage this campaign in 2028, while she holds down the fort in DC as Chief of Staff.

Almost every conversation at work returns to the question of whether President Gardner will run for a second term in 2028. Daniel, whose boyfriend works on Gardner's staff, is the trusted source of insider information. Everyone grills him daily about whether Kieran has heard anything from his higher-ups. Every day, nothing. Every day, Ryan's smile grows more strained.

He vents to Tessa and Matt in private. They soothe him, as they always have. "There's no way he's going to run," Matt says. "He'll be eighty next year. The election is in 2028, so his term would be up in 2032. He'd be eighty-five by then."

"I know. I'm still worried. Incumbents have an advantage. Gardner's advisors will warn him not to throw that away against the Republican candidate — whoever that is." Ryan punctuates the words with an exasperated wave of the hand.

"Gardner implied he would be a one-term president when he offered you the VP spot," Tessa reminds him.

Another exasperated hand wave from Ryan. "That's true, but I also don't trust him on that. People get their hands on this kind of power, and they don't want to give it away."

"The media speculation is picking up." Tessa tosses her copy of The New York Times on the coffee table. "But I doubt that he'll make an announcement before the holidays. I would expect him to call you in for a meeting after the New Year."

"After the New Year." Ryan props his elbow up on the armchair of the sofa, massaging his temples. "I hate this waiting. I just want to know, so that I can make plans. *We* need to make plans."

"Patience is a virtue," Matt counsels. Ryan rolls his eyes at him.

⚬⚬⚬⚬⚬

Tessa spends the New Year with her friends and Ryan. There are enough people around that she and Ryan can't share a kiss when the ball drops. Tessa lifts Leo into her arms and kisses him on the top of his furry head instead, and he licks her on the cheek. They are among friends and away from the media, at Javier and Rosalie's house, so Ryan discreetly takes her hand. She hopes that her 2027 is filled with as much love and joy as her 2026 had been.

⚬⚬⚬⚬⚬

Tessa returns to work on January 3. It is a frigid pre-dawn in DC, and she and Leo are both shivering when they step foot in the EEOB. They are the first into the office. Tessa flicks the lights on, taking in the first sight of the space in the New Year.

"Here's to a good year, Leo. Here's to a lot of wins." Leo wags his tail hard in agreement.

She opens her email, and her inbox updates to reflect 250 new messages. Tessa winces. Her attention is immediately drawn to an email from Ernesto Ortega, her counterpart in President Gardner's office.

There isn't a lot to read. An important meeting request between the President and the Vice President tomorrow, between seven to eight in the evening. The old adrenaline surges through her, the way it did during the lead-up to every previous campaign launch. Tessa looks down at Leo, ignoring the tightness building in her chest. "Here we go again."

⚬⚬⚬⚬⚬

That workday and the next hurtle by at a frenetic pace. Tessa stops work at a quarter to seven and knocks on the door to Ryan's office.

"Come in."

She enters, leaving the door slightly ajar. "I wanted to tell you to get ready." Once Ryan gets started on a task, he hyperfixates for hours at a time, forgetting to eat or drink, or attend to other commitments.

It doesn't look like he is in the middle of anything, though. He stands in the middle of the room, so she must have caught him pacing. He has assumed his calm, composed demeanor, but she can see the cracks in it. Tessa joins him without saying a word, and Ryan manages a smile. "I'm taking a deep breath now."

"You got this. No matter what happens in that meeting."

"I'm trying." Ryan's smile fades. "It's just — I can't bear four more years of this. I'm ready. I'm so ready to lead."

"You can handle four more years of this, if you have to. You've gotten through so much worse."

The memory of Iraq hangs between them. Ryan nods, his typical resolve returning. "You're right."

"As always."

Ryan reaches out like he would put a hand on her arm. Tessa glances at his hand, and he withdraws. "Come to the meeting with me."

"You don't need me there." Tessa almost never attends his meetings with the President. She wishes she could place a hand on his shoulder to comfort him, but all she can do is give him a small smile. "Good luck."

∞∞∞∞

The meeting runs late, and Tessa's friends all leave for the day. Only Matt, as her Deputy Chief of Staff, lingers. They take their laptops into Ryan's office, but they get no work done.

"What would our first steps be, if — you know?" Matt asks.

"The announcement will come from Gardner's office. He'll say he won't seek a second term."

"Should we give it a day or two to build hype, or strike while the iron is hot?"

"Give it a day or two," Tessa decides. "Let the media digest Gardner's announcement first."

"Kahaan–"

"Already wrote two announcements. One in support of Gardner, and one announcing Ryan's intention to run. Ryan needs to approve both and make his additions and edits."

"Alright. We have to hit the ground running with the DNC. Gardner will throw his weight behind Ryan, and that means the DNC has to as well.

Let's put some extra pressure on them."

"I'll call Green as soon as Ryan makes the announcement."

Tessa notices Leo's ears perk up. The dog lifts his head off his paws, his tail thumping on the ground. "Matt."

They shove their laptops aside and rise to their feet. Ryan bursts through the door, his energy barely contained. Tessa knows even before he strides toward them, his arms outstretched. "It's happening."

He throws one arm around her shoulders and one arm around Matt's. Tessa's trepidation vanishes, replaced with Ryan's joy. "I knew it would. Congratulations."

Matt claps him on the back, his eyes shining. "We're with you, man. We're going to do everything to get you into the Oval."

Matt and Tessa bring Ryan up to speed on everything they discussed while he was gone, and he provides a detailed recap of his conversation with Gardner. "He said he wants to stay in office, that serving the country as the President has been the greatest privilege of his life, but he's…" Ryan lowers his voice. "He's been diagnosed with Parkinson's disease."

Matt forgets to keep his voice down. "What?"

"Parkinson's disease. Like Michael J. Fox," Tessa answers. "It's a neurological condition."

"It affects movement." Ryan's expression is faraway. "I have thought that he's seemed different somehow, lately. Physically slower. Less spry. I put it down to aging."

Matt sighs. "At least the media hasn't picked up on it."

"Is he going to disclose the diagnosis when he announces that he won't run for a second term?"

"I don't know," Ryan says. "I can't imagine what he's going through. It's hard enough to tell your family and friends, let alone the entire nation. It's his choice. I'll support him in whatever he chooses."

"If he discloses his diagnosis, it could cast a shadow over the last couple of years of his presidency. Undeservedly," Tessa adds. "He'll be doubted and second-guessed on everything he does."

Ryan scowls. "Congressional Republicans will push him to step down. I want the presidency, but not if it comes to me like that."

"But if he doesn't disclose and the news leaks, or the media starts speculating about it and it gets traction, he'll be accused of being dishonest with the American people. That will cast a shadow over him too — and get the entire Democratic Party embroiled in the mess." Tessa bites her lip as she mulls it over. She doesn't envy Gardner's position.

"What does this mean for you?" Matt looks at Ryan. "Are you going to have to take on more, to take things off his plate, over the next couple of years? While campaigning for President?"

"I have no idea. Gardner said that this isn't a disease that progresses fast. He's doing everything he can to stay on top of it all. Rehab, medication, and so on. Ernesto and the rest of his senior staff are going to pick up more duties, as needed, to support him." Ryan's attention drifts to the grandfather clock in the corner of the room, and he startles. "It's late, man. Go home to your family."

"You guys text me if you need anything, okay?"

They wish him good night, and watch him go. Tessa turns to Ryan. "Matt should be the one to run your campaign this time around." They hadn't gotten into those details tonight.

Ryan runs a hand through his hair, looking unsettled for the first time in their conversation so far. "We'll see."

Chapter Thirty
January 2027

Ryan and Tessa make the announcement to their staff the following day. They don't mention Gardner's reason behind not running for a second term. "Keep this under wraps," Tessa warns. "The President's office hasn't made their announcement yet."

There is no need for the warning. They have never had any leaks come from their staff. No one breathes a word outside of the office, but the topic dominates their hushed conversations for the rest of the week. Everyone begins balancing their current work with 2028 prep. It helps that this isn't their first presidential campaign. The staff knows what to expect.

Ryan makes no comment about who is stepping into the role of campaign manager, even though Tessa, Matt, and Kahaan all press him for further information. "We'll see," he repeats. "I'm thinking some things through right now." He swings between palpable excitement about the challenge ahead, and worry, which is normal. A presidential campaign is one of the hardest professional and personal endeavors to undertake. *No one sane would do this,* Matt told her, once. That explains why Ryan is doing it. Again.

Tessa is overwhelmed by relief when she and Leo arrive at Number One Observatory Circle on Friday night. Ryan's presence makes it feel more like home than her apartment. Over the fourteen months that they have been together, they have added more and more personal touches to the house. The walls hold framed photos of New York City, which will always have their heart, no matter how long they live in DC. There are photos of them with their friends over the years adorning coffee tables and bookshelves. The master bathroom is stocked with Tessa's favorite bath products. Ryan has ceded half the master bedroom closet to her, even though she doesn't need all that space.

The intimacy of sharing space, living together part-time with someone besides Owen, was hard to get used to at first. She has settled into it now. Being with Ryan like this feels natural.

Passion comes before tenderness on this particular Friday night reunion. They trade soft kisses in bed afterward, stroking each other's hair, running their hands over each other's arms and backs. "I missed you," Ryan breathes, even though he sees her every single day.

Tessa presses her forehead to his. "I missed you too."

She doesn't give voice to the worries that have plagued her all week. A presidential candidate comes under immense scrutiny during a campaign. Privacy ceases to be a valid concept. In a matter of months, it will be impossible for them to do this.

ooooo

They sleep in the next morning, work out together in Ryan's home gym, and play with Leo in the backyard. They shower (not together, despite Ryan's teasing), and make bagel sandwiches for brunch. "Do you want to get back to the puzzle?" Tessa puts the last plate into the dishwasher, as Ryan tosses a detergent pod in. "There's a new episode of Freakonomics we can listen to. Unless you listened already?"

"No, I waited for you."

They find their half-completed thousand-piece puzzle on the coffee table in the living room. Tessa pulls out her phone to play the podcast, but Ryan touches her arm, nodding toward the sofa. "Do you want to sit first?"

Her stomach cramps with nervousness. Either he is going to give her his decision about the campaign manager position, or…

Tessa sinks down on the sofa, patting the cushion beside her. Leo sits beside her legs, sensing her increasing stress. Ryan joins her, taking her hand in his. He lifts her hand to his lips, pressing a soft kiss to her knuckles, regarding her with the same pure tenderness he did last night. "I love you so much, my Tessa."

Tessa clasps her other hand on top of his. "I love you too."

"I've been thinking about what's ahead. About us. I…"

Tessa takes pity on him. She kisses his hand, just like he did with her. "Look, I get it. Don't feel bad."

Ryan blinks. "What?"

"I know we have to…" The words stick in her throat, but she forces them out. "I know we'll have to stop this for a while." For the duration of Ryan's campaign, until his inauguration. *A while* is an understatement. The campaign period is almost two years. "It's the smart thing to do."

Ryan's expression reflects his horror. He pulls his hand out of hers. "No. God, no, that wasn't what I was trying to say." He puts his arm around her, drawing her close to him, and exhales a ragged breath. "Tessa, I wanted to ask you if you'll marry me."

Tessa pulls away, aghast. "What? You — what?"

Ryan wilts. "Did I… Did I misread something?"

"No." Tessa grabs his hand. "Ryan, I love you. I already think of you as my husband." Her voice breaks, and Ryan puts his arm around her again. Leo nudges her leg, sensing her distress. Her stomach roils. She pets him and then straightens, turning to face Ryan. "Is this about the campaign?"

"That's part of it. I've been thinking of what the years ahead have in store for us. Almost two more years until I'm inaugurated, and eight years — hopefully — of my presidency. That's a whole ten years. How are we going to sneak around for the next decade? It just doesn't… It just won't work."

Ten years. In ten years, she will be forty-eight. Ryan will be fifty-two. They are young-ish now, but they won't be in a decade. Ten years is a long time to wait. Tessa's shoulders sag. "You're right."

"And I'm giving you scraps right now, with these weekends. We have, what, a little more than twenty-four hours before you have to leave again? I'll have even less time once I take on the presidency. I want to give you more than this. We're not old yet, but we're only going to get older. I want to spend that time with you."

Tessa lets that sink in. She places her hand on Ryan's arm. "I want to give you more than this too. You've been my best friend for twenty years, and this past year with you has been so… I never thought I could feel this kind of love again. I would–" Her voice catches in her throat again. "I would spend the rest of my life with you, if I could."

Ryan rubs her back. "You can, sweetheart. I want you to."

Tessa tries to wrap her mind around all of this. "What — what would that mean for us? Aside from the obvious. I always imagined myself as your Chief of Staff if you got the presidency. Sorry if that's presumptuous."

"It's not."

"That's what I've been preparing for, for my entire professional life. But this–" Tessa struggles to digest it. "I would be the First Lady."

"Yes. You would."

Tessa thinks of Margaret Gardner, Penelope Baiss, Michelle Obama, Hillary Clinton, Laura Bush. They had been so intensely in the public eye — as much as their husbands had been. "Then I wouldn't be your Chief of Staff, as I have been. I wouldn't work with you anymore."

"Not in the way you do now." Ryan's face registers the same pain she feels. "You would be politically active in a different way. You'll travel internationally as a representative of the United States. Laura Bush traveled to seventy-seven countries, did you know that? You'll campaign for Democrats across the country. You can advocate for our policy priorities. Michelle Obama supported her husband's economic stimulus bill by visiting the HUD* and the DOE*. You can champion the policy and social issues that you feel most strongly about."

Tessa hears him. The interviews she has watched and read over the years, every First Lady under the media spotlight, plays in a loop in her mind. Every one of their words analyzed, the scrutiny paid to their outfits, of all things. Their body language, their hair, their makeup. So many speeches. Mrs. Gardner, Baiss, Obama, Clinton, and Bush made so many speeches. In front of the DNC and RNC. In front of thousands of voters and donors and massive audiences, foreign and domestic. Cameras flashing, hundreds of shouted questions. Tessa is no stranger to that, but it has always been on Ryan's behalf. Not her own. She has never been the one in the public eye. She has always been ensconced safely behind the scenes.

Her grip tightens on Ryan's arm. "The media–"

"That… will be an adjustment for you. But you know how great Kahaan is. He'll give you all the training you need. And you don't need much!

Department of Housing and Urban Development
Department of Education

You're absolutely brilliant, and you're always so calm and composed, so thoughtful and compassionate. You'll be perfect. Don't have any doubts about that."

"I'm…" Tears fill her eyes. Leo scrambles up onto the sofa, settling into her lap for support. "My past, Ryan. I can't have that come out. People will ask questions — why I got divorced — why I got a service dog afterward– People from Owen's old support groups might talk, or his medical records might get leaked, or his brother might say something."

"We won't let that happen." Ryan hugs her around the shoulders. "We'll control the narrative, just like we did when I got divorced."

Tessa wipes her tear-streaked face with her free hand, petting Leo with the other. The dog nuzzles close, trying to comfort her. "I can't bear it if they get their hands on old photos of Owen and I. If they put those on TV, on the Internet — I can't see those. I can't."

She is crying in earnest now, and Ryan holds her. "I know. I'll do everything I can to protect you, and your past, and your privacy, through this, if you say yes. But if you don't…" He pulls away, looking her in the eye. "I'll respect that. We'll find some way to make things work."

Tessa struggles to regain her composure. "I'm going to text Matt, Kahaan, and Rosalie. This is bigger than the two of us. We have some things to talk through."

"Of course. Go ahead. Invite them over today, if they can make it."

Their friends are wonderful. The three of them join them in the kitchen within the hour. Tessa makes tea for them, and she and Ryan set out a charcuterie board on the table.

"You didn't have to do all this." Rosalie wraps her hands around her mug of tea to warm them. The snow let up today, thankfully, but the temperatures outside haven't broken the mid-20s.

"Speak for yourself." Matt attacks the cheese cubes.

"It was the least we could do, considering that you all were able to make it at such short notice." Ryan takes a seat at the table beside her. Kahaan looks between the two of them in silent understanding. They aren't public with their relationship with anyone outside of Matt, Rosalie, and Jesy, but Tessa has the feeling that every one of their friends knows the truth.

"Thank you for joining us today." Slipping into professional formality makes this easier. Tessa hesitates, glancing at Ryan. "Do you want to…?"

"No, you go ahead."

She turns back to her friends. They stare back in expectant silence, their plates and tea forgotten. "Ryan proposed to me today." It's still surreal to say it out loud. She can't help but think back to the last time she was proposed to. Tessa suppresses those memories.

Kahaan breaks into a wide grin. "I knew it!" Matt yells so loudly that Leo startles, punching the air with joy.

Rosalie shrieks, covering her mouth with her hands. "Oh my god!"

Kahaan leans over to give her a hug. Rosalie drags her chair over to sit near Tessa and takes her hand, gripping it tightly. Matt pushes away from the table, rising to embrace first Ryan, and then her. "You guys — this is the best news."

"Thank you." Ryan reaches out to her, and Tessa gives him her other hand to hold. "We're not in celebration mode just yet."

"I haven't said yes yet. There are a lot of things to consider."

Her friends' faces reflect understanding. "Yeah, of course," Matt says. "First Lady isn't the role you expected to have."

Rosalie's brows draw together. "Would you have to quit your job? You can't announce an engagement right now out of nowhere, right? You guys would have to go public with a relationship first."

Kahaan rubs his forehead. "Well, let's think through our options."

Matt sets his mug of tea down on the table with a *thunk.* "We're going to lose you?"

He has been her Deputy Chief of Staff for as long as they both have worked for Ryan. Anyone else in his position would have been glad to see her go, because it guarantees him a promotion. Matt isn't like that. Tessa attempts a smile. "It's not like I'll be dead."

This is exactly what she wanted to avoid. Leaving Ryan and her friends, especially on the verge of another presidential campaign. *Don't be greedy,* Tessa chastises herself. She got to have her cake and eat it too, for over a year.

"Tessa," Rosalie says suddenly. "What do you want?"

Tessa glances at Ryan. "It's not about that. We have to do what's right for the candidate. We have to find the best optics for him."

Ryan shakes his head. "Rosalie is right. We've made everything about me for the past twenty years. You tell us what you want. We'll figure out a way to make it happen."

Matt and Kahaan nod, their expressions resolute. Rosalie smiles at Ryan, but Tessa hesitates. It goes against every fiber of her being to think of herself before Ryan. She tries to gather her thoughts, turning inward.

What she wants is to have it all. To be Ryan's wife, without being the First Lady. She wants to be Ryan's Chief of Staff, as she always has.

What she wants is impossible. She can't have both positions. She has to choose what is most important to her.

It takes several moments for Tessa to speak. When she does, the words come slowly, decisively. "I want to spend my life with Ryan. I don't want to leave my job in the administration until I absolutely have to. I want to maintain my privacy as much as I can throughout this process. I want — I *need* the media to be respectful of Owen and Vanessa. I don't want anyone hounding them, asking them to comment on Ryan and I. The two of them need to be able to live their lives in peace."

She still hates that Owen and Vanessa will see the news at all. She could have lived the rest of her life happily without either of them ever knowing.

Ryan sits up straight, as though a tremendous weight has lifted off his shoulders. Matt pulls out his pocket journal and takes notes on her priorities, the way he does whenever the two of them meet at work. "Got it," Kahaan says. "I'll put pressure on those points. Privacy for you, Owen, and Vanessa. I won't entertain any media questions about them, or about your past."

"When the time comes…" Tessa still can't fully grasp the implications of what she is about to say. She is giving up her old dream of being the first woman to be White House Chief of Staff, and replacing it with one she never expected. "I want to be a politically active First Lady. I'll work to promote our agenda in every way I can. I have my own issues that I want to take on as well. I'll campaign for Democrats around the country. Ryan, I know Matt will be your Chief of Staff, but I want to be as involved in supporting you both as I can be."

Ryan opens his mouth, but Matt speaks first. "Yes. Chief of Staff to the President is the toughest job anyone in our staff has ever faced, and you're the one who's been poised to take it on. I'll benefit from your help."

Tessa smiles at him, grateful for his lack of ego. "Yes," Ryan echoes. "You've always been right by my side in decision-making, talking me through everything. That won't change."

"All right," Kahaan says. "Anything else?"

Tessa thinks back to her first meeting with key staff in the incoming Gardner White House, in November 2024. The Office of the First Lady is an entity of the White House Office, part of the Executive Office of the President. She never dreamed that would be relevant to her. "Rosalie, I want you to be my Chief of Staff, if you're okay with it."

Rosalie hugs her around the shoulders again. "I would be so happy to."

"You'll need a communications director and a press secretary too." Ryan frowns at her with mock seriousness. "But you can't take Kahaan or Booker."

Tessa tries to smile. She still can't believe that they're discussing this. "We'll see."

"Okay." Kahaan cracks his knuckles, leaning over to look at Matt's list of priorities. "We know what Tessa needs, and we know what Ryan needs."

"I have what I need. Tessa said yes."

"Right, but we need to figure out the way this is all going to play out. Tess doesn't want to leave us until she has to. Let me know what guys you think of this. Ryan is going to announce his 2028 run soon. It's only January of 2027. He won't start hitting the campaign trail until summer or fall. In this scenario, Tessa resigns this spring or summer and takes another job–"

Tessa tries not to wince.

"—And we let her and Ryan's relationship go public, while putting as much pressure on the media as we can to protect her privacy. It's like what you said, Rosalie. She and Ryan would be dating in the public eye, not engaged yet."

"How are we going to message that?" Matt asks. "You know that people are going to ask questions about how it all played out."

"We'll figure it out. I'll workshop some ideas. We could announce the engagement whenever we want. Maybe a year from now, in January of 2028. Or we wait until afterward, after Ryan wins the election."

"Thanks for your faith in me."

Rosalie chimes in. "Tessa will carry more clout during the campaign if she's engaged to, or married to, Ryan. She'll be the potential First Lady in waiting, rather than "just" the candidate's girlfriend. That lends itself to being politically active like you want to be, Tess. It also means that you'll get a lot of attention from the media."

Tessa stops herself from picking at her cuticles. "This sounds like a good plan." Kahaan mentioned her resignation this spring. She has no shortage of offers from special interest groups. Taking any one of them would feel dishonest when her heart and mind are with Ryan and the 2028 election. A thought occurs to her, making her sit up straighter. "What if I went to the DNC?" The DNC raises funds, commissions polls, and coordinates campaign strategy, independently and in coordination with the presidential candidate. Ryan's eyes widen with excitement. "That's perfect."

"Genius," Matt praises. "You'll still be a political power player, but affiliated with the DNC and not Ryan. He won't be your boss, and you can work with me on his campaign strategy."

"You're good with the Chair, right?" Rosalie asks. "Green?"

"Yes." Excitement surges in her. "And one of the Vice Chair spots is vacant."

Kahaan claps his hands together. "I think we have a plan. Can I start scheduling one-on-one time with you for media training? The sooner we start getting you comfortable with the media, the better. You already know how it's done, from helping Ryan. You just need to apply those lessons to yourself."

"Mm-hmm." Her friends must pick up on her discomfort, because they give her sympathetic looks.

Kahaan, Matt, and Rosalie head out shortly afterward, after a last round of congratulations. Ryan sighs as he closes the front door behind them. "I'm so glad that we could talk this through."

Tessa approaches him, wrapping her arms around him from behind. Ryan turns to embrace her. "I'm so glad you said yes," he says, his voice muffled by her hair.

Tessa pulls back, touching his face lightly. "I'm sorry for how I reacted earlier, and that I didn't say yes at first. I'm sure that wasn't how you expected any of that to go."

"Don't apologize. You thought it through and made your decision, and that's exactly what I love about you. You never jump into anything. If you did, you wouldn't be my Tessa."

"I jumped into kissing you in Tokyo."

"That's true." Ryan grins, but his smile fades quickly. "It was a huge, life-changing question, and I dropped it on you out of nowhere. It would have been a life-changing question even without the context of the presidential run. With it… I get why you were upset."

They go to the sofa and sit close together. "Thank you for understanding."

"I know how unfair this is. You have to make sacrifices for this, while I don't. I'm asking you to give up your career and your privacy, and step into life in the public eye." Ryan rests his hand atop hers. "I know none of that is what you wanted. I feel… I wish that there was another way."

"I'm trying to think of it as a career change, not giving up my career," Tessa corrects. "As for life in the public eye, I'll find a way to deal with it. You've managed for all these years, after all. It's… It's change, not sacrifice. They are major changes, but this is what it takes for us to be together openly, for all the years to come. I'll do it."

"You're too good to me," Ryan says quietly.

"No." Tessa casts her gaze to her lap, smoothing out a wrinkle in her skirt. "It's not unselfish of me. You gave me something I thought I would never have again." Something rare and special, worth treasuring, a love that can last the rest of her life. "I'll do what I have to to hold onto that."

Ryan kisses her on the temple. "I have something that I didn't get the chance to give you earlier. You won't be able to wear it for a while, but I wanted to show it to you anyway."

Tessa's heart hammers. "Okay."

Ryan takes out a small velvet box from his pocket and opens it, showing her what's inside. Tessa's lips part in a silent gasp. She reaches for the box, studying the ring nestled inside. It is delightfully, mercifully different from the diamond ring that Owen proposed to her with, and from the gigantic two-carat diamond that Ryan gave to Vanessa. This is a large oval-cut emerald set on a simple gold band. The depth and luminescence of the green is stunning. Tessa tilts it this way and that, awed by how it catches the light.

Ryan laughs. "You can put it on, you know."

"It's perfect." Wearing another engagement and wedding ring, after taking hers off, will be hard enough. It is a blessing that this doesn't look anything like her first ring, the symbol of her and Owen's commitment to one another. The ring she left behind when she left him.

"I'm glad you like it. It's unconventional, but I thought — I thought this would suit you."

Of course he understood why she wouldn't want a diamond. "Thank you." Tessa kisses him on the cheek. She hesitates briefly before removing the ring from the box and slipping it onto her finger. It is heavy. After more than two years of not wearing a wedding or engagement ring, she became accustomed to the lightness of her hand without. (That same lightness, the absence of the rings she wore for over a decade, made her sick, in the days and weeks and months after her divorce.)

It is heavy, but it feels right, on her hand. It is comforting to look at; a tangible symbol of Ryan's love for her. Tessa can't take her eyes off it. A thought suddenly occurs to her, and her hands drop limp into her lap. "Wait. How did you buy this? You didn't–"

"Don't worry, I used cash. Untraceable. My aunt got it for me."

Tessa breathes easier. "Okay." Ryan laughs again, and she elbows him. "What? It was a valid concern."

"Like I would have been stupid enough to use my credit card." Ryan is still chuckling. "You give me no credit. I would be offended, if I didn't know how much you adore me."

Tessa leans close enough to kiss him, and deliberately stops short. "Do I?" she breathes, caressing his shoulder. "Do I adore you?"

Ryan's gaze drops to her lips. He doesn't bother with a retort, leaning in to kiss her instead. Tessa returns his kiss with equal enthusiasm, unprepared for the upswell of emotion within her. Underneath all the apprehension about the changes ahead, there is excitement. There is so much to look forward to. Another campaign, and hopefully another victory — the victory that will count the most. The chance to lead the nation. She will get to be by Ryan's side for all of that, participating in the change he brings. She will get to spend the rest of her life with him. Not after he is out of office in another ten years, but within a matter of months.

All the hiding and secrets will be over. The crushing anxiety about their relationship being leaked will be over. They can be together openly, without fear.

She is sure there will be new fears, but for now, she wants to focus on the positive. Ryan's lips on hers, his hands on her waist. Tessa climbs onto his lap without breaking their kiss, planting her knees on either side of his hips. She cradles his face in her hands as he pushes her skirt up over her thighs. Ryan strokes her legs, and Tessa moans into the kiss, running her hands over his shoulders and back. She finally, reluctantly breaks the kiss when she feels Ryan trying to unbutton her blouse. She does the same with his shirt.

"I'm glad you like being engaged to me." Ryan is too busy smiling up at her to pay attention to her buttons, and his fingers slip on one. She didn't even see him smile like this on the night when they learned that Gardner wasn't running for a second term.

Tessa unbuttons her blouse for him, and returns to her work on his shirt. "Correction. I *love* being engaged to you."

Ryan slips her blouse off her shoulders, leaving her in just her bra and skirt. Even more than a year into their relationship, he still gives her the same awed look he did on the night they first slept together. He reaches for the zipper of her skirt, and Tessa presses herself up against him and starts kissing his neck. "So impatient," she murmurs, in between kisses.

"Mm-hmm." Ryan's hands find the hook of her bra instead. "I want you in nothing but your ring."

Tessa runs her fingers through his hair, before kissing him again. "I can do that."

Chapter Thirty-One

January – March 2027

Tessa sets up a meeting with Ernesto Ortega, President Gardner's Chief of Staff. She makes the short walk from the EEOB to the West Wing, and Ernesto's administrative assistant shows her in. "Ernesto will be with you soon. He just stepped out for a second."

Tessa stands in the Chief of Staff's office, adjacent to the Oval, and bittersweet emotion rises inside her. She thought this would be her office, someday. She dreamed of being the first woman to be White House Chief of Staff. Right beside Ryan, as she always has been. The most senior political appointee in the White House; the head of the Executive Office of the President.

She will be in the East Wing instead, with her own staff, and Tessa reminds herself that she will work to promote Ryan's agenda and her own. The door opens, jolting her out of her reverie. Ernesto rushes in. Sweat beads on his forehead, his face is flushed, and he has the air of someone in a terrible hurry, which is typical for him. "I hope you haven't been waiting long."

He holds out his hand to her, and she shakes it. "I just got here."

"Good, good. Take a seat."

Tessa settles on the sofa, and Ernesto perches on the armchair nearby. She gets right down to business. "When is President Gardner going to announce that he won't be running for reelection? Of course, we're not making any public moves or private inquiries until the president makes his announcement."

"We want to put it off for as long as we can. I know that hobbles you,"

Ernesto acknowledges. "But you understand that as soon as the president makes his announcement, he becomes irrelevant, in the eyes of the media. All eyes are going to be on your guy and the Republican nominee."

"I get it. I just wanted to make sure that nothing was coming down the pipeline in the next couple of weeks."

"The next couple of weeks? No." Ernesto fixes her with a curious look. "Why? You guys planning anything big?"

"No, we're not."

"Because we should know about it if you are."

He is turning red again. Leo tilts his head at the man, undoubtedly hearing his increasing heart rate. "I promise, Ernesto." Not for the first time, Tessa hopes that the man won't have a heart attack in front of her. She has no idea how someone with such a nervous disposition guided Gardner through a successful presidential campaign, and then made it through two years as Chief of Staff.

"Okay." Ernesto pulls out a handkerchief and mops at his brow.

Tessa takes pity on him, rising from the sofa and picking up Leo's leash. "I'll let you get back to your lunch break."

"What break? I'm meeting the Administrator of the EPA* in five." Ernesto gives her a rare, thin smile, as he opens his office door for her. "This is going to be you in a couple years. I hope you're ready for it."

∞∞∞∞∞

Two PM on Friday finds Tessa and Leo descending into the basement underneath an ice cream shop in Mount Pleasant. It is a tiny, brick-walled space, with a few tables inside and seating at a counter. The scent of freshly baked pizza crust, ripe San Marzano tomatoes, basil, and mozzarella hangs in the air, making Tessa's mouth water. Leo's nose twitches and his ears perk up, even though he is too well-behaved to beg for human food.

Her lunch date sits at one of the tables near the back of the restaurant. Jonah Green waves to her in greeting, and stands up. "I hope you found the place okay." Jonah is in his early fifties, with impeccably styled dark, wavy hair, and a penchant for bow ties. *I want to have his hair when I'm*

Environmental Protection Agency

old, Ryan has commented. *First, you're not old in your fifties. Second, you have to have the bow ties too, then,* Tessa told him.

"I've been here a few times before. My goddaughters love the place. It helps that there's ice cream right upstairs."

"We have to get a cone when we're done here. They have this butter-scotch miso flavor that's out of this world. Oh, and I ordered a white pie with hot dip for us. Sound good?"

"That's perfect."

They chat about work, Jonah's family, and the Super Bowl next month. It is a breath of fresh air to have a cordial working relationship with the Chair of the DNC. Jonah's predecessor hadn't been a friend to Ryan or his staff. Jonah waits for the server to leave after dropping off their pizza, and then plates a few slices for her. "Should I plate one for the dog too?"

"Thank you. I'm sure he'd love that, but he already ate, so better not."

Jonah eyes her as he plates his own slices. "So, you have news for me?"

She doesn't normally joke around with anyone outside of her circle of friends, but she can't resist this one. "News? Why would I have news?"

"Come on. I can't get Ernesto to answer my calls or emails for weeks, and then the Veep's Chief of Staff reaches out and asks for a meeting? Something's up." Jonah lowers his voice, even though there's no one else in the restaurant at this hour. "He's not running for a second term, is he? Chao's going to run instead?"

"No comment. I didn't reach out to you about the election. I wanted to ask if you still have that Vice Chair position open."

Jonah adjusts his bow tie. "Who's asking?"

She works closely enough with Democrats around the country for that to be a valid question. "Me."

Jonah sets his slice of pizza down and pushes his glasses up on his nose. "You."

Tessa meets his gaze, and Jonah shakes his head. "Okay, I get what's happening here. Gardner's not running. Chao is, and he picked Han to be his campaign manager this time around, and your feathers are ruffled. Or–" The color starts to drain from his face. "Is some scandal going to come out soon? Are you jumping off a sinking ship? He's the future of the party! If he's fucked it up I don't know what we're going to do."

Tessa sighs. Between Ernesto, Jonah, and Ryan, she gets more than her fill of drama. "No, to both. Please don't speculate."

"What am I supposed to do? You've been with Chao since you were a kid in college, and now you're leaving?" Jonah squints at her suspiciously. "I know that you've gotten a dozen asks that you've turned down, I know that NOW* and Emily's List have been after you for years and gotten nowhere. Now you want to leave, right on the verge of Chao's big move, throwing away a spot on his administration?"

It is a valid question, and one that she anticipated. "You know the Vice President's history with the DNC."

Jonah laughs. "Oh, you bet I do."

"Consider that it might be helpful for any presidential candidate to have friends on their respective party's committees."

"Aren't the Veep and I friends? He said he was coming to my Super Bowl party and everything." Jonah asks, wounded. He holds up a hand, forestalling her reply. "No, I get it. But why you?"

"Pardon?"

"Chao has a bunch of senior staff. Why are you the one leaving for the DNC?"

"It's a change, Jonah. I've done everything there is to do for the Vice President. I've worked for him for fourteen years. I've run his congressional campaigns, a Senate campaign, and a presidential campaign. I don't want to do another presidential campaign. He knows that. There are no hard feelings between us."

"Why don't you want to do another campaign, though?" Jonah presses. "I thought you'd have a real fire in you to do it. Win this one for your guy, you know."

"I don't want to let him down again." Not everything in this conversation has been honest. That is, though. Tessa ducks her head, embarrassed.

Jonah must see the truth in her face, because he relents. "Fair. It sounds like you two are still on good terms, so you could still get tapped for a spot on his administration."

Tessa takes a sip of her drink and murmurs something noncommittal.

"All right. I'll make some calls to the other Vice Chairs, get you an interview. Now let's get the check so we can get some of that ice cream."

*National Organization for Women

ooooo

February comes and goes. March is more than halfway gone, and there has been no public announcement from President Gardner. Tessa's staff operates in silence, making discreet preparations for 2028.

Friday, March 20 finds Tessa and Leo disembarking at Penn Station. Tessa is wrapped in a dusty-rose colored trench coat, a matching weekender bag slung over her shoulder. This is the first time in years that she hasn't traveled as part of the Vice Presidential entourage on Air Force Two, with the Secret Service in tow. It is a breath of fresh air. It reminds her of riding the train all over the city in college, from class to volunteering to her internships. The crowd at Penn Station is as over the top as ever. One cry still cuts through the crowd. "Tess!"

Jesy stands near the elevator, beaming from ear to ear. Tessa strides toward her, greeting her oldest friend with a tight embrace. "You got off work early?"

"Of course. My girl being back in the city is an event." Jesy steps back, regarding Tessa with delight, and then bending to pet Leo. "You're wearing the coat!"

"Of course I am. I have to match Zahra."

"Z's going to be thrilled. She's wearing hers today too. Here, can I take your bag?"

"No, no, I'm fine."

"How was your trip? Also, what cafe–"

"Grace Street," Tessa says, before Jesy even finishes.

Jesy laughs. "Some things never change."

They start walking over to Koreatown. The eve of the first day of spring is brisk and bright, with cloudless blue skies. "The trip was fine," Tessa says, answering Jesy's question. "I worked the whole time."

Jesy gives her a long-suffering look. "Long train trips and flights are for catching up on movies and shows, not work."

"I wish. Besides, I have to work, considering…" They are hours away from DC, but Tessa lowers her voice anyway. "I have to get everyone ready for the transition. Matt knows his stuff, but I want to have everything in writing for him, to make the process easier."

Jesy takes her arm. "You got the job?"

This is one of several drawbacks to them living in different cities. Tessa keeps everything that she doesn't want leaked off phone calls, emails, and text messages. The only time she can exchange big news with Jesy is when they are together in person. She made a special trip to New York in January, the weekend after she and Ryan got engaged. "I just heard on Wednesday."

"Oh my God. How are you feeling? Have you told anyone yet?"

"No one besides Ryan, Matt, and Kahaan, and you and Rosalie. I haven't made an announcement to everyone yet. I'm planning on doing it on Tuesday, and I'm… not looking forward to that. I'm not looking forward to May 1, either."

"That's your last day at this job, or the first day of the new one?" Jesy nudges Tessa, and points out a Samoyed walking on the other side of the street.

"Oh, that's a beautiful dog. It's the first day of the new one." They step to the side of the sidewalk, dodging a pack of college freshmen in NYU sweatshirts.

"You know all of your new colleagues at the DNC, right?"

"Yes, but it's not the same. I've worked as part of this team for so long. I mean, you get it."

Jesy has been working at her nonprofit since college, and she has made her way up from an intern to the Vice President of Programs. "It's going to be hard. But you'll crush the work, and you're still going to be living in DC. You'll still see everyone. They love you. They're not going to forget about you just because you're not in the office with them."

Jesy has always been way too perceptive. Tessa manages a smile, as she opens the door for them at Grace Street Coffee and Desserts. "Thanks."

ooooo

They hang out at the cafe until Zahra gets done with school, and they meet Tessa's goddaughter with a paper bag full of Korean donuts and a bouquet of daffodils. Zahra shrieks with joy before she even sees the gifts, throwing herself into Tessa's arms. Jesy snaps a picture of Tessa and Zahra in their matching coats and sends it to the group chat.

The rest of the day is wonderful. They have a picnic in Central Park, sitting under blooming red maple trees, a home-cooked dinner courtesy of Jesy's husband, and a movie night on the sofa. After Zahra reluctantly goes to bed, Jesy, Tessa, and Leo remain on the sofa, huddled under blankets.

"I really hope she sleeps, but I think she's so excited for tomorrow that she'll bounce off the walls for a little while longer."

"It's just Legally Blonde Junior and the botanical garden."

Jesy laughs. "You could take Z to see paint dry at the Home Depot, and she'd be over the moon."

Tessa nudges Jesy's foot with her own. "In a couple of summers, she could come stay at the White House." She can hardly believe the words, even as she speaks them. "There's plenty of space to explore. There are the gardens, the pool, a movie theater, and if Zahra's interested, I could use a junior intern in the East Wing."

"A pack of wild dogs couldn't keep her away." Jesy's smile makes the corners of her eyes crinkle. "I still can't believe it. From Elizabeth, New Jersey, to the White House."

"Not yet," Tessa says grimly. "I have to run a whole gauntlet before I get there."

Jesy puts a sympathetic arm around her shoulders, giving her a squeeze. "Media training getting you down? How's it been going?"

"You'll see tomorrow."

∞∞∞∞∞

Tessa takes Zahra to Legally Blonde Junior, out to lunch, and to the botanical gardens on Saturday. The time in New York City with her goddaughter is a delight, the perfect escape from work and the rapidly increasing stresses that come with contemplating her future.

Kids weren't in the cards for her, with the demands of her career. Owen was wary of the idea too, considering his own baggage with his parents. With what happened between them, and their divorce — it is a good thing that they never had a child. It is also a very good thing that she gets to be a godmother and a beloved aunt to Jesy and Rosalie's daughters. Tessa has marveled over how they have grown from newborn babies to girls of eight. When she thinks of the future, she thinks of Ryan's successes as president over the next eight years. She also thinks of college visits, prom dress shopping, and high school and college graduation ceremonies.

It is early evening by the time they get back home to Brooklyn. Zahra practically falls asleep over her dinner, thanks to all the happenings of the day. Isaiah takes her upstairs to get ready for bed, and Jesy, Tessa, and Leo head over to the living room. Leo settles down in front of the fireplace with a huff of exhaustion.

"Poor thing!" Jesy exclaims. "I've never heard him make that sound before."

"He doesn't normally get that many steps in in one day. He's not a New York City dog." Tessa sinks to her knees, stroking Leo's back. She would have been anxious and hypervigilant in the city crowds today, if not for him. It made a difference knowing that Leo was there to protect her and Zahra. Her phone lights up with a notification. "Kahaan will be here in five."

The doorbell rings in five minutes on the dot. Tessa opens the door to see her communications director dressed to the nines in an embroidered navy blue silk sherwani, carrying a large brown bag, and she steps back to let him in. "You look amazing."

Kahaan gives her a one-armed hug, and then bends to scratch Leo behind the ear. "Hey, buddy! So do you. I've never seen you wear this color before."

"Zahra and I went to see Legally Blonde Junior today, and she let me know that bright pink was a must." Tessa looks ruefully down at her blouse.

Jesy emerges from the kitchen as Kahaan slips his shoes off, holding a fragrant mug of tea for him. "That outfit is incredible. Where did you get it?"

"This little place in Queens. I'll take you guys sometime." Kahaan hands Jesy the bag. "Samosas, pakora, and milk sweets."

"Oh, you shouldn't have! This was for your sister's engagement party, right?"

"Please. We have enough food to feed the whole borough."

"It wasn't a problem that you left early?" Tessa asks, as they head back to the living room.

"I won't be missed. There are like a hundred other people there."

Kahaan claps his hands together. "You ready?"

Tessa's phone lights up again with a text from Ryan. *I hope you're enjoying NYC. Good luck with that meeting you have tonight. You'll do great.* His text is punctuated with a smiley face emoji.

She can't suppress a smile. They never let a day go by without exchanging a couple of texts or a brief phone call when they're apart. They make each one sound innocuous. Something that wouldn't raise any red flags or alarm bells if it were to be leaked to the public. All the messages do is let the other know that they're thinking of them. It never fails to brighten her day.

"Three guesses who that is," Jesy stage-whispers to Kahaan.

Tessa sets her phone down. "I'm ready." The text from Ryan arrived at the right time. These practice sessions with Kahaan always leave her sick with nerves, even though the face across from her is a trusted friend. Leo inches closer to her legs, picking up on her increasing anxiety.

"All right. Jesy, you do some media and PR at your job. Any thoughts?"

Jesy studies her. "Can you relax a little, Tess? Your expression is pretty intense right now."

She hadn't been going for intense. She had been going for neutral. This is with Kahaan and Jesy in front of her, rather than some random news anchor and their entire camera crew. Tessa tries to relax, to no avail. "This is just my face."

"I mean, she's right," Kahaan mutters.

"Yeah, but I know that you can get softer than that. Give me the look Z and Ruby get. Give me the look that Leo gets."

Tessa thinks of Ryan and Leo, of Zahra and Ruby, and tries to soften. Jesy and Kahaan nod encouragingly. "That's great. I'm stepping into interviewer mode now."

"Of course," Tessa replies, in her mildest tone. After their first mock interview, Kahaan very apologetically told her that she came across as terse and sharp. "You know how sexist the media — and the public — are," he said. "You know that women and people of color have to be hyper-aware of their "tone" in order to be perceived as likable and non-threatening."

She hasn't cared about being perceived as likable since she left college. But this isn't about her. It's about Ryan. She, and her image, will reflect on Ryan. Tessa chafes against it on principle, but it is what it is. First Ladies and potential First Ladies have to be as charismatic, warm, and engaging as the candidate.

"Blah blah, here's the intro." Kahaan waves a hand. "All boiling down to the first question. Can you tell us more about your early life?"

This is her third mock interview. Tessa still has to steel herself to answer. She rarely revisits her childhood. Her real life started when she enlisted; when she met Rosalie, Spencer, and Ryan. She was reborn in Landstuhl, when Ryan told her about his political ambitions and asked for her support.

"I was born and raised in New Jersey. My mom passed away from pancreatic cancer when I was in middle school." She hates talking about this even to the people closest to her. Now she has to prepare to confess this awful loss to the entire nation. "So it was just my dad and I, until I enlisted in the Army after high school."

Kahaan's eyes shine with genuine sympathy. "I'm so sorry to hear that. That must have been hard for you."

"Yes." She briefly considered speaking a little more about this, at first. She isn't the only person who has lost a parent to cancer. She thought about speaking about the grief and pain, to let those children know that they aren't alone. That they and their pain are seen and heard; that their grief is understood.

She isn't ready yet. Maybe someday she will be able to do that, as the First Lady. Maybe someday she can record a message for any child, youth or adult, who has lost a parent or parental figure to cancer. But for now, she can't do it. "It was."

"What motivated your choice to enlist in the Army?"

This is an answer she, Kahaan, Matt, and Ryan worked and re-worked. *I was young and naive, ignorant and desperate. I bitterly regretted my choice as soon as I learned I would be deployed to Iraq,* is not an answer that will land well with the general public. "Economic opportunity. I was told that the Army would pay for my college education, and it did." The Army paid for a top-quality education, an education that opened a thousand doors for her. All she had to do was kill, and almost be killed, in exchange.

"I don't know," Jesy interjects. "Critics could paint her as, I don't know, greedy, not patriotic."

Kahaan sighs. "Oh, I know."

"I'm not changing my answer. Ryan's with me on this. I'm already whitewashing it enough."

"It can be spun in a positive way," Kahaan allows. "The military pays for college, and that benefits people like Tessa. There are high schoolers who are going to see this interview, see the position and prominence that Tessa has now, and think about enlisting."

Tessa's shoulders stiffen. "That's not what I want anyone taking away from what I said."

"This is the nature of the media, unfortunately. You say what you want to say, but people will take away what they want to from your words."

"Fine," Tessa says shortly. Kahaan is right. She has told Ryan the same thing, in years past. "Let's get back to it."

"Can you tell us more about your military service?" Kahaan mimics the curious tone of a reporter, but regret is written all over his expression. He knows how difficult these questions are for her.

Tessa is grateful for Leo's presence at her side. "I served in Iraq for a year, as a military working dog handler. My partner and I worked together to detect IEDs*." She pauses. "I was injured in the line of duty in the last weeks of my deployment. I received an honorable discharge from the Army after that."

It isn't a lot of detail, but there is nothing that can make her recount her time in Iraq on camera. There is nothing that can make her relive that last firefight, and what happened to Spencer. Undoubtedly all those details will come out, thanks to reporters digging around. But they don't have to hear it from her. They won't.

"Make sure that they don't ask any questions about Spencer, or ask about the burns on her hands, or, I don't know, zoom their cameras in on her hands," Jesy orders. "Can we do that?"

"We'll do everything to ensure that. Ryan said the same thing." Kahaan is being tactful. What Ryan actually said was that if whoever interviewed her set one toe out of line, he would blacklist them and their entire network from the White House.

Kahaan's following questions are easier. He asks why she chose to major in political science after her discharge from the Army, and what

*Improvised Explosive Devices

motivated her to become politically active in college. "Did you meet the Vice President in college, when both of you were volunteering with the New York Democrats?" He feigns the ignorance of a reporter.

"No. I met Ryan, and Matt Han, during our time in Iraq. We were on the same squad. The three of us had an interest in politics, and that informed our career choices after our time in the Army came to an end."

Kahaan winces in a premature apology for what he's about to say. "But you and the Vice President didn't date in college?"

"No." Tessa makes herself stare calmly back at him, imagining some interviewer in his place. She hates that she will very soon owe her life story to the American public. "I had a boyfriend through most of my time at college."

"And that boyfriend became your husband."

"Yes."

Kahaan breaks character, as he has every time he has "interviewed" her. "I'm sorry, Tessa."

Tessa attempts a smile. "Don't apologize. You're just trying to prepare me for what's coming. It's better that I practice this now, with you."

"You and your husband were married for over a decade, until your divorce in 2024. Pausing now." Kahaan looks at Jesy. "We're going to tell anyone who does interviews with Tessa not to follow up on that statement."

"But who says they're going to listen to you?" Jesy argues. "They want ratings. What if they blindside Tessa with something to see her reaction?"

"They're going to listen to us, if they don't want their network's access to the White House yanked for at least four years. Besides, Tessa won't grant interviews to any hack journalist. Trusted figures from trusted outlets only."

Tessa indicates Leo. She decided it would be better to proactively bring up her service dog, rather than wait for an interviewer to ask about him. *There is power in controlling the conversation,* she told Ryan years ago, as he prepared for his first interviews while running for his seat in the House. "I got Leo to help me cope with the stress of the divorce. As many Americans know, even an amicable divorce is a challenge."

"That is genius," Jesy says. "Forty-one percent of marriages end in divorce. Some people are going to act like it's a huge red flag that you and Ryan have been divorced, but it's a normal part of life for people from any political party or race or whatever."

"You worked for the Vice President for over a decade, as his campaign manager and Chief of Staff. You stepped into your new position with the Democratic National Committee earlier this year," Kahaan continues. "What prompted this major career change?"

Tessa gives the same stock answer that she gave to Jonah when he asked her why she wanted a change. Kahaan continues. "You and the Vice President began a relationship just a couple of months after you started the new job at the DNC. Was that just a coincidence?"

This is the question that both she and Ryan have to be careful with, while making it seem like they are being honest. "It was. The professional relationship between the Vice President and I precluded anything but friendship. Once I stepped into a different role with the DNC, the nature of our relationship changed."

"Vague, but it answers the question," Jesy mutters. "People are going to analyze every word you say."

"How did you make that leap, from a longstanding professional relationship to a personal one?"

Tessa repeats the answer that she and Ryan have practiced. "We went from spending every day together to spending no time together. We realized that we missed each other's company, and things developed from there."

"You and the Vice President knew each other well, and worked closely together, for almost twenty years before this. That's as bold as I think any reputable interviewer will get," Kahaan adds. "I doubt that anyone we give the okay to get in front of Tessa will accuse her and Ryan of an inappropriate relationship, especially when they were both married."

Tessa catches herself picking at her cuticle, and immediately stops. Undoubtedly "body language experts" on and off social media will weigh in on her demeanor during any of her interviews. "I think a lot of people can relate to this in their own lives. You can know someone for months or years, and never think of them as something different than a friend. But then you laugh together, or share a quiet moment of understanding, or you're just sitting together talking over lunch or coffee. Something just shifts, and you relate to that person in a way you never have before."

Tessa catches Jesy looking over at the framed photo sitting on the bookshelf, of her and Isaiah on their wedding day. "That's beautiful."

Kahaan breaks character. "That's relatable. We've been operating under the assumption that this interview is going to be watched by millions of Americans who are ready to hate you and assume the worst of you, but that's a shitty assumption. There are a lot of people who are going to relate to what you're saying. About losing a parent, or falling in love with a friend, or falling in love again after a divorce, or enlisting in the military to try and get a better life."

"I know you're worried about other things coming out." Tessa flinches at Jesy's words. "We all hope that they won't. But even if they do. There are so many people who will relate to you, and speak out with compassion and understanding."

"Thank you." It is frightening and exhausting to consider all these aspects of how she might be perceived by the public. Until now, Tessa never had to consider whether there were any aspects of her life, of her experience, that were relatable. Now her life is a story for consumption.

"Do you want to stop?"

"No, it's okay. I know there are just a couple left."

Kahaan transitions into a few softball questions about Ryan, his platform, his campaign, and why she thinks he would make a good President. These are easy to answer. Tessa sighs with relief when Kahaan concludes the "interview," and Jesy claps. "You did great!"

"You're getting better every time," Kahaan agrees. "Your body language and delivery is smoother and more natural, and your answers are good."

"It's going to be harder when it's not you. When there's a whole camera crew around." She has nightmares about it on a regular basis.

"It is, but you're going to be just as prepared as Ryan is before every interview, before every debate. We've got your back."

Jesy hands her a milksweet from the open box on the coffee table. "Here. You've earned a break. Let's watch some TV and chill."

Chapter Thirty-Two
April – May 2027

POLITICO

April 2, 2027

Teresa Halifax set to depart as VP Chao's Chief of Staff

Ms. Halifax's departure marks a rare moment of high-level turnover in an administration that has been remarkably stable.

Teresa Halifax, Vice President Ryan Chao's Chief of Staff, plans to leave her post after over two years in the role, according to a person familiar with the move.

Halifax managed Chao's first campaign in 2012, when he won the NY-14 seat vacated by Susan Calcraft. Halifax served as Chao's Chief of Staff during his years as a Representative, and he called on her to run his Senate campaign in 2020. Halifax returned to her role as Chief of Staff to the then-Senator until 2023, when Chao announced his presidential run. The new Vice President-elect surprised no one when he named Ms. Halifax his new Chief of Staff in November 2024.

Much has been written about Chao's campaigns. The lion's share of attention has been given to his bold—and often polarizing—platforms. Less attention has been paid to the surgically precise execution of each campaign.

"People talk about the Vice President and what a sensation he is. And he is a smart guy, a brilliant guy, in fact," said Linda

Roberts of the Democratic National Committee. "The candidate's brilliance alone doesn't win elections. Understanding the political landscape, field organizing, voter targeting and outreach, get out the vote initiatives, understanding voter issues, thinking through funding, campaign messaging, combating fake news… All of that is the work of the campaign manager. Halifax has a gift for thinking that through. It's all the more impressive when you remember her first campaign win was when she was a fresh college grad."

Ms. Halifax has kept a low profile in New York and DC, despite her extensive professional network. An Army veteran, she is known for being quiet and reserved, shadowed by her service dog. Chao's staff has spoken highly of Ms. Halifax's leadership for the past several years. She is consistently described as capable, calm, and steady, in contrast to the high-octane Chao. "She [Ms. Halifax] is a rock," Daniel Bell, a longtime Chao staffer, commented. "She keeps this office running like a machine. She's the kind of person that anyone can go to with their issues and concerns," Deputy Chief of Staff Matt Han added.

Halifax's departure from Chao's administration comes as a shock, after over a decade of loyal service. Ms. Halifax will step into the position of Vice Chair of the Democratic National Committee. A person familiar with the move insists that there is no rift between the Vice President and his longtime Chief of Staff, and that Chao supports Halifax's decision.

Chao's Deputy Chief of Staff, Matthew Han, is mentioned frequently as Halifax's successor in the role.

∞∞∞∞∞

The professional transition dominates Tessa's conversations with her therapist for weeks. Her sleep is fragmented leading up to her last day of work. Her last day is as emotional as she feared it would be, and Leo sticks to her side like Velcro. Members of the White House IT department parade through her office, confiscating her desktop computer, her laptop, and her work cell phone in turn. She hands each over, unable to shake the feeling that she is giving away a part of herself each time. Her hand feels empty without her work cell phone. She used to check her office's Slack channels about a hundred times a day.

The mood in the office is subdued, despite the lunch-hour party that her friends put together for her. Instead of a signed card, they give her a folder stuffed to the brim with handwritten letters. Tessa clutches the folder close, and looks out over her friends' faces. She blinks, her eyes stinging. She sees them now, in their late thirties like her, established professionals. She sees them as they were five years ago, traveling between New York and Capitol Hill. She sees them as they were in 2012, college grads and students clustered in Ryan's first campaign headquarters.

They have been with her for so long, through so much. Not just with Ryan, but with her. She and Matt, Booker and Javier, are the four senior staff who work the closest with Ryan. To everyone else, she has been the driving force of their office's endeavors.

"This isn't goodbye," Tessa says. "But this is the end of an era. It's been sixteen years. In DC, across New York State, in Queens, across this country on the campaign bus and on Air Force Two."

The mention of the bus triggers a few groans. "Oh, God, that bus," Javier complains, rubbing his lower back. "I guess we're going to have to pull that thing out of storage again soon…"

Tessa smiles. "We've stayed up all night, and slept on each other's shoulders on flights and bus rides, and on the floor in conference rooms. We've solved problems together—and caused more than a few, too, for politicians on both sides of the aisle."

That earns several laughs, and some pleased smirks and grins. "We've laughed and cried together." Tessa remembers the elation of every single election night, and the way several of them wept together when it became clear that Ryan's run for president in 2024 had come to an end. She swallows over the tightness in her throat. "It has been one of the greatest privileges of my life to be here with you."

ooooo

Every staff member stops by her office before they leave work to say goodbye, to give her a hug or a farewell gift, or to make plans for dinner over the next couple of weeks. By nine that night, the only person left on site is the occupant of the office next to hers.

Tessa knocks on Ryan's office door. "Come in," he calls.

A simple interaction that they have repeated thousands of times. Tessa steps inside, leaving the door open behind her. Ryan sits at his desk, fingers steepled together. A frown is etched on his face, and the dark circles under his eyes are more pronounced than usual. He rises when he sees her, coming around to join her.

"I think I'm going to head home." Her voice wavers. She won't come back tomorrow. Matt will be the one who reviews Ryan's schedule with him tomorrow morning.

"Right." Ryan runs a hand through his hair, the way he always does when he's on edge. "It's been a long day for you."

Neither of them move. They stand where they are, a couple of steps away from one another, looking at each other. Ryan is the one to break the silence. "I'm so sorry, Tessa. I know how much this has all meant to you, and I know giving it up is–"

"Don't be sorry. I meant what I said earlier," Tessa reminds him. "This has been the privilege, the opportunity, of a lifetime. This has been the backbone of my life. You gave that to me in 2011. I'm grateful for it."

"You earned it. You earned it every day, every year, every campaign, every election. I was lucky to have you. I wouldn't have had anything near this level of success without you. I owe you so much."

The ache in her chest builds. This is what they have to do. There is no way around it. She still feels like she is abandoning Ryan. He is about to embark on another presidential campaign, and she isn't the one running it or holding down the fort here in DC, allowing him to hit the campaign trail. "You can call me anytime, about anything, okay? Any problems, any issues."

Ryan regards her softly. "I will. Thank you so much, Tessa. For everything."

"It was an honor."

Ryan extends his arms to her, and she goes to him for a hug. This one is different from all the embraces they have shared over the last two and a half years, since they began their relationship. This is the kind of hug they used to exchange during all the years before that, on every election night and inauguration day. This embrace speaks to their years of working closely together; to their long friendship. It is filled with a very different gratitude, tenderness, care, and affection.

They pull away, and they don't have to speak aloud to understand one another. Tessa can see in Ryan's expression that he will miss her as much as she will miss him.

She raises a hand in farewell and turns to leave.

ooooo

CNN

May 1, 2027

Pres. Gardner announces he will not seek re-election

The announcement comes after several months of speculation, with Gardner citing his age as the reason he will not launch a second campaign.

President Gardner formally announced on Tuesday that he will not seek a second term, making him the first president since Lyndon B. Johnson in 1968 who chose not to launch a second campaign. In his address, Gardner highlighted notable accomplishments in his first term, including the creation of nearly 11,000,000 jobs, leading to a historically low unemployment rate. He also cited offering student debt relief for middle-class and working-class families, averting a national debt crisis, signing executive orders protecting reproductive rights, and strengthening America's alliances and partnerships.

"That President Gardner has been able to accomplish this much with a bitterly divided government is incredible," said Ernesto Ortega, White House Chief of Staff. "That is a testament to the strength of the president's leadership, and his commitment to care for all Americans."

Gardner stated that he will continue to focus on his legislative agenda, including action to address immigration reform, access to health care, and the climate crisis.

Republicans and Democrats are mobilizing in response to the

White House's announcement. Several high-profile Republicans, including House Minority Leader Joshua Farmer (R-NE), Senate Majority Leader William Bernard (R-KY), and Senate Majority Whip Richard Salinas (R-TX), have commented in support of Gardner's decision to not seek re-election. Among the Democrats, all eyes are on Vice President Ryan Chao's office. Chao, who fell just short of securing the Democratic Party nomination in 2024, has long been speculated to be a successor to President Gardner.

In response to press questions about whether Chao would seek the Democratic Party nomination, President Gardner responded, "Vice President Chao and I have worked closely together since the inauguration. I'm grateful for all of his hard work on advancing our agenda. As to whether he's going to run, I don't know. You'll have to ask him yourself."

Chao's office released a statement today congratulating President Gardner on his substantial accomplishments during his term. The statement thanked the president for his vision and commitment to moving America in the right direction. No mention was made of a presidential run.

ooooo

The first hours of Tessa's first day as Vice Chair of the DNC are spent on onboarding. The rest of the day is derailed by an impromptu meeting about national campaign strategy in the aftermath of Gardner's announcement.

Tessa's new colleagues at the DNC have a certain manic energy. They turn on her after the news breaks, demanding to know if Ryan is going to run, and not waiting for her to answer their question. "He has to run, right?" Benjamin Ball rubs his hands together anxiously. "He's definitely going to run."

"There's never been a VP as hands-on as him," Lisa Peterson points out. "Why would he do all that if he wasn't going to run?"

Amy Wagner scoots her chair way too close to Tessa, making Leo sit upright and lock a wary gaze on her. "Who's he going to pick as his running mate?"

"He has to move to the center if he's going to run." Robert Quinn taps the table decisively. "That's what hurt him in 2024, wouldn't you agree?"

Alex Torres runs back into the conference room, pushing a whiteboard on wheels in front of him. The whiteboard is covered in dozens of names scrawled in dry erase marker. "Possible Republican candidates." He flips the board over. The other side has only four names. Ryan's is written in the largest print, and circled.

That sets off a new firestorm of conjecture. Everyone talks at the same time, arguing with one another, jabbing their fingers at the whiteboard, and checking their cell phones and laptops for any further breaking news. Tessa takes a deep breath, running her hand over Leo's head. She wishes that she were somewhere else right now. In her old office, preparing her team for what lies ahead.

That isn't a constructive thought. She isn't there. She is here. For more reasons than one, now that she thinks of it. Jonah and her fellow Vice Chairs aren't here in DC all the time. The lack of strong, present leadership is evident in this chaos.

Tessa rises. She never raises her voice, but she does so now. Just slightly, just enough to be heard over the din. "Listen up."

You never have to yell to show authority, Javier wrote, in his letter to her. *People could learn from you.*

Her new colleagues fall silent, turning to face her. "We're going to prepare for a call from the White House Chief of Staff and the Vice President's Chief of Staff." Tessa pauses, letting that sink in. Understanding dawns on their faces. Their expressions range from stormy to excited. Alex Torres bounces on the balls of his feet. "We're going to spend the next two hours outlining the national strategy recommendations for this campaign. Then we're going to spend an hour discussing the potential Republican candidates. This is going to be an orderly discussion."

Some of her friends may have described her tone as grim or severe. But that's fine. She doesn't have to police her tone unless she is in front of the camera, being interviewed, presenting herself to the American public. That isn't her life yet. This is.

"Let's get started."

Tessa sits and opens her laptop. One by one, everyone follows her lead.

ooooo

It is jarring to take a different route to work every morning. Tessa reports to the DNC Headquarters on South Capitol Street instead of the EEOB. She walks into the office with Leo as dawn breaks and is greeted by an entirely different setting, an entirely different cast of characters. New names. New faces that are neither familiar nor beloved. New work styles and personalities she has to learn how to respond to.

Her friends' names light up her cell phone several times a day. They ask how she is doing and send her memes and humorous updates from the office. Tessa misses them so much that it aches. They could communicate in shorthand, in fragments of sentences, and understand what the other person meant. They didn't have to worry about stepping on each others' toes, about hurting anyone's feelings or pride or ego. They were so good about leaving that at the door when they walked into the office every morning. They understood that their job wasn't about them as individuals. It was so much bigger than that. It was about the vision for the American people that they all shared.

Having Leo with her is a lifeline. Tessa pets him in between meetings, and he looks up into her eyes. "I couldn't do this without you."

Her eyes fill with tears of pride as she watches Ryan's speech formally announcing his candidacy. He speaks of his commitment to the American people, and he vows to do better for them. To give them better, to give them more than what they have now. This feeling, like her heart might burst with joy, is even more intense than it was last time Ryan announced his candidacy. This time will be different. She feels it in her bones. This time, Ryan will have the power of the DNC behind him.

There are tears of pride, and maybe something else, too. This is the first of Ryan's campaign announcement speeches she hasn't seen in person. She read the text of this speech before she left her job. But it isn't the same as watching him in person, clasping his hands and congratulating him when he steps away from the podium.

Tessa turns away from the TV screen in her office, grasping at the shreds of her composure. She has gone from seeing Ryan every single day in the office to not seeing him at all. It has left an outsize void in her life. She misses their lengthy conversations and problem-solving sessions about what approaches to take to policy and strategy. She misses their morning and evening touch base meetings, and Ryan's moods during said meetings. (They ranged from upbeat and energetic to thoughtful, or sometimes grumpy.) She misses their working dinners together almost every night, and their working lunches. She misses speculating with him, and being his voice of reason.

She misses his voice. She misses him being on the other side of the office door. She misses sharing little jokes with him during the day, or commiserating with him about other politicians.

Get a grip. Tessa tilts her head up and blinks up at the ceiling. *All of this is so that you can share the rest of your life with him later.*

ooooo

She works every bit as hard as she used to in her old job. She spends long hours on Zoom with Matt, Booker, Javier, and Kahaan, and with every state-level DNC head. She spends hours poring over thousands of pages of 2024's campaign strategy documents, and thousands more pages of post-election analysis. The analysis delves into what went right, what the near misses were, and what went wrong. (They lost Wisconsin, North Carolina, Florida, and Texas.)

With that in mind, Tessa writes drafts of new strategy papers, reflecting the demographic and economic changes that have taken place in the nation between 2024 and the present. She only tears herself away from her office for her morning run with Leo, and his afternoon and evening walks.

Tessa's personal cell phone rings, startling her out of a deep spell of focus. Leo startles as well, where he had been curled up at her feet. A jolt goes down her spine. Ryan's name lights up her phone screen. It is also past ten at night, but that is less important.

Tessa's hand trembles a little as she lowers her laptop screen. "Hello?" This is the first time she has heard from Ryan live, rather than over text, in two weeks. They have texted responsibly, as careful of potential leaks as ever.

"Hi."

It is amazing how much warmth he can put into one word. Tessa relaxes back against her office chair. "Are you still in Wisconsin?" Ryan wasted no time over the past couple of years in trying to make inroads in swing states. That hasn't changed, now that his campaign is officially underfoot.

"I got back an hour ago. Are you at home?"

"Um. No. I'm at the office."

Ryan makes a disapproving sound. "The advantage of leaving the White House is that you don't have to keep White House hours anymore."

"I know. I'm just…"

"Are they working you too hard? You don't have to prove anything just because you're the new one there."

Tessa can't hold back a wry smile at the worried protectiveness in his tone. "It's not like that. I'm actually enjoying the work."

"What do you like most so far? Besides the fact that you have a better boss now, of course."

She can hear Ryan grinning at his own (bad) joke. Tessa rolls her eyes. "Very funny. It's… I'm working at the macro level now. Even when I worked on your race at the national level, it was still at the micro level. Does that make sense?"

"Yeah. You were laser focused. You didn't have to worry about what any other Democrat in the nation was doing. Just me."

If they didn't have to be so cautious about leaks, Tessa would have teased him about how he liked being the only recipient of her attention. "Right. Your race is a huge focus, of course, but I'm also working on Senate seats and House seats."

"The DNC offices at the state levels are lucky to have your guidance. Not all of the Democratic candidates have campaign managers who know what they're doing."

"I know it's a long shot." Tessa stares at the massive electoral map she pinned to the wall. "But I want to get a supermajority in the Senate. I want to get control of the House and the Senate for you." Getting Ryan elected is Matt's job now. But smoothing the way for his legislative agenda? That is something she can do.

A beat of silence. She knows what Ryan would say to her if they were together in person. *That's one hell of a wedding gift.* "That's ambitious," he says, at last. "Democrats haven't had control of the executive and legislative branches since the 2009-2011 Congressional session."

"It's pretty audacious of you to call me ambitious."

Ryan laughs. "That should tell you something."

"I learned from the best." She missed this. She had taken simple conversation with Ryan so much for granted. This call has just been a few minutes, but it has lifted her mood. She is actually smiling.

"So, the reason I called…" Ryan pauses. "I hope that you don't work on Saturdays."

Tessa almost drops her phone. Leo gives her a curious look. Of course. This entire plan involves her and Ryan being able to publicly see one another. She thought that he would wait longer than two weeks. Maybe it would be wise to wait longer. To give it another week or two.

Fuck it. She can't wait another two weeks.

"I don't work on Saturdays, no." She spent the last two Saturdays working.

"Hmm." Ryan loads that with quite the amount of skepticism. Tessa knows very well that he would have spent the weekends working too, especially in light of his campaign announcement. "What do you think about a late dinner at Le Diplomate? Nine PM?"

It is ridiculous that her heart flutters at this. They are literally engaged. Still. Their entire relationship has been spent at Number One Observatory Circle, and as Ryan has regretfully said several times, they have never been out on a date.

Yes. Yes, please, is what she wants to say. She wants to see him so badly. "Is that a good idea?" Tessa plays it out instead, as she should. Anything could be leaked to the public—every text and email they send one another, every phone call they make.

She expected Ryan to banter with her as he always does. His simple response takes her by surprise. "Yes. I miss you."

"Dinner at nine on Saturday sounds good." That is all she can say. She doesn't trust herself to say that she misses him. If audio from this call gets leaked, then anyone will hear the emotion in her voice. That is a chance she isn't willing to take.

"I'll pick you up at eight-thirty." She hears the smile in Ryan's voice again. She knows it is his truest smile, not the polished, camera-ready one he can summon at the drop of a hat. "Go home. Get some sleep."

"I will." She will text him something innocuous, perhaps a link to an interesting news story, as soon as she gets home, just to let him know she made it back safe. "Good night. And Ryan—thanks for calling."

Chapter Thirty-Three
May 2027

Tessa spends Saturday morning at an author talk and book signing with Vasu, Booker, and Mari, followed by brunch. She heads back home with Leo, in better spirits than she has been in a while. Her new job engages her mind, but her time with her friends nurtures her spirit.

She gets ready at seven. She showers, blow-dries her hair, and smoothes sunflower-scented lotion over her skin. Tessa dresses in her typical outfit of a skirt and silk blouse. The only concession to this being a date instead of a work dinner is that her skirt has a modest slit in it. She leaves the top button of her blouse undone. This, as she knows from delightful experience, is enough to drive Ryan mad.

Tessa puts on the necklace and earrings Ryan gave her for her birthday a couple of years ago and gives her reflection a quick appraisal. A violent surge of nerves makes her stomach roil. She turns her back to the mirror, resting the heel of her hand against her temple.

This will be her first time out in public with Ryan as anything other than his Chief of Staff. She is well-known in circles of DC insiders. Outside of that niche community, she is invisible. Anonymous. Just another woman walking down city streets or airport terminals in business attire. That is exactly how she likes it.

Leo makes his way into her bathroom from where he had been sitting just outside. He comes to stand at her side, pressing his nose to her legs, trying to comfort her.

Tessa sinks down, petting him until the pain in her stomach eases. She stands up straight, reminding herself of what she spoke with Taliyah about during her last therapy session. She has faced fears worse than this before. She has lived through a dozen things more terrifying than this.

Tessa leaves her apartment a couple of minutes before eight-thirty, Leo at her side. ("I should pick you up at your door," Ryan groused, when they talked on the phone last night. "That's the gentlemanly thing to do."

"Go ahead," Tessa prompted. "Say it. Say, *back in my day, we picked our date up at the door.* I know you want to." Ryan growled, and she continued. "You can't show up in front of my apartment door with the Secret Service at your back. It'll cause a scene in the building." She can just imagine her neighbors Tweeting about it. Or, God forbid, making TikToks.)

Tessa and Leo go to the building's basement, and through the service door that opens into a narrow alley. A black SUV with tinted windows is parked there. One plainclothes Secret Service agent lingers at the entrance to the alley, and another is posted at the opposite side, ensuring that no one turns in here. Yet another agent stands in front of the SUV.

"Good evening, Agent Decker." Tessa always remembers Agent Decker as being one of the agents unfortunate enough to witness her and Ryan's initial indiscretion in the garden in Tokyo. Even worse, she learned last year that Decker is a die-hard fan of the New England Patriots.

"Good evening, Ms. Halifax." He opens the passenger door for her. Leo hops in first, wagging his tail furiously at the sight of his old friend. "Good boy," Ryan remarks, as he pets Leo. Tessa joins them with a word of thanks, sliding in across from the Vice President. Decker shuts the door, leaving them alone, thanks to the privacy screen separating the passenger area of the SUV from the agents driving up front.

Ryan beams at her. "Hi."

Tessa reacts before he even gets the word fully out, hugging him tight. She revels in the solid warmth of him, breathing in the familiar scent of his aftershave. This is like coming home. "Hi." Her voice is muffled by his dark suit jacket.

Ryan clings to her just as tightly, burying his face in her hair, kissing the top of her head. "Here." He draws her down to sit beside him and hands her the strap of her seatbelt. They cuddle close in the backseat as the car starts moving, grateful for the blacked-out windows. "Thank you for seeing me tonight. I was going crazy."

"Me too." All of her earlier apprehension melts away in the face of being with Ryan in person. There is no need to be cagey and discreet like they are in their texts and emails.

She answers his questions as fast as he can throw them at her. She has been feeling all right, save for her struggles with anxiety. She describes her sleep as adequate, making Ryan frown. People at work are annoying. She is having a hard time adjusting to working with anyone besides her longtime colleagues and friends. With that being said, they are treating her with respect.

"I want to hear about you," Tessa insists. "How have you been received at your trips outside of DC since announcing? Has the DNC on the ground treated you right?" She studies him. He doesn't have dark circles under his eyes right now. His posture is straight, head held high, without the telltale slight slump and the strained set to his mouth that are characteristic of dejected Ryan.

Ryan spills out everything that he has wanted to say to her over the last two weeks. He is so eager to get it out that he abandons some sentences half-finished in order to forge ahead to the next thought. Tessa mentally fills in those unfinished sentences, the way she always has.

They talk until they arrive at the restaurant. She trails off mid-sentence as the SUV stops, smoothing down her skirt in a nervous reflex. *Don't be stupid,* Tessa tells herself. The local or national media aren't expecting them out there. They aren't going to be confronted by flashing cameras and cell phones held high.

Ryan touches her arm. "Don't worry. We're going to go in through the service entrance. I booked a private dining room for us, separate from the main dining area."

"Thank you."

Tessa's nerves scream warnings as they enter the restaurant, telling her that she has no business holding Ryan's hand so openly. They walk into the private dining room, escorted by the Secret Service and the restaurant's executive chef. *Let him go,* her body and mind order her. *Step to a discreet distance.*

Tessa maintains her grip on Ryan's hand. His hand is steady, though hers trembles. She manages to smile at the executive chef, the waiting server, and the sommelier, and reply politely to their greetings. After they are alone, Ryan rests his hand on hers, atop the table. "Are you okay?"

"Yes." Tessa takes a sip of her sparkling water. Her hand still trembles a little. "It's just — it felt like a big step."

"It was, and you crushed it." She has always been the one encouraging him throughout his career, and now he is doing the same for her. "It felt good," Ryan admits. "To be able to hold your hand in public."

It is clear how much he has wanted this. Tessa turns her palm to face his, and intertwines their fingers together. They pick up right where they left off with their conversation. She doesn't release his hand when the server takes their orders and brings their food. The shock of this daring move fades, replaced by awe that this is possible.

They eat their own meals and bits of one another's, as is their custom. Ryan cuts her a chunk of his prime rib steak, and Tessa heaps a scoop of lobster risotto onto his plate. They linger over the meal, catching up on everything outside of work and politics. She tells Ryan what she thinks about the books she is currently reading. Ryan gives her his two cents on the latest episodes of their favorite podcast, which involve a deep dive into the world of museums. They end up discussing their favorite museums and debating over art museums vs. natural history museums. (Ryan comes down on the side of natural history museums — not a surprise — and Tessa opts for art.) Ryan tries to convince her to watch some new horror movie that is coming out soon with him, and then tries to sell her on the benefits of horror as a genre. Tessa remains unconvinced on both counts.

They split a vanilla creme brulee for dessert. They both eat one-handed, their left hands intertwined on the table. The joy and comfort of being with him always makes Tessa feel years younger, erasing all the strain that weighed her down during the week.

They head out just before the restaurant closes. This time, Ryan offers her his arm as they leave. She takes it after only the briefest second of hesitation. The three of them settle in the backseat of the SUV, and Tessa leans against Ryan. He rubs her back. "How did it go?"

"It was good." Tessa looks up at him. "I realized tonight that I think I'm ready for this new chapter. For us being public. I'm still nervous. I still hate that people outside of our circles might know my name. But I'm prepared for it."

"I'm so glad. It isn't easy." (She knows. Back in his days in Congress,

Tessa saw all the death threats that flooded Ryan's public-facing email inbox and Twitter DMs, and the unhinged letters that came in the mail. The Secret Service handles all of that now.) "But I hope that feeling more prepared will help you feel less anxious. On a selfish note..." Ryan rests a hand on her thigh. "I'm glad I'll be able to see more of you."

The touch is what she has been craving since she laid eyes on him tonight. Tessa moves a little closer. "You can see as much of me as you want."

She can tell by the barely restrained eagerness of Ryan's kiss that he has wanted to do this since they first saw each other tonight. They are hampered by their seat belts, but Tessa still wraps one arm around his shoulders, pulling him closer to her. Ryan cradles her face in one hand, stroking his thumb along her cheekbone. The tenderness of the gesture, juxtaposed with the heat of their kisses, makes her consider unbuckling the seat belt and sliding into his lap.

They do what they can while staying put, angling to face one another. Ryan slips one hand up her skirt. The other goes to brush at the hollow of her neck, where the pendant of her necklace lies. "I love when you wear this."

"What?" Tessa keeps kissing his neck. "The necklace or this skirt?"

Ryan traces the back of his hand down the hint of bare skin revealed by the open top button on her blouse. Tessa presses her chest up against him. "All of this."

The drive back to her apartment passes much faster than it should. Which is perhaps a good thing, considering that it spares them from doing anything too inappropriate in the back seat. When the car finally comes to a stop, Ryan and Tessa pull apart with identical groans of frustration and slump against the seat. Tessa pulls her skirt down to a much more respectable length, still breathing hard, and buttons up her blouse. "I want to invite you upstairs, but..."

"There's no chance they let me walk into an unsecured building, on the off chance that one of your neighbors is a domestic terrorist who builds pipe bombs. Ugh." Ryan casts a pleading glance skyward, as though begging for the heavens to intercede.

Tessa tries to make his hair lie flat from where she had been running her fingers through it, and straightens his tie. "Let's plan to go back to your place next time."

"When can I see you again?"

"It has to be next weekend, right? With our schedules." Some things have changed, but some things stay the same. She and Ryan will still wait to get through the week with bated breath.

Ryan heaves a sigh. "Fine."

The goodnight kiss he gives her is long and sweet, and has the (intended) effect of making her melt. When they finally draw back, Tessa rests her forehead against his shoulder. "I love you."

Ryan places his hand on her back. "I love you too."

∞∞∞∞∞

Tessa doesn't get online until the following afternoon. She checks her work email and Slack first. There are a few fires across the field, but none that she has to put out yet. She will monitor those situations for further developments.

She opens another browser and types in a web address she has been visiting for years — since 2016, as a matter of fact. It started as stress relief during a contentious election season. *www.reddit.com/r/deuxmoi* — a subreddit dedicated to discussing celebrity gossip.

Today's thread is titled *Sunday Spotted — Weekly Discussion Thread.* Tessa scrolls through the comments, resting her free hand on Leo's back. She finds what she was looking for near the middle of the thread.

Idk if this counts as a celeb sighting but my bf said the VP came into his restaurant last night with a date. The short sentence is punctuated by the eyes emoji.

The comment has a few replies. *That totally counts, he's all over the news every day*

Chao is celeb hot, he could get it lmao

who was the date though?? I'm jealous lol

Tessa strokes Leo's fur and reminds herself to be mindful of her breathing. The original poster has replied to the final comment. *Idk he didn't recognize her from anywhere but he said she was pretty and her dog was cute!*

Tessa stares at the screen for a while before shutting her laptop. If she doesn't, she is going to keep refreshing that thread, waiting for new replies to be added.

ooooo

The news hasn't broken, even after two months of weekly dates. It would have gone much faster if Ryan made dinner reservations for them in restaurants' main dining rooms, or if they visited the Dupont Circle farmers' market on a busy weekend morning, or if they walked down the Waterfront Park in Georgetown during sunset instead of after dark.

Tessa has no particular eagerness to be thrust into the spotlight. Ryan still wants to spare her, even though his new presidential run has re-ignited tired rhetoric on conservative channels about how unconventional it is to have a serious presidential candidate, let alone a president, without a wife and children. All of the Republicans who have begun to announce their candidacies flaunt their families, and their "family values." They attack Ryan for his divorce, and his aunt for owning a LGBT burlesque bar. Op-ed rebuttals on The New York Times and The Atlantic abound, striking back on the idea that a serious candidate or a president has to be married and have children.

"I could kiss Chanda Raja for writing this article." Tessa brandishes her phone at Ryan, The Atlantic article pulled up on her browser.

Ryan peers at her phone and affects a serious demeanor, trying and failing to hide his smile. "I appreciate that he's speaking out in support of me, but please don't."

They walk one of their favorite paths along the Washington Mall later that night, arm-in-arm. The memorials and monuments are lit up, along with the reflecting pools in front of the Lincoln Memorial and the World War II Memorial. Leo trots at Tessa's side. The Secret Service, as always, follows behind. "Let me know when it would be helpful to go more public. If you ever want to distract from the Republican candidates' attacks, or if you want to take some of the spotlight off any one of them." She knows the importance of controlling the narrative, and making the media cycle work for the candidate.

"There's no rush. I'm not in a hurry to throw you to the wolves. Besides…"

He trails off, and Tessa prompts him with a nudge. "What?"

"I want to hold it off as long as possible. This is the last bit of normalcy you're ever going to get. By this time next year, you'll be the First Lady in waiting. Then you'll be the First Lady, and then you'll be the former First Lady. You'll have Secret Service protection for the rest of your life."

It is foolish of her, but she hadn't thought that far ahead in the context of anything besides spending the rest of her life with Ryan by her side. Tessa recalls every televised presidential inauguration she has seen. The former Presidents and their spouses always sit in their own special section. Ryan — and she — will serve the nation for eight years. But they will always be public figures. They will lead the Chao-Halifax Institute, focusing on public health and ensuring equal access to mental healthcare.

Tessa imagines future presidential inaugurations, in decades to come. She imagines herself and Ryan watching the ceremonies, hand-in-hand. Growing older together, her hair silvering, more lines appearing on Ryan's face. She shivers and leans into him, and Ryan draws her even closer.

ooooo

It is close to eleven on Sunday night, and Tessa is listening to the latest episode of the Freakonomics podcast while flossing. The host's voice cuts out, replaced by her ringtone. Tessa drops her floss stick, snatching her phone up from the counter. She never gets calls this late at night. Worry makes her fumble. If something has happened to Ryan, to Ruby or Zahra, or her friends–

Kahaan's name lights up her home screen. "Hello?"

"Hey, Tessa. Sorry to bother you so late at night."

Tessa walks over to Leo, finding him where he rests on her bed, and pets him. "It's fine. What's up?"

"Someone submitted a photo of you and Ryan to CNN. They're going to drop a story on it over the next couple of days. CNN just reached out asking me if we have a comment."

Tessa sinks down on the bed. "The photo…"

"Taken from one of you and Ryan's dates over this summer. You guys are leaving some restaurant. We'll release our comment."

She knows the comment he's referring to. She helped write it. Tessa takes a shaky breath, running her fingers through her bangs. "Okay. Have you called Ryan?"

"I just got off the phone with him. He said he's going to call you in a sec. And Tessa?"

"Yeah?" Her voice sounds thinner than she would like. CNN is ubiquitous. It will only be a matter of time before Owen and Vanessa hear the news.

"It's going to be okay. I promise."

∞∞∞∞

The call with Ryan doesn't bring any surprises. She can't get Secret Service protection until she and Ryan get engaged, but Ryan and his aunt both have connections with high-profile private security. "They can't follow me around at work." Tessa tries to shake the ridiculous mental image of two bodyguards tailing her at the DNC headquarters. "The building has good security, anyway."

"Fine. But I want them around your apartment, and with you during your commute and when you walk Leo."

∞∞∞∞

Tessa has had news alerts on herself and Ryan for a while now. There are no words for how surreal it is to reach for her phone at seven in the morning, an hour into the workday, only to see her home screen lit up with dozens of notifications.

Her stomach lurches. She navigates to CNN's home page and is greeted by a photo of her and Ryan arm-in-arm, leaving Thip Kao. *Vice President Chao steps out with fmr. Chief of Staff.* Tessa clicks. A cursory scan of the article reveals that there is nothing unexpected here. She can only take in short phrases at one time. *The Vice President and current presidential candidate was previously married to New York interior designer Vanessa Martinez, until Martinez filed for divorce in 2023... The couple had no children... Ms. Halifax served as the Vice President's Chief of Staff for several years preceding the inauguration. She managed all of his campaigns, including his Presidential run in 2024... Ms. Halifax left her position in the White House earlier this summer, taking on a role with the Democratic National Committee... CNN reached out to Chao's office for a comment...*

Tessa stares at the rest of the article without registering it. She reaches for her keyboard and types. *foxnews.co*

She stops before finishing the URL. She has talked about this in therapy, and with Ryan. *I need to know how the opposition is going to spin this,* she argued. *My job is to get Ryan elected. This is work-related, not personal.*

Taliyah and Ryan, and all of her friends, vehemently disagreed. "Stay off Fox, Reddit, Twitter, and all social media," Matt recommended. "You know how ugly it gets out there. You don't need to expose yourself to that. Kahaan will give you the gist of what you need to know."

Tessa turns her phone face down on her desk and returns to work.

ooooo

She has never faced a work day like this. Not even on her first day back to the office after *that* day. She had been so fragile, trying desperately to hold it together and be strong for her staff. And yet, Tessa knew she was safe. If something happened, if she broke down weeping in the conference room, every single one of her staff would have reacted with the utmost compassion.

This is a different animal. It has just been two months, so she isn't particularly close with the other DNC staff. "They're intimidated by you," Booker pointed out, the last time they got coffee together. "You won your first election as a fresh college grad. How many of them can say that?"

Her colleagues filter into the office as the work day gets into full swing. Half of them attempt to conceal their stares. Half don't. Their expressions, in conference rooms and Zoom calls, run the gamut between judgment, shock, and wonder.

Tessa retreats into her armor. The only thing she allows herself to care about is Democratic candidates. Democratic races nationwide. Democratic strategy. She doesn't care about the conclusions that people are drawing. About the connections that they think they are making between her departure from the Vice President's office and this new announcement. She doesn't care about the connections that they think they are making between her long-standing professional association with

Ryan, and his divorce. And hers.

They can say what they want. They can believe what they want. All that matters is that she shepherds Democratic candidates to victory. Including — *especially* — their Presidential candidate.

ooooo

Work becomes a coping mechanism, a protective shell, just like it was in the last months of her and Owen's marriage. There is no time for pain or distress during a campaign. Focusing on work keeps Tessa from dwelling on how strange it is to have her own small plainclothes security team. (Two women who trade shifts, one roughly her age and one slightly older than her. Both are proficient in Krav Maga.)

Focusing on work keeps her from the temptation to check the op-eds and articles on CNN or The New York Times during her few minutes between meetings. Tessa takes the additional steps of deleting the Reddit app off her phone, and shoving her personal laptop under her bed. She has never been so glad she doesn't have any social media accounts.

She thought she was ready to see her name in the news, in headlines, in this new context. She was wrong. It is impossible to be prepared for that. Her voicemail and email inbox fill with journalists' interview requests. Tessa deletes them. There will be enough time for that later.

Ryan calls every night to check up on her, even when he is out of state, on the campaign trail. He brushes off her attempts to ask him about work. "How are you doing with everything?"

"I'm…" Tessa catches herself before she can respond with an automatic *fine.* "It's challenging. It's a transition. But I'm dealing with it all right."

"I know you are, publicly. But are you really?"

Tessa doesn't hesitate. "Yes." Autumn of 2024 was just over three years ago. It feels like a lifetime ago. The memories of that autumn and winter are vague and indistinct, her mind's attempt to protect her from the trauma. "I've been through much worse."

Interlude

May 2027 – April 2028

There are a few things that help her get through the months that follow.

At least once a day, Tessa reminds herself that she has survived worse. The media and public speculation is intensely uncomfortable. But it isn't painful, like her losses have been. Unlike her grief after her losses, there is a clear end in sight, as Ryan and her friends remind her. "You know the news cycle as well as we do," Booker says, when she meets up with him and Mari for dinner. "The most intense phase of this scrutiny will be over in a week. Two, max, especially because you're so private, you and Ryan are discreet, and our office isn't fanning the flames. By the time you and Ryan announce your engagement next spring, I bet that it won't even make much of a stir."

She learns from Ryan. They spend hours talking about his experience in the public eye on a national stage, and Ryan passes on all the lessons that he has learned over the years. There is something about being taught by Ryan that makes the experience less nerve-wracking. He builds her confidence with the idea of interviews and public speaking, bit by bit. He sits across from Tessa and holds her hands, looking into her eyes. "You can do this," he says simply. "You have a long history of communicating well under pressure. Remember everyone that you've talked to, every situation you handled, during every campaign and legislative session."

"That wasn't in front of an audience," Tessa hedges. "I was just doing my job."

"It was in front of an audience, just on a smaller scale. You've been a leader for your whole career, and every leader has an audience. You've handled some intense stuff, Tess. Remember when we had to deal with the hurricane? We lost power for days, the office flooded, the election was in less than a week, and you still kept operations going and morale high. Now, with this stuff you're stepping into — you're going to make speeches with notes. That's nothing, compared to what you've done professionally."

Tessa sighs at the memory of the hurricane, rubbing her temples. "Well, when you say it like that…"

Everyone she is closest to — Ryan, her friends, her therapist — encourages her, as she slowly grows in confidence. They support her through her very first interview with a New York Times journalist, and the aftermath, positive and negative. They support her through the resurgence of media attention when she and Ryan get publicly engaged in March 2028, and after Tessa makes her first tentative forays into the campaign trail on Ryan's behalf.

Matt, Ryan, and Kahaan don't tell her where to go. She selects her campaign stops herself, in swing states that align with her work as DNC Vice Chair. Tessa speaks to the Georgia Association for Women Lawyers and the Georgia Commission on Women. She meets with Georgia's five Democrat House members and their two Democratic senators. The following day, she addresses a group of three hundred senior citizens at the AARP* Chapter in Michigan, and speaks to a larger crowd of the Michigan League of Conservation Voters.

Her palms sweat, her heart races, and she picks at her cuticles, but Tessa gets through each event — the speeches, and the question and answer sessions that follow. She models her demeanor after Ryan's, trying to mimic his ease, his charisma. She tries to read the attendees' body language to see if she is connecting with her audience; if her message resonates. Each time, a small line of attendees forms to come talk to her after the question and answer session ends, so that must be a good sign.

Sometimes they ask her more questions on Ryan's and the Democratic Party's stances on issues she hadn't addressed in her speech, like agriculture, kindergarten through grade twelve education reform, and trade. Sometimes the questions are more unexpected. "How do I help my granddaughter get involved in politics?" one older man at the AARP event asks

*American Association of Retired Persons

her. "She's fourteen. If she's going to vote in four years, she should know more about what this is all about, right? But all these events, like this one, they're during the hours she's at school, so I can't bring her."

One man comes up to her just to show her the picture on the lock screen of his cell phone — a black-and-white collie. "I have one just like yours at home." A lady approaches her next, and politely asks to take Tessa's hand for a closer look at her emerald ring. "I own a jewelry store in Detroit, you see. Oh, this is a good-quality stone."

Kahaan attends the events in Michigan. "How did I do?" Tessa asks, as soon as they have a chance to talk afterward.

He hands her the black protective finger gloves that cover her cuticles, keeping her from picking at them. She will be able to wear them during the drive to the state capitol to speak with the governor on DNC business. "You were great." He hesitates. "I know that Ryan is your inspiration with all of your public-facing appearances, but from what I've seen, you're actually doing something different, and it's working well."

"What?" Tessa asks, alarmed. "What am I doing?"

"Ryan's notable traits in his public speaking are his intelligence and his energy. You're giving the audience intelligence, in a slower, more thoughtful way. That's a good thing," Kahaan hastens to add. "You're… measured. That calms people down, slows them down and makes them think, which is especially valuable in these swing states and with undecided voters. And you're just… I don't know. Kind. Ryan is too, obviously, but people seem to respond to that more with you. That AARP crowd loved you."

Tessa touches his arm, moved. "Thank you."

She realizes, as they arrive at the state capitol, that she hadn't remembered to put on her finger gloves when they got into the car. She still hadn't picked at her cuticles once.

Chapter Thirty-Four

April 2028 – July 2028

POLITICO

April 18, 2028

> *President Gardner to join DeNiro, Beyonce and Jay-Z, Tom Hanks, and more at New York Democratic Fundraiser*
> *The president is expected to urge his party to support Vice President Ryan Chao, who will also be in attendance at Friday's event...*

ooooo

"This is so ostentatious." Ryan speaks through gritted teeth and a smile. Their first private moment to themselves comes two hours into the evening. Every Democrat at this party wants to get a few minutes of face-time with the future president of the United States.

Tessa has made the rounds among the hundreds of attendees as well, thanking them for attending, and remarking on the Democratic candidates in their districts. After Ryan is waylaid again, Tessa finds and introduces herself to the youngest person in the room. Valeria Moreno, one of TikTok's biggest stars. "Gonzales has a fighting chance in Miami-Dade County because of your work on social media. I can see you having a measurable impact in other counties in Florida and Texas as well."

Valeria beams. "Thank you so much, Ms. Halifax! I'm a huge fan. Your speech at Duke last week was amazing. Could I please get a selfie with you?"

"Oh," she replies, taken aback. She still isn't used to being asked to be part of people's pictures, even after her speech at Duke went viral. "Yes, of course." Valeria angles the selfie so that Leo is in the shot too, and Tessa gets her phone number and email address. Valeria will be good to connect with after Ryan — and she — have taken their respective offices.

She chats with about four dozen others before she finally runs into Ryan again. Tessa takes his offered arm. "How much do you think went into this event?" he continues, his voice barely audible over the chatter of the crowd and the live band.

Multiple crystalline chandeliers adorn the ceiling of the ballroom, and the walls are taken up by enormous arched windows offering a striking view of New York City at night. "The venue alone would be upwards of thirty thousand," Tessa estimates. "And we're not counting the catering, the music, the flowers…"

Ryan doesn't let his smile slip. "It's so wasteful. This one night's event could have paid for multiple annual salaries for field staff nationwide."

"This one night's event is expected to bring in over ten million dollars." Spending for the last couple of presidential elections, in 2020 and 2024, reached an outrageous fourteen billion dollars.

"We need to address this somehow."

"We do, though I'm not sure there's much we can do. Both parties will fight us on limiting campaign spending." Tessa rests her hand on his arm. "I'll be right back."

The bathrooms are just as opulent as the ballrooms. Thankfully, they are empty. Her social battery is running low, and they have at least three more hours left in the night.

Tessa pats her hands dry, before smoothing on the complimentary hand cream. Her nails are painted a deep, shimmering claret red, matching her dress. Leo turns toward the bathroom door, his ears perking up, and she mirrors him.

The bathroom door swings shut, and Vanessa's mouth falls open. "Oh." She takes one small step back, her heels clicking on the marble floor. "I can go."

"No," Tessa replies hastily. She takes her own step back, away from the sink, toward the other exit. "No, you're fine. I didn't know you — I didn't know that you were here. I didn't see you earlier."

Leo looks up at her, sensing her distress. It is ridiculous that she is this incoherent, even after months of media training and public speaking. She has acquitted herself better in conversation with the President and First Lady, various foreign dignitaries, and celebrities. But if anyone would, if anyone could have this effect on her — it would be Vanessa. Her fiancé's ex-wife. How could this happen? How did Vanessa end up on tonight's guest list without anyone giving Ryan a heads-up?

Vanessa's gaze falls on Leo, and Tessa realizes that he is new to her. Back when Vanessa knew her, she didn't have — or need — a service dog. "It was a very last-minute thing. We weren't going to make it, but our meetings in Paris fell through, and Caleb really wanted to come."

Caleb Hamilton, the President and CEO of OpenAI. "That's great." The strain in her voice would be evident to anyone who knows her well. Then again, she and Vanessa had never been that close. "And also — congratulations." There is a new ring on Vanessa's left hand, even larger than the two-carat diamond Ryan gave her once. Ryan mentioned Vanessa's engagement in January, and that he sent her a card.

"Thank you." Vanessa's smile is small, but still striking. More than twenty years have passed, and Tessa still feels like the awkward young woman she was when she and Vanessa first met. Vanessa's looks and poise, her sense of fashion, her glamor, left her feeling so flustered, so inadequate.

Now here they are, in New York City again. Vanessa is stunning in her glimmering gold evening gown, her dark hair cascading in loose waves down to the small of her back, her red lipstick immaculate. "Congratulations to you too."

If Tessa were in a better state of mind, she could analyze Vanessa's tone. She could search for any bitterness in her expression. But the shock of seeing her here is so fresh, her nerves so raw, that Tessa just flinches.

Vanessa takes a few steps forward, approaching the mirror. She inspects herself in it, tucking a loose lock of hair behind her ear. Her eyes find Tessa's in the mirror. Tessa almost doesn't recognize herself. She looks pale, guilty, *afraid.*

"Don't look at me like that." Vanessa's voice is low, matter-of-fact. "I'm not upset at you."

"What?" This time, anyone could pick up on the way her voice wavers.

"I don't envy you, Teresa. You're the only woman who can put up with Ryan's ambitions, his obsession with his own vision." She removes one of her diamond-tipped hair pins and rearranges a few locks of hair, before sliding the clip back into place.

Vanessa has never commented publicly on Ryan or his career in the years since their divorce. Tessa stares, taken aback by the vehemence of her words. "Ex-excuse me?" She bites back the instinct to defend Ryan. She has enough tact to know that isn't appropriate.

"You heard me." Vanessa turns to face her. "I'm happy that I'm not the one in your shoes. I'm glad to have a partner who actually cares to spend time with me."

"I-I'm glad you're happy." Vanessa deserves happiness. It doesn't fully absolve Tessa of the guilt she carries. The guilt of knowing that Ryan loved her before he ever met Vanessa. That part of him never truly stopped loving her, even during the years of his marriage. But it does ease some of that guilt.

Vanessa studies her for a few long moments. Her scrutiny is even more uncomfortable than the media attention that has been leveled on her. This is personal. Tessa doesn't flinch from her gaze. She tries to convey everything she doesn't dare to say out loud. *I never wanted your husband. I was fully in love with, fully committed to, my own.*

Vanessa turns away, checking the clasp on her bracelet. "Good luck." There is nothing bitter in her tone now. "You're going to need it."

She has no idea what to say to that, and she tightens her grip on Leo's leash. "Good night, Vanessa. And congratulations, again."

Tessa almost collides with Emmy, one of her protection agents, upon leaving the bathroom. She gasps, and Emmy puts a steadying hand on her arm. "Sorry about that. I was just about to come and make sure everything was okay."

"Everything's fine. I was just catching up with an old friend."

Emmy looks unconvinced, but she lets it pass. Tessa returns to the ballroom, looking around for Ryan. Her phone is heavy in the concealed pocket of her skirt. She wants to text Jesy and Rosalie. She wants to find Ryan. She does not want to get embroiled in conversation. But a dozen people fall upon her in quick succession, and it is easily half an hour until Tessa finds Ryan again.

"There you are." He gracefully excuses himself from his conversation. Ryan wraps an arm around her, drawing her to a quiet spot at the perimeter of the room under the guise of making their way over to the appetizer table. "Are you okay? You look rattled."

Tessa makes sure no one is in earshot. "Vanessa is here."

Ryan very nearly trips over Leo. "Sorry," he apologizes to the dog. "But — what?"

"She and her fiance are here tonight. I have no idea how we didn't know they were on the guest list."

"Oh, God, Caleb too." Ryan throws a paranoid look over their shoulders, as though he expects Caleb Hamilton to materialize out of thin air and punch him in the face. "Where did you last see them?"

"I ran into Vanessa in the bathroom."

Ryan looks aghast. "How did that go?"

"She was gracious enough to me. She was, ah, less so about you."

"That tracks." Dinner will be served soon, so there is no crowd around the appetizer table. They linger there, as if deciding what they want to help themselves to. An unusual expression crosses Ryan's face. A flicker of shame, of regret. "I wasn't a very good husband to her. I mean, there wasn't… But, you know."

She knows. There were no extramarital affairs. No abuse. Ryan hadn't been that kind of bad husband. But as one of his closest friends, she had a front-row seat to Ryan and Vanessa's marriage. There had been plenty of benign neglect. Vanessa took the back seat to Ryan's political career and his ambitions. Everyone could see that.

Ryan rests a hand on the small of her back. "I'll do better for you," he says quietly. "I promise."

She trusts him, and she knows that faith isn't misplaced. He isn't the same person he was years ago. The relationship that they share is different from the one he and Vanessa had. Vanessa may think that she is being a fool, but Tessa doesn't doubt him at all. "I know you will."

∞∞∞∞

Everyone asks about how running into Vanessa made her feel. Jesy and Rosalie interrogate her about Vanessa's "micro-expressions" and tone of voice. "Thank God she hasn't done any interviews," Jesy says. "The media would have a field day. Twitter would blow up." She is right about that. People would take Ryan's mistakes and failures as a husband, and use those flaws in character as reasons he would be an unfit president.

"Did it give you a sense of closure?" Taliyah asks Tessa during therapy. "You've been living with this apprehension, this anxiety, about Vanessa for so long."

"It was more than anxiety. It was like — dread." Apprehension and anxiety manifest as a tightness in her chest. Dread is heavier. Dread is a shadow looming over her, a cold fist wrapping her in an iron grip.

"Dread, then. How do you feel now?"

"I wish it gave me a sense of closure. It did the opposite. It's like this door was just ajar for all this time, and now it's been pushed wide open." Her schedule is hectic enough that she should sleep like the dead every night. Instead, Tessa wakes up at three o'clock every morning, soaked with sweat.

Taliyah leans closer to the screen, her brows drawing together in concern. "What do you mean?"

Tessa averts her eyes, looking at Leo instead. "Owen." The word lodges in her throat like she has swallowed a cherry pit, hard and bitter. "I keep — now that I've seen Vanessa, now that I ran into her like that, I keep thinking that I'm going to see Owen again. That I'll turn a corner while walking and he'll be there. I keep trying to rationalize myself out of thinking that way. It would be damn near impossible for that to happen. I don't walk Leo alone in the park anymore. I get my groceries delivered. Owen and I don't have the same social or professional circles. It doesn't make sense, but I still… Every day, I still…" Leo lifts his head, nuzzling against her hand.

"You don't have to try and make rational sense out of this fear. Is it fear?"

"Not… Not quite. I don't know. I'm not afraid that he's going to hurt me, or Ryan. I'm afraid of how seeing him would make me feel. It was difficult enough to see Vanessa, and she wasn't my spouse. My partner." Her heart. Her everything. Everything that Ryan is to her now, Owen had been that for her, once.

"You're right that it's unlikely that you'll see Owen like you saw Vanessa.

I still want to explore these feelings. Is that all right with you?"

Tessa looks at Leo, drawing strength from his presence. "Yes."

∞∞∞∞∞

She talks about it in therapy, and she stays busy with work and the campaign. Eventually, the fear of encountering Owen recedes. Tessa makes a decision jointly with Ryan's campaign and the DNC, determining that they are going to unleash her on the Southwest. "I want to speak at the University of Arizona in Tucson, Arizona State in Phoenix, and the Navajo Nation in Apache County. I'll switch up the venues in Colorado and New Mexico, but I want to talk about affordability in Colorado, and jobs and the economy in New Mexico. And…" Tessa pauses, anticipating the pushback. "I want to add half a day to speak at Utah State and BYU*."

Jonah waves a dismissive hand. "Don't waste your time in Utah."

"Are you kidding? Utah?" Matt squints at her in the Zoom screen. "What's next? Are you going to speak at some Baptist association in Arkansas?"

"Bill Clinton was the governor in Arkansas." She is just as bad as Ryan now when it comes to dropping (unasked for) presidential facts.

Jonah and Matt exchange a nonplussed look. Ryan cuts in. "Tessa is right not to count Utah out. We don't win hearts and minds by writing off entire states like that."

"I'm not going deep into Utah," Tessa points out. "Utah State and even BYU, by virtue of being universities, are going to learn more liberal than rural Utah."

"Liberal." Jonah puts air-quotes around the word.

"Do you think you can even pull a crowd in Utah?" Matt asks.

"Yes. We'll lean on the Young Democrats of Utah, and Women in Politics and BYU Democrats. I want Republicans on campus to attend too, even if just out of morbid curiosity. I might say one thing — just one thing — that resonates with them. Maybe that cracks a door open. Maybe that door doesn't swing all the way open for two or more election cycles, but it's something."

Brigham Young University

"Exactly," Ryan agrees. "Let us know how it goes. If you think it's a good idea, I'll add Utah to my list too."

There isn't much space in Ryan's schedule for new additions. They are booked almost completely solid until the day before Election Day. They are running into certain immovable limitations at this point — the hours it takes to travel between states, and back to DC for Ryan to fulfill his responsibilities as Vice President.

As is their custom, Tessa and Ryan linger on the Zoom call after Matt and Jonah leave. "Thanks for backing me up on Utah."

"Of course." Ryan smiles at her.

"Don't start dreaming about me turning Utah blue in this election. Even I know that's not going to happen." Even 2032 would be the longest of long shots, as likely as Kentucky voting blue.

"It's not that. I'm proud of you, baby. All these years, you've driven my campaign strategy, and now you're the one giving the campaign speeches. You're the one not just writing, but delivering, the talking points. You're the one drawing big crowds."

Tessa's face goes warm. "Yes, well…"

Ryan crosses his arms over his chest, making a thoughtful sound. "Chao 2028 and 2032. What do you think of Halifax-Chao for 2036 and 2040?"

"First of all, those sound like fake numbers. Second, I'm going to hang up on you now."

Ryan beams into the camera. "I love you."

"I love you too."

ooooo

Tessa's Southwest trip is a whirlwind. Four states and eight speeches in two and a half days, followed by a lengthy debrief on the plane back east with Ryan, Matt, Jonah, and the other DNC Vice Chairs. She sits in her office at the DNC Headquarters at half past eight that night, staring at her map of the states with all of their electoral college votes written in. CNN plays in the background, speaking on the Republican nominee's visit to Pearl Harbor in Hawaii.

A knock sounds on her office door, prompting Leo to sit up. "Come in."

Agent Morgan, one of Ryan's Secret Service protection detail, enters. He holds an envelope in one hand. His body language — the length of his steps, the set of his mouth — betrays slight unease. "Good evening, Ms. Halifax. You received this yesterday. We just finished screening it for you."

This is standard procedure now. Every piece of mail she receives gets screened by the Secret Service. They test it for anthrax or other toxins, and they make sure that none of her mail contains any threats. Agent Morgan places the torn-open and resealed envelope in her hand. Tessa catches a glimpse of the return address, and her fingers go numb. "Thank you, Agent Morgan."

Leo picks up on the change in her voice. He sits upright, leaning against her legs. "Of course, Ms. Halifax," the agent says quietly, before exiting her office.

Ryan's Secret Service agents know. They are the only people who do, save for her friends and her divorce lawyer. Tessa hadn't wanted to tell the agents, but Ryan insisted. *They need to know if there's anyone who would have any reason to harm you, or us.* He held her hand, and he couldn't bear to look her in the eye.

Her breath comes fast and shallow. Leo paws at her leg to snap her out of it, and Tessa makes herself shift her focus to him. His eyes are wide and concerned. "Good boy," she whispers. She pets him until the fear subsides. Then she picks up her phone.

Ryan picks up on the second ring. "Hello?"

"Hi. Did you just land?"

"Just two minutes ago. What's wrong?"

Of course he would have noticed. He notices when she doesn't like her food, when she is unhappy or irritated with the path a conversation is taking; when she is frustrated by a challenge at work. Tessa can't bring herself to explain out loud. "I got some mail, and I–"

Ryan doesn't wait for her to finish. "I'll come right home."

"Thank you."

"Don't thank me. Drive safe."

She is so preoccupied that it is difficult to keep her focus on the road, and getting back to the house is a relief. Tessa settles on the sofa to await Ryan's return. Leo comes to sit on her lap, comforting her with his presence. She clutches the letter in her free hand, unable to face the prospect of opening it; unable to let it go.

What would Taliyah tell her? The contents of this letter won't change anything. She will still marry Ryan. She is still in love with him.

The key clicks in the front door. Ryan steps in, his laptop bag slung over his shoulder. He is visibly tired from the long day, but he proceeds right to her without bothering to take off his overcoat or shoes. "No, don't get up."

Tessa sinks back down, holding her arms out. Ryan embraces her. "What happened, baby? What did you get?"

The envelope rests facedown on the sofa, the return address hidden from view. Tessa wordlessly picks it up and hands it to Ryan. His reaction is immediate. A quick, sharp inhale, his brows drawing together. He puts an arm around her shoulders, easing her close to him, like he would protect her. "Oh, Tess."

"I can't open it."

"Do you want to throw it away?" There is no judgment in the question, and no pressure.

Tessa hesitates. "N-no. I think that if I did that, I would always wonder…"

"Right. Yeah, of course." Ryan rests a hand on her back. "Do you want me to read it with you?"

Tessa leans against him, grateful for his support. "Would you — would you mind reading it first? I know the Secret Service screened it, but…" They would have just screened it with her physical safety in mind, and passed it through to her as long as it didn't contain any threats to her or Ryan.

"I can, if that's alright with you. I know how personal this is. I don't want to intrude."

"It's not an intrusion, but–" Tessa covers her face with her hands. "I'm so sorry for asking you to do this."

"What? No, it's not–"

She ignores him. "This has impacted every part of our relationship. We had to wait to have sex. You're so careful never to get really angry around me, or to raise your voice. We're engaged now, and I still have all this baggage. I'm so sorry I've put you through all this."

"Please don't apologize." Ryan looks pained. "Look, I hate that this happened to you. I wish you never had a moment of pain in your life. But at the same time, I never wish that you were different, that your history was different. Does that make sense?"

Tessa pets Leo. "I guess."

"I love you just the way you are. Nothing that I do to accommodate your needs is a chore, or a burden. I have baggage of my own, and you help me carry it every day."

He holds her gaze until she nods, forcing herself to acknowledge that objectively, he is right. Tessa nestles against his side. She keeps her eyes averted as Ryan withdraws the letter and begins to read. Sometimes he makes tiny, involuntary noises when he is reading something. A thoughtful hum, or a soft sound of annoyance, surprise, or consideration. He remains silent now, leaving her to pet Leo.

Ryan finally rests a hand on her leg, getting her attention. "It's fine for you to read. Whenever you're ready."

Will she ever be ready? She hadn't been ready for Owen's injury, for the abuse, for their divorce. Every single one of those things just happened to her, leaving her stumbling, reeling, trying her best to react and cope.

Tessa takes the letter, and presses a soft kiss to Ryan's cheek. One calming breath, and she unfolds the letter and begins to read.

The handwriting itself is a gut punch. It is far from Owen's handwriting pre-injury, but it isn't the shaky, crooked script he had in the weeks and months post-injury. *It looks like a toddler wrote this,* he said, disgusted, the first time he saw his own handwriting in rehabilitation.

The letter isn't long. *Dear Tessa,* it begins.

I hope it's okay for me to reach out like this. I'm sorry if it isn't. I don't want to cause you any more pain. You don't have to reply.

I've seen you on the news lately. I don't watch it much, but election talk even makes it to the Alaskan backwoods.

I've been wanting to write for months, since the news came out about you. It ended up being pages and pages of stuff better fit for my journal. I don't want to burden you with all of that, all those thoughts and feelings.

Tessa closes her eyes, wiping the tears from her lashes. She used to willingly take on all Owen's thoughts and feelings, as he did for her. They talked about everything, just as she does now with Ryan.

With effort, she continues. *All of the things you're going through look so hard. The interviews, the speeches, the media being in your face, talking about your past. You look great doing it, though. You look smart and classy. You're going to be a great First Lady, Tessie. I always knew you were going places, from the first time I met you.*

Tessa's shoulders heave with a sob. Ryan holds her, and Leo moves closer, like he would hug her too.

I want you to know I'm happy for you. I'm happy that you have someone to love you and take care of you, someone who you can be safe with always, who will always treat you right. I love you, but I can't/couldn't guarantee those last parts anymore and you deserve better than that.

I have thought about it a lot and I had a hard time figuring out if it was better or worse for me that it is Ryan. Then I got it. It's better for you that it's him, and that means it's better for me, too. It's not like you're with some random guy now. I know that he really loves you.

I wish you the best of everything, Tessie. I'm sorry for everything.

Love,

Owen.

Ryan and Leo are there for silent support as she cries in shuddering sobs. She hasn't wept like this for Owen since the first couple of years after their divorce. This letter should have been healing — and it will be. But right now, it just opens up a fresh wound.

When the tears finally stop, she curls up against Ryan as he rubs her arm. "I'll make you some tea when you're ready," he offers.

"Thank you." Tessa wipes at her face. "I think… It was good that he wrote that."

"I think so too. Did it — did it help you?"

"I think it will."

Ryan looks her in the eye. "What do you need from me right now?"

Tessa just holds out her arms again, and he holds her close.

Chapter Thirty-Five

July – August 2028

She is preoccupied and withdrawn for days after receiving the letter. Talking about it with Ryan, Rosalie, and Jesy helps, as does discussing it in therapy with Taliyah. Tessa spends long hours just sitting with Leo as she processes it. The silence with Leo is just as helpful as the talking with everyone else.

July turns into August, heralding the last month of summer. The Democratic National Convention takes place in Boston. It is emotional for both of them, after over a decade and a half of attending this convention together, all while striving for this moment. Two former Democratic presidents give keynote speeches, and Tessa gives her own keynote. Her voice remains steady throughout, as she faces the crowd of more than fifty thousand delegates, journalists, and party officials in attendance. President Gardner delivers the final keynote. Ryan formally accepts the Democratic Party's nomination for President, making history, as Tessa stands at his right side.

The election grows more contentious after both political parties' conventions, and they all help Ryan prepare for the first presidential debate in September. Tessa's melancholy finally eases its grip, leaving behind a quiet sense of peace. Her schedule and Ryan's are more booked than they have ever been before. They travel, together and separately, six days a week. They stay up late and wake up early, poring over polls and having calls to discuss what those poll results mean for their campaign strategy. They write and revise endless speeches to dozens of different audiences across dozens of states.

Tessa still finds time to hold Ryan's hand when she can. She looks into his face, appreciating the features and expressiveness she knows and loves so well. She still finds time to sit outside and reflect, just her and her pre-dawn morning tea, for a few minutes before getting to work.

"You're so Zen," Rosalie comments, as the two of them catch a flight to Georgia. "I haven't seen you like this in a long time."

"How are you so chill?" Matt asks. "Meanwhile, I'm losing my hair and Ryan has high blood pressure."

"It's barely elevated," Ryan argues. "I wouldn't call it high blood pressure."

"Your hair is fine," Tessa assures Matt. "And — I don't know. I guess I'm just trying to keep all of this in perspective." For all these years, she took Ryan's elections as matters of life or death. There is more at stake in this one than in any preceding. This is Ryan's greatest chance to take the White House; to lead this country out of the woods. He can finish what President Gardner started, and take that progress further than any other Democratic president has before. The future of the nation hinges on the outcome of this election. This is what Ryan has been relentlessly advancing toward for the past two decades.

If he lost, it would be a devastating blow. To Ryan's spirit, to all of them, to the country. And yet. Even if the worst happens, even if they lose, she can still envision a future for herself. Even if they lose, she and Ryan still have a future together.

ooooo

Ryan goes off to Texas for a weekend of campaign events - without her, for once. He is scheduled to return on Sunday evening. Tessa gets back from Wisconsin early enough on Saturday night that she has time to consult one of her favorite recipe websites for inspiration.

Ryan breaks into the biggest smile upon walking in the front door to see her leaning in the doorway to the kitchen. "That smells amazing." He kicks his shoes off, tosses his coat onto the back of the sofa, and greets her with a kiss when she goes to him.

Tessa lifts the laptop bag off his shoulder. "I picked up the shrimp from the municipal fish market at the wharf this morning." She had been unrecognizable, with her hair put up in a bun, large sunglasses on, wearing leggings and a Georgetown t-shirt.

Ryan takes a few minutes to wash up, while Tessa feeds Leo and plates their food. Ryan joins her at the table, kissing her forehead. "I feel like the luckiest guy in the world right now."

Tessa smiles, giving him a playful shove on the arm. "I don't even know how the shrimp turned out."

She asks him all about how things went in Texas as they eat. He obliges, answering her questions in detail. "Enough about me." Ryan takes another heaping spoonful of his rice. "What have you been up to today, besides being a gourmet chef?"

Three years of therapy has made her more comfortable with recognizing her emotions, acknowledging them to herself, and taking the leap of expressing them to others. Tessa unfolds her napkin and then re-folds the corners. "I've been thinking. We should get married."

Ryan looks between her face and the emerald engagement ring on her finger. "Well, yes. That's the plan."

"I meant that I want to do it sooner rather than later."

Ryan raises his eyebrows. Their plan was to get married in the interim between the election in early November and the inauguration in late January. "Why? Optics? Stealing the spotlight from Salinas?"

"No. It's the principle. I don't want to wait until we know that you won this. I want to be with you, committed to you, no matter what the outcome of this election is. Win or lose."

"Oh, I'm going to win." Ryan takes her hand.

"You get what I mean."

"I do. And I'm touched. Really." Ryan's eyes crinkle with his smile. "You know what my schedule is like over the next few months. But I'll talk to Matt tomorrow and get him to move some things around."

"We only need a couple of hours. It's just a quick trip to the courthouse."

"Yeah, well. I was thinking we could have a ceremony. A little ceremony," Ryan hastens to add, catching sight of her expression. "Very small. Tiny. Just my aunt and our friends. And Leo in a bow tie."

Tessa narrows her eyes. "Tiny, you say."

"Miniscule."

"So, C-SPAN and CNN and MSNBC will not be invited."

"We'll exile all the journalists in Vermont if you want. Round them up and drive them to New Hampshire."

Tessa laughs, and then she stops laughing. "Wait. Vermont?"

"You know what they say. Vermont is for lovers." Ryan rubs the back of his neck. "Also, I impulse bought a cabin there a couple years ago."

"You impulse bought a cabin?" Only Ryan. A big impulse buy for her is a candle from Anthroplogie. "Also, do you remember what I used to say about Vermont?"

Ryan sighs. "That you would quit your job and retire to Vermont to make jam. Your favorite threat."

"Exactly."

"That's why I bought the cabin, actually."

Tessa inspects his face. "Oh my God, you're not joking."

"I would never joke about Vermont, cabins, or you. I thought it could be, like…" Ryan starts laughing. "Your jam workshop. I had this whole rom-com with you and I plotted out in my head."

"You are the strangest person I know." Tessa goes to sit in the chair next to him. "Do you have any pictures of this jam workshop-slash-wedding venue?"

∞∞∞∞

The week following their discussion is less pleasant. Ryan's campaign team and DNC leadership spend hours in calls and meetings, exchanging hundreds of emails a day. They anticipate every word out of their opponents' mouths, crafting messages to draw in centrist voters and the undecided. They craft counter-messages to rebut the Republicans' criticism of Ryan and his platforms.

Ryan Chao has been Republicans' favorite target for almost twenty years now. The venom they spew rises to a fever pitch. Right-wing outlets fixate on how his policies, like housing as a human right, tuition-free public college, abolishing ICE, and Medicare for All, will "bankrupt and ruin America."

They make the commentary bizarrely personal, painting Ryan as a spendthrift. Fox News runs a story "analyzing" the cost of Ryan's shoes, suits, coats, and haircuts. They play photos of him leaving "expensive DC restaurants" with Tessa on his arm. They zoom in on her engagement ring and speculate about how much it cost. "Easily six thousand." A so-called "expert" shakes his head. "Meanwhile, everyday Americans are struggling every time they're at the grocery store, struggling every time they're filling their cars up at the pump."

Tessa calls Ryan's second most loyal defender as soon as the "story" crosses her TV screen. "Did you see it?" Matt asks, in lieu of hello.

"How dare they?" Tessa paces the length of her office. "Commenting on his clothes, his shoes, when they mocked him during his first term in the House for dressing like "he bought his work clothes from a thrift store." He flew economy all those years in Congress! Who else did that?"

Leo looks downright alarmed. It is rare that she loses her temper like this. Tessa mouths a silent apology and reaches down to pet him, while Matt tears into the anchors. "The audacity of them, to try to make him out to be some out of touch elite when he's the one whose policies actually support the average person."

Tessa gets off the phone with Matt when Ryan calls, fresh off a campaign stage in Des Moines, Iowa. "You did a good job with–" she starts.

"I can't believe they brought you into this. Talking about the cost of your ring?" Ryan fumes. "Insinuating that you're some high-maintenance partner who needs nice jewelry and fancy restaurants? I swear, I'm going to call them myself after I get off the phone with you."

Tessa's shoulders stiffen in response to the fury in his tone. She holds a hand out to Leo. "Don't do that. Kahaan just texted me. He has a comment ready to go."

"Okay. Fine." Ryan exhales, fighting to calm himself. "Not sure if Matt told you, but we shifted some things around this morning to free up the third weekend in September. How does that sound for a wedding date?"

That is a welcome change in topic. Tessa pulls up her own calendar to confirm, and smiles for the first time that day. "It's perfect. It's nice to have something to look forward to."

"I picked it because fall foliage should be at its peak then. It'll be beautiful." All hints of anger are gone now. Ryan sounds just as wistful, as longing for just the two of them in the woods in Vermont, as she feels.

ooooo

Tessa barely has any time free from thinking about - obsessing about - the election. This happens every election cycle. The restlessness, the disrupted sleep, the agitation. In her sporadic moments of free time, her thoughts drift to the wedding. Jesy comes to visit, and Rosalie comes over, and the three of them sit huddled around Tessa's laptop on the sofa. A giant bowl of chilled, sliced watermelon garnished with mint leaves sits on the coffee table, as well as a pitcher of iced fruit tea and their half-full glasses.

"What are you thinking?" Rosalie cracks her knuckles as if getting ready to hit the boxing bag.

"Not white." Tessa tries, and fails, to suppress memories of her younger self, scouring the $99 rack at David's Bridal. She had been so young. So hopeful, so happy. "I–" She stops. Both Jesy and Rosalie look at her. They know her too well.

"What is it?" Jesy asks.

She would have brushed off the question a few years ago, deflecting it with a comment about how white doesn't suit her complexion anymore. Therapy and experience have taught her better. She can open up about her feelings to her friends with the knowledge that listening to her won't be a burden for them. They want her to confide in them, just like she wants them to confide in her.

"I feel stupid," Tessa admits quietly. "You're only supposed to do this once. You guys only did it once. Last time, I… I never imagined that I would do it all again, without Owen."

"Hey." Jesy takes Tessa's limp hand in her own. "You're not stupid. You didn't do anything wrong, or fail, or any of that. Life never fails to surprise us. There are a lot of reasons why getting married once doesn't always work out."

"Thousands of people get remarried every year, for so many different reasons. And that's a good thing," Rosalie says bracingly. "It's a blessing to get the chance to go the distance with the right person."

Tessa wipes at her eyes. "You're right. Sorry."

"No being sorry," Jesy reminds her. "So, not white. How do you feel about gold?"

∞∞∞

"...And I am excited," Tessa finishes, during therapy the following week.

"Even though it was a tough start?"

"Yes. Once I got out of feeling that I shouldn't be shopping for a wedding dress again." Tessa pets Leo. "It's a beautiful dress. When I put it on, I felt happy, and so excited for the future. It just felt right." She thought of how Ryan would smile when he saw her, and that made her smile, too.

"That's what you want to feel, I'm sure. But I want you to know that it's normal if those feelings of sorrow recur as the wedding gets closer."

"I know. I expect that. I think…. I think it's all right. Everything that I went through - it brought me here. I'm okay." That isn't a lie, the way it was when she first started seeing Taliyah.

"I'm so glad to hear that. If you want to schedule any appointments the week of the wedding, I'll hold some spots open for you."

"Thank you." It is time to put some of the communication skills she has learned in therapy to use. "Taliyah?"

Tessa falters, until Taliyah prompts her with a gentle, "Yes?"

"Thank you. I remember when I first started seeing you. I was a mess." She blinks away her tears. "The only reason I was even still alive was my friends and my job."

"You were trying your hardest, Tessa," Taliyah replies softly. "Even when you were at rock bottom, you were committed to climbing up. You found me. You found Leo. You armed yourself with the support you needed to survive, and then thrive."

Tessa manages a smile. "Now I'm about to get married again. I would have never thought, never dreamed that was possible. Thank you for helping me heal enough to do this."

"It has been my privilege to walk along this path of healing with you." Taliyah smiles at her. "Thank you for allowing me to do that."

Chapter Thirty-Six
September 2028

Normally, she would never take a weekend off so close to the election. She would be too terrified of missing an important move from the opposition, or missing a national or global crisis, or even coming back to an out-of-control email inbox.

There is no fear, as Tessa loads up the car with Ryan during sunrise on Friday morning. "I can't believe you talked them into letting you drive." She runs a fond hand over the top of Ryan's old Prius, and settles the folded garment bag carrying her wedding dress in the back seat.

"In the middle of their convoy, but I'll take what I can get." Ryan hasn't stopped smiling since the two of them turned off their work phones in unison and tossed them into the depths of her purse. "I made a playlist for our road trip."

"When did you have time to do that?" Tessa pets Leo as he climbs into the backseat, sniffing around the unfamiliar car.

"Um… around one in the morning. I couldn't sleep. Too excited."

The long drive north to Vermont is a delight. They don't listen to any news podcasts. They listen to an audiobook, and Ryan's playlist, and talk. Ryan keeps one hand on the steering wheel and the other resting atop hers. They reminisce about past road trips across the country in the loathed campaign bus, and the NYC to DC drives in college.

"I'm still surprised your road rage video hasn't been leaked by now."

Ryan grins. "Remember when you drove back that one summer, and you made Matt and I listen to Eminem the whole drive back?"

Work has allowed her to meet dozens of celebrities, but meeting

Eminem at a campaign event in Detroit is still one of her personal high-lights. Ryan and Matt teased her for months about how starstruck she got. Tessa laughs at the memory. "Hey, that's why he made it onto this playlist, right?"

"I'm going to expect you to start rapping along when he comes on." Ryan glances over his shoulder at Leo in the backseat. "Our last road trip together, just the two of us, was to pick this little guy up from upstate."

"It's been a while. We should do this more often."

"We'll come up to the cabin whenever you want. It'll be a nice change of pace from the White House."

The congested highways of the DC area give way to long, winding roads lined with spectacular displays of fall foliage. Golden-yellow, rich orange, and vibrant red, interspersed with lingering patches of green. This election season and 2024's brought them to New England in autumn, but the shine hasn't worn off.

The two of them are the first of their friends to arrive at the cabin. The weather is pleasantly cool, and Tessa takes a deep lungful of the fresh air as she lets Leo out. Her dog hops down from the backseat, tail wagging. Four Secret Service agents beat them here, having arrived yesterday morning to do a complete sweep of the cabin and the surrounding woods. Tessa stares around, taking it in.

Ryan puts an arm around her. "What do you think?"

"It looks like a postcard." Tessa gazes up at the trees above them. The cabin is in the middle of the forest. Sunlight filters down through the canopy of colored leaves, dappling the small clearing out front that serves as a parking area. There is a front porch with two Adirondack chairs set on it, the perfect spot to have her morning tea with Ryan, Leo, and a book. "Are those blueberry bushes over there near the porch?" She remembers a blueberry cheesecake recipe her mom used to make, with fresh berries. She hasn't made that in a while.

"Yes, and wait until you see the inside." Ryan is almost hopping with excitement.

The cabin's interior is just as picturesque. An abundance of natural light streams in through the windows, and there are plenty of tempting spots where they can curl up with a blanket. Tessa links her arm with Ryan's as they finish the tour. "We're retiring here."

"Oh?" Ryan kisses her forehead. "I thought we were headed back to Queens."

They fill up the kitchen with the coolers of food and supplies they brought, and take a leisurely nap spooned together in bed. They have a pot of stew bubbling on the stove and cornbread in the oven when the rest of their party begins to arrive in the evening. The clearing fills with cars, and the cabin fills with friends and family. Matt made the halfhearted suggestion that a couple of people stay behind at campaign headquarters, but both Ryan and Tessa shot him down. "Absolutely not, man," Ryan said, and Tessa agreed. "Jonah and the other DNC vice chairs can keep an eye on things for one weekend."

Andrew and Booker bring in cases of wine. Mari, Daniel, and Daniel's husband stagger in under the weight of an Instant Pot and huge bags from Costco. Vasu and his wife surprise Tessa and Ryan with large, fragrant garlands of jasmine and marigold. Ryan's aunt Sherry brings cakes from their favorite New York City bakery. Rosalie and Javier, Jesy and Isaiah, Matt and Grace, and Kahaan bring yet more food and flowers.

The cabin, empty for years since Ryan purchased it, comes alive with warmth and light, with laughter and conversation. The air fills with the aroma of samosas and dumplings being fried on the stove, and the Instant Pot full of chicken and rice, and sweet potato fries and pita bread in the oven. Alicia, Oliver, Zahra, and Ruby have taken over the music, and alternate between playing K-pop and Latin pop.

"I'm glad you didn't wait until December to tie the knot," Booker comments.

Daniel nods, gesturing out the open windows at the autumn tableau outside. "These vibes are impeccable."

Tessa takes a sip of the apple cider cocktail that Mari whipped up for them. "The timing was right. Everybody deserves a break."

It is wonderful to relax for the first time in months; to be together with friends, without talking about politics or the campaign. Tessa stays by Ryan's side, her arm around his waist, his around her shoulders. She hasn't felt so light, so unburdened, so free, in a long time.

It is past ten when everyone decamps to their hotel, after ignoring Tessa and Ryan's claims that they can handle the cleanup themselves. They get ready for bed and return to the living room, comfortable in their pajamas.

Ryan settles on the sofa and holds the throw blanket out to her. Tessa accepts it gladly, snuggling up against his side, as Leo situates himself at their feet. She sighs with contentment, leaning her head onto Ryan's shoulder.

He kisses the top of her head. "Today was perfect."

"We still have tomorrow."

Ryan holds her closer still. "I know we're just getting started with our work — but I love this life we've built anyway."

It is rare to hear him express contentment so openly. This is a relatively recent development, dating back to when they began their relationship. For all the years before that, Ryan kept an obsessive focus on always striving for more. Looking for the next career accomplishment, the next step up the ladder. "It's nice to hear you say that. No matter what happens in November, we still have this." Tessa gestures at their living room, so recently filled with friends and family.

They watch the fire crackling in the hearth. "I'm so excited about tomorrow," Ryan bursts out. "It's hard to sit still. I feel like — like a can of soda on the inside." Tessa laughs, and he grimaces. "I put all my language skills into writing speeches, okay?"

"I get what you mean." She nudges him. "I'm excited for this fresh start. That's part of why I wanted it to happen sooner rather than later."

"I'm so glad you're as excited as I am," Ryan confesses. "I was so worried that this would feel like — like a consolation prize, to you. Like second place, compared to what you've wanted all this time. To make history, to be the first woman to be White House Chief of Staff. I took that away when I proposed to you. I was worried that this would be… bittersweet for you."

Tessa shakes her head before he even finishes speaking. "No. Marrying you, getting to start our lives together, could never be a consolation prize. It could never be second place to anything. That's the most ridiculous thing you've ever said. Ryan." She takes his hand, squeezing it. "I'm not going to be your Chief of Staff in name, but I'll be by your side, working toward every goal you have, just as much as Matt is. Even if I'm a little more behind the scenes. I don't feel like I'm missing out on anything. I promise you that. I'll get to be one of your most powerful allies, and your wife. Win-win."

Ryan hears the sincerity in her voice, and he relaxes. He reaches out, gently stroking her temples. "I'm so lucky to have you."

Tessa smiles at him. Instead of mentally correcting him as she always used to, thinking that she was the lucky one to have found someone so willing to deal with her trauma, she allows herself to accept his admiration. It was true that she carried a lot of trauma and emotional scars out of her first marriage. That doesn't make her a bad partner for Ryan. It doesn't reduce her love and devotion to him. "We're lucky to have each other," she says, meaning every word.

"I know you don't like when I make comparisons." Ryan rubs her back. "But this — I've never felt this way before. I didn't feel this way the night before I married Vanessa. This kind of excitement, this courage and optimism, knowing that I can handle whatever life throws at me from this point on, because I have you."

Tessa reaches up, running her fingers through his hair. Her chest hurts, but not with sorrow or anxiety, for once. Her heart feels full. "I'm so happy that I can make you feel like that." Not for the first time, she reflects on how lucky she is to have experienced true love. Twice. She folds her hands in her lap, reminiscing. "I can't believe I met you when I was eighteen."

"You were such a kid. Even Matt and Curtis and I — we were so young."

"Right? That was twenty-two years ago. Getting older… is a privilege." Both her parents died young. Ryan's parents, too.

"Yeah, it is." His eyes are shadowed, and she knows he isn't thinking of his parents. He is thinking of Iraq. So much loss of life, and so many of the lives lost were young men, women, and children. An entire lost generation.

"It's also scary. The thought of losing your health, of illnesses like dementia or cancer–" Cancer killed her mother. That ax hangs over her head, too. It is why she is so rigid about daily exercise, and eating plenty of fruits and vegetables, and being sparing with her alcohol intake. Even that isn't necessarily enough to protect someone. Her mother ate healthy and exercised too. That ax hangs over her head, and the heads of everyone she loves.

Ryan squeezes her hand, and Tessa rests her head against his shoulder again. "It's scary," she repeats. "But the thought of growing older with you, the way we have for the past twenty-two years, makes it bearable. It reminds me that I'll have joy in the years ahead — when we're fifty, or sixty, or seventy or eighty, even. It won't all be fear and loss and pain."

Ryan makes a soft, dismayed sound, and Tessa winces. She rarely opens up about her fear of death and cancer to anyone besides Taliyah. Ryan cradles her hands in his. "Of course it won't all be pain and loss. There will be that, and we'll be there for each other. But that's not all there will be."

Taliyah has reminded her of the same. Sometimes she still cries with anticipatory grief at the idea of losing Leo or any of her friends.

"We're going to retire here, apparently," Ryan reminds her. "We're going to travel the world. We're going to give our godkids career advice and go to their college graduations. We're going to be the king and queen-makers to the next generation of Democratic party leadership. We're going to see Matt take the presidency someday, and Booker too." Ryan wraps an arm around her shoulders. "And then we'll come back home. Together."

Tessa buries her head in his chest, and allows herself to bask in this warm, hopeful vision of their future. "I would like that."

∞∞∞∞

The following day is so busy that there is no time to dwell on the memories of her last wedding day. Ryan handles the deliveries of the ceremonial arch, the catering, and the tables and chairs for the outdoor dinner later. Tessa watches from an upstairs window as she blow-dries her hair, smiling at how someone from every delivery team asks for a selfie with Ryan. He obliges, of course. (He has a gift for selfies, and no bad angles. It is unfair.)

Jesy and Rosalie arrive an hour and a half before the ceremony, both of them stunning in matching cranberry-colored dresses. They zip Tessa into her dress, and Rosalie helps Jesy sweep Tessa's hair into a relaxed braided chignon.

"This is definitely going to influence next fall's bridal looks," Jesy remarks, while Rosalie applies eyeshadow to Tessa's lids.

"Tessa Halifax," Rosalie announces. "First Lady. Influencer."

Tessa makes a gagging sound. Rosalie swats at her shoulder, while Jesy laughs. "Stay still!"

When she is finally allowed to open her eyes, Tessa stands and stares at her reflection in the mirror, astonished. She tried on the dress, a simple A-line one-shoulder chiffon in deep emerald green, with her usual make-up-free face, hair clipped up in her typical updo. She loved it then. Paired with Jesy's hairstyling and Rosalie's subtle touch with makeup, the effect is even more striking.

She looks very different than she did at her first wedding, when she had been a young woman wearing a white dress. She looks older now, of course. She also stands taller. She had been a fresh college grad then. In the years since, she has become one of the most prominent political figures in the country. Life has hardened her, but maybe that hasn't been a bad thing.

"I love it. Thank you."

Rosalie and Jesy admire her, and their work. "Very Roman," Rosalie observes. "Or Greek. Or something. Very classic."

"And the necklace and earrings from Ryan? Perfection."

This is the second time they have styled her hair and makeup on her wedding day, and stood by her like the sisters she never had. Like the mother she lost so long ago. Tessa holds her hands out to them, and they take her hands. "You've been with me through it all. The mess I was after Iraq. You helped me get on my feet after Owen. You made me a part of your families. Even when… Even after the divorce, I knew I wasn't alone."

"Don't cry," Rosalie warns, blinking hard herself. "We don't have time to redo any makeup."

Tessa looks at Leo to keep herself from tearing up. Her dog sits nearby, in a burgundy-colored bow tie Ruby and Zahra picked out for him. "You kept my secret. One of the biggest secrets anyone could keep. I know that you guys are going to be with me always, just like Ryan. I feel lucky for that." Especially now, standing on the precipice of another huge life change.

"Consider that we're the lucky ones." Jesy dabs at the corners of her eyes.

"Come here." Rosalie folds both of them into her arms.

∞◌◌◌

Tessa walks herself down the short aisle in the clearing, as she did last time. As she did last time, she remembers her mother and father, gone for over two decades now. *Be at peace,* she thinks.

She smiles at her friends, standing for her. Instead of self-consciousness because they have seen her like this before, walking down the aisle to marry another man, there is gratitude. Almost twenty years later, they are still her closest friends.

Ryan waits with Matt, who is performing their ceremony, at the simple bronze ceremonial arch. Tessa has seen Ryan in the fanciest of suits, hair styled impeccably, more times than she can count. He is still stunningly handsome. The way he gazes at her, brimming over with joy — she can tell that he feels the same way, even though she is no more dressed up than she would be for any black-tie fundraiser.

Before joining Ryan and Matt, Tessa pauses to pet Leo, sitting at the front row of the small crowd. "My sweet boy," she whispers. She takes Ryan's hand, and steps up to join him and Matt.

"I'm not going to go on forever," Matt starts. "I'm not Ryan making a campaign speech, after all." Laughter ripples over their small party, and Ryan makes a jokingly wounded expression.

"I want to talk about care today. About caring. Everyone here has been the recipient of Ryan's caring and Tessa's. Tess never let any of us work late, or come into work on holidays or weekends. Even when she was up to her eyeballs in her own work and life, she always knew — always remembered — what was going on with us and our families. She remembered the Halloween costumes, and who had laryngitis, and who had a play or a concert or sports game coming up that they were really excited about. She always made it so very clear that we mattered to her, and that the people we loved mattered to her too. That is truly precious, in a boss and a friend." Matt smiles at her. He turns his gaze to Ryan, with the usual blend of fondness and exasperation he regards Ryan with.

"Ryan's generosity is legend. I know you all remember the hotel laundry mishaps we've had on the campaign trail over the years, and all the times he's literally given us the shirts off his back. Like Tessa, he always goes above and beyond — asking the Getty to stay open late for us to see that Graphic Design in the Middle Ages exhibit, or getting us tickets to the NBA Finals, or reservations at nice restaurants in any city we travel to. He's never too busy to come to the career days at our kids' schools and impress the heck out of everyone there.

"Ryan and Tess are two of the most caring people I've ever met. I also want to talk about care as the foundation for a relationship. For a marriage." Matt exchanges a smile with Grace in the audience. "Attraction and chemistry are nice and all, but caring is what a long-lasting, loving relationship is built on. I've known Ryan and Tessa for over twenty years now. I've seen how they have cared for one another, how they looked out for one another, in different ways, large and small. Often small — like Tessa always reassuring Ryan that he was a good squad leader in Iraq. Like Ryan putting his coat over Tessa whenever she fell asleep at her desk, or on the campaign bus."

Tessa squeezes Ryan's hands, and he squeezes them back.

"But there have been so many small moments of caring over the years. Every day, something. Tessa and Ryan have always looked out for one another's happiness, comfort, and safety, even when they themselves aren't aware they're doing so."

Tessa realizes that he is right. She and Ryan have cared for one another for months, years, decades, before they even kissed.

"Caring for one another is second nature to them. Truly as natural as breathing. I am so happy–" Matt clears his throat, collecting himself. "I am so happy that we can all be here with them today, as Ryan and Tessa begin their next journey together, with decades of caring for one another behind them, and ahead of them. With that, I'll begin the ceremony."

Both of them used the traditional wedding vows in their first marriages. *To have and to hold from this day forward, for better or worse, for richer or for poorer, in sickness and in health. To love and to cherish, until death do us part.* They don't repeat those this time. They are beautiful vows, but it is too sore of a spot for her. It always will be.

Ryan speaks his vows without taking his eyes off her, a soft smile on his face. Tessa has seen him ecstatic and triumphant before, but the only times she has seen him glow with this kind of soft contentment is when he is with her. "Tessa Halifax, I give you my hand, my heart, and my love. Now and forever."

Tessa echoes him, her voice calm and steady. "Ryan Chao, I give you my hand, my heart, and my love. Now and forever." As she speaks, she remembers the airfield at Camp Victory in Baghdad in December 2006, and her first time laying eyes on him. That moment changed the course of her life forever.

Matt lets them seal their vows with a kiss. Tessa cups Ryan's face in her hands, and he hugs her tight, kissing her deeply. The joy that courses through her is so pure that it even surpasses their first kiss in Tokyo, the night they got together at Thanksgiving, the day they got engaged. So much of her life has been marked by pain and uncertainty. This feels beautifully, staggeringly right.

∞∞∞

Drinks, dinner, and dancing follow the ceremony. Their friends strung up the surrounding trees with golden twinkle lights, and the lights illuminate the clearing in an ethereal glow as the sun begins to sink beneath the horizon. Tessa's friends tease her, referring to her alternately as Mrs. Halifax-Chao or First Lady Teresa Halifax-Chao. "Five words." Grace gives her an unusually mischievous grin. "It's so long it sounds royal."

Ryan's Secret Service agents present them with a signed card and a framed photo they snapped of Ryan, Tessa, and Leo during an official visit to Canada a few years back. It is a touching gesture, especially considering that these agents have been witness to her and Ryan's developing relationship. They enabled that secret. No one ever breathed a word to the media, or to any of Ryan's political rivals. Ryan beams at the agents, shaking each of their hands in turn. "Thank you so much." Tessa cuts all of them slices of cake, ignoring their protests about eating while on duty.

It is more fun to dance with Ryan here, dirt and twigs catching on the hem of her dress, than it is to dance in any DC ballroom. They hold one another close as they sway to the music. "Thinking about us at the inaugural ball?" Tessa asks, as Ryan twirls her around, and then gently spins her back into his arms.

"No." Ryan kisses her forehead. "Just thinking about how happy I am to be dancing with you at our wedding."

The party disperses earlier tonight, because tomorrow is Sunday, and all of them have to head back to NYC and DC in time for work on Monday morning. They head inside, followed by Leo. Ryan's hand is on the small

425

of her back, and she leans into him. "This has been one of the best nights of my life. I'm so…" Tessa blinks her sudden tears away. "Thank you for always making me so happy."

"I will, always," Ryan vows, pulling her close. "Always."

Epilogue

Teresa Halifax-Chao

Teresa Halifax-Chao (née Halifax, born November 26, 1988) is a political operative and author. Halifax-Chao served as the First Lady of the United States from 2028 to 2036, married to <u>President Ryan C. Chao</u>.

Raised in <u>Elizabeth, New Jersey</u>, Halifax-Chao is a <u>US Army</u> combat veteran and a graduate of <u>Barnard University</u>. In her early political career, she worked as Chief of Staff to Ryan Chao during his tenure as a Representative, Senator, and Vice President. In 2027, Halifax left the Chao administration to take the role of Vice Chair at the <u>Democratic National Committee.</u> Halifax, along with DNC Chair <u>Jonah Green</u>, is credited with helping Democrats take control of the House of Representatives, the Senate, and the White House in 2028.

Teresa Halifax married then-Vice President Ryan Chao in September 2028. Halifax campaigned for her husband's presidential bid throughout 2028, delivering a keynote address at the <u>2028 Democratic National Convention</u>. She has subsequently delivered acclaimed speeches at the <u>2032</u>, <u>2036</u>, and <u>2040 conventions</u>.

Halifax-Chao was involved in national and global concerns during her tenure, especially regarding <u>public health</u>. Her key areas of advocacy involved increasing funding for <u>cancer research</u>, <u>pandemic preparedness</u>, and expanding access to mental healthcare for all Americans — specifically treatment for <u>post-traumatic stress disorder</u> and <u>grief support</u>.

Halifax-Chao was considered an "extremely" politically active First Lady. This sparked controversy among the <u>right wing</u>, as she became deeply involved with political discussions and engaged Republicans in public disputes.

She was an outspoken advocate for her husband's policies, and campaigned for Democratic candidates nationwide in the 2030 and 2034 midterm elections. After the elections, nineteen out of the twenty candidates Halifax-Chao campaigned for won. David Dean of CNN noted Halifax-Chao's popularity, writing, "The First Lady is treated like a rockstar on the campaign trail – with local Democrats lining up for selfies and autographs – as she crisscrosses the country to help candidates."

Halifax-Chao traveled extensively within the United States, speaking out in support of President Chao's legislative agenda, Democratic candidates, and her areas of advocacy. The First Lady represented the United States at seventy-seven trips abroad over the eight years of her husband's presidency.

Halifax-Chao's influence has remained high after leaving the White House. In 2040, she topped Gallup's poll of the most admired women in America for the third year running. Alongside her husband, she remains an active figure in the Democratic Party, serving as a consultant for Democratic candidates around the nation.

Halifax-Chao currently works as the co-President of the Chao-Halifax Institute for Global Health, along with former President Chao. The couple splits their time between their residences in Queens, New York and Rutland, Vermont.

Acknowledgements

Thank you to my husband, David, for being endlessly loving and supportive. Our long talks about politics while sitting at the kitchen table are one of my favorite things we do together. David, I knew you were the one when you shared my love for watching Scandal (only partially kidding).

I could never have written this story without our love to draw inspiration from. Thank you for giving me so much joy every day, and a home filled with love, light, and warmth.

This novel wouldn't exist without David. It also wouldn't exist without my editor (and this project's first reader), Kira. Kira wholeheartedly loved this idea back when it was just a spark, back in July 2021. Her love for this spark of an idea, and her relentless encouragement, helped this grow into the novel it is. Writing a novel can be a lonely, frustrating, challenging process - and she kept it from being that way. Kira has been my beta reader for hundreds of thousands of words of my writing since 2020. Writing is a joy, and that joy is magnified so many times over by getting to share it with her. Thank you, good egg.

Thank you so much to all of my friends. In alphabetical order, Alanna, Carolina, David, Deborah, Emily, Eri, Hallie, Jenny, Katy, Kira, Laura, Mar, Natalie, Rachel, Shruti, Steve. You bring such warmth and caring to my life. Tessa's relationship with her longtime friends Jesy and Rosalie is a tribute to all of you. It was inspired by you, and the warmth and sense of closeness I feel when I spend time with you. Thank you for being there for me during the good times, and for your kindness and support when I'm at my lowest.

Thank you to Alanna Tran, who designed this cover, and to Carolina Gwinn, who typeset this novel. I am so grateful to both of you for visually bringing this project to life, turning it from a long Google doc to the real novel of my dreams.

Thank you to my parents, who gave me a love of reading and stories from a young age. Thank you to my parents-and siblings-in-law, Mary and Doug, Anne and Adam, and Tiara and Derek. You are all so kind and supportive, and I deeply appreciate that. Tessa's love for her goddaughters Zahra and Ruby is how I feel about my sweet nieces.

Thank you to all of my friends on Tumblr and Archive of Our Own who have supported my writing over the years. Every comment, every message sent on Tumblr, and every kudos, gave me the confidence to try my hand at writing a novel.

Finally, thank you to my beloved cat, Westin. Westin has been my writing buddy, sitting on my lap or beside me, for countless hours of writing from 2020 to today. As I write this, he sits on my lap, purring. Tessa's love for her dog Leo, and the amount of comfort she gets from Leo's presence, was inspired by Westin. Thank you for being my bestie, Westie.

Colophon

Minion Pro is an Adobe Original typeface designed by Robert Slimbach. The first version of Minion was released in 1990. Cyrillic additions were released in 1992, and finally the OpenType Pro version was released in 2000. Minion Pro is inspired by classical, old style typefaces of the late Renaissance, a period of elegant, beautiful, and highly readable type designs.